The Crusade
of
The
Black Angel

by
Phil Walker

ISBN-13:978-1887982047
ISBN-10:1887982043

Dedication

To the Military Veterans, past and present, whose courage, sacrifice and devotion to our country makes it possible for all of us to live in safety with our families and look forward to a brighter tomorrow,

Characters In order of Appearance

The Frost Family
>Cody Frost The Black Angel
>Ashana Frost Cody's Wife
>Charlie Frost Cody's Son
>Rosy Frost Cody's Daughter

The Moretti Family
>Adolfo Father
>Carlotta Mother
>Enrico (Rico) Son
>Alia Daughter

The Church
>Bishop Vincent Paglioni Director of Covert Ops
>Pope John Luke I, (formerly Robert Stroud)

The Kurds
>Masoud Barzani Kurdish Leader
>Kamal Barzani Son of Kurdish leader

The Americans
>Carson Palmer President of the United States
>Tom Bostwick Director National Security Agency

Israel
>Ari ben Cannan Prime Minister of Israel

The Iranians
>Manek Faroush, President of Iran
>Mitra Faroush, Daughter of the President

Turkey
>Farid Sensek, Prime Minister of Turkey

ISIS
>Hassan Al Aswiri, Leader of Islamic Caliphate

Table of Contents

Foreword

There are a few important points to keep in mind as you read 'The Crusade'. It's not possible to write accurately about the Middle East simply because you are only capturing a snapshot of a moving object, which continues to move after you take the picture. Therefore, you are going to find all sorts of anomalies in the story because of the constantly changing struggle with ISIS.

Nevertheless, no matter how the ISIS issue is finally settled, the most important components of the story are all the facts, actual events and forecasting of how the political, ethnic, religious and economics of the Middle East should be addressed.

For example, the descriptions of the historical Crusades are very different from what is commonly taught in Western schools, but are still true.

The manner in which the winning countries of World War I, England and France parceled up the Middle East is entirely accurate. It is also true President Woodrow Wilson dispatched Chicago businessman Charles Crane and the American theologian Henry King to determine the real wishes of the people of the region. Wilson grew ill during this time, and the report was never presented until long after France and England had arbitrarily redrawn all the borders.

The thousand-year battle between Sunni and Shiite Muslims is also accurate. No resolution of discord in the Middle East will appear until this issue is addressed.

The overture by prominent Muslim leaders to the Roman Catholic Church is also historically correct. In 2006, Muslim clerics all over the world prepared thoughtful and critical laws to encourage peace and good will responses after the pope's comments on the use of reason. It also made a direct criticism of Muslim extremists.

A year later, in 2007, a much longer dictate by Muslim leaders addressed the Christian leaders East and West, Roman Catholic, Orthodox, Protestant, and Evangelical. It was called *A Common Word Between Us and You*.

In the long history of Muslim-Christian relations, this unprecedented group of Muslim thinkers, from different parts of the world with differing views, collaborated on a positive overture to Christians.

Thus far, the Western world has not responded.

The grim facts are Christians and Muslims comprise 55% of the world's population. If there is no peace between them, there can be no peace.

The story of how the Crusade of the Black Angel unfolds may seem like a total flight of fantasy. In my judgement, when the final solution to Middle Eastern harmony arrives, it will contain many of the very components I suggest.

Chapter 1
A New Generation

Positano, Italy

Sweat poured from Cody Frost's face. He wiped his eyes and stared at the two figures facing him. They had grim looks on their faces.

Suddenly, they attacked simultaneously. Cody swerved to the right and parried a thrown punch with one arm, while slipping underneath and doing a leg sweep that threw the other to the ground.

The first attacker blocked two quick blows Cody threw and countered with a shoulder throw that rolled him to the ground. He kept rolling and sprang back to his feet to face the second attacker who was closing with a vicious leg kick. Cody was able to dodge most of it. He countered with a leg kick of his own, and the second attacker caught his leg and twisted it, throwing him off balance.

As he regained his balance, he moved to the left this time and stood facing both attackers again. They sprang forward and began hammering him with flying fists. He was able to counter most of the blows but twice he took hits in his midsection, and almost lost his breath.

He made a quick step to the side of his first attacker and threw him over his hip and onto the ground.

Before he could recover, the second attacker locked him in a vise grip around his neck. He arched his back and then pulled forward, throwing the attacker over his shoulder.

Then he fell flat on his face and pounded the ground for mercy. He got none. The two attackers were on him in an instant, tying him up with their bodies, and continuing to rain blows to his arms, side and back.

"Stop, stop!" screamed Cody.

A face with red hair poked her nose into his face and said, "Had enough, Dad?"

"More than enough," gasped Cody.

"I'd say that was enough," said Ashana, looking up from the book she had been reading in the soft lounge chair. "You guys haven't stopped for almost an hour."

Charlie climbed off Cody and helped Rosy pull him to his feet.

"Next time we'll use the mat," said Cody. "The ground is too hard."

"You were the one who said we should set up an ambush," said Charlie.

"But I was carrying a fresh glass of lemonade to your mother," said Cody, "I think that deserves some consideration."

"Surprise is your most valuable tactical weapon," said Rosy.

"I'm pretty sure we read that in a book somewhere," said Charlie.

"You didn't read it in any book," said Cody, "I taught you, myself, quite a few years ago."

Charlie looked at Rosy, "He's just sore because we beat him up." They slapped hands together.

"I'm sore alright," said Cody, "I doubt very much I will be able to grill those steaks for you tonight, because of my serious injuries."

"You don't even have a bloody nose," said Rosy.

"Well, I still think its lousy way to treat your old man on your first day home from school."

"We just wanted you to know we haven't lost our edge," said Charlie.

"In case you hadn't noticed," Ashana said, "while you children were playing, I went in and got myself another glass of lemonade and also brought out the steaks. It's just a good thing you didn't knock over the grill. Then I would have mopped the floor with the lot of you."

"I'm a fearless man," said Cody, "but I'm scared to death of you."

"No you're not," said Ashana, "but you should be."

Cody smiled at his beautiful wife. The years had been good to her. She still had the bloom of youth to her. He loved her more today, then when they married twelve years before.

In fact, Cody was in excellent shape. It took him nearly a year to heal completely from the multiple wounds he had sustained in his mad rush out of Iran. After that, he put himself on a strict rehabilitation regimen, and recovered most of his physical skills. Most people who knew him in his younger years would say he was every bit as lethal now as before. Cody knew differently. Now, at the age of 51, he could feel the years. His stamina was half what it had been. His many injuries over the years, especially those he suffered in his escape from Iran, bothered him more.

❖

In the early years, after his final mission so profoundly changed the optics of Middle-Eastern politics, Cody pulled the covers over his eyes to everything going on in the world. His primary goal was to help Ashana raise the children. Ashana always homeschooled Charlie and Rosy, and Cody felt this should continue, particularly since he was now home all the time.

Cody's caretaker of the villa, Adolph Moretti and his wife Carlotta had two children near the ages of Charlie and Rosy. It was Ashana, who suggested the Moretti children, Enrico and Alia, should also join the classroom. Both of the Moretti offspring had sharp, inquiring minds, just as Charlie and Rosy. School time was lively and varied. In just a few months, Enrico and Alia were completely fluent in English, and Charlie and Rosy became fluent in Italian. This was easy for them because they both were raised speaking Spanish every day in Zapata, Texas. They taught Enrico and Alia to speak the language. Cody also began teaching everyone to read, write, and speak Arabic and Farsi. Before the first year was over, the household became a cacophony of languages. Cody established a day each week when they spoke one of the five languages exclusively. On the other days, it was a free for all, with one person speaking English to another, who answered in Arabic. Often, a third person would sum up the conversation in Italian.

Cody and Ashana moved the children's education along at the fastest rate they could absorb. Soon, all four of them were years ahead of other students their age. They received a first class education in history, literature, mathematics, computers, and a wide range of sciences from physics to philosophy. In almost all cases, Cody's eidetic memory was the final arbiter in disputes over facts, and figures.

The years passed happily. As Charlie and Rosy grew, learned, and matured, Cody included self-defense in their curriculum of studies. He taught with intensity and seriousness on his subject. Ashana knew the importance of such skills with her own eyes, and supported Cody while taking part in the training. Even though they were small, the children found size did not matter much with the right moves and techniques. Before they were teenagers, Cody counted them as being among the most skilled martial arts students he would ever engage. Ashana joined in and turned out to be unexpectedly deadly. Not only was she fearless, she held nothing back. Cody had to be especially careful to insure she did not seriously injure him.

Another training element Cody included was the use of weapons of all kinds. The children could break down a Glock and reassemble it, blindfolded, before Rosy's ninth birthday. There was no fear of loaded weapons in the Frost home, the kids knew what they were and respected them.

At least once a week, Cody took the family into the hills above Positano for live fire exercises. They trained with a number of different handguns and rifles.

Cody was able to acquire a new sniper rifle. After giving it a lot of thought, he chose weight over distance. Some of the rifles had a range of up to 2700 meters, but they also weighed 27 pounds, too much to lug around when mobility was at a premium. He selected the Canadian Timberwolf C-14. It had an effective range of 1500 meters, but only weighed 15 and a half pounds with a five round, detachable box feed system.

He started Charlie shooting when he was only 11-years-old and needed a tripod to hold the rifle steady. By the time, Charlie was 16; he could handle the Timberwolf with ease and was routinely hitting targets at the maximum range of the weapon.

Rosy got her chance with the Timberwolf when she was 13. Although she was very good with handguns, she lacked the aptitude of Charlie with the sniper rifle. When Charlie asked his father about this he said, "Rosy is almost as big and strong as I am. She can handle the Timberwolf easily. How come she's not as good?"

Cody said, "It's not a matter of speed, or even accuracy, Charlie, it's being willing. Rosy knows the whole purpose of the Timberwolf is to kill people at long distance. That's a horrible thought for her, and she lacks the will to do it."

"I guess that's a good thing," said Charlie.

"It's a very good thing, son, Rosy is deadly when she's working defensively to protect herself and others, but she sees the Timberwolf as an offensive weapon. That's where the Lord has told her to draw the line."

"What does that make us?" asked Charlie.

"Pragmatists," said Cody. "I don't see the Timberwolf as an offensive weapon at all, but just another tool for protecting the lives of others."

If Rosy seemed less than perfect with guns, she absolutely excelled in computers. Her skills exceeded Cody's by a wide margin, which was saying a lot. When she was 13, Ashana discovered she'd hacked into the Positano city computer system and downloaded the names and addresses of all the local police. When Ashana asked her why she had done this, Rosy just shrugged and said, she wanted to know who might be watching her. The indiscretion cost her reading three extra books, and writing reports on them. Cody hired an expert computer tutor and told him he wanted Rosy to be the best computer scientist in the world. Rosy learned quickly and she taught Alia, what she had learned. Between the two of them, they made a formidable team.

The overriding core value in the Frost family was its dedication to God. It was not the "in your face" evangelical kind of dedication. Cody and his family simply tried to follow the will of God in all their actions throughout each day. It made for a joyful, peaceful home, filled with the blessings the Lord promised for those who made that commitment. The family went to mass, every Sunday. The Moretti's always went with them.

At the onset of their lives together, Cody and Ashana mutually agreed Cody's past was not something for discussion. The children remembered spending time at the White House, but Rosy barely remembered. Charlie remembered everything about the visit to see President Mitch Colter, and asked about it often.

The cover story Cody and Ashana devised simply explained Cody was in the military with advanced training. His skills in martial arts, and shooting came from that. They told the children their new father was a very small part of the planning process, which resulted in the detonation of six nuclear weapons in Iran. His appearance as a priest had been only a misdirection to allow him to work more openly. It was a story from which they never deviated or enhanced. Adolfo and Coretta had a thorough briefing on the story. Both of them knew a good deal more, since they were with Cody for many years, and saw the scars he brought home with him. They knew he was not just some minor analyst for the U.S. government, but a very active operative, and a priest, who risked his life every time he left. Still, Cody had never provided any details on his jobs. Nobody ever heard the term "Black Angel" in the Positano home.

When Charlie was 17, Cody and Ashana decided they'd taught him all they could. They had Charlie take his ACT and SAT tests. His scores were impressive. He got a perfect 36 on his ACT, and 2300 on his SAT. Charlie had shown a real aptitude and passion for International Studies, so Cody had him apply for admission to the College of William and Mary in Williamsburg, Virginia. By any standard Cody knew, William and Mary was the best university in the world for International Studies.

The resume Cody and Charlie wrote to accompany his admission application included documentation of Charlie's fluency in Spanish, Italian, Arabic, Farsi, German, and, of course, English, since he was applying as a foreign student living in Italy. He mentioned he had dual citizenship in both the U.S. and Italy. Cody also had Charlie write an analysis on the current state of world politics. It was very comprehensive and insightful. Cody was proud of Charlie because he provided almost no input to the content.

As he fully expected, Cody was not surprised when Charlie received a letter a month later, saying his application was accepted. He was just grateful it had not been necessary to reach out to any contacts to help him along.

In July of that year, the family drove Charlie to the airport in Naples and sent him on his way. It was a tearful and bittersweet moment. The first chick had left the nest.

Ashana missed Charlie and clung to Rosy. For that reason, she was truly upset when the computer tutor, Cody had hired, came to the villa two years later with exciting news.

"Microsoft put out a new operating system. Rosy installed it on her computer and was annoyed with all the glitches. She was able to hack into the Microsoft code for the system and wrote new programming language to correct the problems."

"I contacted a friend of mine, who's a senior programmer for Microsoft, and showed him the improvements. I got a call back from him last week. He was astonished anybody could break into their system, and nearly went into shock when I told him who did the improvements. Today, I got a long email from him. You need to see it."

Ashana and Cody sat down at their computer and read the email. Their eyes grew wider with every line they read.

The email was essentially a job offer. Microsoft wanted such a talented programmer in their company. They also wanted Rosy to move to Silicon Valley and were offering an employment contract with a huge salary, all the benefits, and a two million dollar signing bonus to pay for the work she had already done.

Ashana exploded, "She's only sixteen years old! I'm not sending my daughter into that Godless world!"

Cody felt exactly the same way, and said so. He took Ashana in his arms and held her tightly. Then he said quietly, "There's no question this is a genuine offer. However, the company is failing to address the legitimate concerns of her mom and dad. On the surface we can't agree to these terms, but we can change the debate to make them acceptable."

Skeptically, Ashana asked, "What would those be?"

Cody began ticking off points, "I'm unwilling to put Rosy into the corporate center. There are far too many variables inside we can't control. What's more, working for the company doesn't get Rosy the college education and degrees she'll need in later years."

"I agree with that," said Ashana.

"What we need to do is put a security bubble around Rosy, as close to what we have here as possible. I suggest we counter Microsoft's offer in the following ways. First, I think Alia should go with her. The two of them will provide mutual support and slice away at the inevitable loneliness Rosy would feel being alone."

"Next, we require Microsoft to allow Rosy to do her work for them remotely. I had in mind Stanford University. My guess is both girls can test out of a lot of the undergraduate courses, and move to more advanced studies rather quickly. A campus environment is more user friendly than a corporate complex. Therefore, we surround them with kids closer to their own ages.

"I believe they'll still need the support and counsel of an older person. You would be the best person for that, but *I* couldn't bear being without you. I think you should go with the girls and hire a woman to stand in for you. I trust your judgement to pick the right one."

"We should have the girls take their ACT and SAT tests now. I'm sure they'll score high enough to allow Microsoft to put pressure on the University to accept them, especially since they both have so many other qualifications, like being fluent in five languages. We get Microsoft to pick up the bill for everything, tuition, books, an off-campus apartment, and generous living expenses."

"I must say all you suggest makes me feel a lot more comfortable," said Ashana, "but Rosy, is still only 16-years-old."

"Charlie was only a year older when he went off to William and Mary. He was completely alone, but he's doing just fine."

"How certain are you Microsoft will agree to all this?" asked Ashana.

"Completely. The company made it clear Rosy is a commodity they have to have. They'll agree to anything, which gives them that. We'll even have them make sure, Rosy and Alia get graduate credits for the work they do for them. Of course, we'll accept their original offer, with our amendments to the agreement."

It turned out exactly as Cody imagined. In less than two months, Ashana boarded a plane, with Rosy and Alia in tow, for San Francisco. Fifteen candidates went through before Ashana felt comfortable with her choice of a companion for the girls. She found a nice apartment, in a safe neighborhood, close to the Stanford Campus. Microsoft cleared the path. Rosy and Alia, got considerably more attention and special treatment from the academic department, than other students in the elite school did.

Both the school and the company benefitted. Rosy and Alia excelled in every way. They rose to the senior level of classes, in two years and got full acceptance by their fellow students, despite their youth. Microsoft was delighted with the new, innovative breakthroughs they achieved.

"Since this is pile up on Dad day, I might just as well start grilling these steaks." He fired up the big grill and started sorting out the steaks. Ashana, Carlotta, Rosy, and Alia went back into the villa's kitchen to bring out all the rest of the food for this special homecoming meal.

Rosy and Alia brought their constant companion and dear friend, Hettie, with them back to Positano. She had never been to Italy. The beauty of the Amalfi coast, the charm of Positano, and the lavish, homey Frost villa overwhelmed her. Hettie went in with the other women to help in the kitchen, leaving Adolfo, Charlie, and Enrico to watch Cody cook the steaks.

Charlie, now 23, was trim and fit. He had filled out to be six foot-two, and weighed 210 pounds. Handsome with a long face, noble nose, and a square chin, he inherited his mother's blue eyes. Appraisingly, he looked at Enrico.

"I can't believe how much you've changed in the past two years, Rico," said Charlie. "I think you're in better shape than I am."

"Credit your dad for that," said Rico. "With nobody here for him to spar with but me, he's made a habit of it."

Rico was a little shorter than Charlie, but far more muscular. He held himself like a lion poised for a leap.

"Just be glad Rico didn't come in on my side for our little tussle," said Cody, "he would have cleaned up both you and your sister."

"I believe that," said Charlie with a big grin, and hugged Rico. "Actually, I've missed you a lot, brother."

"And you, as well," said Rico.

As they visited, the ladies of the villa came out, loaded with trays of food.

"Perfect timing, my love," said Cody, "the steaks are ready, and looking for mouths to eat them."

Everything went into the oversized gazebo. It was set in the midst of a beautiful garden with thousands of flowers in raised beds, walkways winding about, elegant shrubbery, and a spouting fountain in the center. The table in the gazebo opened to seat nine.

Ashana and Carlotta set bowls of baked potatoes, steaming corn, fresh bread and all the condiments around the table. Then everyone took a seat.

Cody reached out his hand for Ashana, and the rest of the family joined hands as well.

"Heavenly Father, we thank you for the blessing of this happy reunion. We are all together again. You have filled our lives with joy, peace, happiness, and success. We live in triumph according to your will. Bless the wonderful meal you have provided. We pray in the name of Christ Jesus, our Savior. Amen."

"In consideration for our guest and good friend, Hettie," said Cody, "the language for this meal will be English. Enjoy your dinner."

As they were eating, Hettie said, "I don't know how to thank you for bringing me here. Everything is just breathtaking. I praise the Lord for the day Ashana brought Rosy and Alia into my life."

"I think we're the lucky ones," said Ashana, "the girls have blossomed in your care."

"That's not entirely the case," said Hettie, from what I saw it was difficult to tell the professors from the students, most of the time. Rosy and Alia cut a wide swath in Computer Sciences at Stanford, and Microsoft.

"One thing I didn't know," continued Hettie, "was Rosy's skill in martial arts. I watched you three today and it was something to behold."

"We told both Rosy and Alia to keep as low a profile as possible," said Cody, "we wanted them to operate under the radar and not attract any undue attention."

"They did that," said Hettie, "I was the one who had to get them out of the apartment and have a little fun once in a while. I've never seen such, disciplined individuals, and so young."

"We had fun," said Rosy, "we made our schooling fun. It was a hoot watching our instructors trying to keep up. As for the kind of socializing you wanted us to do, neither Alia nor I could stand the backwards political philosophies of most of the students. I'll tell you, Dad, the State of California is more screwed up than you warned us it would be."

"I didn't have quite the same experience you've had," said Charlie. "William and Mary College is far more level-headed. However, I experienced much of the same kind of idiocy whenever I stepped off the campus."

"I suppose you kept the same low profile as your sister?" asked Hettie.

"Absolutely," said Charlie, "I was regarded as the studious bookworm type. The only time in the past five years I had to throw a punch for real was when a couple of guys tried to mug me in Washington, DC. I had to drive fifty miles to find a domo where nobody knew me, so I could keep sharp."

"To tell you the truth," said Cody, "what worried me more than anything was how the kids were going to adjust to a formal school environment. Neither of them had ever been to a public school before they left here."

"You and Ashana homeschooled all these guys?" asked Hettie.

"We did," said Cody.

"Well, you certainly gave them a fine education. It's too bad more parents don't take a more active role in their children's early learning."

The rest of the conversation during the meal was about Positano, and the Amalfi coast. Ashana spilled many juicy tidbits about the whole area. Hettie was fascinated and thrilled with all she had seen. Ashana promised to give her a much bigger tour during her visit.

"After we finish cleaning up, I want to show you the view from the upstairs veranda," said Ashana. Cody and I never tire of sitting out and enjoying it."

Everyone helped in cleaning off the table. Ashana shooed Carlotta away so she could go to the Moretti home for a long conversation with Alia. Rico and Adolfo were just as interested to catch up on all the news of the last two years, so they went along.

At present, only Cody and Charlie stayed in the gazebo.

"I read your Master's thesis on the current situation in the Middle-East," said Cody. "I thought you did a first-rate job of summing up all the conditions of the region. I suppose you have job offerings everywhere. Completing your undergraduate studies and getting a Master's degree in just five years is quite an achievement."

Charlie said, "If I thought I could actually make a difference, I would go into government service. Heaven knows the new administration is trying to clean up the mess of eight years from the previous one. However, the situation is so dangerous throughout the area, nothing less than a global effort by many countries will stem the tide of terrorism and atrocities on a daily basis. What's worse, terrorism occurring all over the world is causing most countries to work full-time just to keep their own people safe."

"I gather from what you're saying, you've decided to go on a different path," said Cody.

"If I'm really going to make a difference, I need to solve a few mysteries beginning clear back when I was just a kid. To do that, I have to do a lot of research and end up with a Doctorate thesis, which I hope will wake a few people up."

"A noble enterprise," said Cody, "where are you going to start?

"I have to get to the bottom of the Black Angel Operation."

Cody's blood ran cold.

Chapter 2
Pointed Questions

The Villa, Positano

Cody sat quietly for a moment, and then said, "I think that's a dead end for you. Certainly, all the real files on the operation are still heavily classified. You won't be able to access them."

"That's what I thought too," said Charlie, "However, there is quite a bit of information on the subject. The best resource I've found is a book by an Israeli named Noki Nevshahir. He claims he was part of the secret operation that brought the nuclear weapons into Iran, concealed in propane tanks. These went out on food service vans servicing all the secret Iranian nuclear installations.

"Of course, there have been many books and papers written about the operation. Most of them I've discounted as being too far-fetched to have any credibility."

"No doubt," said Cody. "Tell me what you know or suspect to this point."

"Let's start with the outcomes of the operation," said Charlie, "following the nuclear explosions in Iran, with what we know."

"Go ahead," said Cody.

"Following the nuclear explosions in Iran, the country found itself with about five million dead. Nevertheless, these detonations occurred in largely, sparse populated areas. The capital in Tehran escaped major damage, as did other big cities. The single exception to this was the city of Qom. It was wiped out, and so were all the senior Shia Ayatollahs, driving the hatred of America and Israel.

Charlie continued, "The Colter relief plan and reconstruction, much like the Marshall plan after World War II in Germany and Japan, brought many Christian Americans into the country to implement the reconstruction. Large numbers of Shia's from all over the world joined them. It was these Shias, who influenced the more moderate government of Iran to take a more tolerant world-view. There are about

200 million minority Shias in the world. The majority Sunnis have always persecuted them. The Shias comprise only about 15% of the world's billion Muslims. This conflict goes back over 1300 years, when the question of who would succeed Muhammed produced a schism that has never been resolved.

"Iraq also has a majority population of Shias. However, following the unilateral division of the Middle East by the Europeans after World War I, the Sunni, Baathist party, ending with Saddam Hussein, ran the country.

"With the withdrawal of the American military at the end of the Iraq war, the vacuum left behind allowed the rise of ISIS, the Islamic caliphate. These were also Sunnis, but the brand of Islam they follow is positively medieval. It imposes extreme Sharia Law, not seen in the Middle East for a thousand years. On top of that, ISIS is essentially just a vicious gang of cutthroats, thieves and murderers, hiding behind the religion of Islam as the basis for their authority. They're phony religious fanatics and more interested in power, rape, needless slaughter of innocents, especially Shias, and the accumulation of wealth."

"That's a very good history lesson," said Cody, "when do we get to the real meat of the situation?"

"I'm sorry, Dad," said Charlie. "Most Americans don't have the least idea of the divisions in the Islamic world. To them, it's all the same. Muslims are Muslims, and they are committing hideous atrocities and terrorist attacks all over the world. I guess I kind of forgot who I was talking to."

"Charlie, that's okay," said Cody. "Continue with your analysis."

"Well, the rise of ISIS was already a fact when the much bigger threat of a nuclear Iran was destroyed by the Black Angel Operation. The collapse of Iran made the country a very tempting target for ISIS, after their occupation of all of Iraq and Syria. Much of the Iranian military was still intact, but was unable to prevent an ISIS invasion of the country. The result was the incursion of American troops into the country to take on ISIS head on.

"Even though a grateful Iranian government through oil revenues paid for the costs for this, the American public saw it as just another war in the Middle East with Americans dying. The anti-war sentiment in America cost the White House for the Republicans when Mitch

Colter went out of office. The new president was a charismatic, but feckless woman with little or no understanding of foreign relations. She cut the Colter plan drastically for eight years. The Iranians couldn't understand this. They had come to think of America as an ally against the Sunni ISIS. The good will toward America still existed in Iran, but troop withdrawals of American forces put them in a tough spot to fight ISIS on their own, until now."

"What's changed?" asked Cody.

"ISIS has always been an organization of opportunity, attacking in places where the opposing forces are weak. That's one reason they've not been able to defeat the Kurds. At least this part of foreign policy stayed the same, because we don't have any troops there. We have armed the Kurds and they are ferocious fighters.

"My best friend at William and Mary was my roommate, Kamal Barzani, the son of the Kurdish leader. I think the Lord was at work in putting us together. He was worried about his English, and was thrilled with having a roommate who spoke Arabic. I helped him with his English, and we spent many hours on the mats sharpening our fighting skills. I was very sorry to see him go when he graduated and went back to Kurdistan."

"I didn't know that," said Cody, "but I certainly agree God had a plan for you when he put you two together. Anyway, go on with your main points."

Charlie gathered his thoughts and said, "What is happening is the numbers of terrorist attacks around the world have increased exponentially. The hideous attack in Paris was France's 9-11. Hundreds died, many hundreds more were injured. These were coordinated attacks, six of them at the same time, all organized by ISIS. As I said before, the European countries are just trying to protect their own people. The effect is causing whole populations to freeze in place. International travel is down, because people are afraid to fly in planes that blow up everywhere.

"Fortunately, for us, the American people swung back to a more militant stance at the last election. Having terrorist attacks occur in the United States got their blood boiling and the new President, Carson Palmer, restored our defenses and quietly restarted much of the Colter plan."

"You haven't told me anything I don't already know, Charlie,"

Cody said. "What's that got to do with your Doctorate thesis?"

"A great deal of the current geo-political conditions in the Middle East started with the Black Angel Operation. The groups of people who conceived and carried out that mission were clearly the absolute best. Mitch Colter gets a lot of credit for authorizing the action, but I believe there was another player. Without any footprints leading anywhere, someone thwarted the attack on America and caused the Iranian bombs to go off in their own country. From everything, I know, Dad, the actions in Iran and elsewhere, was not a big combined operation with a lot of input, but was in fact, the work of a single man. The Black Angel was not a thing, but a person."

Cody silently listened to Charlie lay out his case, and was grateful he actually still didn't know very much. However, he knew there were hundreds of books, blogs, articles, and papers on the Black Angel. Most of them were complete hogwash, but a lot of them contained at least one tiny kernel of the truth. Cody knew Charlie would sort through everything available, putting tiny pieces together, here and there. Afraid Charlie might discover most of the truth, at this moment of relief he still had time.

"I wish you good luck on your quest," Cody said. "Don't be surprised if the mystery turns out to be impossible to solve."

Charlie asked, "Will you give me a hand and speak to Mitch Colter for me?"

"Mitch won't divulge anything to you. You'll be wasting your time."

"But you know him, apparently pretty well. I remember our time at the White House very clearly."

"Social events are one thing," said Cody, "asking the former President of the United States to disclose top secret information is entirely different. He won't do it, even if I asked him."

"You weren't there for a social event," said Charlie with frustration, "there was a lot more going on, and you were right in the middle of it. Then after going to the White House, we went to Rome. They treated you with a lot respect, and I don't think you were just telling them what the President said. Is it possible my best source is going to turn out to be a dud?"

"May I respectfully tell you I'm as subject to the same restrictions of disclosure concerning classified information as anyone else in the government?"

"But I…"

"Charlie! Drop it! I can't tell you anything more than you already know."

"I won't put you on the spot, Dad. But I'm going to find this out."

There was no more discussion about Charlie's quest the following morning. Cody sighed in relief. He did not lie to his, son, but he talked it over with God in his morning devotions.

"Father, I wonder if I did the right thing with Charlie. The struggle we had to overcome the Iranian nuclear threat was unbelievable. You kept us alive to complete it. I would spare Charlie from that. I've no idea what you plan for us in the future, but I trust you completely."

For the next several days, the family just had fun. Ashana zipped around Positano with Hettie, Rosy and Alia, in the ATV, shopping and seeing the sights. There were excursions to Paestum, Sorrento, Vesuvius, and the town of Amalfi. They swam in the ocean and sunned on the rocky beaches. Every night they sat on the upstairs veranda and watched the sun go down and the lights of Positano twinkle in the night.

Cody organized workouts of martial arts, this time on mats. The only people who did not actually participate were Adolfo, Carlotta and Hettie. All the rest took part. Hettie could not believe what she was seeing. With Cody doing more supervising and teaching than fighting, the matches raged furiously between, Charlie, Rico, Alia, Rosy and Ashana. Hettie had never seen real people doing what she saw. She thought all this martial arts stuff was just Hollywood stunts, but seeing them fight before her eyes, gave her a new perception of real, deadly hand combat.

The best battles were the ones between Charlie and Rico. Charlie had lightning fast reflexes, but Rico used the careful training from Cody, and had better techniques. Most of the time, Charlie had to slap out. He was not angry at losing, and complimented Rico on his advanced skills.

"If we ever had to do this for real," said Charlie, "I'd want you next to me, for my own protection."

Ashana was older, and did not have the speed or the stamina of the younger girls, but often won points with superior techniques. Hettie watched with admiration of Ashana and made a mental note to get some basic training from her … as soon as possible.

Near the end of the week, the families saw news of the latest ISIS atrocity. This one was more horrible than any before. Cody's elaborate communications system was able to bring in satellite feeds from all over the world, and all watched as the ghastly event unfolded.

Cody was not surprised the U.S. networks spared the public all the grisly details, but that was not the case for the Arab network of Al Jazeera. ISIS rounded up 1,000 Christians from all around Iraq and Syria, and proceeded to execute them all, by cutting off their heads. Groups of twenty at a time were dragged up to cutting blocks, and burly ISIS men, wearing black masks, would force the men, women, and children down onto the blocks and use large swords to chop their way through 1,000 people.

It was, by far, the most extensive execution ever seen from ISIS. The cries of the victims during the killings heard the crowd reply with 'Allah Akbar'. A steady stream of speech by hooded men insisted Islam was the only true religion of the world. All people not accepting this religion would die. They boasted all Christian bastions would soon see the black flag of ISIS rise over them.

"That's the most awful thing I've ever seen," said Hettie.

"I didn't know there were still that many Christians remaining in the Islamic Caliphate," said Charlie.

"Obviously, there were," said Cody. "This demonstration was designed to show the Western world the power and resolve of ISIS. I'm sure these Sunni fanatics have done much the same with the Shia population in Iraq and Syria who were not able to escape to Europe or to Iran."

None of the people in the Frost villa knew things were about to get much worse. One week later at St. Peter Square in Rome, the pope celebrated a public ceremony in front of the church with 150,000 people in attendance. The warm, sunny day in June had television cameras recording the event for the Vatican archives, the people of Rome, and recordings by other networks, who were hoping the pope would say something to acknowledge the slaughter of 1,000 Christians in Iraq.

An elderly, intelligent pope elected after the death of Pope Francis four years before, rose to the task. In fiery Italian, he declared that

Muslims all over the world could not possibly condone the actions of the extreme regime of the new Caliphate. He called for all people, Christians, Jews, and Muslims to seek ways to stem the tide of horrific barbarism, practiced by this lunatic brand of Islam, and not seen in the world for over a thousand years.

As he was finishing his address, the cry of 'Allah Akbar' rang through the square. Suddenly, four huge explosions blasted near the area of the pope. The church of St. Peter collapsed and demolished the entire front. Thousands of people lay dead or injured; among the dead, laid the pope himself.

A group of twenty men rushed forward, shooting the unarmed Swiss Guards as they went into the Basilica. Moments later, after more gunfire, two of them appeared on the dome of St. Peter's and hoisted the black flag of ISIS over the church.

The Italian Gendarmerie police moved in immediately and engaged in a firefight with the ISIS gunmen inside St. Peters. In only a few minutes, they had killed all the ISIS attackers, but the two remaining in the dome, detonated suicide vests of high explosives. The great dome of St. Peters, designed by Michelangelo in 1547, shattered in pieces.

Every news organization in the world began wall-to-wall coverage of the events in Rome. Soon, this was the only thing anyone could find on television, the internet, or in papers all over the world.

Cody and his family were not watching the Vatican ceremony when the attack occurred, but quickly caught up as the news spread, literally from home to home in Positano.

Everything came to an abrupt stop as the news reports poured out. The Frost and Moretti family huddled around television screens to see the massacre and destruction with their own eyes, and watched it, repeatedly.

After spending at least 24 hours glued to the news, Cody summed it all up, "This is the limit to what ISIS can do. I can't imagine anything that will infuriate the Christian world more. From now on, their days are numbered. The response will be beyond belief."

"What's going to happen, Dad?" asked Rosy.

"There will be a lot of teeth gnashing, threats and the beginnings of mobilization by a lot of countries over the next few weeks," said Cody. "The problem is everyone will have their own idea of what actions to take. Some kind of a central authority is going to have to emerge. Probably, the United States will take the lead, but other countries will have to be brought into a coalition from somewhere to get any real response prepared."

"The use of nuclear weapons will, almost certainly, not be part of the response," said Charlie.

"Your right, son, the memories of Iran are just too fresh and close to the surface for that."

"If other people are as angry as I am," said Ashana, "we'll have rioting in the streets unless something is done soon. When was the last time a pope was assassinated?"

"There are a lot of allegations on that," said Cody, "but the last actual documented killing of a pope was in 999, when Pope Gregory V was poisoned."

"Boy!" said Hettie, "you sure pulled that fact up in a hurry. How do you do it?"

"Dad has an eidetic memory," Rosy said. "He never forgets anything."

"It's not always a good thing," said Cody, "there are lots of memories I wish I could forget. In addition, there's a lot I don't know. If I haven't seen or read it, I'm just as dumb as the next guy."

As it turned out, Cody was right. The United Nations condemned ISIS for its actions, a number of countries, including China, declared ISIS to be a terrorist state. Sanctions of all kinds fell on ISIS. However, the world had still not made up its mind about military action against the Caliphate.

Ashana could sense a thunderstorm headed their way. She had no idea how it would play out, but knew they had to clear the decks for action. The first thing she decided to do was to get Hettie as far away from the family as possible. It was near the end of her trip, and so she, Rosy and Alia took her to Naples a day later to catch a flight back to California.

"I've never seen a family like yours," said Hettie, just before she said goodbye at the airport. "One thing is for sure, I'm sure we haven't heard the end of your family's involvement in these terrible events that have occurred."

"Unfortunately, you're probably right," said Ashana, "don't be surprised at anything that happens, but I must ask you to forget everything you know about us, and speak to no one on that subject."

Hettie said, "I promise." She hugged Ashana, and gave long hugs to the girls. Then she took her bag and disappeared into the airport security lines.

❖

In Rome, Cardinals from around the world gathered to choose a new Pope. Many of the senior Vatican Cardinals, who would have been candidates, died in the attack on St. Peter Square.

After several long days of debate and deliberation, the College of Cardinals selected a 55-year-old German Cardinal to fill the shoes of the fisherman. It was obvious the church wanted a vital, young man to take on the daunting task of rebuilding St. Peter's Basilica, and to defend the church from threats. His name was Robert Stroud, and the name he chose for his papacy was John Luke. It was the first time a Pope selected that particular name.

When the choice became public, Cody sat straight up in his chair. He knew this man. He was one of the team members to Bishop Marcello Bernelli in the super-secret Vatican Black Ops division. His impression of Stroud was a very smart, charismatic, and effective leader. Cody wondered if his selection as Pope had something to do with his background.

His suspicions were further aroused a few days later when his secure phone rang, the first time in twelve years. On the other end was Bishop Vincent Paglioni, who had taken over Vatican covert operations after the death of Bernelli a few years earlier. Cody liked Paglioni. He was very good at his job and Marcello trusted him, completely. Cody expected Marcello had clearly chosen him as his successor, and knew it when Paglioni became second in command.

"Good morning, Cody," said Paglioni. "I suppose you know why I'm calling. We lost a lot of good people in the attack on the Vatican and I'm calling everyone I know to get all the help I can. Is Ashana with you?"

"Yes," said Cody.

"Then I will do most of the talking," said Paglioni. "Your skills are vital to the church, now and even more than ever. In particular, your ability to conceive comprehensive plans from limited information. We realize your field skills are now limited, owing to your age and many nagging injuries, but your mind is intact and we need it. Can I count on your help in this?"

"Yes," said Cody.

"I understand," continued Bishop Paglioni, "Charlie has gotten his Master's Degree in Middle Eastern studies, and did it in just five years. That is quite an achievement. We need him.

"Rosy is now one of the best computer minds in the world. One of our biggest problems is disrupting the social media campaigns by ISIS. We are of the opinion she could have a big impact on that.

"I hear the whole family is deadly in martial arts, especially Alfonso's son, Enrico. What's more, I know all of them can hit a silver dollar with your Timberwolf from a grand. It sounds like you've raised a new team."

"Yes," said Cody.

"We have a new Pope," said Paglioni. "He was chosen, as all Popes are, a man for the times, in addition to his dedication to God and the Church. You know Robert Stroud. Probably your eidetic memory can tell me more about him than I know.

"In any case, Pope John Luke is not wasting any time getting all the balls rolling. He is not even waiting for his formal coronation. He's in the Papal chambers, hard at work, as we speak. I know because I just came from there. He sure remembers you, everyone does. You wrote the book on most of the procedures we use today."

Paglioni paused for minute and then said, "Cody, I know you've raised your family to make them as safe as they can be in this world of ours. I know the last thing you want to do is to put them at risk, but can you imagine how they would feel if you came in and worked for us again, and then lost your life? None of them would be able to live with themselves, wondering if they could have done something. Isn't that right?"

"Yes," said Cody.

"Very well, I'm giving Charlie, Rosy, Alia, Rico and Ashana full access to everything we do. The pope wants to meet with you tomorrow. Can you be here by two?"

"Yes," said Cody.

"I don't envy you the next few hours in your home, but your family will have to be told the whole story."

"Goodbye," said Cody, and rang off.

"Five yeses and one goodbye?" Ashana said, "Not very much information for a call that had to be pretty important."

"It was a terrible conversation," said Cody, "however, not unexpected."

"They want you back don't they?" said Ashana

"Not for field work. They know my limitations as well as I do."

"It looks like our quiet life is over," sighed Ashana.

"To tell you the truth, I'm surprised it's lasted this long," said Cody. "It's possible they were just keeping an eye on me, letting us raise our family, and see what kind of people the kids turned out to be."

Ashana looked confused, "Why do you say that?"

"Because the new head of Vatican Ops, a Bishop named Paglioni, rattled off our life history like he was reading a book. I guess I've been careless about watching what's going on around me. Paglioni talked about Charlie and Rosy. He knew everything about them. I think the Vatican had us under surveillance, more or less continuously, both here and at the kid's schools for years. It's as if they knew I was going to train Charlie and Rosy to be as good as my original team. Since that's exactly what I did, the Vatican wants the whole family involved in whatever the new Pope has in mind to do."

Ashana was alarmed, "risking you, even from behind the scenes, is bad enough, but dragging the kids into this is something I can't stand."

"Me neither," said Cody. The trouble is we have two grown, adult individuals. Who's to say either or both of them won't just volunteer?"

"If that's the case," said Ashana, "I'd rather they were with you."

"I hate this!" said Cody. "Paglioni told me it was going to be a few tough hours in our house, and he's right. I have to go to Rome tomorrow and meet with the Pope. Charlie and Rosy have to go with us."

"Guess we've got some explaining to do."

Ashana went off to find Charlie and Rosy, to bring them back to the second floor with the beautiful veranda and view of Positano. Cody stood there looking out at God's masterpiece. Tears welled in his eyes, while the strength of God's love bolstered his belief. Take heart, and know I have overcome the world echoed from St. John's written scripture. Cody rubbed his eyes.

"Dear Lord, we are at the edge of the abyss, and stepping into frightening waters. I know you are with us this moment and for all the moments still to come. I'm not afraid for myself, but I pray for your mercy on my family. I trust you, Jesus."

Charlie and Rosy came into the room, with Ashana following them. They all sat in a circle around the big coffee table. Cody read their eyes, and shook his head. "There's no easy way for me to tell you this. I ask your forgiveness for any deceit or misdirection I've done over the years. My prayer was for us to live out our lives in peace and happiness.

"I was born an orphan and raised in a Catholic orphanage in Philadelphia. As you might imagine, they spotted my gift of memory very early in my life and I moved along in school, about like both of you have, as fast as I could absorb it. When I was 17, I joined the Marines, where I learned how to shoot the way I do, in sniper school. Later, I went to Seal training in San Diego, and after I graduated, I spent four years with the teams.

"Then, suddenly one day, I was given new orders and told to report to a new duty station in Rome. Here I learned the church had not forgotten about me, and all the time had intended my service to be in a special, secret branch of the church.

"There's never been anything in my life more important than God, so when I had the chance, I went to seminary and became a Priest."

"You mean your masquerading around like a priest was not just a cover?" asked Rosy.

"No, honey, it wasn't. When you first met me, I was an actual priest. Later I quit, and the pope approved it, but I agreed to do one last job"

"How come you quit?" asked Charlie.

"Because twenty years before I met your mother and you, I lived a much different life. My job involved dangerous situations, with evil people to eliminate threats. My team and I went into some horrible places, and did unspeakable things to give innocent people a chance to live their lives as they chose.

"I did all of these things for the church, and their super-secret covert operations branch. The organization remains secret from all but a handful of people in the world even today. When I came home from a job in Guatemala, I told my boss I'd had enough. I never was a real priest in the traditional way, I was a hired gun for the church, and I was burned out."

"Let me guess," said Charlie, "along came the Iranians."

"Right," said Cody. "What you, and anyone else in the world don't know is, the Iranians were actually successful in smuggling six nuclear weapons into the United States. We let them do it. Then we wiped them out and stole the bombs. After that, we smuggled them back into Iran and blew them up."

"So that's what you were doing in Texas," said Charlie, "and that's why we went to the White House, and then on to Rome. You were not the tiny part in the strategy like you said. You were right in the middle of it, probably doing most of the planning."

"Guilty as charged," said Cody. "There goes your doctorate thesis. Sorry for bursting your bubble."

"How come?"

"Because the Vatican called me today. After the tragedy at St. Peter's Basilica, they asked for all the help they can get. I'm going to answer the bell one more time. However, this time, the Vatican wants me to bring along my new team."

"You mean us?" Rosy said with breathless shock.

"You two, and Rico are as good as anyone I've ever worked with," said Cody. "I did a thorough job of training you."

Charlie asked, "Any chance we can meet the Black Angel?"

"Usually, you aren't so slow to connect the clues, Charlie."

"What does that mean?"

"It means the simple truth is *I am* the Black Angel."

Chapter 3
The New Mission

Cody made a late night call to Bishop Paglioni. He was less than courteous over the quagmire Paglioni had put him in, and the risks he was taking with his own flesh and blood.

The Bishop was sympathetic, but said, "The Church has suffered a terrible tragedy. Not only was our Pope killed … the first in over a thousand years, but our magnificent basilica is in ruins. You will find a lot of very angry people when you arrive."

"Do we come to Ops first, before my meeting with the Pope?" asked Cody.

"That would be best. To save time, I'm sending a helicopter to pick you up at 6 a.m. I think we should give you as much time as possible to catch up on the latest Intel before your meeting with the Holy Father. He's likely to ask you some very direct questions, give him direct answers."

"We already know each other, so he'll be prepared for me to speak bluntly."

"Do so," said the Bishop, "he needs clarity at this moment, and you're the one to give it. Since you've worked together before, and he's read your entire file again, he'll trust your judgement."

While his family slept, Cody scanned the internet for everything relating to the Middle East in the past twelve years. He'd kept up with the basics in a casual way, but now was looking at the information with the eye of an analyst, trying to find answers and possible ways to proceed. A number of scenarios formed in his mind. He filed them all away in anticipation of what Pope John Luke would say.

Early the next morning, Cody slipped into his bedroom, and found Ashana already awake. "Did you sleep alright, sweetie?"

"Not so good," said Ashana. "I kept dreaming of the time you came back from Iran, and how badly wounded you were. I'll bet you didn't sleep at all."

"I catnapped here and there, while I was getting caught up on all I've missed these last few years."

"Have you figured out how to save the world?"

"Hardly, but I do have several ideas to present to the Pope this afternoon. I'll have an even better understanding when I see some of the raw intelligence in the Ops Center."

"Will the kids and I get to see this nerve center of international intelligence?"

"Certainly," said Cody, "the Bishop would not have reached out to me unless he thought I could make a real contribution. He also believes Charlie and Rosy are valuable assets as well. You're not exactly a silent partner. You understand the big picture better than 99% of the world. Paglioni is going to think he's getting a very effective package deal. I'm sure they'll treat us with honor and respect. In fact, the kid gloves treatment has already begun. Paglioni is sending a helicopter to pick us up at 6 o'clock."

"I'll go and wake Charlie and Rosy," said Ashana.

Both were already awake when she went to their rooms. They set their alarms and packed a bag before they went to bed. A glow of anticipation emitted from both of them. Everyone gathered in the dining room for breakfast. Carlotta was also up early, and prepared a big meal.

The family joined hands and Cody prayed, "Father, please forgive us for our fears this morning. We trust you, and know you have an exact plan for all of us. We are stepping off such a huge cliff of unknowns. We ask for your help for we are only human and the future has clouds of uncertainty. Be with us today and help us all follow your will in all things. We pray in the name of Christ Jesus, who is our Savior and redeemer, Amen."

As Cody looked up, he found Rosy smiling at him. Charlie had a look of amazement and wonder on his face. "If you think this is all a big revelation now, Charlie, ask Bishop Paglioni to let you read my entire file. Not only does it contain the operations for all the years before we became a family, it has the entire Iranian operation in it. You're going to get a look into things known only to a very few. I hope it satisfies all the questions you've had, and gives you a better insight on what your real Doctorate Thesis could have contained."

"It'll fill in a lot of blanks," said Charlie. "Even if I never get to write about it, I'll have the satisfaction of knowing I was right in my conclusion the Black Angel was a person and not a thing. I just never expected the real Black Angel would turn out to be my own father."

"I never cared for that nickname," said Cody, and I've come to hate it even more over the years with all the far-fetched and idiotic stories written about me. Besides, remember the Black Angel died in the Iranian Operation. Maybe now I'll get less notice so I can do the work I need to do, whatever that is."

The family was waiting as the silver, unmarked helicopter sat down in front of the villa. Cody ushered everyone aboard, and the craft took off immediately.

"There aren't any markings on the helicopter," said Charlie.

"When it relates to intelligence, nothing the Vatican does is ever marked," said Cody. "Did you notice they didn't come in over Positano? That's so we attract the least amount of attention possible. The early hour only adds to being inconspicuous."

The flight to Rome took less than an hour. Charlie and Rosy stared out the windows to see the ground below. Cody and Ashana sat back and took a nap. The familiar dome of St. Peter was not on the horizon as they approached the Vatican. The front of the basilica showed heavy damage, but the most heart-breaking sight of all was the ruins of the dome, which had collapsed into the interior of the church. An army of workers was all over the scene, laboring to remove the unusable rubble and restore pieces with painstaking selections to save what remained.

The helicopter sat down on the plaza in front of the Administration building. Waiting for the craft to land was a group of people, led by Bishop Paglioni. Cody and the family exited and Paglioni walked up to him immediately, with a smile on his face and his hands out.

"It's so good to see you, Cody. I feel better just knowing you're here."

"Thanks, Bishop, have you met my wife Ashana?"

"I have, although she probably doesn't remember. I was at the hospital when they brought you back from Iran."

"Yes, I do remember you, and I'm glad to see you again," said Ashana. "You were very kind. It's good to see you after all these years. Here are the rest of your protégés, Charlie and Rosy."

Charlie took the lead in the exchange, "Well, Bishop Paglioni, I can't say Rosy and I care very much about your spying on us all this time."

Paglioni actually laughed, "Welcome to the wonderful world of intelligence. I can assure you Charlie, and you too Rosy, our time looking at you was entirely benign. We were delighted to watch you both perform so magnificently in school, and still keep your personal lives so tidy. Cody taught you well, you both drove long distances to gyms where nobody knew you did your workouts. I must say, I've never seen such a deadly duo as you two."

"In that case," said Rosy, "we forgive you, lead us to the war."

Paglioni laughed again and grinned at Cody, who just shrugged his shoulders.

"If you will just come this way, I'll take you to the Ops Center."

Cody could see some changes as they went inside. The long stairway near the entrance was gone, replaced by an elevator in the hallway. The group stepped in. Paglioni put a key into a slot, pushed a button, and they went all the way down to the bottom floor where the sprawling intelligence center was located. At the end of the hall, the administrative offices and Paglioni's apartment stood across from the Ops Center on the other side. Paglioni opened the door and ushered the Frost family into the deepest, darkest secret place in the whole world. There were at least a hundred people in the room, more than ought to be there, for normal operations.

Cody led the way into the Center. As he came into the room filled with computer screens, and a big array of special equipment, the entire group of people stood up. There was complete silence in the room. Caught completely off guard, Cody recognized a few faces of people who had seen him work in the room during the Iranian operation. Otherwise, everyone was a stranger, and a young group at that.

Cody took a moment to figure it out. The people in the room grew up hearing stories of the legendary Black Angel and his brilliant solutions to so many different missions and operations. Most of the people sincerely believed he was dead. Now, here in person, the tough intelligence officers seemed overwhelmed. Here he was, alive and well.

"After you accept I'm not a ghost, don't you people have something to do?" asked Cody.

This broke the ice with laughter and followed with applause and cheers. People crowded around Cody to shake his hand. Ashana had expected this response, but Charlie and Rosy had not.

"I'm not going to start bowing and scraping," said Charlie in Cody's ear, "but it's nice to know you're appreciated."

Bishop Paglioni clapped his hands for attention. "Alright, let's get back to work. Everyone get where their supposed to be." He turned to Cody, "We've been preparing for your arrival. The main intelligence piles are over there, with a terminal set up for you to use. Charlie, we have a team ready to brief you on the things they didn't teach you at William and Mary in International Studies. Rosy, we have some folks trying to disrupt the social media websites and twitter accounts of ISIS. We think you can help with that. Ashana, your expertise is in probing personalities and character elements of people. We have some on our list, we think deserve another look, both good and bad."

"It looks like you've done plenty to keep us busy," said Cody. He turned to the family. "OK, gang let's get started on what we came to do."

Cody walked over to the desk with a big computer terminal on it, and several piles of files. He sorted through the piles and separated several of them, then started scanning them. Turning pages so quickly, the people watching him wondered if he was really absorbing the mountains of data.

When he finished reading the selected files, he turned to the computer terminal and his fingers began to fly over the keys, bringing up one box after another. He was doing it so fast, the other analysists did not know what subjects could help him.

Charlie was involved in an animated conversation with several men and women around a table with a computer they passed around to emphasize points. What he was seeing and hearing was well beyond the history, projections, and analysis of the current world situation, especially as it related to the Middle East. Charlie was able to confirm through the intelligence files, many suppositions he suspected were true.

The most noise in the room was coming from the group surrounding Rosy. There were half a dozen people working on computers. They were following her lead in punching holes, and exploiting soft spots in the ISIS computer network. Several times, there were cheers as the programming wizards, following Rosy's lead, were able to take down big hunks of the ISIS network. Rosy even wrote a virus that infected their entire system. The biggest thing she was able to learn was the location of their main servers.

After three hours of furious work, Cody called for a meeting. Ashana, Rosy, and Charlie joined Bishop Paglioni and his principal department heads at a big conference table in a room across the hall from the Ops Center.

"Let's start with you, Charlie," said Cody.

"There are multiple problems, both politically and religious among all the countries involved in the active operations of Daesh, or ISIS. In many ways, ISIS is its own worst enemy. The type of Islam they are imposing on their conquered territories has been absent for almost a thousand years. Their return to a purist kind of Islam debases women, and forbids teaching in science, literature, and civics. They have banned almost all forms of entertainment, including religious music. The core of the ISIS personnel use an extreme form of authoritarian rule, which includes rape, mass executions, and torture among any group who does not subscribe to their fundamentalist Sunni beliefs. The good news shows a huge dislike of ISIS among the majority of Muslims, including other Sunnis.

"The execution of a thousand Christians was an atrocity, but the people who are really taking it on the chin are the minority Shia. ISIS is killing them wholesale. In a perverse way, this is regarded as a good thing among many Sunni controlled countries including Saudi Arabia, Qatar, Libya, Yemen, and to a certain extent Turkey, who is buying some of the ISIS oil. Lately however, Turkey has begun bombing ISIS targets. The country is close to a civil war because of their hardline President. The military was opposed to allowing American warplanes to use Incirlik Air Base, but he went ahead with it anyway. One of the biggest problems the Turks have is the Kurds, who now hold ten percent of the seats in their parliament.

"Speaking of the Kurds, they're the best thing we have going for us against ISIS. They have not only held their own against them, but have made advances in Iraq, and Syria. The Kurds have a minority Shia population, mostly in northern Iran, but they think of themselves as Kurds first, and Muslims second.

"From a public relations standpoint, the worst thing ISIS could have done is to kill a Pope and destroy much of the Vatican area displaying respect for St. Peter. Public sentiment against ISIS has risen dramatically since the attack. There are a billion Catholics in the world telling their governments to do whatever it takes to destroy ISIS."

"Good job, Charlie," said Cody. "Everything you've said squares with my intelligence research."

He turned to Rosy and said, "Your group was making a lot of noise. What have you got?"

"It seems the computer operations and social media push is coming from Raqqa, in Syria. We can bomb these guys forever and fail to put them out of action. However, from the inside we can cripple or even sabotage their effort. I was able to hack into their system and install a virus that will take days to unsort. While they're busy unscrambling the mess, I believe I can write a code that will make them think they're delivering all their messages to Facebook and Twitter, when in fact all their junk will actually be sent to a ghost Facebook and Twitter which we should have time to build. It isn't easy; Bishop Paglioni, but you have some real sharp computer nerds here. In any case, I don't think ISIS can build a firewall strong enough to keep us from breaking into their servers and make their social media effort choke."

"That's very good news," said Paglioni, "You are definitely everything my sources reported to me."

Cody reported, "I've been exploring the military options we might employ. While the world has muddled around, worrying about their oil and natural gas supplies, and taking a defensive stance regarding ISIS, this group of fanatics have grown and expanded. Today, they control all of Iraq and Syria. I estimate their active fighting force at 60,000 men. They have plenty of equipment, lots of money, and are intent on making the whole world compliant to their brand of Islam. I believe it will take 50 brigades of real troops, about 200,000 men, complete air superiority and a coordinated assault from several fronts to defeat them. Mobilizing the whole world, while convincing the 1.2 billion Muslims to just stand by and watch us do it, will take a major miracle."

"The goal here is to convince the mainstream Muslim public that ISIS does not represent the true faith at all. We need to marginalize them without doing the same to the Islamic religion. As Catholics, we believe fervently Jesus was sent by God to reconcile humanity with the Holy Spirit. Muslims feel the same way about their beliefs. We must always speak the name of Allah with reverence. In the end, the creator of the universe will make the final choice on everything."

"Will you speak to His Holiness in the same manner?" asked Bishop Paglioni.

"I will," said Cody. "If you want to know what I think my biggest problem will be with the Pope, is to find a way to restrain him."

"You're about to find out," said Paglioni, "Your appointment is in 15 minutes."

"Oh that's a relief," said Cody, as he winked at Ashana. "I thought I was going to have to work under pressure."

The Papal apartments, the Vatican Museum, and the Sistine Chapel did not suffer damage in the ISIS attack. It broke Cody's heart to see the ruins of the main cathedral. Workers had a temporary cover over the hole where the dome had collapsed, to keep out the rain and elements. One of the pieces of art not damaged, to Cody's surprise, was Michelangelo's Pieta. If it had blown to pieces from the explosions outside, the devastation would wound the feelings of Christians everywhere; yet here it was, as beautiful as ever. Cody said a quiet prayer of thanks for that.

A monsignor anxious to get Cody to his Papal appointment on time cut short his brief look at the Cathedral. They walked up the stairs and to the floor where the pope lived, and entered into the offices of Pope John Luke, the First. He was sitting on his tall chair at the end of the room, and seemed in deep thought or prayer when Cody entered and stood respectfully quiet. At last, the Pope looked up and smiled grimly. Cody knew the look.

One of the files he reviewed was that of Robert Stroud, the man who was now the leader of the Catholic Church. He had known Stroud very well in the intelligence center, even though he was there less often. What he remembered was a very vital, pragmatic, realist who viewed the world as it was, not as it should be. This made him quite different from other senior leaders of the church.

The pope was as tall as Cody, seemed to be in perfect health, and appeared to be close in age, even though Cody knew he was a few years older. His face was not as beatific as other popes often appeared. John Luke's face seemed chiseled from granite. It was square, with widely spaced brown eyes. There was strength and determination about him. Cody knew his decisive resolve matched his looks. He was the best man the Cardinals could have chosen for this time of crisis.

Cody already had decided to dispense with all the trappings of formality and get right to business, so he approached the pope, bowed politely, and said in German, the pope's native language, "Your Holiness. This is a lousy time to renew our acquaintance, but these are not normal times."

John Luke smiled and replied in perfect English, "Thank you for greeting me in my own tongue. I hear so little of it around here." He rose and came over to shake Cody's hand. "I hope you're not too angry with Bishop Paglioni for bringing you here. It was We who believed you and your family could aid our current situation. We were the one who ordered him to pull you out of Positano and back into the eye of a storm." Assuming his new papal position and mantel also carried the understanding, he now was 'One with Christ'. The pope said, "Pardon my effort to discuss our predicament with ISIS. We are in a steep learning curve to represent my Savior."

"I thought as much," said Cody. "Well, we're here now and already hard at work. I can't say I like the odds of us solving this peacefully. Moreover, I won't bet on a chance to get the outcome we want."

"No question about that," said John Luke. "We are forced to use the tools at our disposal and if we have to fight, we fight."

"You've been looking at this longer than I have," said Cody "Why don't you tell me your thoughts on our first steps."

"We were thinking of a modern Crusade."

Stunned by what he just heard, Cody had the same thought while sorting the filed options this morning. Nevertheless, he rejected the possibility as a lose/lose proposition. ISIS would not tolerate setting Christianity directly among Islam. John Luke must have thought about it, and unless he was delusional, should have come to the same conclusion.

The statement was so incredible Cody lost all sense, with whom he was speaking and said, "Robert, that's suicidal. We'll end up with a war about religion, which is never a good idea, and it will fracture the entire world."

"I said 'modern Crusade.' I'm not so stupid, nor will I allow the church to fall into the quagmire of the old Crusades. They made a disaster for Europe, and almost lost all of Christendom, by Islamic occupation. Use your brain and tell me what actually happened."

Cody sat for a minute gathering his thoughts and then responded, "When Muhammed began his wars in the seventh century, Christianity was the dominant religion of power and wealth. As the faith of the Roman Empire faded, it spanned the entire Mediterranean, including the Middle East, where it was born. Therefore, the Christian world became a prime target and remains so right up until today."

"The warriors of Islam struck out against the Christians, shortly after Muhammad's death and were extremely successful. Palestine, Syria, and Egypt, once the most heavily Christian areas in the world, easily fell. By the eighth century, Muslim armies conquered all of Christian North Africa and Spain. In the eleventh century, the Seljuk Turks conquered modern Turkey, which had been Christian since the time of St. Paul. The old Roman Empire, known to modern historians as the Byzantine Empire, became little more than Greece. In desperation, the emperor in Constantinople sent word to the Christians of Western Europe asking them to aid their brothers and sisters in the East."

"This is what gave birth to the Crusades. They were not the conveyance of ambitious popes or greedy knights, but a response to more than four centuries of conquests where Muslims had already captured two-thirds of the old Christian world. Christianity, as a faith and a culture, had no choice but defend itself or fall to Islam. The Crusades were that defence."

"Pope Urban II called upon the knights of Christendom to push back the conquests of Islam at the Council of Clermont in 1095. The response was remarkable. Many thousands of knights prepared for war."

"One would think, three centuries of Christian defeats in the Middle East, except for the first one, would have soured Europeans on the idea of Crusades, but it did not. Actually, the Europeans had little choice but to keep fighting. Muslim kingdoms were becoming more, not less, powerful in the 14th, 15th, and 16th centuries. The Ottoman Turks conquered the entire region further unifying Islam. The Ottomans continued to move west, capturing Constantinople, and then attacking all of Europe. By the 15th century, the Crusades were desperately fighting for Christendom to survive. Europeans faced the real possibility that Islam would conquer the entire Christian world. Actually, it was a miracle they didn't."

"Excellent summary," said Pope John Luke, very succinct and entirely accurate. What happened then?"

"The Renaissance happened," said Cody. "Along with that came the Protestant Reformation. The Catholic Church lost much of its power to control the hearts and minds of people, and the Kings. The result was the rise of secular institutions and independent countries. The social and political landscape changed dramatically. The West began to surge forward. The discovery of the Americas caused countries to adopt Colonialism as a matter of national policy. Then the Industrial Revolution got rolling. Europe became the dominant force in the world. Basically, the Middle East became a quaint backwater, until the largest reserves of oil in the world, showed up there."

"You're doing fine," said John Luke. "Now tell me the results of European Colonialism."

"That's a very broad topic," said Cody. "I assume you mean how it relates to the Middle East."

Pope John Luke nodded.

"The story should begin with the Ottoman Empire, founded in 1299, which controlled all the modern Middle East. With conquests in the Balkans, the Ottomans became a transcontinental empire. In 1453, the Ottomans conquered Constantinople, present-day Istanbul, and overthrew the Byzantine Empire.

"During the 16th and 17th centuries, at the height of its power under the reign of Suleiman the Magnificent, the Ottoman Empire was a multinational, multilingual empire controlling much of Southeast Europe, Western Asia, the Caucasus, North Africa, and the Horn of Africa. At the beginning of the 17th century, the empire contained 32 provinces and numerous vassal states. Some of these were later absorbed into the Ottoman Empire, while others received various types of autonomy during the course of centuries.

"With Constantinople as its capital and control of lands around the Mediterranean basin, the Ottoman Empire was at the center of interactions between the Eastern and Western worlds for six centuries. Following a long period of military setbacks against European powers, the Ottoman Empire gradually declined in the late nineteenth century. The empire allied with Germany in the early 20th century and joined

The Great War, with a desire to recover its lost territories, and achieve this imperial ambition. While the Empire was able to hold its own during the conflict, it struggled with internal dissent, especially in its Arabian holdings. It collapsed following the war. This resulted in the emergence of the new state of Turkey under Ataturk.

"The winners of World War I, principally France and Britain planned to divide the Middle East in arbitrary ways, independent of cultural, religious, and geographical considerations.

"President Woodrow Wilson proposed a different solution; it was an obvious idea. First, a survey to find out if the residents of Syria would accept a French mandate. Next, another survey conducted in Palestine and Mesopotamia, or Iraq, as we know it today, to measure their willingness to accept British rule. President Wilson said, 'We should find out what people in those regions wanted.'

For two months, the Chicago businessman Charles Crane and the American theologian Henry King travelled through the Middle East and interviewed hundreds of Arab notables. Although the British and the French did all they could with propaganda to influence the outcome of the mission, their findings were clear. Locals in Syria did not want to be part of the French mandate, and those in Palestine opposed inclusion in the British mandate. London was successful in preventing the Americans from conducting a survey in Iraq.

"In August, King and Crane presented their report. They recommended a single mandate covering a unified Syria and Palestine and granted it to neutral America instead of to the European colonial powers.

"Today, nobody has ever heard of the King-Crane Report, but in hindsight, it represents one of the biggest lost opportunities in the recent history of the Middle East. Under pressure from the British and the French, and because of Wilson's serious illness, in September of 1919, the public did not see the released report until three years later. By then, Paris and London agreed on a new map for the Middle East, which diametrically opposed the recommendations made by King and Crane. France divided its mandate area into the states of Lebanon and Syria while Great Britain took on the mandate for Iraq, but not before swallowing up the oil-rich province of Mosul. Between Syria, Iraq, and their mandate area of Palestine, they established a buffer state called Transjordan. Saudi Arabia was consolidated under the Saud family, the states of Kuwait, Bahrain, Qatar, the Arab Oil Emirates, Oman, and Yemen, all formed along ethnic, and economic lines, especially as it related to oil."

"No doubt about your memory, Cody," Pope John Luke said. "You have good insights into many of the conditions we have today."

"So I've given you a nice lesson in history," said Cody, "now tell me what that has to do with a 'modern crusade.'"

"I have some information you don't have, and I believe it could represent an unknown breakthrough."

"Okay," said Cody, "What is it?"

Pope John Luke added, "Within the last several years, there have been two serious efforts by Muslim leaders to reach out to the Christian world. The first was an open letter to Benedict XVI a month after his lecture at the University of Regensburg. There was a lot of violence in the Muslim world after the speech, but the letter, completely ignored by the American press, was more significant. From it, Muslim leaders all over the world proposed thoughtful and critical laws to encourage peace and good will responses after the pope's comments on the use of reason. It also made a direct criticism of Muslim extremists."

"A year later, in 2007, a much longer dictate by Muslim leaders addressed the Christian leaders East and West, Roman Catholic, Orthodox, Protestant, and Evangelical. It was called *A Common Word Between Us and You.*"

"In the long history of Muslim-Christian relations, this was an unprecedented group of Muslim thinkers, from different parts of the world with differing views, who collaborated on a positive overture to Christians. From the beginning, Islam chose to be a harsh critic of the Old Testament teachings of Christianity. This document composed comprehensive testimony from the New Testament to argue that Christians, like Muslims, should teach the love of the one God, who is the first and greatest religious truth.

"The authors linked the words of the Prophet's message directly to the biblical tradition. By saying "there is no god, but God," these Muslim leaders concluded, the Prophet Muhammad was echoing the first and greatest commandment in the Bible... to love God with all one's heart and soul. Perhaps Muhammad tried to restate the Bible's first commandment before he died."

Cody said, "There is no doubt the face of Islam, worldwide, has changed and is changing. Still, I find it hard to believe they are turning away from the complete line, 'there is no god, but God..., and Muhammad is his prophet.'"

"They've opened the door for a debate and a conversation. We are going to see if it can be opened much more."

Cody was exasperated, "Fine, let's do that. Just tell me what you have in mind as a 'modern Crusade'."

"Frankly, I don't have the slightest idea how to bring it about," said the pope. "This is why I brought you back. You have the most insightful mind anyone has ever seen. I want you to take the entire conversation we had back to your Ops Center, and come up with a plan. I brought you in here today to get you thinking in the right direction."

Cody switched back to German and said flatly, "You spent a lot of time in the Ops Center, Robert. We can do a lot, but you know we can't have a few meetings and come up with a strategy involving the whole world."

"Why not?" said John Luke. "You just told me yourself a couple of countries got us into this mess."

"For certain, but the first thing I need to know is whether all those worldwide Muslim leaders are serious. Having a worthless dialog to come to an accommodation with Christianity could become a trap. Is it possible for you to have a face to face meeting with each of them to see how deep their motives run?"

"In that area, at least, I was thinking ahead of you," said the pope. "We've sent private messages to everyone who was either a signatory or a recipient of the last correspondence we had. Next month, all of them will meet in Geneva, very secretly, to see how sincere they really were."

"Which means ... that's how long I have to come up with a plan," said Cody.

"That would be correct, my friend," said John Luke.

The two spoke for another hour, with the pope assuring Cody he would not sit still while St. Peter's dome lay in ruins.

Chapter 4
On To Kurdistan

Rome

By the time Cody got back to the Ops Center, most of the staff was gone for the day. Only his family and Bishop Paglioni remained. Ashana jumped out of her chair, and hugged and kissed her husband, "You were gone so long. You must have had quite a conversation with the Pope."

"It was cataclysmic," said Cody. The church has the right man for the job. It looks like he's willing to go all in, and make some fundamental changes to the whole world."

Cody then proceeded to repeat the entire conversation in detail. When he was finished, Bishop Paglioni's face was white.

Charlie was more pragmatic. "Both of you left out an important detail in this. At the end of World War I, the Kurds expected to end up with a sovereign country of their own. It didn't happen, and they've thought of little else since then."

"You spent four years as a roommate with the son of the Kurdish leader," said Cody. "Is the creation of the country named Kurdistan more important than religion?"

"Definitely," said Charlie, "If they got that, they would be a stabilizing force for the entire region. They have already proved it by embracing the Iranian Kurds, who are almost completely Shia, with the Sunni majority. They live in peace with each other, much like Protestants do with Catholics, respecting their differences for the greater good."

The first piece of the puzzle given to him by the Pope fell into place for Cody. "If you went to Erbil, would Kamal be able to get you in for a serious conversation with his father, Masoud?"

"I'm sure I can meet Masoud," said Charlie, "whether I have a deep political talk with him, is not so sure. I'm the same age as Kamal, and won't carry the same weight as his other advisors."

"You will if you tell him who you really are."

Charlie shook his head in confusion, "I thought everything about you was supposed to be Top Secret?"

"It is, and it will stay that way if you speak to Masoud in private. What you say is simple. Tell him I'm alive and working internationally to redraw the boundaries of the Middle East, this time with consideration for the ethnic, national, religious, and cultural desires of the people in the region. What I want from him is the minimum size and location of the new Kurdistan. If the claims are reasonable, I will work to get it for him. The quid pro quo is that he must commit his entire army to defeating ISIS, under my operational control."

"You won't have any trouble in getting them to fight ISIS," said Charlie. "They've been doing just that for the past decade and winning most of the time."

"But they're no closer to having a country of their own, than when they started fighting ISIS," said Cody. "What I'm going to offer is that reality."

"Exactly how are you going to do that?" asked Charlie.

"Frankly, I'm not sure. However, a string of a plan is starting to form in my mind. I'll have to give it considerably more thought. However, I told you this morning we need 50 brigades to defeat ISIS. I'm hoping the Kurds can give me a dozen of them."

"When do you want me to go?"

"Right away, can you call Kamal now and set up a meeting?"

Charlie pulled out his notebook and looked up the number. "How do I get an outside line here?"

"Just push nine, and dial the number," said Paglioni.

In just a moment, Charlie was talking to Kamal in Arabic. "Hey bud, this is Charlie." He listened a few seconds and then said, "It's great to hear from you again. I was thinking about dropping in for a visit. Would you like that?" He listened for another minute and then said, "All that sounds perfect. How about I fly up there the day after tomorrow, would that be too soon?"

He listened a moment more, and then said, "I'll text you the flight details. This is great! I always said I would visit you one day, and eat all your groceries." He said goodbye and looked at his dad, "Kamal is real excited to see me. He says he's looking forward to introducing his whole family."

"No private jets for you this time, Charlie," said Cody. "Right

- 40 -

now, you're way under the radar. Let's keep it that way. Just one school friend visiting another. We'll book you on a commercial flight."

"I'll take care of that," said Paglioni. "It's been a long day. Why don't all you go out and have a nice dinner?"

"I'm glad somebody finally thought about food," said Rosy, "I'm starved."

"I know just the place," said Ashana.

Paglioni pushed a heavy envelope across the table to Cody, "Since we've dragged you into all this, you might as well go back on the payroll."

Cody peaked in the envelope. It was full of money. "Thanks, Vincent, we'll make sure we have a really good dinner."

The meeting broke up and Cody led the way to their rooms. When they got there and went in, Ashana said, "These are the same rooms we stayed in when we first came to Rome years ago. Do either of you remember?"

"I do," said Charlie. Rosy wasn't so sure, but said it was a very elegant suite.

"If the place you have in mind is the Borgia Antico," said Cody, "I need to make reservations."

"That's the one," said Ashana.

Cody made a call. "They're checking it out, and will call us back. While we're waiting I think we all have time to shower and put on better clothes."

Rosy and Charlie went off to their rooms. Cody and Ashana went to the master bedroom.

"Lots of memories in this room," said Ashana. "It hasn't changed a bit. At least the condemned will have a good dinner and a pleasant night's sleep."

While Ashana was showering, Cody got out a bottle of wine. The phone rang. He answered it and somehow found out reservations at the exclusive roof top restaurant would be ready in an hour. At least that part of the church's punch had not changed, and they were within walking distance of the Vatican.

The family enjoyed a glass of wine, then dressed in their best, went out across St. Peter's Square to the restaurant. They received a royal greeting, escorted to the best table in the house, along a railing overlooking the vast glow of Rome and the hills.

They had a fine meal, while Ashana, Rosy, and Charlie laughed and talked about all sorts of memories. Cody didn't talk much. Ashana could see he was deeply thinking, so she left him alone.

The pope's concept of a modern Crusade kept coming back to Cody's mind. He knew the pope was not talking about the historical crusades from the middle ages, but sought Cody's ability to create a plan with the same attacking effect to defeat the false Islam in Syria and Iraq, as his target objective. Without a doubt, ISIS and their brutal tactics, and their classic adherence to ancient Islamic law infuriated the whole world.

On a much bigger stage, Cody was attempting to envision a Middle East that was fundamentally different from the one presently existing. He examined his memory to recall any facts or background that might give him some frame of reference. It was daunting. For the first time in his memory, he could think of only one single plan of action he might propose to the pope. It was so complex and involved with so many other people and nations it frightened him. One thing was sure; he could not able to solve this problem without excellent help.

That line of thought led him to the men and women with whom he had interacted or worked with over the years. This was more productive. He had contacts all over the world. Some of them were in positions of authority. Many of them had gotten to these positions because of their link to Cody. Ultimately, this crisis would require calling in every favor anyone owed him. Mentally, he began compiling a list of those he would call, and those who would be the most valuable here at the beginning.

If he was going to pursue this scenario, he imagined the contact. Ironically, the first people he needed to speak to, he'd never met. Furthermore, if he revealed his real identity, there was no way to know how these people would react. He needed to goad, incite, and observe the fascinating possibility. Unfortunately, his trail would lead him back to Iran.

"Don't you think so, honey?"

Cody realized Ashana was speaking to him. He smiled and said, "Sorry, I was a million miles away."

"It's okay," said Ashana putting her hand on his arm, "you haven't really been with us tonight. Got anything figured out?"

"Maybe, but it's a real long shot. Charlie, I'm going to write a letter and a detailed analysis for you to give to Masoud Barzani. It's for his eyes only and should be destroyed after he reads it, okay?"

"Whatever you say, Dad."

The following morning the family went to the Ops Center. Ashana knew Cody had not slept, laboring all night with his thoughts. Still, he seemed to be in good spirits. As they entered Ops, the technicians and analysts again stood up in respect.

"This is stupid," said Cody. "It's also counterproductive. All of you are busy, competent people. If you stop when I come in, it disturbs your train of thought, which could be important. Please get used to treating me just like any other person in this room."

The techs seemed satisfied, and sat at their stations to resume what they were doing.

"Ashana, sweetie, you're our expert in reading people, understanding their thoughts and seeing through them to the core of their being. What I would like you to do this morning is to study Masoud Barzani. His support in the plan I'm developing is critical. I also want a synopsis on the current leader of Iran. I don't even know his name, but I have to meet him in the next few days. Knowing what sort of man he is will be very helpful."

"Rosy, in addition to your continuing efforts to disrupt the social media campaigns of ISIS, I want you to find their satellite servers. They're bound to have some backups. We've hit their headquarters in Raqqa a number of times and the social media is still operating. I need to know the location of those auxiliary servers."

"That brings me to you, Charlie. You're heading up to Erbil tomorrow. I want you to deliver the letter I'm going to write. You can read the letter before you seal it. I want you to give it to Masoud Barzani personally. Tell him who wrote the letter before he reads it. Kamal can be present when you do, but no others. I will leave it to your judgement to decide whether you want to tell Barzani you know its contents. Your mother will give you an analysis on his hot and cold buttons before you leave. Basically, I'm going to outline the conditions of how an independent Kurdistan can come into existence, and suggest what those borders should be."

"Today, I want you to do an analysis for me on which countries in the world have managed to avoid violence between Sunnis and Shias. I guess it's the secular governments, which have declared religious freedom for everyone, and keep a separation between the state and any religious groups. Who is the best at this? I know the moderates are now in control in Iran, and view domination of social and political power by the Ayatollahs as being a disaster for their country. But other countries have achieved a level of stability. You need to cherry-pick these countries and prepare a report. Let's get busy."

The Ops Center hummed with activity.

During the afternoon, Rosy came over and said, "You were right about ISIS having other servers. They got their social media operation back up in record time. That means they must have another way of sending out their propaganda. They've been bouncing their signal off IP addresses all over the world. Still, we think we've found their other source. It's in Mosul."

"That makes sense," said Cody. Mosul is a city with over a million people. ISIS is embedded there in the middle of the civilian population, which is why no airstrikes have targeted the city."

"We don't need airstrikes," said Rosy. "We used a procedure called ddosing. It sends so many requests for information to the servers they are not able to function properly. Once we got the servers disabled, we were able to write a number of little codes that will be very difficult to find, and will keep the servers malfunctioning indefinitely. ISIS will have to install new servers and start over. I think we've compromised their ability to use normal channels of social media since the information they send out is unreadable."

Cody went back to his comprehensive study of the Sunni-Shia dispute. It was as old as Islam itself, and centered on who the rightful heir to Muhammad should be. The violence between the two groups had ebbed and flowed for centuries. One of the outcomes of modern history was the fall of the Shah in Iran, and the ascendancy of the Ayatollah Khomeini. He made many public speeches calling for an end to Sunni and Shia divisions, saying they were all Muslims. His political life was not the same. He did little to improve the lives of the Sunni minority in Iran. Instead, he gave the people a common foe to oppose...Christianity and Judaism. More specifically, he targeted Israel as the Little Satan, and the United States as the Big Satan, vowing to wipe these countries out of existence. The result was a full generation of Iranian terrorism throughout the Middle East, with proxies of the Hezbollah in Lebanon and Hamas in Palestine. Worse, he began a program of independently developing nuclear weapons. These, he hoped to use to improve Shia positions in the Arab world as the ultimate weapon of mass destruction to hold over the head of all the countries in the Middle East.

The result of that program was the smuggling of six nuclear weapons into the United States. This is what drew a reluctant Cody into the middle of the crisis. His successful plan took the weapons back to Iran and detonated them. Even though only a handful of people in the world had actually seen him, or knew who he was, the entire world knew about the heroic efforts of the Black Angel. It was a strange dichotomy. If he had not taken on the mission, he never would have met Ashana and the children. For this, he thanked the Lord every day.

What he did not expect was the vacuum produced by the change of Iran to be just another big oil exporter, and far more thoughtful country. The United States removed all their troops from Iraq by executive order, long before they were ready to stand on their own.

Into that void came the rise of ISIS, a much more vicious, brutal and dangerous enemy of all people, Muslim or Christian, who did not subscribe to their narrow interpretation of what the Islamic religion was all about, or the progress it had made over the years in becoming a less militant culture.

With all this in mind, Cody wrote a letter to Masoud Barzani, along with a very insightful and detailed narrative of his emerging plan through which the Kurds could finally achieve sovereignty as an independent nation, and the price they would have to pay to get it.

As he was just finishing his 20-page document, Ashana and Charlie came to his cluttered workstation. Rosy joined them as well.

"Is this a good time to interrupt you?" asked Ashana. "You've been working so hard and absorbing so much information, we didn't want to disturb your thought process."

"I've finished all I wanted to do," said Cody, "so this is a good time to take a break and listen to what you've learned."

"I've been trying to get a measure of the man who is the leader of the Kurds," said Ashana. "He's very focused and practical. He's learned the art of diplomacy, because he had to. It's not his favorite thing, and he gets very impatient when people don't come right to the point. He only has one wife, named Enwa, and no mistresses. He loves his family. He regrets he doesn't get to spend more time with them, but he works like a galley slave to keep his coalitions together and his opponents in line, off balance, or appeased. He's a realist, who knows how difficult the challenges facing him are."

"Sounds like I wrote the right things to him," said Cody. Great job, sweetie, I know your analysis will help Charlie."

He handed the letter and analysis he had written to Charlie, "I've thought about it some more. I want you to read this before talking to Barzani. Now tell me what you've learned in your research today."

"Islam, like Christianity, has somewhat evolved over the centuries. In the beginning, the Muslims were hell bent on conquering the world and converting it to Islam. To date, they have moved into 50 countries and withdrawn from none. That's not something Christianity can say."

"There are approximately 1.2 billion Muslims on the planet. Of these, 85% are Sunnis. The minority Shias, about 200 million of them, are concentrated in six countries, Iran, Iraq, Azerbaijan, Syria, Kuwait, and Bahrain."

"There are minority Shia populations in all the Muslim countries. Relations have not always been peaceful, far from it. The discriminated Shias are in almost every country. They don't have a voice in government.

"The largest Muslim country is Indonesia. There the secular government has cracked down on Sunni-Shia violence. Their constitution says all people will have freedom of religion. The same is true in India, where large populations of Muslims live, with the same percentage of Shias. However, the secular government guarantees all freedom of religion.

"In Azerbaijan, the policy works the other way. In this country, the majority is Shia, and the government has to protect the Sunnis from abuse. Right on the border between Azerbaijan and the majority Sunni Kurds, we see very little unrest. I don't believe the Kurds have a territorial interest in Azerbaijan, despite the fact they are so rich with oil.

"We all know what happened in Iran. The secular government took a backseat to the Ayatollahs and their emphasis on religion as a government policy. With the operation, you led to block Iran from blowing up American cities, which ended up destroying their nuclear infrastructure. The moderates, who have always been present in Iran, were able to wrest control of the government from the Ayatollahs; most of them were already dead when one of the bombs went off in Qom.

"Perhaps the most striking result of the tragedy in Iran was the United States taking the same attitude about them, as they had with Germany and Japan after World War II. In this instance, there was no evidence America had anything to do with the nuclear explosions, but we shared our help, nevertheless.

"It was certainly a shock to most Iranians. They called our nation infidels, and planned to destroy America because they were Christian. Yet suddenly, a huge number of volunteers came to clean up the mess on the ground, give food, and medical services. President Colter did a masterful job of treating religion as a non-issue. The Americans and other western countries, which came to rebuild Iran never tried to convert Muslims to Christians. They respected the religion of Iran, and expected the Iranians to do the same about Christianity.

"Today, a secular administration runs the government. They wrote a new constitution that guarantees freedom of religion to all. After twelve years of hard work, the country is doing very well. Almost all their oil production is back on line. The people are a lot happier without the crushing burden of Sharia law running their lives. Actually, the Shias have always been more progressive than the Sunnis. They take a more practical approach to the world, and reject the precepts of the first four Caliphs of Islam, which is the basis of Sunni Islam."

"In the reconstruction of Iran, there were no foreign military forces, another Colter innovation. He wanted the Iranians to know the United States was not moving in to occupy their country. He took a lot of heat for that, since none of the workers had weapons. A number of ugly incidents occurred, when hardline Shias killed some of the workers. The new government stepped in and provided security. Despite the nuclear detonations, a large portion of the Iranian military was still intact. It was a very strange picture, Iranian soldiers protecting American workers from harm by other Iranians.

"There were no military units in Iran, until ISIS began attacking their borders from Iraq. Then the United States stationed two brigades along the border at the request of the Iranian government. They're still there, protecting the oil fields, and occasionally mixing it up with ISIS. Iranian soldiers fight shoulder to shoulder with Americans. The common enemy makes cooperation between Iranian and American commands very effective.

"Of all the shifting alliances in the Middle East, the Iranian one is the strangest. I suppose we shouldn't be surprised. Japan and Germany were our mortal enemies in World War II, now they are among our strongest allies, with booming economies. Much the same is true in Iran. They're so busy modernizing the country, and enjoying the benefits of Western society, religion has taken its correct place inside families and the general society,"

"An excellent report, Charlie," said Cody, "It gives me the information I need to move forward. I'm very glad about the good will in Iran. I'm going to need it when I go there, and risk my life."

"Why are you going to Iran?" asked Ashana.

"Ever since my meeting with the pope yesterday, I've been thinking about a really intricate idea. I've no idea if what I'm pondering is even feasible. Actually, I keep asking myself if this is the best, I can do, when so much is on the line. Anyway, I haven't thought of anything better, so I'm going with what I have."

"You didn't answer my question," said Ashana.

"If what I have in mind is going to work at all, I need the cooperation of the Iranians."

"The same Iranians who would do anything to get their hands on the man who blew their country to bits?" asked Ashana.

"I told you the idea is risky, especially when I'm going to have to tell them who I really am."

"Are you out of your mind!" blurted Charlie.

"Really, dad, you could think of a better way to commit suicide," said Rosy.

"If we're going to spend our best man," said Bishop Paglioni, "I think we deserve to have a little more insight into your thinking."

"Oh, all right!" said Cody with disgust.

He walked over to a big map displayed on a computer screen of the Middle East. He slammed his hand onto Iraq, and then Syria. "Who is in control of these countries?"

"ISIS," said Charlie.

Cody nodded and said, "And who is ISIS?"

"Radical Terrorist Jihadists," said Charlie.

"And what religion do they purport to be?" asked Cody.

"Muslim," said Rosy, "everyone knows that."

"You're making the same mistake as the rest of the world," said Cody. "You're putting all the Muslims into one group."

He pointed at the map again, "Who are the majority of Muslims in Iraq and Syria, Charlie?"

"They're Shia Muslims," said Charlie.

"And what are the fighters in ISIS?"

"They're Sunni," said Charlie with growing understanding.

"What's the majority of Muslims in Iran?"

"Almost totally Shia," said Charlie.

"Very well," said Cody. "What is the breakdown of Muslims in the world?"

"About 85% Sunni," said Charlie.

"How much persecution have the Shias endured over the past thousand years at the hands of the Sunni?"

"As I said, almost endless," said Charlie. "More Shias have died in Iraq and Syria than any other minority."

"You've just listened to Charlie's report on Iran. I don't think the circumstances are remotely the same." Cody said. "Therefore, we have an opportunity for the minority Shias of the world to actually have a true homeland of their own, as well as the Kurds."

"The Shia had a homeland in Iran," said Bishop Paglioni, "look how that turned out. There must be some Ayatollahs left who would love to use you, Cody, as a reason to regain control. You would become as the Shah."

"I know that," said Cody, "but I need to talk to the President of Iran and hope he doesn't still harbor a grudge for the Black Angel."

"How are you going to arrange that?" asked Paglioni.

"I was thinking of having the pope set up a meeting for me with the President of the United States."

"Is it your intention to take this plan to his Holiness?"

"He told me he wanted a modern Crusade. This is as close as I can come to arranging our plan."

Paglioni stroked his brow, "But your plan calls for a coalition of Christians and Muslims. I can't imagine the pope will approve such an endeavor."

"I'm going to ask him anyway," said Cody. "If he says 'NO', then we'll just have to think of something else. Can you set up a meeting with him for tomorrow morning?

"I'll make a call now and let you know later this evening."

"In that case," said Cody, "I think we've done all we can do today. It's been a long day and we're beat from the heavy lifting we've been doing. I'm going to take my family back to our apartment and let them relax for a while before I get them fed. Then we're going to work a little more. I need to brief Charlie for his visit to Erbil. Is the Vatican kitchen still running?"

"Better than ever," said Paglioni, "they think good food is good for Vatican morale."

"Smart person in that kitchen," laughed Charlie, "maybe you should bring him down here."

It truly was an historic meal in the apartment for the family. They ate late; since Cody made sure everyone got a good rest. He was happy they all slept. The Vatican waiters served the meal with superior grace. Charlie and Cody both had luscious filet mignon, with béarnaise sauce, mashed potatoes, and white asparagus. Rosy and Ashana had big salads and a plate of chicken in a creamy pasta. All enjoyed Cody's choice of wine.

After dinner, the family sat down on the soft couches around a carved coffee table.

"Let me just say, I think you all did a great job today," said Cody. "Each one of you brought valuable information to the situation in which we find ourselves. In fact, as a result of your efforts, I'm beginning to think my plan might actually work."

"I'm glad you're so confident," said Charlie, "but you don't have to go to Erbil tomorrow."

"The most important thing you must do requires establishing your credibility with Masoud Barzani. Otherwise, he would just read the letter I wrote and consider it just another wild mission. Insightful, but of no operational significance.

"As it turns out, I've actually met Barzani. It was many years ago when he was just another of the Peshmerga fighters. The church sent me in to protect a community of Christians who lived along the border between Turkey and Iraq. Barzani didn't give a hoot about the Christians, but the attacking Turkish forces had his full attention.

"His position was about to be overrun by the Turks, but I had my full team with me at the time, and we were able to kill enough Turks to force them to withdraw. On their way out, they made one last effort to shoot up Barzani's squad. We got in the middle of that and saved his life.

"When he asked me why we protected them, since obviously we came there to help the Christians, and clearly were not Arabs or Kurds, I said, 'The enemy of my enemy is my friend'.

He smiled and said, 'You must be the Black Angel about whom we hear so much.'

"I said I didn't care for that term very much, and he should forget it. Then I said 'Allah Akbar' and we disappeared into the night."

"Well, that's certainly news to me," said Charlie, "I'm sure he'll remember. However, you're supposed to be dead. What am I supposed to say when he says that?"

"Tell him, I still don't care for the term The Black Angel very much. Then you can give him the letter, and the accompanying analysis."

Cody filled in the details, dates, and location of the skirmish. Only someone who was actually there would know them. He was certain Barzani would believe Charlie and immediately take him into his group of advisors.

"You should expect to stay in Kurdistan for quite a while, Charlie," said Cody. "You're my point man for the Kurdish portion of my operation. I'll join you in Erbil as soon as I can, until then your roadmap is the analysis of how the Kurds should prepare to run their operations."

He handed Charlie a larger than normal cell phone. "This is a secure phone that will allow you to contact me anywhere in the world. Use it to bring me up to date on how your meeting with Barzani goes."

He looked closely at his family, "Here's a phone for you, Rosy and for you, honey. After tonight, we're going to get scattered all over creation. I pray to God, he will bring us all back together, unharmed. However, let there be no doubt in your minds we are about to embark on the most complicated and dangerous mission I've ever seen. It makes our operation with the Iranian nukes look like a cakewalk.

After a few more minutes of happy family talk, Charlie and Rosy went off to their rooms. Ashana and Cody were alone.

"Is it alright to tell you I'm shaking in my boots," said Ashana?

"Me too," said Cody. "I love you with all my heart, Ashana. Despite this walk into mortal danger, always remember that."

"I love you too, my brave husband," said Ashana, putting her arms around his neck and kissing him with passion

"Why don't you try to get some sleep," said Cody, "I still have some work to do."

"What more is there?"

"I have to get all this into some kind of coherent shape for the pope to read tomorrow morning before our meeting. Paglioni thinks he's going to throw it back in my face as being too big and too dangerous. He didn't talk to John Luke, as I did. The pope is going to push this plan forward at full speed."

"God help us," said Ashana.

Cody worked for several hours putting his comprehensive plan down on paper. As he worked, a number of new ideas occurred to him, and he added those to the report for the pope. By the time he was finished, he had convinced himself his plan was not so bad after all. In fact, he was sure it would work, if he could get the right support from the right people.

He called the Ops Center and told the night crew to come over and pick up his report and deliver it to the pope the first thing in the morning. A few minutes later, a courier knocked on the door and Cody gave him the thirty-page document. Then he realized how tired he was, and went to bed, cuddling with Ashana before he fell into a deep sleep.

Chapter 5
The Pope Girds For War

Rome

The next morning the family was up early. Charlie was leaving for the airport, and Rosy was anxious to get back to Ops to see if her latest nasty lines of code did what she expected.

Ashana presided over breakfast, knowing this might be the last good meal any of them would have together for some time to come.

Cody was fresh enough, even though he worked late preparing his report for Pope John Luke. He said a long and heartfelt prayer before they began eating, asking God for his help and protection for the many months before them.

Cody asked to Charlie, "All ready to go?"

"Not much to take," said Charlie, "just my passport and a couple changes of clothes. Of course, I'll have my phone and your papers for president Barzani with me all the time. My flight will arrive in Erbil in time for dinner. I'm looking forward to seeing Kamal again."

Ashana asked, "When do you expect to meet with the pope?"

"He's an early riser. I expect he's already ready my plan."

As if Cody had just spoken in code, the phone rang, and he answered it. He listened a moment and then hung up.

"The pope wants me in his office by nine. I guess that means you and I will be leaving at about the same time, Charlie."

"I'm going with him to the airport," said Ashana. "Not much for me to do while you're talking to the pope."

"I could be there awhile," said Cody.

"I'll be in Ops seeing how much more we can screw up ISIS propaganda," said Rosy.

While Rosy and Ashana were in their rooms getting ready for the day, Cody sat down with Charlie.

"Remember Charlie, you're a Christian in a Muslim community. I'm sure President Barzani will have his people keep an eye on you for your safety. Just remember all your years of training. You're as good as anyone I ever had with me. Don't hesitate to use it all if the need arises. You may have to do some very scary work. New people without testing in battle make the Peshmerga suspicious and cautious. I mention these things in private to you. I wouldn't want to further frighten your mother."

"I'll be careful, dad," said Charlie. "Right now, I wish I'd gotten even more training."

There was a car waiting for Charlie and Ashana. Cody gave his son a hug, and said, "Think you can remember the plan?"

"Funny," said Charlie, "Bye now, I love you."

"Good luck on your meeting, Dad," said Rosy, and headed off to the Ops Center.

The car drove off.

Cody went back into the Vatican and navigated his way to the office of the pope. A Monsignor asked about his business. He gave his name and sat down in a chair. The wait was not long. Cody was ushered into the office of the pope, who was sitting at a table with papers spread out. John Luke looked up and said, "I said to plan a modern Crusade, but *this* represents a redrawing of national boundaries all over the Middle East!"

"Oh don't give me that crap!" said Cody irritably. "You knew perfectly well I was going to think this entire situation through to a conclusion. You also knew it would require something of this size and complexity to solve our problem. How many times have your read that analysis this morning?"

"All of it three times, and parts of it considerably more," said the pope with exasperation.

"Well, if you've got a better idea, now's the time."

"Regrettably, I don't. Your logic is undeniable.

"Let me just hit the high points again for you," said Cody, sitting down at the table. "I told you it would take at least 50 brigades and total air superiority to defeat ISIS. However, we can't use 50 American army brigades or even 50 brigades from any totally Christian countries. That would be the same thing as declaring war on Islam, which would surely look like another ancient Crusade throughout the global Muslim community.

The only way to approach this is to use a coalition of military units from both Christian and Islamic countries. When I looked at the facts, I learned there are three such groups who would join us for their own self-interested motives.

The Kurds will join because we will promise to give them a sovereign nation of their own. The Shias will join because they get some control of Iraq where the population is a majority of Shias. All 200 million Shias in the world will thank us for breaking the grip of the Sunni domination and their Islamic beliefs."

"We're going to have to give our best sales pitches," said the pope.

"No question about that," agreed Cody. "I've already started the ball rolling with my son, Charlie. He left this morning for Erbil. We caught a break there. His roommate at William and Mary is Barzani's son. I wrote a long message to Barzani, basically, telling him we'll give him a country if they will join our crusade."

The pope asked, "How would that work out?"

"They already control most of northern Iraq. Lots of oil money there. I think I can get the Iranians to yield by treaty the northern corner of their country to the Kurds, even though they are 100% Shias. However, the Sunni Kurds don't have the same regard for the Shia. For them, being a real country trumps religion every time. The real crunch comes when we start talking to Turkey about giving away *any* of their territory to the Kurds. The Turks and the Kurds hate each other. Some kind of a quid pro that benefits Turkey, such as the Kurds building oil pipelines and becoming the proxy for them, against ISIS will be our best chance of getting them to agree to limited land swaps."

"How do you see the Americans in this grand alliance?"

"The Americans are already allied with Iran, as strange as that seems from modern history. They put two combat brigades on the border with Iraq to help the Iranian military ward off ISIS. It's not a peacekeeping mission. The U.S. army is involved in real fighting. From an operational standpoint, that means at least ten combat brigades are on line. The U.S. rotates personnel on a regular basis."

"What about Israel?"

"I wondered when you would get around to the Jewish question," said Cody. "Okay, let's look at the facts. The elimination of Iran as a nuclear threat to Israel was a big win for them, but the real victory is the reduction by Iran of their support for Hezbollah in Lebanon, and

Hamas in Palestine. Israel now has more influence in the Middle East. They've consolidated their control of the Golan Heights, come to agreement for a permanent cease fire with the Palestinians, improved their relations with Jordan, and have prevented the incursion of ISIS into either Lebanon or Jordan. They stopped ISIS cold in the Becca Valley of Lebanon when they tried to invade, and Jews are now welcome in Beirut. They have respect for protecting the Muslims in their sphere of influence. Whether or not they could be included in a Crusade coalition is a rather big unknown. A lot of this will depend on you."

"How so?" asked the pope.

"They're still Jews. The hatred for them goes back a long way."

"I know that, but what about the other thing you said?"

"You gave me the idea for all this with your messages from Muslim leaders worldwide to meet with the Christian church in hopes of coming to an understanding that there is no god, but God. Period. If we could come to common ground on worshiping the same God, we might be able to push past the Jesus and Muhammad dichotomy."

"There is no dichotomy as far as Jesus is concerned," the pope said firmly. "He is your Savior, and the hope for a future mankind."

"No argument with me there," said Cody, "but tell that to a billion Muslims who get down on their knees and pray to God in the name of Muhammad five times a day."

"So you are saying I should tell the council of Muslims and Christians that Jesus and Muhammad are less important?"

"Not less important John Luke, less imperative. God almighty is our sovereign leader. He is universally, revered by all three religions. That's the point you need to drive home. Not our differences, but our commonality."

"The terrible scourge of ISIS is sweeping through the Middle East murdering, raping, stealing, intimidating, blackmailing, and taking fear with them, wherever they go. Without God, as far as I can foresee, your line of reasoning might possibly succeed."

"I have the greatest confidence you'll be successful in winning them over, particularly if I'm able to give you some concrete steps we can take in the next month."

"Ah yes, your meeting with the President Palmer. It's set for tomorrow at noon in Washington. I spoke to him and asked him to invite President Faroush to the White House. There is absolutely no way I'm going to let you go to Iran on your own. You are far too valuable to risk in such a stupid way. You should have thought that one through better. Otherwise I think you're doing fine."

"You are a sly fox, my old friend. Meeting the Iranian President in Washington is a much better idea. As for my analysis, you already made up your mind to go ahead with it before I came in."

"Call it my belief you would say all the right things, which you did."

"Thanks, for that," said Cody, "I was beginning to think the years had dulled my senses."

"Quite the contrary," said John Luke, "You seem to get better with age. By the way, I insisted to the President that NSA Chief, Tom Bostwick, be present for this exclusive meeting. Is there a reason?"

"Tom Bostwick knows who I am. It will grease the skids a little with a president I've never met."

The pope smiled, "Time to take the Black Angel out of mothballs?"

"In that very limited way

"On another subject, allied to your search for fighting brigades," said the Pope, "I have a couple more to add to your list."

Cody seemed surprised, "Who would that be?"

"The Swiss Guard."

"You'll need to explain that to me," said Cody.

"In the terrorist attack of St. Peters, a great many of our Swiss Guard were killed. The Swiss didn't take that very well. I got a call the following day from the Prime Minister of Switzerland. He told me his country was ashamed of falling down on their 600-year tradition of serving as the pope's personal guard."

Cody said, "The Swiss served as mercenaries to European Kings for hundreds of years. They were the best fighting men in Europe, but Switzerland outlawed all of that when it became an official neutral country, except for the Swiss Guard at the Vatican."

"Exactly right," said the pope. "However, the country has apparently changed its mind about the size and scope of the Swiss Guard. They have assured me they are prepared to send two fully armed brigades to Rome, for me to use in whatever manner I wish."

Cody shook his head in wonder, "Including using them to fight

ISIS?"

"I believe that is exactly what they expect."

"Wow!" Cody said. "Not only will the Swiss be a potent force in our attack against ISIS, they also represent a huge symbolic gesture in the credibility of our entire mission."

"Use that line of reasoning with the United States. I think it will make a difference in how you work to convince the Americans to give their support to our operation. We need public support in America, or, at least, the President needs it. He already has the support of the millions of Catholics. This just adds sauce for the goose."

"When does my plane leave?"

"Tonight," said the pope, "it will get you to Washington in plenty of time for your meeting with President Palmer in the morning."

"Say your mass for me tonight, your Holiness," said Cody.

"I will," John Luke said, "and may the Lord bless us in this work we will do in His name."

"Amen," said Cody.

Erbil

As Charlie's plane came in for a landing, he looked at the city of nearly a million people. If there was a war going on 50 miles away in Mosul, somebody had forgotten to tell the Kurds.

There were modern hotels, wide freeways, and a look of a resort town. It reminded Charlie of Dubai. There was construction going on everywhere.

As he exited the plane and headed for the embarkation center, Charlie spotted his name on a big sign. Waving it was his friend Kamal, who broadly smiled. Charlie grinned and waved back. The two men greeted each other with hugs, playful slaps on the shoulders and stomach, and two-handed handshakes.

"It's just wonderful to see you, Charlie," said Kamal. "Welcome to Erbil."

Kamal had spoken in English, so Charlie replied in Arabic, "I'll bet you haven't had much of a chance to speak English. Still, I appreciate it."

"I have a car waiting for us," said Kamal, "do you have luggage?

Charlie lifted his modest carry-on bag, and said, "I travel light. This is all I have."

"Then let's get to the car, and head for home."

The car was actually a big, black limousine with official flags on the front bumpers. There were also two police motorcycles in front and back of the limousine. Charlie and Kamal climbed in, and the motorcade drove off.

Erbil was really a beautiful city. Kamal pointed out the sights as they drove along. He pointed to a great stone structure sitting on top of a cliff near the center of the city. "That's our Citadel. For your information, Erbil is the oldest city in the world, our Citadel dates back thousands of years."

Soon, they took an off-ramp from the freeway and drove down a wide street separated by lovely landscaping and walkways. The Presidential Palace came into view at the end of the street, where it split off in two directions.

The Palace was a grand affair. It gleamed, white in the bright sunlight. It was a square building with ornate siding, not columns, but like fluted vertical arches. It was very impressive.

"Is this the best you can do for a place to stay?" said Charlie with a grin.

"We somehow manage to make do with what we have," Kamal shot back." Both of them laughed.

The limousine pulled up to the wide stairs leading to the entrance of the palace. People came running out and grabbed Charlie's meager luggage. He held on to his shoulder bag that contained his phone, the letter and report for Kamal's father, and his passport, money and a book he'd started on Kurdish history.

Inside the lavish entryway, stood a woman, who had a smile on her face. Kamal took Charlie to her. "This is my mother," said Kamal.

Charlie bowed and said, "It is my honor to finally meet you Mrs. Barzani."

"It's so good you've come to visit us. Please call me Enwa," said Kamal's mother in passable English.

"Thank you," said Charlie, responding in Arabic. He shook hands with Enwa. She was of medium height, but was slim and supple. Her hair was dark, and spun up into a bun. Her face was pleasant and friendly with a wide mouth and shining teeth.

"It's so good to have a guest speak to me in Arabic. All our other American visitors think the whole world speaks English exclusively."

"I also speak Italian, Spanish, and Farsi, if you feel like trying something besides English or Arabic. Sorry, I don't speak Kurdish well enough to be conversational."

"It's quite alright," said Enwa, "My husband is busy with state matters, but he asked me to welcome you, and said he would join us for the evening meal.

"I look forward to it," said Charlie.

"Come along, Bud," said Kamal. "Let me show you to your room."

The two went up one side of a pair of wide stairs to the second floor. The staircases curved, separated by a long walkway fronted by a beautiful balustrade. Charlie followed Kamal down the long, wide hallway, highlighted with ceramic tiles and very expensive looking rugs.

Kamal came to the end of the hallway and opened the double doors. For a moment, Charlie thought he had just walked into the apartment in the Vatican. Comfortable couches, a large television, and open curtains leading to sliding doors that opened onto a wide veranda, filled the large living room with decorations. There were two large fans whirling from the tall ceiling, so the room was cool and comfortable.

"I suppose I can manage here," said a grinning Charlie. "It's a little bigger than our dorm room at William and Mary."

"Your bedroom is off to the side. It has a full bath."

"I could use a shower," said Charlie, "It's been a long day of travel."

"Then I will leave you to freshen up," said Kamal. "Dinner is at seven. I'll come and collect you to take you there. The whole family is looking forward to meeting you."

After Kamal left, Charlie explored the room more carefully. He was not only admiring the décor, but was also looking for any spy devise hidden in the room. He didn't find anything, but that didn't mean they weren't there. He opened the sliding doors and went out onto the veranda. Below was a lovely garden. He couldn't imagine how much precious water it took to keep it so green and lush.

He glanced at his watch. It was getting late. He just had time to shower and put on the best clothes he'd brought with him for dinner.

Just before seven, Kamal knocked gently on the door. Charlie opened it and breathed a sigh of relief. Kamal was dressed in, more or less, the same kind of casual clothes Charlie was wearing.

"We only dress for formal state occasions," said Kamal. "The rest of the time we don't bother when it's just family. Since you are family, come on along and I'll get you acquainted with the rest of the family."

The two went back down the big stairs and through several formal rooms for state events. Finally, they arrived in more homey surroundings. This was the private residence quarters for the Barzani family. Kamal led the way into a big dining room. In traditional fashion, the "table" was just a raised platform from the floor, and the family sat around it in a big circle.

They all rose when Charlie and Kamal came in. There were a dozen people in the room. Charlie bowed and said in Arabic, "May the blessings of Allah, be on this house, and all who are here."

Smiles appeared spontaneously around the table. An older man came forward. He was short and had a face scarred with acne and one clearly marked from some violent act in his past. His eyes were almost black, but had the same kind of penetrating stare Charlie recognized in his father. He smiled pleasantly, and said, "Welcome to my home. I am Masoud Barzani. I thank you, for your very kind greeting, you are most welcome. Kamal has told us so much about you; I feel I already know you."

"It is an honor to be here. You are a great man, with such heavy responsibilities."

Barzani sighed, "Alas, some of them kept me from being here to greet you properly when you arrived. My apologies."

"None are needed, Effendi," said Charlie, "The serious matters of the Kurdish people must come above all."

"You are most gracious," said Barzani, "Kamal, you did not mention your friend was such a courteous and gracious young man. I can now understand better what made you so close at the University."

"Charlie made my time in America a most pleasant experience," said Kamal.

"Please be seated," said Barzani, "we are ready for our meal."

All touched their foreheads in praise. Charlie was not the last one to do so.

The meal was very sumptuous. There was roast lamb, a delicious bean dish that you dipped with unleavened bread, and many kinds of vegetables. Charlie ate with relish.

The meal turned into a very happy and funny affair as Charlie and Kamal told many stories of their lives at William and Mary. Charlie did most of the talking, and the Barzani family hooted in laughter when he told of Kamal's exploits and embarrassments. When it was over, everyone had enjoyed themselves, and Charlie truly felt like a member of the family.

As Barzani rose to his feet, Charlie stepped up to him, offering a hand as he did. Barzani took Charlie's arm and smiled, "Old bones make me wish for a taller table."

"I wonder, Effendi, if it might be possible for Kamal and I to speak to you in private for a few moments?"

"If you wish," said Barzani, "we can go to my office."

Barzani led the way down a hallway and turned into his private office. Charlie firmly closed the door, holding tightly to his shoulder bag.

Barzani sat down at his desk and said, "What is it you wish to share only in private?"

Charlie took a deep breath and began, "In July of 1991, you were with a small force of Peshmerga, just across the border in the town of Gelsian, when you were attacked at dusk by a much larger force of Turkish soldiers. You were hard-pressed to defend yourselves, when suddenly three men appeared in your midst and began killing Turks with modern weapons and very skillful movements of martial arts. You learned later these men had come to protect a small community of Christians, but the Turks were there to kill you all. With their help, you were able to kill most of the Turks, and drive them into retreat, but a small group of them attacked you and three more of your men as they were leaving the area. The strangers killed all the Turks, the last one of which had attacked you with a knife and wounded you.

The leader of the strangers stepped in and saved you, killing the Turk with his own knife. As your wound was being dressed by one of the leader's companions, you asked him why he had done this. He said, 'The enemy of your enemy is my friend.' You said, 'You must be the Black Angel of which we have heard so much', then he said, 'I've never cared for that term very much' then he said, 'Allah Akbar' and disappeared into the night."

Barzani looked at Charlie with wide eyes and an astonished look on his face. "All you have said is just as it happened, how could you possibly know this?"

"My father told me," said Charlie.

"Then he must have been one of the men with the legendary Black Angel that night. May Allah bless his soul; he was the greatest fighter I have ever seen. I heard many other stories about him after that night. One of them was he was involved in the explosions of the nuclear bombs in Iran, but the official story I got was that he was killed in South America and his body was never found. Did you ever meet him?"

"I have," said Charlie, "he wants me to tell you he still doesn't care for the term 'Black Angel' very much."

"Are you telling me the Black Angel is still alive? That can't be possible!"

"That's exactly what he told me you were going to say."

Barzani put his hands to his face, and then looked straight at Charlie. "The Black Angel is your father?"

"His real name is Cody, but yes, I am his son."

Barzani leaped out of his chair and embraced Charlie for a long moment. Kamal just sat in his chair, not knowing what to say.

"I cannot begin to express my joy," said Barzani. "The Black Angel lives, and now his son is here standing in my office. May Allah be praised!"

"My father says you might not be quite so pleased when you read the letter and the papers I've brought with me."

"He's written to me?"

"Yes, Sir," Charlie opened his shoulder bag and pulled out the letter, and the bundled folder of papers. He handed them to Barzani. "Would you like some privacy, Effendi?"

"Do you know what's in all this?"

"I do. Some of it I helped to write, but not the letter. My dad intended it just for you."

Barzani broke the seal on the letter and opened it.

"The enemy of my enemy is my friend," it began. Barzani was speaking out-loud, "And you still are my friend. Come, let us reason together."

His voice trailed off as he continued to read. Charlie and Kamal sat quietly as he read on.

Barzani's eyes grew wider and wider as he read. He finished the letter and snatched up the paper bundle, opening the cover to read the contents. After he'd read a couple a pages, he stopped and said, "This will take me a while to read and understand. Why don't you boys go out and have some coffee. I'll join you when I can."

Charlie and Kamal left the room. Barzani did not even hear them close the door as he read on in frenzy.

When they got outside, Kamal turned to Charlie and said, "My father has told us stories about the Black Angel, especially of the night in which he saved his life. I had no idea you were even connected to him let alone being his son. What else haven't you told me?"

"I didn't know any of this either until just the last few days. Trust me the news had an even bigger effect on my sister and I, than it did your father. All my life, I thought my dad was just a former military man, where he learned all his fighting skills, and his uncanny ability to shoot a rifle. After the attack on St. Peters with a dead pope, the Vatican called him and asked him to come back to work. I didn't even know he used to be an actual Catholic Priest."

"Let me see if I understand you," said Kamal. "Your father, the real Black Angel, was actually an agent for the Catholic Church, and ran many years of covert ops for them? Is that what my father is learning now?"

"All of that and much more. What your father is reading right now is a proposal that will create the sovereign nation of Kurdistan."

Kamal said, "I can't imagine anything that all Kurds would support more. Are you saying to include freedom of religion, which the new state must guarantee, and should not permit any religion to exercise political control? Yes, I would say that a country is more important than religious bickering."

"Peace should be practiced by individuals and their personal relationship with God."

"You didn't learn that at William and Mary," said Charlie, "you learned it at your father's knee."

"That's true. I've heard my father say privately, he gets a little tired of people engaged in endless debate over the missionaries of God, and killing people over it. God is God. He's God for you, God for me and even God for the Jews. There is only one God.

"Am I correct in my assumption that the reason why I was invited to join the meeting with my father was because you trust me to keep my mouth shut about everything?"

"Amen, brother," said Charlie. "Also, Kamal, bear in mind the day may come when it will be you in your father's chair. If that happens, what goes on here over the next several days will stay with you forever."

It turned out to be two hours before Masoud Barzani emerged from his office and waved Charlie and Kamal in.

"What I have here is the ultra-most top secret document in the world today. Charlie, you included Kamal, why?"

"Because he's smart, would know what to do with this information, and I trust him."

"Very good answers," said Barzani, "I agree. Now tell me, where is your father right now?"

"I would imagine he's just about to go in for a meeting with the President of the United States."

Does he intend to try and get the Americans to join this Crusade?"

"He will convince them," said Charlie, "because it's the correct solution to this extensive problem. America will agree, just as you will."

"What assurances do we have that the world powers will keep their word?"

"Simple geography, Mr. President," said Charlie. "Possession is nine tenths of the law. If you have occupied the lands as outlined in your brief, it will be very difficult for anyone to force you out of it, particularly since you are about to have one of the best-trained, best-equipped armies in the world. Most likely, other new countries near Kurdistan will be too busy consolidating their gains to bother with yours. I'm sure my Dad made that point."

"He did, and I must admit the proposition is very compelling. How quickly can your father come to Erbil and speak to me directly."

"I can't speak to that," said Charlie, "but I do know he considers you to be one of the three main allies in this coming war. My guess is he will be visiting with you in a very short period of time."

"Can there be any negotiation in the boundaries of the new Kurdistan?"

"Again, I can't speak for my father. Frankly, he thinks at a level that I would never attempt. However, my guess is you may find it easy to negotiate with the Iraqis, and the Iranians. It's the Turks where you'll have real problems."

"Will you be speaking to your father soon?"

"I hope so," said Charlie, "Kamal and I studied International Relations, we didn't think we would be involved in making it, anytime soon."

"When you speak to your father, convey my love to him, and say he should proceed along the lines he's outlined, and I will do all I can to live up to our part of the bargain."

"That's great news, Mr. President.

Chapter 6
Deadly Snipers

Washington, D.C.

As the big unmarked jet set down at Andrews Air Force Base, Cody Frost gathered up all his papers, talking points, and thumb drive containing all his graphics, Rosy did such a masterful job in preparing. During the flight, he made a number of phone calls. Among them was one to Adolfo Moretti in Positano. The two talked tensely for some time.

He had also spent a lot of time on the airplane studying President Carson Palmer. Palmer won his election simply by being smarter than everyone else. He had never held a public office before, but somehow managed to communicate his message in a soft-spoken way that people just trusted.

At the beginning of his second term in office, reelected by a landslide, President Palmer had righted the ship of America. The economy surged back with the repeal or elimination of the mountains of regulations that saddled the business community. The United States was now the largest producer of oil in the world. The Keystone pipeline was running at full capacity.

The Teddy Roosevelt quote of speaking softly and carrying a big stick was now truer than ever. In the world, the United States had respect simply because it was the most deadly. The President put a high priority on national defense and national intelligence. The country had not had a single case of terrorism, while other countries could not make that boast.

Cody respected this President and gave more than the usual amount of preparation for his meeting. He thought about, and dispensed any number of ways to dress for the meeting. He even gave thought to appear as a Priest, or in the full dress uniform of a naval officer. Eventually, he'd decided to appear as who he was without a lot of ceremony.

There was a limousine waiting for him as he stepped onto the tarmac. Cody noticed, with satisfaction, there were no security guards, just a driver, who opened the door for him. He climbed in the car drove off toward the city and the White House.

"There's something going on here," said President Palmer to his National Security Advisor, Tom Bostwick. "At first, when the pope called, I thought he was going to ask for money to rebuild St. Peters, but that wasn't it. He just said he was sending his representative to Washington to discuss important matters. He was very specific about it. He wanted the meeting to be completely private, except for you, Tom. The pope asked for you by name. Do you have any idea what this is all about?"

"I'm afraid I'm as much in the dark as you Mr. President," said Bostwick.

"I guess we'll know soon enough," said the President. "The church representative will be here in just a few minutes.

The two spent the time waiting by discussing some National Security matters. As usual, President Palmer had looked beyond the standard morning security briefing and probed into the backstories the briefing did not explain. Bostwick was used to the intuitive insight of this President, and appreciated it. The country was far safer and better prepared to react to global issues than it was five years before, because he asked the tough questions and sought advice from anyone he believed could help him make tough decisions.

One of the staff opened the door of the Oval Office and said, "The representative of Pope John Luke is here."

"Send him in," said Palmer.

Cody came through the door. He was wearing battle fatigues with bloused brown boots. He had no rank or insignia on the uniform. The President was a little shocked. He had expected some kind of ranking church member, but this man looked like he was just about to jump into a war.

Tom Bostwick rushed across the room. "I was so much hoping it would be you who came. Praise the Lord!" He and Cody hugged each other in jubilation, literally bouncing up and down.

President Palmer watched the exchange with interest. At least the question of having his National Security Advisor present alone for the meeting had its answer.

He said, "Do I have to be here for this reunion? Would you guys like to be alone?"

Bostwick recovered and turned to the President with a big smile, "Mr. President, it's my great honor to present Cody Frost."

"It's a pleasure to meet you, Mr. Frost," said Palmer, "I would have paid big money to see such a display of emotion from my normally all-business National Security Advisor."

Cody turned to the President and the two of them looked deeply into each other's eyes, as they shook hands. Both of them were impressed with what they saw.

"Please call me Cody, Mr. President "I get a little uncomfortable around a lot of pomp and ceremony. Most of the time it's just for show, and hides a dozen hidden agendas."

"Well spoken," said Palmer, "I feel exactly the same way, Cody. It's so seldom to encounter such a direct approach. I appreciate it."

"Mr. President," said Bostwick, horning into the conversation after giving Cody an inquiring look and getting a sign of approval, "I must tell you a great weight is lifted from my shoulders, with the arrival of this man. He speaks perfect clarity, thoughtful decisiveness, and with all due respect, sir, he is someone who is the smartest man in the room. His real name is Cody Frost, but you know him better as The Black Angel."

In the light of what he just learned, the President cocked his head in wonder, and looked Cody over again. Palmer was one of the few people who had taken the time to read Cody's complete file, unlike his predecessor, who had not bothered since his agenda was one of appeasement and non-confrontation.

Palmer waved everyone to seats on couches and said, "Everything I've read about you, told me you were dead."

"Real close," said Cody, "but the docs fixed me up. I did retire, however, and was living a quiet and happy life until this latest crisis with the church came up. They knew I was alive too, and didn't hesitate to call for assistance from anyone they thought could help."

"From everything I've read, you did a good deal more than help," said Palmer. "Your solution to the Iran crisis was a world-changer."

"I didn't anticipate the Sunni fanatics would make a power play of their own, so quickly."

"So the pope has sent you here to offer a new solution?"

"Exactly," said Cody, "Boy it's nice to talk to someone who sees the facts as fast as I do. Do you have an eidetic memory?"

"Not quite," said Palmer, "but I can usually remember anything I read. I'm sure you do have an eidetic memory. It's not possible for someone without such a gift to intuitively solve as many problems as you have over such a long period of time."

Cody turned to Bostwick, "Have you given him my entire file?"

"There's only one copy, and I keep it locked in my safe. Mr. President, Cody being here is an expectation for me. I knew Cody was still alive, because we have continued to promote and pay him. He's actually a two-star Admiral in the U.S. Navy."

"I haven't served in the Navy for almost thirty years, Mr. President. All of this is just for show and to provide me with lots of money."

"Very well," said the President, "let's see how you plan to solve our current crisis."

Cody knew no preamble was required for this man, so he reached into his bag and took out the bound report he had prepared and handed it to the President. He was not surprised to see Palmer flipping through the pages almost as fast as he could.

Within minutes, the President finished absorbing the entire 50-page document. He looked up at Cody and said, "Brilliant. What are the chances of this succeeding?"

"With the help of the United States, and whoever you can include in the coalition, about 80%. Without your support, the odds go down to less than half that."

"This is the first time I've ever read a report, other than sent from the academic sector, that actually understands the difference between Sunnis and Shias. Almost all my advisors are still clumping the Islamic world into one group. Tom, here, is one of the exceptions."

"I share your high opinion of Tom's insight and competency," said Cody.

"What, exactly, do you need right now?" The President asked.

"I need an immediate and private meeting with the Iranian President, Manek Faroush. I don't know him, but you have a good relationship with him."

"Are you going to tell him who you are?"

"I don't know another way to get his undivided attention."

"There are still many Iranians who would like to see you dead."

"I don't think Faroush is one of them. Besides, my offer to him will be hard to resist."

"What else?" The President asked.

"I need to talk with the Israeli Prime Minister Ari Ben Cannan. Furthermore, I'd like to meet with them both, together in this office."

"The Iranians may not be yelling 'death to Israel', but I don't think they regard each other as friends."

"They don't have to be friends. They just have to listen to what we say, and agree to work together to wipe out ISIS. Surely, both will see this is in their best interest."

"I could maybe get them to meet together, if nobody else knows about it," said Palmer. "I'll let you know. What else?"

Turkey is scared to death the next ISIS target is them, which is true. The only thing standing between them is the Kurds. You need to convince them that the Kurds will not cause any trouble in Turkey, and will stand between them and ISIS. What we need from Turkey is their willingness to stay out of the active fighting for now, but let us use them for forward bases and a supply chain."

"There's a weakness in your plan," said the President. "The Kurds and Turks have been fighting for hundreds of years."

"Tell the Turks it will be the Kurds who die in the upcoming conflict, not them. That should satisfy their willingness to support our plan."

"Fair point," said the President. "Is there anything else you need?"

"It will take me some time to put all this together, train the troops, and coordinate our offensive. I need the United States and your allies to pick up the pace dramatically on the aerial bombing of ISIS. In particular, we need to shut down their money source. Concentrate on disabling their oil exports, blow up all their oil fields."

"We're already doing that," said the President.

"One last thing," said Cody. "The Catholic Church has elected a young and militant pope. In about two weeks, he will be meeting with clerics from every Islamic country in the world. He's going to declare a modern Crusade for the world. This time it will be a coalition of Muslims, Christians, and Jews, acting in the name of our common God. The coalition will destroy an enemy who is not acting in the name of God at all. They are actually a huge collection of gangsters who are hiding behind the name of Allah to accomplish their own self-interests. You need to publicly announce full support for this Crusade, and mobilize the country for a war."

"Tom," said the President, "you haven't said a word in this discussion. Now I want your honest assessment."

"To tell you the truth, Mr. President, if anybody except the Black Angel had walked in here with this plan, I would have had a lot of questions and objections. However, Cody is probably the best field operative in history. I believe he can do this."

"I agree," said Palmer. "We will proceed with your plan, Cody. Where are you going next?"

"Back to Rome, the pope needs to hear the results of this conversation firsthand. After that, I'll head to Erbil. I have a lot of work to do with the Kurds."

"May the Lord be with you," said Palmer, rising and shaking hands with Cody. "It was a real pleasure to meet you in the flesh. Tom's right, you're the best I've ever seen."

Erbil

"You have a guest, Charlie," said Kamal.

"Boy, those bill collectors will follow you anywhere."

"No," said Kamal, "you really have a guest looking for you."

"That's strange. Not many people know I'm here."

Charlie followed Kamal out of the palace and to the guarded front gate. As he got closer, a very familiar face was smiling at him.

"Rico!" cried Charlie. He ran to the gate, with Kamal following him. When he got to the gate, he said to the guards, "It's OK, I know this man. Let him in."

Kamal had to repeat the order in Kurdish, and the guards swung open the gate. Charlie ran over to Enrico and hugged him.

"Wow, the strangest people show up when you least expect it. Kamal, this is Rico Moretti, he and I grew up together in Positano. He's like a true brother for me."

Kamal was a little surprised when Rico stepped up to him and said in Arabic, "I'm so glad to meet you finally. Charlie has talked about you a lot."

The two shook hands and Kamal said, "You are welcome.

Unexpected, but welcome."

"Give me a hand with this stuff," said Rico.

There were two large canvas bags on the ground. Charlie picked one of them up and staggered a little under its weight.

"What have you got in here?" he asked.

"Stuff that sure couldn't come on a regular airplane. Sneaking it across all those borders made me nervous. The touch and go took me two days."

"I've only been gone for two days," said Charlie.

"Well, your dad called my dad on his way to Washington and said I should bring all this to you, and that you'd know what to do with it."

Rico hefted the other bag and the three men returned to the palace. They did not stop until they reached Charlie's room and locked the door.

Each dropped a bag on the floor and Charlie unzipped one of them. He looked with astonishment at the contents.

So did Kamal, and said, "What a beautiful weapon,"

"It's my Timberwolf sniper rifle," said Charlie. He set the rifle on the floor and began hauling out the rest of the contents of the bag. There were 8 five-round magazines for the Timberwolf, his Gilley suit, and camouflage fatigues, a Glock 18 automatic hand gun with two 100 round magazines, an eight inch knife, a couple boxes of MRE's, a canteen, and a backpack. There was also a note, taped to the Timberwolf in Adolfo's handwriting. It said, "Call your sister."

"What the Hell!" said Charlie, "I suppose your bag has the same stuff in it?"

Rico nodded, "Are you going to call Rosy?"

"I guess I'd better. Maybe she can give us a better picture of what this is all about."

Charlie took out his phone and called Rosy. She answered almost immediately.

"Hi there Charlie, looks like you get to have all the fun, while we computer nerds are slaving away in this dark hole."

"Cut the crap, Rosy," said Charlie. "Tell me what's going on!"

"We re-tasked a satellite to give us a better look at the Mosul computer center, where most of their social media feeds are originating, and we found out something very interesting.

"Every day, the senior staff in that center, come out for evening prayers. Then they have a leisurely meal around a big table behind the building. They smoke a lot. I'm sure they can't smoke inside with the computers. We've been able to do facial recognition on the group and have identified at least eight very high-value targets in the ISIS command structure, including the number three man in the whole of ISIS.

"If we could sneak a team of snipers into Mosul, we could take out all or most of these men. The result would cripple their entire computer system. These guys are the cream of the crop, the best hackers, and operators they have. It would scramble not only their propaganda arm, but significantly affect their entire command and control system."

"We're only fifty miles from Mosul," said Charlie.

"That's why dad sent Rico with all your equipment. Think you can do it?"

"I'm sure we can take out the targets," said Charlie, "It's getting in and out that is the big question."

"Then you have some planning to do," said Rosy. "Call me back when you know more."

Charlie had his speaker on while he was talking to Rosy, so Kamal and Rico heard the whole conversation.

"Well, Rico, we've been practicing all our lives for this kind of operation, but this time it's for real and dad has given us a really difficult and dangerous mission. Do you think we can do it?"

"I'm ready if you are," said Rico.

"Kamal, this is your territory. Can we sneak into Mosul and out without getting killed?"

"The road from Erbil to Bagdad is open. There's quite a bit of traffic on it. It's still very dangerous. People die all the time. ISIS has roving patrols looking for people in the wrong place, and they always shoot first before talking to anyone. Plus, there are many landmines and IED's along the roads, which are a real hazard."

"But you can get people in and out of Mosul?"

"We do it all the time," said Kamal. "Mostly the Peshmerga go in to rescue a family or to assassinate a target, if one can be located."

"What are your losses?" asked Charlie.

"Maybe 30%."

"How would you get Rico and me into Mosul and to the spot where we can do the shooting Rosy mentioned?"

"I'll see what can be done," said Kamal. "But, you don't know the location of the building Rosy talked about. If she can give you an exact location, we can make a better plan. There's just one condition. I'm going too."

"Out of the question," said Charlie. "You'd just slow us down, and your father would never allow it."

"Who was it who went with you and was your sparring partner all those years in Virginia?" said Kamal. "I may not be as good as you and probably Rico, but I can fight with the best of them. As for my father not allowing me to go, *your* father not only said you should go, but sent all the tools to do it."

"All right," said Charlie, "you've made your point. I'll call Rosy back and have her send me all the data on this place, the people involved, and how quickly we have to move."

Two hours later, Kamal, Charlie, and Rico were in the office of President Barzani. Charlie projected onto a screen from his phone the photos, street maps, and general location surrounding the computer center. He showed the pictures of the men involved and gave their names and general background of most of them, especially Abu al Kushari, the number three man in ISIS.

"The computer center is in this office building," said Charlie, pointing to the site. It backs up to the Tigris River. It probably was luxury corporate offices before ISIS moved in.

"Across the Tigris River is a marsh. You can see there is a bluff above the river, which will provide perfect cover. What we need is transportation to a place where we can move undetected to this spot, right here." He pointed at it.

"There is a major highway skirting the marsh connecting the Erbil-Bagdad road right here. It's about a mile walk to our position. We will be out in the open the entire time. That means we have to go in the night before and wait through the day until our targets come out of the building. Once we've completed our mission, we should be able to move, mostly under the cover of darkness back to the rendezvous point, here. Your Peshmerga commandos need to deliver us to the drop off point and then return the following night to pick us up. We should be out of Mosul and on the road back to Erbil before anyone realizes what's happened. Then all we have to do is to avoid any roving ISIS patrols until we're back in our safe zone."

"How far is your position from the target?" asked Barzani.

"It's just under a mile," said Charlie.

"Is it possible to make that kind of shot?"

"Rico and I have done it before."

"One question," said Barzani, "Since we know the location of the building and who's in it, why don't we just send in planes to blow it up?"

"A very good question, Effendi," said Charlie. "The answer is getting a major propaganda victory of our own. We could blow up the building, but the people of the world have grown tired of seeing it happen. What we need is documentary proof we have carried out this mission in the center of ISIS controlled territory and killed some of their major leaders. Of course, the Kurds will get all the credit for doing this, and the world will cheer your victory. The standing of the Kurds will go up dramatically on the world stage. This works to our advantage in two ways. First, it shows the world the Kurds are capable of such an action, and second, it will provide valuable leverage for the Kurdish people when the time comes to form your own country. I should also add your personal image will rise significantly with the less than cooperative Kurdish tribal leaders with whom you are always bickering."

"Two men against the entire ISIS army," said Barzani, "Yes the credibility of our cause would go up dramatically."

Kamal said, "Correction father, three people. I'm going too."

"I forbid it!" said Barzani, "You are my youngest son. I will not have you take risks like this."

"If I may repeat something Charlie said this afternoon, when we had the same conversation, Charlie's father not only gave this mission to his son, he provided the weapons to do it. And besides, someone has to run the camera while Charlie and Rico are blowing the ISIS pigs to pieces."

After another half hour of wrangling, Barzani finally approved the mission, including Kamal. However, he insisted on sending in a dozen Peshmerga commandos to cover the withdrawal of the assassins. They would drift in, in two's and three's, disguised as taxi drivers transporting people on the dangerous road to Mosul. Their passengers would be Peshmerga, some disguised as women. After dropping the team off, they would go to a safe house and wait for the following night to pick them and return to Erbil.

It took a couple of days to organize the mission. Barzani brought in two of his top men to brief them on the operation. "Your job is to deliver three assassins to this spot in Mosul, and then return the following night to cover their withdrawal and bring them home. My son, Kamal, will be part of the team. However, you will take your orders from the man who will lead the hit team. I should tell you these are very skilled agents. They are also Christians who have joined our cause. I want all of them brought back, dead or alive, including Kamal."

The Peshmerga commander surveyed the set up and said, "Nobody can make a shot from that distance."

"The two shooters are going out today to calibrate their weapons and shoot at targets. You are welcome to take your men with you to watch them work. Then, if they prove unable to make the shots, which I also have doubts about, we will cancel the mission."

The Peshmerga leader, a tough character with many missions under his belt, just bowed and said his team would observe these, so-called, long-range shooters.

That afternoon, Rico and Cody piled into a truck with Kamal and the dozen Peshmerga fighters who would take part in the operation, and drove to a shooting range on the outskirts of Erbil.

Charlie, Rico, and Kamal were wearing their camouflage fatigues and brought along all the rest of their equipment. Charlie wanted the practice to be as close to the real thing as possible.

The truck came to a stop, some distance from the firing range. The three men put on their Ghillie suits, and hoisted their backpacks filled with everything they would take on the real mission. Then they ran, in zigzag patterns across the rough ground and disappeared into a clump of bushes. The Peshmerga watched them throughout this process, and followed as the team moved into position. However, as soon as they went into the bushes, they became invisible.

The Peshmerga commandos then turned their attention to the targets. They had to use powerful binoculars to see the targets a mile away. They were man-sized figures, set in the ground in two rows, simulating what Charlie and Rico would see when they got to their firing positions in Mosul.

There was silence for a few minutes. Then the bark of the

Timberwolves rang out in quick succession. The Peshmerga turned their binoculars to the targets. The shooting was over in less than ten seconds. The Kurds watched with amazement as one target after another blew to pieces. All the shots decapitated the targets. The soldiers could not believe their eyes. Ten shots, ten hits. None of them had ever seen such shooting before. As Charlie and Rico emerged from their hiding places, the Kurds gathered around them, smiling, cheering, and pounding on their backs. Kamal was very proud. From that moment on, he knew these tough fighters would follow Charlie and Rico into whatever awaited them.

The word spread fast through the Kurdish ranks. Two strangers, and Christians at that, had done what others considered impossible. Masoud Barzani got the word through the chatter among the guards in the palace. He smiled. The Black Angel had raised another team perhaps more deadly than any he ever had.

Setting the mission for the following night, Charlie checked with Rosy to make sure the evening meal ritual still happened. Timetables were set, the support team gathered, and at midnight, two vans, marked as taxis were loaded with men and equipment.

The trip to Mosul took only an hour. There was little traffic and the vans were able to pull off the road where Charlie, Rico, and Kamal jumped out. The vans sped off. The team climbed off the road and out into the marsh. They stayed away from the bluff overlooking the Tigris River, so they did not show their outline.

Charlie kept checking the soft, wet ground underneath his feet, calculating how fast they could make their way back to the road. It was slower going than he wanted. The muddy ground clung to every step. It took 15 minutes for them to jog across the mile to the place they had selected as their firing position.

Then on hands and knees, they crept to the edge of the bluff. There was heavy grass at the margin of the marsh, and the three men dug into the ground, pulling bushes and weeds over them to conceal them for the long wait.

None of the three spoke. The plan was set before they left, and all knew what would happen, if all went as expected. They slept in shifts through the remainder of the night, with one of them always awake to scan the horizon with powerful binoculars.

With the rising of the sun, Charlie checked their position again and carefully pulled more foliage over them to make them invisible. All were wearing camouflage cream to minimize any glare. Wrapped in brown and gray cloth, the Timberwolf rifles similarly made them undetectable.

One rule for being a sniper insisted no movement at all, or very little, once they were in position. Charlie and Rico worked well in this discipline, but Kamal did not. He spoke in the mumbling voice used by snipers to communicate, "I have to relieve myself," he said to Charlie.

"Just go," said Charlie, "but don't move. Don't worry, my friend, it'll all wash out."

The only time any of them moved during the hot day was to sip water from their canteens and eat some of the rations they brought with them. Charlie had pulled these things out of his backpack during the night. Now his backpack supported the barrel of the Timberwolf. Rico had the same set up.

The hot day went on. Charlie was glad for the cool wetness from the marsh underneath him. Still, it was a long day. At noon, the back door of the building opened and a group of men came out to smoke. Charlie checked his cell phone to confirm the men were the same ones who would be their targets when they next appeared. There were more than ten of them, however. Charlie wondered if that would be the case the next time. "How fast can you get another magazine into your Timberwolf," he mumbled to Rico.

"Faster than you," said Rico without bravado.

"If more than ten come out the next time, we'll have to keep shooting till their all down," said Charlie. "We can't have anyone left to run inside and sound the alarm."

"Right," said Rico.

Kamal was suffering the worst through the heat of the day. His Ghillie suit was like an oven. He tried to take his mind off it, by checking and rechecking his powerful camera that would record the coming action.

Long shadows began to cover the back of the building. "No wonder they come out there," mumbled Charlie. They have a nice view of the river, and stay in the shade."

It was dusk before the men came out for their evening prayers and their meal. They all faced south, toward Mecca, and bowed and prayed. Then they rose and gathered around the long table for the meal. As earlier, there were more than ten men around the long table.

"They must have brought in some techs to try and break through all Rosy's malware," said Charlie.

It was getting dark. Charlie wanted to wait until the last minute to take advantage of that for their escape. So, he scanned the targets through his powerful scope on the Timberwolf. He flipped down his night scope for a better view. Rico did the same. Kamal pulled his camera into position. It was set for high resolution in dark light, so he did not miss any of the action.

Charlie waited until he saw the men pile up their plates and smoke their last cigarettes. "Count down from ten," mumbled Charlie. Rico nodded and flipped off the safety on his Timberwolf. "Ten, nine, eight," Charlie said quietly as he counted down.

When he reached zero, both Timberwolves began sharply snapping. Both Rico and Charlie got off four rounds each before the first bullet struck the ISIS commander in the back of his head, splattering blood, and gore across the table. Charlie fired his final round in his magazine and snatched for another. Rico was, indeed, quicker than he was, and was shooting again.

In less than a minute, every person around the table were either laying on the table with no head, or had fallen backwards, just as dead. Kamal recorded the entire scene.

"Time to cut and run," said Charlie. The three backed away from the bluff and began running at full speed for the road. Charlie was barking into a radio to alert the waiting Peshmerga they were on their way.

Both vans were waiting for them when they reached the road. The three and a few Peshmerga jumped into one of the vans and both sped off toward the main road to Erbil. They turned on to the road and slowed down a little to be less conspicuous. All three of the men shed their Ghillie suits and backpacks, then pulled out the Glocks.

They had only gone a few miles before they could see two pickups had crossed the road as a block.

"A routine checkpoint, or has someone sounded the alarm?" asked Rico.

"Don't know," said Charlie, "but we have no choice but to shoot our way through." He radioed the lead van and told him to crash into the rear of one of the pickups." It had a 50-caliber machine gun mounted in it. "That should make enough room for us to get by. Looks like about 20 ISIS soldiers at the roadblock." He yelled up to the driver to pull up and skid parallel to the two pickups with the sliding door facing the enemy.

"We have to do this quick," said Charlie. "We'll start shooting as soon as we get in range."

The lead van hit the back end of the pickup on the right side, and shoved it back ten feet. The other van turned sharply, and Peshmerga soldiers, Charlie, Rico, and Kamal rushed out behind them. There was gunfire from both directions. Rico picked off the man behind the 50-caliber machine gun.

The Peshmerga were dropping the surprised ISIS fighters quickly. Two of the Kurds took bullets and slumped to the ground.

Now the two groups were close enough to engage in close quarter combat. Charlie and Rico waded into the largest group and began whirling in a flurry, throwing kicks and punching ISIS soldiers in their throats. Together they disposed of at least a half dozen of the enemy with blazing speed in only a few seconds.

The Peshmerga were winning their individual combats as well. They were too preoccupied to admire Charlie and Rico's fighting skills, but as the seconds went by, there were fewer and fewer ISIS to take down.

Suddenly it was very quiet, except for the gasps of air all the combatants were breathing. "Let's get out of here," shouted Charlie. Is that lead van still running?

"We got lucky on that, "said one of the Peshmerga, "our heavy duty bumper saved us from having to leave it behind."

As the team was running back to get into the vans, one of the fallen ISIS soldier rolled over with a gun in his hand and started firing. A bullet quickly killed him, but one of his bullets struck Charlie in his right shoulder. He staggered and screamed from the sharp pain he felt. Both Rico and Kamal grabbed him and threw him into the van. Then both vans speed off into the night. Within an hour they reached Erbil with no further enemy encounters.

A Peshmerga medic treated Charlie's wound as best he could, stopping most of the bleeding and giving him a shot of morphine to ease the pain and keep him from going into shock.

As they passed the Presidential palace, one of the vans turned off to report to an anxious Barzani the outcome of the raid. The other van roared to the hospital. One of the Peshmerga was dead, and two other seriously injured, but all the attention was on Charlie, who had passed out from the painkiller, and still oozed a lot of blood from his shoulder.

Nurses and doctors came rushing out of the hospital to put the injured men on gurneys and went inside.

Rico used Charlie's phone to call Cody, who was in the Ops Center at the time. He had just watched on a satellite feed, what had happened at the ISIS command center, and was grinning with pride over Rico and Charlie's deadly marksmanship.

When he answered his phone, Rico told him about the fight at the roadblock where Charlie took a hit.

"How bad is it?" said Cody in the calmest voice he could muster.

"Bad enough," said Rico. "The doctors are operating on him right now. I pray to the Lord he's going to be alright."

"Ashana and I will leave for Erbil immediately," said Cody. "Tell Masoud we are on our way. I'll call before we land so he can pick us up and take us to the hospital."

Chapter 7
Chicken Soup

Rome

Earlier when Cody returned to Rome, he went to see the pope right away. The Pontiff was busy writing his speech for the "All God" conference, as it was now known and just three weeks away. All the people John Luke had invited were coming, including the Muslim clerics who had written to the Vatican in the first place. Also attending were representatives of all the major Protestant churches, as well as the Russian and Greek Orthodox churches. It was the largest conclave of churches who worshipped the one true God in history.

Not only would there be speeches by each church leader, they also scheduled a number of smaller conferences addressing the pressing issues worldwide. At the top of the agenda, the proposition read by all the conferees would agree to take on the scourge of ISIS. Pope John Luke understood and felt the same.

John Luke was happy to see Cody, and anxious to hear what news and progress he had made in implementing the plan Cody had written. The two sat down together on a couch and drank espresso coffee.

"We're half done in assembling our coalition of nations to destroy ISIS and redraw the political boundaries of the Middle East," said Cody. "The United States is on board. I must say, Your Holiness, President Palmer is one smart cookie. In minutes not hours, he digested my report, and agreed with the plan to accomplish our goals.

"The United States is running full bore to restore its military as the best in the world. It's one of the most encouraging things I've heard."

"The President agreed to reach out to the Iranian President and the Israeli Prime Minister and hopes to get them to come to Washington for a meeting with me. We would speak to each other directly on the ISIS issue. One could only hope this common enemy might lead them to set aside other issues festering for so long."

"Excellent!" said the pope. "I'm glad I ordered you not to go to Iran. It was a risk we do not need, and I thought your plan to do so, was an example that even the best of us are capable of thinking poorly. What about your talks with the Kurd's?"

"I sent my son, Charlie, to Erbil on the pretext of visiting his college roommate. His real purpose was to give his father, President Masoud Barzani, a letter I had written him, after Charlie told him all the details of an event years ago in which I saved Barzani's life. Charlie was to reveal I was still alive, and give him our analysis of how we intended to defeat ISIS and carve out a new nation for the Kurds. He did that, and Charlie called me back to say the Kurds will agree to our coalition."

"Even better," said John Luke.

"There's more. My daughter, Rosy, is working in your Ops Center and has successfully disrupted the flow of information coming from ISIS to the rest of the world. Rosy is a truly gifted computer expert.

Rosy not only located the main terminal from which all this propaganda was emanating, in Raqqa, Syria, but was able to give information to the United States that bombed the center and destroyed it. When she learned the propaganda was still going out, she was able to locate an even bigger source of this trash produced in Mosul. Ops got the U.S. to re-task a satellite and get a look at their operation. She found the building and learned that at least ten high-value ISIS targets were working in the building, including the Number 3 ranked commander of ISIS, and were exposing themselves to attack by us."

"I sent the son of my manager of the estate in Positano, with all their weapons, to Erbil. Both Charlie and Enrico are excellent snipers and among the best in the world in martial arts. Erbil is just fifty miles from Mosul. As we speak, Charlie is mounting an operation to assassinate all these ISIS leaders and their best computer analysts.

"We hope to get all this documented on video and show how competent the Kurds are at dealing with ISIS."

"But aren't your son and his friend going to do all the shooting?"

"The world won't know that. All they are going to see is the killing of top ISIS leaders. It will be far more effective than just sending in a squadron of bombers to blow up the building. This will be personal retaliation for the endless ISIS atrocities. It will certainly make your job in Geneva easier."

Pope John Luke added, "It fits the church's position on all your operations for twenty years. We publicized results and improved lives for hundreds of thousands of people. The faces behind the work were irrelevant. Of course, you turned out to be so good at it, you became a global folk hero."

"Ashana and I raised Charlie and Rosy to feel the same way I do. Naturally, I worry a lot about my son's safety. This will be his first live operation, and I handed him a tough one."

The pope stretched his long arm to put his hand firmly on Cody's shoulder, and said, "I will pray for him and Rico."

"Thank you," said Cody.

"I wonder if you have time to do something else for me."

"Sure, what's that?"

"Will you read the draft of my speech I will deliver in Geneva and offer some helpful hints?"

"Of course, Robert, hand it over."

The Pope smiled and gave Cody a copy of the speech.

"Now, if you don't mind, I'd like to go see my wife and daughter. I came here first. If Ashana knew that, she would put a bullet in my head, and Rosy would break my arm."

"By all means, Cody, go have a wonderful reunion, and many, many thanks for all you have done and will do."

Erbil

Charlie was dreaming. It was a wonderful dream. His mother was leaning over him, smiling and saying, "How about some soup, honey."

Then he opened his eyes and tried to focus his vision. He was not dreaming. His mother really was there, with a spoonful of soup in her hand and a glorious smile on her face.

"Mom!" said Charlie, "is it really you?"

"In the flesh, handsome," said Ashana, "Now really, have some of this soup. It's delicious."

She spooned a mouthful of the soup into Charlie's mouth.

Charlie looked around the room. His Father was smiling at him, and Rosy was grinning too.

"What are you guys doing here?"

"It's a dumb question, Bro," said Rosy, "where did you expect us to be?"

"We got here last night," said Cody. "That was the night after they wheeled you in here. You've been asleep until now."

"Well, what did you expect?" said Charlie "This is the first time I've been shot. It sucks."

"It does," Cody said, "but you're going to be OK. In a couple of weeks, you'll hardly notice the pain."

"Something to look forward to," Charlie said sarcastically.

"Here's something else for you to look forward to," said Cody, "You are now an unofficial Kurdish hero."

"Huh?" asked Charlie.

"It's like this, son, as far as the world knows, the Kurdish Peshmerga single-handedly took out the number three man in the ISIS command, and killed no less than 30 others, counting the sniper shots on their computer geeks, and the massacre of the ISIS platoon at the checkpoint. The greatest defenders against ISIS in the world are the Kurds. Ordinary people are starting to ask why they don't have their own country. President Masoud Barzani is getting the credit as the supreme leader of the Kurds, for dreaming up such a bold and dangerous plan.

"However, within the ranks of the Peshmerga, the stories about you and Rico's exploits are taking on incredible proportions. Not only do they regard both of you as the greatest sharpshooters in the world, but also more importantly, your battle with the ISIS soldiers at that checkpoint is big news up and down the ranks. They are saying you were personally responsible for saving the entire extraction team with your incredible feats of martial arts. Your current nickname is Ardishur, which means 'Great Warrior'".

"What hogwash," said Charlie, "I was just doing what I do."

"Well, it didn't work for me either," said Cody. "But now, we're going to put those names to good use."

Charlie flexed his arm, "They must have done a good job. This doesn't feel so bad. When do I get out of here?"

"Tomorrow morning," said Cody, "and then tomorrow night there's a huge banquet in yours and Rico's honor at the Presidential Palace."

Cody leaned over and put his hand on Charlie's, "You did a really great job, son. I'm very proud of you."

"Thanks, Dad, I guess all that training paid off."

At this Rosy exploded, "What am I, a fly on the wall. Who was it who found that computer center in Mosul? Who was it who found the building? Who was it who re-tasked the satellite so we could get a look at the bad guys? Who identified who they were? Who handed the battle plan to you on a silver platter? Who..." Rosy's voice trailed off as she looked at Charlie's tears running down his cheeks. She ran over to her brother and said, "I'm so sorry, bro, I was running my mouth to hear my head roar. You may have gotten support from others, but you pulled the trigger. I love you so much, Charlie, and I thank the Lord you're alive."

The brother and sister held each other for a long moment, and both of them cried. Cody and Ashana stood quietly behind with their arms around each other's waist. Tears flowed down their faces as well.

As Rosy stood, still holding her brother's hand, the two of them looked at their weeping parents.

Cody wiped the tears from his eyes and said, "My poor children. Both of you are sad and I can see the hurting pain in your eyes. You need to know none of this is your fault. I've always lived in a dangerous and evil world. When you were children, I wanted to spare you from all that, but I knew I couldn't. Therefore, I prepared you for the worst, with tools that would prevent you from being victims of dark souls. They are part of Satan's plan to create the most fear and terror in humanity. At this moment, I feel so helpless. I have pulled you into what is now the worst that exists on Earth. I deeply regret the pain I'm am causing you, and pray to God Almighty to forgive me for what I have done.

"The gruesome truth is this is going to get much worse, not better, in the near future. You must pray every day to seek God's will and, each of you must do all you can to follow it. I can't promise more than to do all I can to preserve us as family.

"It gives me great pain to see my son, laying in a bed with the scars of war already on you. Both of you have already done so much to battle the evil forces we face. Yet, it also fills me with gratitude. The two of you have caused our enemy to be less than they were yesterday.

Rosy rushed across the room and into her Father's arms. Ashana went to her son in his bed and embraced him. Silently, the entire family cried many tears.

Charlie got his emotions under control first and said, "When I was lying in cover on the bluff over that building and saw all those people coming out, I remembered something you told me. You said, 'Charlie, it's not a matter of being fast, or even accurate. It's being willing'. When the moment came and I knew I was going to pull the trigger, I was willing. I have you to thank for that, Dad. You saw into a future I couldn't know and gave me the strength to do what was right. I pray the Lord can forgive me for taking all those lives. It makes me sick."

Cody said, "Then you've learned the most important truth of all, Charlie. Any ungodly idiot with a gun, can murder. I believe, the Lord's finger was on the trigger with yours, and He surely knows the difference."

❖

The family spent most of the day together. Kamal came to see Charlie and they talked about what they had done. Kamal summed it up nicely, "What you did was not Christians killing Muslims in a Holy war with the name of Christ, but men of Allah, who knew they were serving God for a greater purpose."

"I hope so, my friend," said Charlie, "You were probably the bravest of us all. All you had was a camera. I suppose you got good pictures as you did your job."

"The pictures are certainly out there. You can see the whole thing on the internet. Of course, the major media of the world won't show such gruesome pictures to a sensitive public, but it doesn't matter. The You Tube video has gone viral and over 30 million people have seen it."

"None of those pictures show me and Rico, do they?"

"Of course not," said Kamal, "as you said, this was an entirely Kurdish operation. You should see all the commentary about it. We are getting more press in favor of a country of our own than at any time in history. It has really lifted the spirits of all Kurds.

"One of the most interesting things I've read is an analysis by gun experts, who calculated the time of the shot till it hit the target. They know the shots came from a mile away. They also know there was more than one shooter. I know ISIS is reading this and are probably scared to death that shots can arrive from such a long distance. I'll bet they're moving all their perimeter flags out 500 meters."

"What about their 'You Tube' videos?" Charlie asked.

"There aren't any," said Kamal. "An hour after we took out their senior leadership, the U.S. Air Force came in and leveled the building. ISIS is using friendly media to scream out their protests and promises there will be heavy repercussions."

"I feel like I'm missing out on all sorts of things," said Charlie. "I can't wait to get out of here."

"I'll pick you up tomorrow morning," said Kamal. "The doctors say you've recovered enough to stand a day of celebration at the palace."

"What's happened to my anonymity?"

"I can assure, this will be just a family celebration. Your Father is as careful about keeping your identity a secret as his."

Just as night was falling and Charlie was starting to get sleepy, Rico stuck his head in the door. "I've had to wait in line all afternoon to get in here."

"Rico! I'm so glad to see you. I'm really sorry I'm getting all the attention when you were at least as important in our little jaunt to Mosul as I was."

"Are you kidding? I've spent the last two days with the Peshmerga commandos who went with us, and a whole lot more. I'll bet I've had to tell our story fifty times. Both of us are now part of their own. The word 'Timberwolf' is now part of their vocabulary and everyone wants me to teach them to shoot like us. They continue to mob me. I think I'm going to open a sniper school. Having long range shooters like us will be a big advantage for the Kurds."

"No doubt," said Charlie, yawning as he tried to flex his shoulder to a more comfortable position.

"I just dropped by to make sure you're OK, bro. We have a big day tomorrow, so I'm gonna leave now and let you get a good night's sleep."

"I guess I could use it," said Charlie, but thanks for coming."

"See you tomorrow," said Enrico. As he slipped out of the room, Charlie was already snoring lightly.

The next morning Charlie woke early and grumped around until someone finally brought him a cup of coffee, and soon after a decent breakfast. Then the doctors came in and changed his bandage again while fitting him for an arm sling. He found a new set of clothes in his closet and had to call for some help to get them on. All the staff of the hospital treated him as if he was royalty, and said they would miss him; hoped never to see him under the same circumstances; and wished him good fortune for the future.

During the ride out of the hospital, in a wheelchair he hated, many people came out of their offices and stations to applaud him, which embarrassed him.

Outside were two gleaming limousines. Standing in front of them were Charlie's Mother and Father, sister Rosy, Kamal and Enrico. In addition, President Barzani was standing with the group. All of them wore smiles of relief.

Cody came over to Charlie, helped him out of the wheelchair, and said, "President Barzani wants you and Rico to ride alone with him in his limo. We'll follow to the palace."

"What's up?" asked Charlie.

Cody said, "The President wants a private word with both of you. He didn't tell me what he needed to say."

Charlie just shrugged his shoulder and got into the limousine with Rico and President Barzani.

Barzani settled to face the two heroes. "We will have a big day of celebration today. I wanted to take this opportunity to say a few words before others dominate all your time.

"Charlie, your father handed me a plan last week. It is an excellent plan, but will be very difficult to execute. One of the problems is our inability to come together as a people. What you two did erased many of those disputes. The Kurdish people believe our attack on the ISIS command center came solely from us. So does everyone else in the world. We know it's not true. We helped, certainly, but the plan, intelligence, and execution was all yours, both of you. Anonymity seems to be a family trait. Cody's is still secret in every way possible. I pledge yours will be the same. At any rate, I wanted to have these few minutes alone with both of you to give you my heartfelt thanks. If there is ever anything the Kurdish nation can do for you, all you have to do is ask."

"Thank you, Mr. President. My Father says the road gets tougher from here. I think we can say we won the first battle."

"Indeed we have," smiled Barzani, and he shook the hands of both young men with enthusiasm.

Later that evening, Charlie had to admit the Kurds really knew how to throw a party. He ate until he was stuffed, laughed, and was propositioned several times by some very attractive young women. Enrico latched on to one and seemed on the verge of giving in. Charlie was not interested in being a trophy for any woman, so he was polite, charming, and kept his distance. Once his Mother came walking by and whispered to him, "Your Father had temptations like this on a regular basis. I'm glad to see you've learned more from him than just how to fight."

There was one final banquet that night. President Barzani had carefully planned it with one giant round table in the center of the room. A number of tribal leaders were there at his invitation, along with all the men who were on the mission to Mosel. Barzani sat with the leader of the Peshmerga force on one side of him and his son, Kamal on his other side.

Cody and Ashana sat together with Charlie, Rosy, and Enrico about halfway around the table. Near them were sprinkled other Kurdish leaders and their wives, and the table was rounded out with the Peshmerga commandos.

It was a boisterous affair with waiters circling the table and offering any number of dishes, meats, and tasty delights. Charlie's sling made it difficult for him to eat, so he took it off so he could eat with his right hand. Muslims always ate with their right hands and Charlie didn't want to appear out of place by eating with his left hand, since the Muslims considered this unclean. It was a little painful, but he ignored it and joined in with the festivities.

There were a number of speeches by various participants, mostly celebrating the victory over ISIS and saying what a great victory it was for the Kurdish people.

Cody sat quietly through most of the dinner. That day, he read the draft of the pope's speech to the combined leaders of the Muslim and Christian churches. Certainly, the pope had struck the right note by pronouncing that God was the Supreme Being, and creator of all peoples, and all real discussion should begin with that common thread that had no fundamental disagreement. His arguments were reasonable and logical. However, from Cody's point of view, something was missing. The speech did not really have a kicker, a strong statement that would make all the other points follow in logical progression. He thought about it throughout the day, and had come on an idea. He decided to give it a "test run" with these people. A good number of them now knew he was the real "Black Angel" and his own credibility would rival the pope's when he gave his speech.

The opportunity came when Barzani rose and addressed the assemblage, "My friends, comrades and honored guests, I believe the time has come to announce to you a plan is now in motion that will result in a true country for the Kurdish people."

There was a second of silence, then the entire group cheered and applauded. Barzani waited for the tumult to subside and then continued.

"There is not a person here who does not know the Iranian nuclear threat was neutralized some years ago. It changed the face of the Middle East, some of it not good. It allowed the radical jihadist of ISIS to rise and impose their will over much of Iraq, and Syria. However, none of us would be willing to return to the days in which an equally radical Iran threatened to destroy us all. Despite what we have today, the world is better off without the Iranian threat."

None at the table disputed this great truth.

"An entire body of literature has grown up concerning how the Iranians were brought to their knees. Almost all of it is wrong or pure fantasy. The truth is every part of the plan to keep the nuclear weapons out of the United States, and return them to Iran where they were detonated, was the work of a single man. Most of us have heard his codename was The Black Angel. I can assure you the stories of this man's exploits as a secret agent for over 20 years are entirely true. Most of you believed he died in the Iranian operation, but that is not true. He lives today, and his great mind has devised the plan that will give us our independence."

As he spoke, there was complete silence around the table.

"It was his idea to seat us today at a round table as equals. We have Sunnis, and Shias present for this banquet. We also have Christians, and one of them is the Black Angel. I call on him now to reveal himself and speak to us about the future he envisions for the Middle East."

Once again, there was silence around the table. It was almost deafening. At last, Cody pushed back his chair and stood up. There was a lot of noise in the room. People were talking, some of them were applauding, but all eyes were on Cody. He stood quietly for a long moment until the room was once again silent.

"Is there any person in this room who does not believe there is only one god, and He is God?" Murmurs of agreement went around the table. Cody went on.

"Is there any person in this room who does not believe the universe was created by God? Do any of you not believe God's will is our greatest truth, and we are born to follow His will in all parts of our life?" Is there anyone here who does not believe our God was the God of Abraham, Ishmael, and Isaac? Is there anyone here today who does not pray to God every day and all-day to give us the wisdom to follow the will of God and to resist the Evil one, who is God's enemy and seeks to bring deceit and misery to all of Mankind?

"I believe all these things and I believe you do too. The Jews believe it. All three of our billions around the world worship this common God. Yet we still have hatred and divisions that come from something other than the true will of God."

"Doesn't it occur to all of you there is something fundamentally wrong with this? Do you believe God honors such hatred and unrest among his people?

"If we all love God and seek to follow his will every day, then what have we been fighting about for over a thousand years? Surely, the time has come for us to set aside our differences and unite in the worship of our God, as He clearly intended. God does not care how we found Him, he is only happy we did."

"Given what I have just said, and in the spirit in which I offered it, will you stand with me now and let the love-light of God fill your hearts?"

Ashana was the first on her feet, followed by Charlie, Rosy, and Enrico. President Barzani was the next to stand. His wife came to her feet next to her husband. Slowly, every person was standing.

"Brothers and sisters, greet each other now in the manner in which God intended, and let our lives be forever changed."

There were tender embraces among all around the table. Cody thought it was significant he and his family received the same respect as the Muslim Sunnis and Shias were giving to each other. In his mind, Pope John Luke would do the same. It worked.

Chapter 8
Alliance of Enemies

Washington, D.C.

Back in Washington, Cody saw how hard it was for President Palmer to bring Iranian President Manek Faroush, and Israeli Prime Minister Ari Ben Cannan together for a meeting. The good relations Palmer had with both leaders made the meeting possible, but under a cloak of secrecy from both governments.

Cody's original planning analysis, now augmented with new ideas included the after action on the Mosul attack from Erbil. It had grown from the original 20-page document he'd written for Pope John Luke, to a 60-page report. He showed it to the President before they went in to confront the Iranians and Jews. Palmer seemed to know a good deal about the action in Mosul. Cody thanked him for taking such quick action, bombing the building, after the assassination of the men in the command center, and Palmer thanked him for being able to identify the ISIS leader so close to the top.

Palmer gobbled up the report in short order, and then said, "So the rehearsal for the pope's speech was successful in concentrating your audience on the main argument"?

"Admittedly, I spoke to a small group who already regarded Charlie and Enrico as Ardishur, great warriors," said Cody. However, the logic was sound enough. If we can get the Muslims and the Christians to take Jesus and Muhammad out of the discussion, we can force them to concentrate on the real power in the universe. I'm not going to stop believing Christ is my Savior, who delivered me from sin and reconciled me with God, any more than the Muslims are going to stop regarding Muhammad as their great prophet who speaks for God through the Qur'an. The point is not to marginalize either, but simply reframe the debate in a way that provides both with a common reference."

"Very elegant," said Palmer, "and for the purposes of our destruction of ISIS, who all parties believe is nothing more than opportunistic gangsters hiding behind their faith, might work."

"When have you scheduled the meeting of Faroush and Ari Ben Cannan?"

"Tomorrow morning."

"Smart," said Cody, "Sunday morning, not a holy day for either of them, and the press corps has probably adjourned to the golf courses,"

"Exactly," said Palmer. "I guess Mona and I can miss church one week. Speaking of family, where's yours?"

"I brought them with me this time," said Cody. "Charlie is still recuperating from his wound, Rosy is getting code happy from looking at a computer screen 16 hours a day, and my long suffering wife, Ashana, just needs a rest. So, they got to come to Washington this time to relax and see the sights."

"Bring them over here," said Palmer. "You can let them enjoy a little White House hospitality."

"Thank you very much," said Cody, "I'm sure they will all enjoy coming back here."

"They've stayed at the White House before?"

"Yeah, during the Iranian operation they came with me and stayed with Mitch Colter and his family. I'm not sure Rosy remembers much, since she was just five, but Charlie and Ashana have very fond memories of their stay here. Sure you have the room?"

"Plenty," said Palmer, our mutual combatants didn't arrive with anything but grim looks on their faces."

"I'll call Ashana. Can you send a car for them?"

Ashana and the kids were delighted with the invitation to stay at the White House. They arrived in less than an hour. President Palmer and his wife, Mona, greeted them as they came in.

"Actually, I wanted to meet in person somebody who can make a half-dozen bullseyes from over a mile," said Palmer to Charlie. "You do realize that, besides your father, there are fewer than a dozen men in the world capable of such a shot?"

"I don't think I really knew that," said Charlie. "For Rico and I it was just a part of our education, nothing special."

"You have your Father to credit for that," said the President.

"I wonder if you realize how big of a target this makes you, Son," said Cody. "Too many people already know about you. The intelligence services of the world are going to scour their records to discover your identity.

"Which leads them to you, Cody," the President said. "One of the great hazards to your plan is it will bring you out in the open. This makes you vulnerable. One of the easiest ways to get to a man like you is through his family. I think it's time we put some extra security around Ashana and Rosy. I think you're safe enough here in the White House, but we need to develop some contingency plans to protect them when they're not. I mention this because, as smart as you are, this is one area in which I don't believe you have thought enough about it."

"Carson is right about that," said Mona, "Our children are grown and have families of their own. Yet, I worry about them all the time."

Cody ran all the scenarios through his head as Palmer and Mona were speaking. They were right. He had not thought much about the subject, believing the whole family's training would be enough to protect them. Of course, that was not true.

"Remind me to discuss this with you," said Cody to the President.

"I will," said the President, "although I seriously doubt a man with your marvelous memory would really forget it."

"Not to change the subject," said Rosy, "I feel a little gypped. I've been to the White House before, but I was so little, I don't have many memories about it. All you guys take a visit to the Executive Mansion as if it were something that happens every day. How about letting me look around a bit?"

Mona laughed, and said, "Come on along Rosy, I'm in charge of getting you settled. Why don't us girls go off and let our esteemed husbands save the world all by themselves?"

Everyone laughed at that. Ashana, Rosy, and the First Lady excused themselves and went off on their own, leaving Cody, Charlie, and the President standing there.

"By the way," said the President, "it looks like we're all going to be together a lot. Why don't we all get on a first name basis. We'll be the three 'C's', Cody, Charlie and Carson."

"Thanks, " said Cody, "Charlie and I will remember the proper public protocol."

Soon the President went off to handle the myriad of other things for the Chief Executive. Cody and Charlie went to join Ashana and

Rosy, so they could see where they would be sleeping, and to marvel at the great history of this historic building.

Later in the day, Palmer called for Cody to come to the Oval Office. "I've made copies of your expanded plan and delivered them to Faroush and Ben Cannan. It seemed to me they needed to start concentrating on the problem at hand, rather than rehash old feuds."

"If neither of them get up and go home, we can assume they're at least willing to discuss their mutual problem."

"Well, I sent the report in to them a couple of hours ago, and I haven't heard anything from either of them so far. I still think the biggest risk we're taking is you disclosing it was you who caused the bombs to go off in Iran."

"Sooner or later, it's going to be common knowledge. We might just as well face the most damaged party first. By the way," said Cody, "I want Charlie to sit in on the meeting. Both the Iranians and Israelis know the action in Mosul was most likely not just the work of the Kurds, their own intelligence services will have told them that. He might be the edge we need to get the conversation moving in the right direction. Also, I intend for him to be my second in command when the global operation gets started, so he needs to know what I do."

"What do you mean by your second in command?" asked Palmer.

"Who do you suppose is going to run this Crusade?" said Cody. "All of these coalitions of unlikely allies are not going to allow themselves to be commanded by any of the other's in the coalition. It has to be a neutral party, which means me."

"You're hardly a neutral party," said the President, "You are an agent of the Catholic Church."

"None of these countries knows that. As far as any of them are concerned, I'm just a freelance agent who's written the plan that will give them the stability they want and need."

"I guess we'll find out about that," said the President.

❖

The following morning, Cody put on his battle fatigues for the meeting. It had no rank, insignia, or identification of any kind on it. All he wanted to show, was he was a warrior, ready for battle. Charlie was dressed the same.

The President was already in the conference room when Cody and Charlie arrived. "I've asked President Faroush and Prime Minister Ben

Cannan, to come in together, with escorts, through two separate doors."

They didn't have long to wait. Both men came into the room carrying their copies of the report. They faced each other across the table, neither showing much emotion.

"I don't believe either of you gentlemen has ever actually met each other," said the President brightly. "This is Prime Minister Ari ben Cannan from Israel, and Manek Faroush, President of Iran. The two men glared at each other, but condescended to shake hands across the table.

"May I also introduce both of you to Cody Frost and his son, Charlie. Mr. Frost is the author of the report you've brought with you."

Both men looked at Cody with some signs of grudging approval. Cody reached across the table, and took both men's hands in his and said. "Let us pray." He spoke first in Farsi, saying, "In the name of Allah, I pray for good will and patience for these difficult times." He repeated the prayer in Hebrew, "In the name of God Almighty, I pray for good will and patience for these difficult times."

Before either of the men could react, Cody said, "I have just prayed to the one true God, who's will, all of us seek to follow. Both of you must know, I have just spoken to the same God, all in this room worship. Can we, at least, all agree this is true?"

"A clever way to seek common ground at the outset," said ben Cannan.

"All meetings should begin in such a manner," said Faroush.

"Please be seated," said the President. "It's fortunate we all speak English, otherwise Cody would have to be translating the whole time.

"I agreed to this meeting, only after President Palmer suggested American aid might be disrupted if I did not attend."

"President Palmer made exactly the same threat to Israel," said ben Cannan.

"Are either one of you mad at me for writing this report?" asked Cody.

"I'm not angry," said ben Cannan, "but I think you are a little naïve to believe it can be a workable plan."

"Really," said Cody, "exactly what parts of it do you consider unworkable?

"You assume Israel will allow itself to be involved in a dispute, which is entirely Muslim in nature. We have become considerably stronger since the decimation of Iran. We are more secure than at any other time in our history. There is no compelling reason for Israel to become involved."

"Except for the fact all Middle Eastern countries still deny your right to exist and believe you have usurped lands that are rightfully Arab. What do you suppose will happen if ISIS is successful in conquering all the Middle East and then turns all its resources toward wiping you out?

"We have come to a peaceful settlement of the Palestinian issue. They now enjoy independence and freedom to choose their own future."

"They still have not recognized you as a country and would be happy to grab all you have."

Ari ben Cannan was quiet for a moment and then said, "we admit ISIS is a very destabilizing force in the Middle East. In fact, we believe they are nothing more than a vicious gang, who is hiding behind the pretext of religion."

"That's the first thing you've said with which I can agree," said Faroush. "You may not feel threatened at this moment by ISIS, but Iran is engaged with them on a daily basis."

"In other words," said Cody, "you could use all the help you can get."

"Not from infidels such as the Jews," said Faroush sharply.

"Isn't it funny you felt the same way about the United States before your catastrophe, but now regard them as comrades in arms against a common enemy," said Cody.

Intensely, Faroush said, "I was never a hardline Ayatollah, who controlled our country with nothing but religion, never taking into account the real needs of the people, such as a population that was not growing and a 22% unemployment rate. We brought about our own destruction by trying to smuggle nuclear weapons into the United States and ended up with them actually coming back and killing five million of our people. We believe we have learned from that hard lesson and have returned control of the government to people other than religious fanatics who were operating on a single agenda."

Cody was silent a moment, giving a quick glance at Palmer, "So you admit the tragedy in Iran was of your own making? You were the aggressors and were somehow stopped by a counter stroke that made what happened inevitable."

"It was a foolish move on our part," admitted Faroush. "We did not account for anyone being capable of devising such a devious plot. We have never even been able to learn the identity of this evil genius, or for whom he was working. The only thing we do know was that he was killed escaping Iran, and was known as the mysterious Black Angel."

Cody would be forever grateful President Palmer interjected smoothly, "Reading this analysis and it's execution, from purely a tactical standpoint and no other, how would you evaluate it?"

"It's brilliant," said Faroush. "Not only does it solve our immediate problem of a murderous group of cutthroats running countries in a manner not seen for centuries, it also provides a roadmap that will finally establish a truly level playing field for the millions of Shias in the world who've been discriminated against since the beginning of Islam."

"What is your assessment, Prime Minister?" asked the President turning to Ari ben Cannan.

"It's the first Middle Eastern plan that takes into consideration the true social, ethnic, and political realities of the region. It's just too bad some smart person didn't think of this, 50 years ago. Israel would not have had to invest so much blood and treasure into surviving as a nation. On the subject of the Kurds having their own country, we completely agree. We've enjoyed better relations with them than anyone else."

"Isn't it strange that both of you have similar points of view on this means of approaching our operational strategy to solve so many problems?" said the President.

"My congratulations on your insightful document," said Faroush to Cody. "It's just too bad that such an analysis is such a stretch of ingenuity."

"I heard much the same objections on the last plan I wrote for solving a crisis in the Middle East," said Cody mildly.

"And what plan was that?" said Faroush with distain.

"The one I wrote to foil your attempt to attack the United States with six nuclear weapons."

Faroush's face turned into a blank mask of astonishment. Finally, he said, "Are you telling me, you were the architect of the mass destruction in my country?"

"May Allah forgive me for the pain and suffering I caused you. I just couldn't think of another way to stop your Ayatollah's single-minded obsession to bring the world to the brink of chaos."

"Chaos it would have been," said ben Cannan. "The detonation of six nuclear weapons in the United States would have set off a wave of retaliation that would have destroyed civilization as we know it."

"Maybe you should be glad I wasn't killed in our rush to leave Iran, as you both have believed," said Cody. "At least now you have a way out of another crisis, just as deadly."

"You are the actual Black Angel," said Ari be Cannan, with astonishment?

"It was a stupid nickname when I was in the field, and it's a term I've never liked at all. I'm just Cody, if you don't mind."

"Ever since I came to the Presidency ten years ago," said Faroush, "I have often wished you were still alive so we could execute you in front of the whole country."

"So," said Ari ben Cannan, "you were an American operative the whole time.

"Completely wrong!" said Cody with exasperation. "I've never worked as an agent for the United States."

"Then for whom do you work?" asked Faroush.

"I serve the will of Allah, or Jehovah, or God, take your pick. He is the same for all of us, which is the point I've been trying to make since we sat down."

"Even knowing what I know now," said Faroush, "and giving you full marks for your superb plan, we could never get the other countries of the Middle East to agree to your 'Modern Crusade'".

President Palmer said, "Bahrain has, Lebanon has, Jordan has, the Emirates have, and Kuwait has."

"To say nothing about the Kurds, who are getting locked and loaded as we speak," Cody said.

"The Kurds have a lot to celebrate after that big raid on Mosul last week," said Faroush.

"I hate to be redundant," said President Palmer, "but that plan was also Cody's. What's more, the intelligence for it came from his daughter Rosy, and Charlie here did the actual shooting, which is why he wears this sling. He was wounded while saving a whole commando squad of Kurds."

"Those shots were made from over a mile," said Ari ben Cannan. "I had the Mossad look into it. You are one very special marksman, young man."

"I had the world's best teacher," said Charlie, speaking up for the first time.

The atmosphere in the room was warming considerably.

"How do-able is this plan?" asked Faroush.

"With the full support of the United States and its coalition of allies, including Israel, and Iran, about 80%," said Cody.

"Exactly, what would Israel demand for their support in this operation?" asked Faroush.

"The right to live in peace within the new family of nations in the Middle East," said Ari ben Cannan sincerely.

"Which is nothing more than we would ask," said Faroush. "Still, even though I might agree to this, the sales job for just about everyone else is a steep hill to climb."

"Then there is good news for you," said Cody. "In about three weeks, the religious heads of all the Muslim and Christian nations are gathering in Geneva at the invitation of Pope John Luke. Your Jewish religious leaders will also get an invitation, Prime Minister."

"This meeting came as a result of the Muslim leadership reaching out to the pope in two long letters written a few years ago. The implication in their correspondence contends it's time for these two world religions to start searching for common ground."

"The pope is going to remind everyone we all worship the same God. We all have different names and different ways of demonstrating our beliefs, but God is God, the creator of all, and the master of our fates. If we can remember who is in charge, the symbols of our various denominations may become accepted as commonplace."

Faroush said, "If this is an effort to marginalize the Prophet Muhammad, it will be a waste of time."

"That's exactly what the Christians are going to say about Jesus," said Cody. "The pope and I believe some of the other great religious thinkers, are going to say these men were inspired by God, and lived their lives in a manner that was relevant for the people of those times."

Cody faced Ari ben Cannan and said, "For the Jews, who still believe the Savior has not yet appeared, it's the same story. Many of us actually laugh when you let your hair grow in curls, or keep two refrigerators to remain kosher, or set the elevators in your tall buildings so they automatically stop on every floor to prevent Jews from breaking their commandment to do no work on the Sabbath. However, we would not kill you for doing it. That would be petty and absurd.

"So tell me, what is the real difference from Muslims praying five times a day, or fasting during Ramadan? What is the real difference if Christians regard Sunday as the Sabbath, and who worship the resurrection of Christ on the third day following his execution as a common thief? Is genocide justified by these examples?

"As ordinary men, we come to worship these symbols of God's love, as if that was the heart of the religion. However, when our true God, who rules over us all and will gather forgiven believers to his heart, after we leave our earthly bodies, He has given us these holy examples to keep Him at the center of our worship.

"Meanwhile, our true enemy Satan has lied, deceived, and warped the real truth, and laughed as evil men overran half the Middle East, and blew themselves up all around the world at the cost of so many innocent lives. Satan has even used the very religion of our God to justify rape, torture, beheadings, stealing, corruption, and the usurpation of the right of every man and woman to live their lives in peace, happiness and without fear.

"Yet, despite all these obvious signs and the display of the truth of God, we still had to bring you two men, bickering and screaming, into a meeting where you actually had to talk to each other. I ask you, isn't it obvious there's something wrong with that?

"Sometimes I just want to jump up on a table in the midst of all this strife and scream, 'Stop this! You people must be kidding! You must be kidding or you wouldn't be acting this way!'"

Manek Faroush was staring at the wall. Ari ben Cannan had his head down. There was a deep silence in the room.

Finally, Faroush looked at Cody and said, "I must admit you are even more persuasive in person, than you are in writing."

"Maybe it's nothing more than your plan and analysis being an active 'How to do it' operational document, while what you say is more *Why* we should do it," said ben Cannan.

"It's time for your noonday prayer, Manek," said Cody. "This time, why don't you break all the rules and speak to Allah directly about all of which we have spoken. You might be surprised what comes into your heart,"

"We should all take a break," said President Palmer. "If it's any comfort to either of you, I was listening to Cody speak as well, and believe I might have a somewhat different perspective."

Cody rose and put out his hands. This time all five men joined hands around the table.

"Merciful and all-knowing God of creation, we each thank you, in our own ways, for the wisdom to take away a more full knowledge of your Holy will, Amen."

President Palmer could not help but noticed that the Jew and the Shia Muslim both went out the same door this time, each smiling a little at the other, before going their own ways to their rooms.

For the three remaining in the room, Charlie spoke first, "When Rosy and I were growing up my Father always told us to speak the name of Allah with praise and reverence. I guess I never truly understood the reason until today."

"Before we came into this meeting," said President Palmer, "I estimated only a small chance for any success at all. Now, I think we have a good chance. Manek was right. You really are much better speaking in person than on paper. I kept thinking of points you should make, and you made them all. You did them better than I could do."

"I was speaking to you as much as I was Manek or Ari," said Cody. "You also need to come to the same level of worship as they do."

"Mission accomplished," said Palmer. "I purposely didn't plan a luncheon, but I did put another meeting on the schedule. I admit I didn't think it would ever happen, but now it most certainly will. You might just find yourself actually getting into your operational plan."

"I'm hoping for that," said Cody, "I don't expect these guys to kiss and make up like reconciled lovers, but I do think they will pray in privacy to the Lord, and I think He will give them insights they've never addressed. After that, both of them will dive back into my strategy and read again, what's in it for them. I think they will look with fresh eyes on what the outcome of the decimation of ISIS will actually mean, and begin to believe we aren't making idle proposals, but expect to do exactly what I wrote."

Cody looked with appraising eyes at the President, "You do pledge the United States will see this through to the end, don't you?"

"Of course I do, I'm just thinking about the endgame when we have accomplished our purpose."

"Tell you what, Carson," said Cody. "Start thinking about a Pan-Muslim constitution. It will have things in it regarding freedom of religion and equal rights for both men and women. This means, not all the countries will sign it, most notably the Saudis who still treat their women like property. However, our constitution will gut big hunks of Sharia law, or at least confine them to individual families."

"Who do we get to approve all this?" asked the President.

"After the subject countries have done it, we submit the entire matter to the United Nations."

"The Russians and the Chinese will block that in the Security Council."

"Maybe, maybe not. However, the combined countries of the United Nations can act independently of the Security Council. I suspect there are lots of countries who would like their votes actually to mean something. Instead, they're always being saddled with the decisions made by the elite members of the Security Council."

"It gives me another component to add to my already long list of things I have to do," said Palmer.

"We have a war to win first," said Cody. "My belief is that the pope will start it with his call for a Modern Crusade. You need to start revving up public interest in this conclave, so it gets worldwide media attention. Start with the destruction of St. Peter and simply say the church can't stand by and have their holiest site destroyed without creating some kind of response."

"Do you think this new pope is up to the challenge?"

"I've actually known him for quite a few years. I can tell you he's the militant the church needs at this point in history. Of course, much will depend on his address to the conclave. If it's any comfort to you, he asked me to help him with his speech, and you can bet a lot of what I just said in our meeting with Iran and Israel, will be in his impassioned call for worldwide action."

The second meeting that afternoon between Iran and Israel went just as Cody had predicted. The two men greeted each other cordially and then sat down to dissect the strategy Cody had proposed in his report. He was certain God had spoken to the two men in their own way. His opinion satisfied any doubts they had on the value of aligning themselves with a previously mortal enemy.

"Your strategy calls for the Israeli army and air force, moving behind an American strike force of 6 brigades, to strike ISIS from the west, through the Golan Heights and Jordan with additional forces moving north to the Becca Valley. The population of the valley has decreased dramatically over the years because of unrest in Lebanon caused by Hezbollah. However, those who remain are largely Christian, Druze, and Shia Muslims. The valley itself is about 100 kilometers long. It comprises about 40% of Lebanon's arable land. Is it truly your intention Israel annex this land?"

"I don't believe fertile land is the main thing on the mind of the Lebanese. What they want is stability, and a chance to turn Beirut back into the huge tourist resort it was before the civil wars in the country destroyed most of their infrastructure. They are a polyglot population that always advocated religious freedom. Israel will give them that, and both countries will benefit greatly from commerce and trade. An open border is the key to your success. Israel cannot be viewed as a colonial power."

Ari ben Cannan needed further information. "I don't see how that's possible since you call for us to occupy all the West Bank."

"In your agreement with them, following the collapse of Hamas, and a much more compliant Palestinian authority, you gave them autonomy over Gaza. I propose to give the Gaza strip back to the Egyptians, and create a country for the Palestinians in Jordan. The new agreement will create an independent Palestine and put an end to any other disputes over who owns what. It's a win-win."

The Prime Minister sat back with a smile on his face and said, "Thanks for letting me go first, Mr. Farouk. I'm sure Iran has a lot more questions than we did, since our military involvement will move in and occupy land, and then serve as a holding force against ISIS in the south, and use all our air power in the battle."

"You are welcome," said Farouk, "Now, Cody, since that is what you insisted we call you, this battle plan is for the Iranian army, augmented with the American army, to strike west into Iraq, all the way south towards Bagdad, with our primary objective being Basra. Your strategy has outlined all of this. My question is what do we do with Iraq after we are victorious?"

"There are two principal scenarios," said Cody. "Either withdraw back into Iran and let the Iraqis determine their own destiny, or stay in Iraq and attempt to bring the country into a bigger Iran. There are serious problems with both possibilities."

"No kidding," said Farouk, lapsing into Farsi, without realizing it.

Cody responded in Farsi, causing both President Palmer and Prime Minister ben Cannan to get funny looks on their faces. Charlie was able to keep up.

"If you stay," said Cody, "you have a third of the population in southern Iraq, however they are almost totally Shia. But you are Persians, whereas the Iraqis are Arab. There's no assurance they would be willing to become part of Iran. You could have an even bigger fight on your hands.

"If you withdraw there is the distinct possibility of battles between the minority Sunnis and the majority Shias. It would be bloody and protracted and could destabilize the region for years. Sunnis from all over the region, particularly Saudi Arabia, might flow in to rescue their brothers, and we could end up in the same position we are today.

"If you fellows are through speaking where we can't understand," said President Palmer, "you might give us a synopsis in a language we know."

Faroush and Cody looked at each other, realized what they did, and then both laughed out-loud. Cody filled in the details.

"I suppose you have a solution for these contingencies?" said President Palmer.

"Actually, I don't," said Cody. "There are too many variables. I know what I would like to happen, but we have a war to win first, and a very tough, battle-tested, army to beat. I suggest we concentrate on that and let the outcomes determine the results."

"I can't help but notice that neither of you guys," said Cody, pointing to Faroush and ben Cannan, "have done any bickering about how much you hate each other, with threats to wipe each other out."

"Times change," said Faroush, "you will remember that not too many years ago we were busy trying to bring America to its knees. However, it was us, who went to our knees, and guess who was there to pull us back on our feet? Why, it was none other than our supposedly mortal enemy. If that's the way Allah...God...Jehovah works, then who am I to question His will."

"Well spoken," said Ari ben Cannan. "The people of Israel can certainly live with that pledge, and we will." He put out his hand to Faroush and they both shook hands enthusiastically, and smiled at one another.

Cody said, "Congratulations, men, you're allies, and it took less than a day to accomplish it."

Chapter 9
Preparation

Washington. D.C.

The next two days were historic. The main strategy of the coming offensive, dissected in detail, gave information, which was far more comprehensive as both men revealed military capabilities heretofore unknown to anyone, including Cody. He collected what he knew of what each country could bring to the fight, but by hearing previously Top-Secret information from both, he was able to make adjustments and changes to his original plan. Discussions about timetables, troop disbursements, and a series of phone calls to each of their military commanders began moving the pieces into place.

President Palmer was doing the same thing with the U.S. military, ordering two more brigades into Iran, and putting ten more on alert to launch from Israel. He was also speaking to other allies in England, France, Germany, and Australia, asking each of them to commit a brigade of their best to the operation. The first to sign on were the French, who had suffered so much in the ISIS terrorist attacks in Paris.

President Barzani flew to Washington to take part in the wargames as the critical role of the Kurds, already in contact with ISIS on a daily basis, agreed to play. To say Barzani was surprised to see the Iranians and the Israelis coordinating would be an understatement. However, it was not long before the principal allies of Iran, Israel, the United States and the Kurds could see that Cody's plan would work.

With simultaneous assaults by the Kurds in the north, the Iranians from the east, the Israelis from the west, and the Americans starting west, but heading north into Syria, Isis did not stand a chance. Then the brutal job of retaking Iraq and Syria from them could begin.

Cody was certain ISIS would never believe it possible to assemble such a coalition. It would have been impossible if ISIS had not risen and savagely subdued all opposition not following their narrow interpretation of the Qur'an. As Cody had reasoned, the oppressed

Kurds, Shias and Israelis were willing to set aside centuries of antagonism with each other, to defeat a common enemy, whose stated goal was to crush them all.

As the meetings between the four allies continued, the conversations often turned to some of the long-standing issues. For Israel, it was an admission of their legitimacy as a country. For the Shias, it was an end to the discrimination by the majority Sunnis. The Kurds focused entirely on finally having a country of their own.

For Cody, he insured his principal allies, and experienced a sea change of relationships. The ammunition he would need to give Pope John Luke's call some teeth for a Modern Crusade. There were all sorts of meetings on a wide number of subjects, some of which had nothing whatsoever to do with politics. One of the touchy subjects was concerning women. The Shias were more progressive than the Sunnis regarding the place women had in a society. After a dozen years of secular control of the government, Iran was seeing a much more active role by women in society. The universal decree by the Ayatollah that all women should wear burkas changed. Now it was common to see women walking around dressed in Western clothing. Still, the crushing oppression for women under Sharia Law prevented half the population from contributing to the general society.

Carson Palmer came up with the idea of inviting the leader's families to Washington in hope the female view of society could be helpful in decisions, yet to belong on the new face of the Middle East, after the elimination of ISIS.

The families arrived the next day. It changed the dynamics considerably. With some objections by Faroush and Barzani, Cody was able to convince them that bringing their wives into the inner circle of planning would give everyone insights the men had not considered.

Ashana took the lead in integrating the women into the sweeping changes of alliances. She found that Ari ben Cannan's wife was as outspoken as her husband and didn't hesitate to state her opinions. Faroush's wife was far more subdued. Even though she didn't arrive with a full burka, she still wrapped her head in a scarf and wore a long dress. Faroush's daughter accompanied her mother, and was entirely scornful of women playing a silent role in the lives of Iranian families. She was a graduate of an English university and had experience in the world, which certainly did not make women second-class citizens.

Her name was Mitra. She was a raven-haired beauty with widely spaced eyes that shone from her lovely face. She was also very fit and healthy. Ashana liked her, and wondered what Charlie would think of her.

On the morning after the arrival of the women, Cody called a meeting with all parties. They had to use a bigger conference room. After they had all filed in and taken their seats, Cody stretched out his hands and all joined around the table. Let us pray, "Dear Lord, we come to you today with willing hearts and minds to hear your voice and to ask your blessings on our great mission, which we undertake in your name. May we all serve you in a manner that you can honor."

Cody repeated the prayer in Arabic, and Farsi. Then he looked up and said, "I believe it's always a good thing to have multiple minds concentrating on an issue. This is why we have invited you lovely women to attend our session this morning. What you are about to hear is our nearly complete plan for defeating ISIS, who we are convinced are being driven by Satan himself. You will also hear our preliminary plans for a redrawn Middle East following our victory. Only a handful of people in the world know of what we speak so I don't have to caution you that discretion in your talks with other people is of key importance.

"Much of what you will hear today will come from my trusted allies, brothers in arms, who have worked tirelessly to develop and refine our planning. This is how we will defeat ISIS. This is Operation Desert Fire."

For the next two hours, each member of the alliance spoke of their part in the operation and made a point of explaining why they had joined the alliance and what they expected to receive as a result. The women sat wide-eyed with the complexity and scope of the plan. Mona Palmer and Ashana were the least surprised since their husbands had put them in the information loop from the beginning, but Sara ben Cannan, Enwa Barzani, and Kevi Faroush were hearing all this very male scheming for the first time. Mitra Faroush had an intense look on her face, and was the first to speak.

"Without offense to all you able leaders, but this plan couldn't have appeared from just three days of talks. Somebody here was the architect, and has not only thought about it for quite a while, but is also very smart and very experienced. Will the mystery man please stand?"

Manek Faroush stirred and said, "You must forgive my daughter. I would like to say she got her abrupt manner from the English School she attended, but truthfully, she's always been this way. She used to beat up the boys in our neighborhood for irritating her."

Cody laughed, and so did Charlie. Rosy just sat there with her arms folded as if she had just heard the best question of the day. "I suppose you should know the whole story, Mitra," said Cody, "I was the one who dreamed up this scheme about a month ago."

"Then you're the smartest man in the room," said Mitra, "I'll bet it was your idea to include women in this little war council."

"Guilty, again," said Cody. "Manek, tell her the rest of the truth."

"My dear," said Manek, "let me introduce you to Cody by another name, perhaps more familiar. This is the Black Angel."

"I like you, Cody," said Mitra, "tell me the whole story so I can forgive you."

Cody was forced to tell the short version of his part in the plan that resulted in six nuclear weapons going off in Iran."

"I suppose that was your plan as well," said Mitra when he was finished.

"It was," said Cody, "not that I'm very proud of it."

"Are you kidding!" said Mitra, "you saved every woman in Iran from a life of abuse and domination by their husbands. Besides, I don't think you had much choice."

The rest of the women around the table seemed to echo Mitra's opinion. Enwa Barzani looked at Cody with a new tone of respect. She was a great admirer of Charlie and wondered where he'd gotten his skills. Now she knew. Sara ben Cannan smiled broadly at Cody, "You sure did save all of Israel from a life of fear and suspicion. It's no wonder my husband is such a fan. I can't imagine anything else that would have motivated him to accept an alliance with the Iranians."

"If you ladies don't mind, I've never wanted the term 'Black Angel'. If possible, I ask you to forget you ever heard it. I surely would like to forget it. My name is Cody."

"But now, all of this makes sense to me. Only a person of your stature could have put this coalition together," said Mitra. I gather these are your children?"

"Rosy and Charlie," said Cody.

"Why the arm sling?"

"Little scuffle in Kurdistan."

"Were you involved in that big raid on ISIS in Mosul that made all the papers."

"Just a little bit," said Charlie shyly. This woman was a very seductive handful.

"Oh don't be so modest, Charlie," said Masoud. "Young lady, you're looking at the leader of that raid, and the man who shot six people from over a mile."

Mitra gave Charlie an appraising look. Charlie rolled his eyes and looked away in embarrassment while his cheeks turned red.

"Did you get shot by someone else shooting from a mile away?"

"No, the shot happened later at a road block, when they made their escape. Charlie took out at least four ISIS fighters with his bare hands," said Masoud.

Ashana watched Charlie from across the table. He'd never been much interested in girls, but she could see he was somewhat smitten by Mitra.

Kevi Faroush raised her hand a little timidly. Cody said, "Go ahead, Kevi, do you have something to add?"

She responded in Farsi, "I see where one of your resolutions of the region's geography includes Iran absorbing southern Iraq, after the ISIS animals are all dead."

"That's one of the scenarios," said Cody, "do you see something wrong with it?"

Kevi looked hesitantly at her husband, who nodded for her to proceed. "With all due respect, Cody, I don't think that will work at all."

"Southern Iraq is almost totally Shia," said Cody, "I should think it would be a natural match."

Almost defiantly, Kevi said, "But it isn't. They may be Shia, but they are Arabs, not Persians. They don't speak our language, and would find it very difficult to adopt our customs. The women are still living under a strict Sharia Law, and would either resent, or reject any efforts forcing them to conform. Furthermore, the Arab women are… should I say, not very clean people. Our women would find them a tremendous burden. If you were seeking to permit equal rights between men and women, I would applaud. Those dirty Arab girls would use their emancipation to create trouble, not harmony."

- 113 -

"And that is the reason why you women are here," said Cody. "I could not have looked at it from your perspective."

"It looks like you're going to have to find a different solution, honey," said Ashana. "The women of Islam may be invisible to the public, but they wield immense power inside the homes."

"I apologize, Enwa," said Kevi, "for speaking so bluntly regarding Arab women. I was making a broad generalization and meant no offense to you or your family."

"None taken," said Enwa, "I know exactly what you mean."

Cody had to stop and translate the entire conversation to Ari, and Carson, who did not speak Farsi. When he was finished Carson Palmer said, "I don't think this is an Arab or Iranian thing about women at all. The only place I'm allowed to make a mess is in the Oval Office, Mona runs the household, pays the bills, and she even keeps about half my schedule."

"Since we are all coming clean," said Ari, "I have to admit I have to tip-toe around my house and work real hard to keep from displeasing Sara."

The whole room roared with laughter.

After that, the women were far more willing to give their opinions of the grand plans of their men. However, to a person, all supported the coalition and the determination to eliminate ISIS.

❖

President Palmer oversaw an endless list of high-priority issues. He drove the military to be ready to jump and ready to fight on a very short timeline. Finally functioning with full support from their Commander in Chief, and receiving the funding necessary to fuel the military surge, across all services, the chain of command was humming at breakneck speed.

The upcoming meeting of Muslims and Christians in Geneva, now only two weeks away, was one of Cody's priorities. Social media was alive with comments, and now the mainstream media were catching on. It looked like Pope John Luke was ready to make some major announcement, according to the Vatican. The media continued to show and reshow the collapse of St. Peter's dome. Catholics worldwide were in a continual state of rage, demanding their countries do something.

Cody spoke to the pope on a regular basis. He forwarded his suggestions for changes to the pope's address, always pushing for a much harder line. As he was making progress within the allied coalition, the very heart of the Modern Crusade, Cody continually updated the pope and urged him use the information in the last part of his speech when he would rally the troops to join his Crusade. Cody also sent him the exact wording he had used in Erbil, and in the White House regarding the supremacy of God over all life, everywhere.

He was sitting in the President's office for his latest call.

"I've read what you wrote, Cody," said the pope, "In many ways it's almost exactly what the Muslims wrote in their letter to Christianity in 2007."

"I know that," said Cody, "where do you think I got all the good ideas?"

The pope chuckled, "I truly believe this is the way to bridge the gap and create an atmosphere of cooperation. It must be so, or you wouldn't have gotten the Iranians and the Israelis to work together if they weren't scared to death. They know that God is God, the true God, and the real God. He is master of all. He is the one to whom we must turn in this crisis. He is the communal thread."

"No arguments here, your Holiness," said Cody.

"I believe Satan is ruling the minds of the men of ISIS," the pope said forcefully. "God demands we be true to Him and do what must be done. We aren't asking anyone to deny Christ or the Muslims to deny Muhammad. We are asking them to turn to the God of all to deliver us from this evil."

Cody said, "We've got the world's mainstream press focusing on your conclave. I think there will be millions, even billions of people watching what you say. Call on all believers of God to throw down this evil specter, stalking the world. Do that and you'll have the Modern Crusade you asked me to create."

"The entire doctrine of the Christian Church, be it Catholic or Protestant is centered on Jesus Christ, just as the entire doctrine of the Muslim religion is centered on Muhammad," said the pope. "Millions of people have died because of that single fact. All I'm trying to do is to reframe the debate in a new and different way, long enough to get through this stubborn mess."

"Here's my plan," continued Pope John Luke, "I'm going to begin my speech by using the same language we found in the Muslim letter. I will endorse and support all they said. There is nothing like hearing confirmation of another's point to get people on your side. Then, I'm going to move to the section where I say I believe ISIS is actually agents of Satan, and God demands we respond as our faith dictates."

"That sounds right," said Cody.

"Then I will really turn up the heat. I plan to display anger, such as no Pope in modern times has ever done. I will show again our broken St. Peter's dome and say it's the same thing as blowing up the Black Stone in Mecca. Then I'll call for a new Crusade, of Christians and Muslims."

"What's your guess on how that will play out?" Cody asked.

"The Bishops, Cardinals, and Ayatollahs will go home and call meetings of all their subordinates, and tell them what was decided. Then these men will spread out throughout the world and begin firing up the masses."

"That may not be very necessary if we get the widespread coverage I'm expecting on the media."

"It will give legitimacy to the anger and desire to have the people do something."

"There's a downside to this," said Cody, "the majority of the Muslims attending the conclave will be Sunnis. It won't escape their attention, the Crusade you are advocating points mostly at them. Let's pray they preach neutrality and not a counter-crusade to oppose us."

"The latter is not likely," said the pope. "The Muslims want to have themselves viewed as being on the side of the God."

"Probably," said Cody. "One last thing John Luke, so far we have kept most of this under wraps, but a wider and wider group of people are finding out who's the Commander of Operation Desert Fire. I'm not too worried about the Kurds. Their big hero is Charlie. He now has a name of his own. They call him 'Ardishur,' Kurdish for Great Warrior. I'm about to send him back to Erbil to start making his presence known to the troops he will lead."

"I guess we've done all we can," said the pope. "You've done a masterful job in putting this all together. May the Lord be with you."

"And with you, your Holiness," said Cody, ringing off from the call. He sat quietly and urgently prayed to God, he was doing the right thing.

While he was concentrating, the President's phone rang. He answered it and listened for a few minutes. Then he said, "Keep the airlifts pouring into Erbil." Then hung up.

"Cody, if I might disturb you for a moment," said the President. "That was the Secretary of Defense. He says we are flying twenty C-130's a day into Erbil, filled with arms and equipment. As you asked, 100 Timberwolf sniper rifles and all other supplies you requested were on the first plane. The Secretary says for me to tell you Enrico is putting all this to good use. He says you would know what that means."

"Enrico was Charlie's partner on the Mosul raid. To tell you the truth, he's actually a little better shot than Charlie, but I also had a few more years to train him. He's the son of my villa manager in Positano. He and Charlie grew up together and think they are actual brothers."

"The Peshmerga and our teams of Navy Seals, are already engaging ISIS," said the President, "apparently with real success. They've pushed ISIS out of three towns west of Mosul."

"That's good," said Cody, "let ISIS continue to believe the main offensive will come from the north. They'll move men and equipment up there. That will make it a little easier when the assaults begin from all the other directions."

"I was reading about Operation Desert Storm in 1991," said the President, General Schwarzkopf took four months to get all his forces in place and trained before he let them jump off into Iraq against Saddam Hussein. How long do you estimate it will take before you're ready to begin the offensive?

"Nothing like that," said Cody. "In the first place we don't have the time, but more importantly we already have a Kurdish army with 20 brigades in place and engaged with ISIS in the north. We have two brigades of Marines in Iran, along with 15 more Iranian brigades and they've been training and skirmishing for years. We have a very tough and well-trained Israeli army of five brigades, plus their very effective air force. We drop the 82nd and 101st airborne into Israel and that's six more brigades. Additionally, the French, Italian, German and British are all sending a brigade each."

"That's 52 brigades," said Palmer, just what you said you needed to beat ISIS."

"I'm also counting on the pope to hitch up his britches and make a hell of a speech," said Cody. "That ought to start a popular uprising against the Sunni minority in and around Bagdad by the Shias. The real problem is to keep many Saudi Arabian Sunnis from launching a counter-offensive in our rear, or keeping Saudis from declaring war. It's our single greatest weakness."

"How likely is that?" asked Palmer.

"The pope is going to emphasize this is a Holy war to defeat the forces of Satan. That should be a restraint for most Sunnis, so I think the likelihood of a mass Sunni uprising is small. Of course, when the Shias start killing them, they're sure to fight back.

"As a further update," said Palmer, "we are moving the 82nd and the 101st to Israel starting tomorrow. The rest of the brigades from our other allies are doing the same. We expect to have all the troops and their equipment on the ground in two weeks."

"Don't forget to remind all your Generals their Commander will join them soon and give them the tactical battle plans."

The President said, "I've already done that, Cody, did you think I was just sitting there in all your meetings and not paying attention.

"Sorry, Carson, I keep forgetting you're smarter than me, and think ahead just as well as I do."

"I'm only implementing your plan, my friend; this is a stupid time to compare IQ's. Anyway, in terms of thinking on multiple levels, you have me beat all to pieces."

Cody nodded and reached for the phone.

Erbil

President Masoud Barzani was anxious to return to Erbil. His time in Washington was worthwhile and very illuminating, but now he considered all the preliminaries at an end and was eager to put the plans for attacking ISIS into action. Enwa was with him, and Charlie, who spent the previous two weeks growing a beard.

As the Presidential jet set down at Erbil International Airport, Charlie could see a big crowd had gathered.

"It looks like the people are glad to have their President back," said Charlie.

"I rather think most of this crowd has come to see you, Ardishur," said Barzani.

Much to Charlie's embarrassment, Barzani was right. The huge crowd, held at a safe distance by security forces, was chanting "Ardishur, Ardishur, Ardishur"! He was glad he had changed into battle fatigues, and had sprouted a decent beard. At least he looked the part.

President Barzani and Enwa were the first off the plane. The crowd cheered. Charlie was the last off, and when he appeared at the doorway of the plane, the crowd started chanting "Ardishur" again. Barzani looked over his shoulder and said, "We do so love our heroes."

At the bottom of the stairs were a number of Kurdish officials and army officers. They greeted Barzani warmly, saying they had a lot to report. Barzani said he had a lot to report as well and called for a meeting at the palace that afternoon. Several of the officers came over to Charlie and said, "Welcome home, Ardishur, we look forward to you being back in the field with your comrade."

Out of the group came Enrico. He ran to Charlie and they hugged each other. "Great to see you, bro," said Charlie.

"You too, we've been busy. Thanks for sending all that gear and the Timberwolf rifles, we've put them to good use."

"Are your snipers hitting anything yet?"

"Once in a while, but they sure do scare the Hell out of the ISIS soldiers. I have a school running full time and some of my guys are shaping up to be first class snipers. There's a good bit of turn-over since I weed out the guys who can't make it pretty fast, but there are always twenty guys ready to take their place."

"Anything special you have planned?"

"The regular Peshmerga captured three more towns. We're thinking about taking a crack at the big enchilada, Bahji, just west of Tikrit. It's on a main road. If we could take it and hold it, we'd straighten out a bulge that threatens Kirkuk and the oil fields. It'll be a tough fight. However, we're starting to receive some heavy equipment from the Americans. We have a dozen Bradley's, a bunch of Humvees and we even have a couple of Abram's tanks."

Charlie asked, "What's the opposition?"

"We think ISIS has reinforced with at least a brigade and they have Bradley's of their own, compliments of the retreating Iraqi's."

"Can we get any air support?"

"We can get some F-22's, out of Incirlik in Turkey and Blackhawk gunships from Erbil."

The two men realized they were holding up the motorcade, discussing battle tactics, so they jumped into a bulletproof SUV and rode off toward the Presidential Palace.

"Are you still staying at the Palace?" asked Charlie.

"When I'm around, I've been from one end of Kurdistan to the other, several times. I get the same hooraying as you do. I give hope to the people that, soon, they will have their own country, but, to get it, they must fight hard, together. In addition, I'm running a sniper school and that takes all my time. Most nights I just crash at one of the officer barracks. They're good people, Charlie, and I want to help them."

"Dad's been flying in load after load of modern weapons. Are they getting to the right people?

"They sure are. Our Peshmerga army is now one of the best equipped in the world. How do you think we got back those three towns?

"I'll go with you on the attack to take that town…what's it called?

"Bahji, having you run the operation makes me feel a lot better."

"Listen, Rico, the pope is going to make a speech in Geneva to a conclave of Muslims and Christians. We believe it will set off the new Crusade. Can you wait a while to launch your assault?

Chapter 10
Our Common Father

Geneva

At last, Pope John Luke arrived in Geneva expecting to find his biggest challenge would be the combined imams and ayatollahs of Islam. After two days of meetings with fellow Christians, he was not so sure.

His speech to the entire assembly remained tucked in his pocket. He had written it almost entirely on his own, with some suggestions from the logic of his friend, Cody, plus the practical intelligence he gave John Luke on the size and scope of the coalition gathering like a coiled spring, waiting for its release.

The pope found himself dealing with intense men and women who could not understand why his Crusade had to include any Muslims at all, or even Jews for that matter. They all agreed ISIS had to be defeated, and defeated so badly it could never rise again. However, they regarded the collateral damage as a Holy war against Islam as a religion, because they did not accept Jesus Christ as their Savior.

Repeatedly, John Luke had to patiently explain why Muslims and the country of Israel were so critical in the overall plan and how a Crusade in the traditional sense of Christians battling Islam face to face would be a disastrous failure. He found himself having to explain the real differences between the Shia minority, and the Sunni majority. For centuries, since the time of the death of Muhammed, the battle had raged, and the Shia minority had suffered.

He used the Protestant Reformation as a perfect example of how people who fervently worshipped Jesus, could nevertheless, argue endlessly over which denomination of Christianity had the correct interpretation of what, fundamentally, was the same God.

In exasperation, John Luke had to show the thoughtful insights of the best Muslim leaders in the world, and use the long letter written to a previous pope in 2007 entitled "A Common Word Between You and

Us." His hope was to save the substance of this letter to form the basis for his speech. However, without some unanimity within the Christian world how could he expect to convince others living an entirely different faith? The reasons why this Crusade had to be different from the Medieval Crusades took issue with many of the Christian leaders who had scant and even completely wrong beliefs. He gave copies of the letter to all of them, along with a paper written for the Catholic Education Resource Center by Thomas Madden, a former Chair of the History Department at Saint Louis University in St. Louis, Missouri.

An afternoon and evening of reading the pope's information, finally brought the Christian leaders to come around to his point of view. This made it possible for the pope to reveal the strategic objectives of the Crusade. He showed them how it would forever rewrite the map of the Middle East. Afterwards, John Luke became a military genius, and received the complete support of the Christian delegation.

The pope often wished Cody could have made the presentations; he would have made the process a good deal shorter. John Luke just repeated Cody's original plan, followed by the inevitable question of who was going to lead the coalition. He announced his selection of a man everyone would find to be a most able General, who did not formally align with any member of the coalition.

As it turned out, the pope's appeal to the distinguished Muslim clerics, proved to be an easier proposition. In a meeting with them, John Luke just gave back their own words from the letter they had written. He quoted from the letter:

"Finding common ground between Muslims and Christians is not simply a matter for polite ecumenical dialogue between selected religious leaders. Christianity and Islam are the largest and second largest religions in the world and in history. Muslims and Christians are more than a third to over a half of humanity respectively. Together they make up more than 55% of the world's population, making the relationship between these two religious communities the most important factor in contributing to meaningful peace around the world. If Muslims and Christians are not at peace, the world cannot be at peace. With the terrible weaponry of the modern world with Muslims and Christians intertwined everywhere, as never before, no side can unilaterally win a conflict between more than half of the world's inhabitants. Thus, our common future is at stake. The very survival of the world itself is perhaps at stake."

"And to those who nevertheless relish conflict and destruction for their own sake or reckon that ultimately they stand to gain through them, we say our very eternal souls are all also at stake if we fail to sincerely make every effort to make peace and come together in harmony. God says in the Holy Qur'an, *'Lo! God enjoineth justice and kindness, and giving to kinsfolk, and forbiddeth lewdness and abomination and wickedness. He exhorteth you in order that ye may take heed.* Jesus Christ said, *'Blessed are the peacemakers'*, and also: *'For what profit is it to a man if he gains the whole world and loses his soul?'"*

"So let our differences not cause hatred and strife between us. Let us collaborate with each other in righteousness and good works. Let us respect each other, be fair, just and kind to one another and live in sincere peace, harmony and mutual goodwill. God says in the Holy Qur'an:

"And unto thee have We revealed the Scripture with the truth, confirming whatever Scripture was before it and a watcher over it. So judge between them by that which God hath revealed, and follow not their desires away from the truth, which hath come unto thee. For each we have appointed a law and a way. Had God willed, He could have made you one community. But that He may try you by that, which He hath given you. So compete one with another in good works. Unto God, ye will all return, and He will then inform you of that wherein ye differ."

The Sunnis were the majority at the conference as they also were globally, and had a difficult time defending the Sunni led ISIS.

John Luke offered a simple solution. "This, so-called, Caliphate is made up of disenfranchised Muslims, who no longer follow the most fundamental of civilized norms. Their sins are so brutal, so inhuman; they no longer deserve to be included under any Islamic umbrella of faith. They hide their barbarity behind a cloak of religion that has nothing whatsoever to do with the God we all worship."

Many of the ayatollahs were involved as authors of the *'A Common Word Between You and Us.'* document, and so any real dissent disappeared, simply because they still believed in this principle.

The conclave now came to full sessions with all the religions of

God mixed together. Even the small, but very noticeable group of rabbis from Israel, received polite reception.

A number of speeches evolved. The Muslims confirmed they were serious about their position as written in their letters to the Catholic Church. Nearly all of them condemned, in one way or another, the violence and departure from Muslim doctrine, as they understood it.

The video of the most holy religious construction, attacked and ruined, made a ground swell leading to the keynote speech from the pope of the Catholic Church.

Pope John Luke sat alone in a room waiting for his time to step into the glare of the worldwide media gathered to hear his speech. On an impulse, he phoned Cody. When he answered, Cody said, "If you are looking for a pep talk to get you ready for this, then we're all lost. You're the one with all the cards and the support right now." Cody spoke in German to do exactly what he said he was not doing. Calm the pope.

John Luke said, "I don't need the pep talk, but I did want to hear one last friendly voice before I step out to the podium. I also wanted to know if there was anything new in your planning that I should include."

"You have all the latest numbers as of yesterday," said Cody. "I assume you're going to open the military portion of your speech with your own army, the Swiss Guard?"

"Yes, of course," said the pope. "There will be more impact if I show I'm willing to deploy the troops at my disposal first and foremost."

"We're all watching, Robert," said Cody, "Break a leg."

The pope rang off, feeling much better. He knelt and prayed to God with his full heart. Then he rose and went down the hall to the entrance of the assembly room. He waited as the moderator made his introduction. Then when he heard his name called, he walked out onto the dais and up to the lectern with a single microphone.

As he came onto the platform, the entire conclave rose and welcomed him enthusiastically. He smiled and raised his hand in response. Most notably, he did not use the common papal sign of the cross. After a few minutes, the several hundred people in the hall followed his sign for all to take seats. The rows of television cameras and their commentators grew quiet.

Cody, Ashana, and Rosy were in their apartment in the Vatican. Charlie was watching from the Presidential Palace in Erbil. Kamal, Enrico, and the entire Barzani family were there.

"All praise to God, the master of us all, creator of Heaven and Earth to whom we all owe allegiance, trust, and service to His will," began the pope. "I speak today in the name of Allah, Jehovah, Yahweh, and all the names we use to praise our God. There is only one god and He is God."

"In order for us to find the common ground we all seek, we should turn first to the Holy prophet Muhammad who spoke and wrote the words that will give us the unity we seek."

"Of God's Unity, God says in the Holy Qur'an, *say: He is God, the One! God, the Self-Sufficient Besought of all!* Of the necessity of love for God, God says in the Holy Qur'an, *So, invoke the Name of thy Lord, and devote thyself to Him with a complete devotion.* Of the necessity of love for the neighbor, the Prophet Muhammad said; *"None of you has faith until you love for your neighbor what you love for yourself."*

In the New Testament, Jesus Christ said; *'Hear, O Israel, the Lord our God, the Lord is One. And you shall love the Lord your God with all your heart, with all your soul, with all your mind, and with all your strength. This is the first commandment. And the second, like it, is this: 'You shall love your neighbor as yourself.' There is no other commandment greater than these."*

In the Holy Qur'an, God Most High enjoins Muslims to issue the following call to Christians and Jews—the *People of the Scripture, Say: O People of the Scripture! Come to a common word between us and you: that we shall worship none but God, and that we shall ascribe no partner unto Him, and that none of us shall take others for lords beside God. And if they turn away, then say; Bear witness that we are they who have surrendered unto Him."*

"There is true commonality in these messages from the Prophets of our religions. It is my belief Muhammad understood this message very clearly. He wrote that despite all the seemingly important manners in which we worship, that everything begins first with our understanding God is supreme in all ways and with all people. Everything begins from this singularity."

The members of the conclave rose as one to applaud the words of the pope, and to endorse the moral high ground from which he spoke. In Rome, Cody nodded his head, "So far, so good."

"Muslims and Christians together make up well over half of the world's population. Without peace and justice between these two religious communities, there can be no meaningful peace in the world. The future of the world depends on peace between Muslims and Christians.

"The basis for this peace and understanding already exists. It is part of the very foundational principles of both faiths: love of the One God, and love of the neighbor. These principles appear, over and over, in the sacred texts of Islam and Christianity. The Unity of God, the necessity of love for Him, and the necessity of love of the neighbor is thus the common ground between Islam and Christianity.

The following are only a few examples, the words: *we shall ascribe no partner unto Him* relate to the Unity of God, and the words: *worship none but God*, relate to being totally devoted to God. Hence, they all relate to the *First and Greatest Commandment*. According to one of the oldest and most authoritative commentaries on the Holy Qur'an the words: *that none of us shall take others for lords beside God*, mean 'that none of us should obey the other in disobedience to what God has commanded'. This relates to the Second Commandment because justice and freedom of religion are a crucial part of the love of our neighbor.

"Thus in obedience to the Holy Qur'an, and the Bible we as Muslims, Christians and Jews should come together on the basis of what is common to us, which is also what is most essential to our faith and practice: the *Two Commandments* of love."

"While Islam and Christianity are obviously different religions— and while there is no minimizing some of their formal differences—it is clear the *Two Greatest Commandments* are common ground and a link between the Qur'an, the Torah, and the New Testament. What prefaces the Two Commandments in the Torah, and the New Testament, is the Unity of God—that there is only one God. For the *Shema* in the Torah, starts in Deuteronomy, *Hear, O Israel, The LORD our God, the LORD is one!* Likewise, Jesus said in Mark, *"The first of all the commandments is: 'Hear, O Israel, the LORD our God, the LORD is one"*. Likewise, God says in the Holy Qur'an, *Say, He, God, is One. God, the Self-Sufficient Besought of all.* Thus, the Unity of God, love of Him, and love of the neighbor form a common ground upon which Islam, Christianity, and Judaism is founded."

Once again, the conclave rose in unison to applaud the words of John Luke. He was laying the groundwork for the stunning proposal he now was about to propose. The room grew quiet, again John Luke began that process.

"My brothers, we all know it's possible to extract some morsel from either the Qur'an or the bible to justify actions that seem moral because they came from these sources. However, in light of what I have just said, there is a blasphemous heresy continuing to rise in the Middle East. It is ISIS. Their behavior cannot be the true will of God. God would never honor the slaughter of innocent lives, which have sought to follow the will of God, but do not follow the exact distortion that ISIS follows. It is a clever deceit from the enemy of us all…Satan, who captures the minds of these men, and drives them to commit barbaric atrocities. Satan is using them to hide behind a false faith.

"I condemn all they have done and declare ISIS to be our true enemy in the battle between our God and the enemy who despises God and all his works!"

A mighty ovation swept through the assembly hall. Many shouted cries of retaliation and retribution.

Cody sat on the edge of his chair, saying to Ashana and Rosy, "He's got them! We will have our modern Crusade."

Pope John Luke cried, "I call for a new Crusade, different from any ever known in the world before. This Crusade will be a coalition of Muslims, Christians, and Jews, to wipe from the face of the Earth this scar on the face of God!

"I will lead this Crusade with soldiers of my own personal forces, The Swiss Guard. Switzerland has agreed to modify its neutrality in this manner for the five-hundred-year commitment to the Vatican.

"Additionally, we are now allied with the Kurds, who will fight for us, and finally be the largest ethnic group in the world not having a country of their own, to have one. The Iranian army will attack Iraq from the east, the Israeli Army and air force will attack from the west, the United States, and its allies, England, France, Italy, Germany, and Australia will begin their assault from Israel. In total we will field an army of 250,000 men, Muslims, Christians, and Jews, who will fight together to utterly destroy all of ISIS and repatriate the millions who now suffer ruthlessly persecution.

"When the battle is over, we shall go to the United Nations with a Pan-Muslim constitution which establishes freedom for all, and define the boundaries of our new Middle-East. Our new countries will erase the arbitrary borders given us by Christians with no concept of the ethnic, cultural, geographical, or religious differences of the region, after World War I. That action was a sin by Christianity and we offer our sincere and heartfelt apologies for the heartaches and suffering of Islam because of it.

"May the Lord, our God, our one true God, give us the strength, wisdom and resolve to move forward in His name; and may Satan finally see this Armageddon destroy his evil plans with all who oppose him."

❖

The time for questions, commentary, and analysis were yet to come, but this was not that moment. History would record the major media as the world sat silently and absorbed the twenty minutes of continuous celebration that followed Pope John Luke's call to the Modern Crusade.

In Rome, Cody, Ashana, and Rosy hugged each other and cried tears of joy. In Erbil, Charlie, Rico, Kamal, and the Barzani family were doing the same.

The mainstream media of the United States and the rest of the world began analyzing the speech, and wondering how they had managed to miss such a huge story. The press, especially in the Western counties, prided themselves in being able to sniff out a story through their multiple contacts. They were the ones asking the questions. Now they were playing catch-up, and their full resources focused on learning all the back-stories. They faced the reporting on the biggest story in centuries of years. In the back rooms, networks were working full time to root out what they discovered by vying with each other to gain the slightest edge.

Almost universally, hailed as a tremendous triumph, Pope John Luke's address succeeded in uniting the whole world to a cause that was just, and far too late in coming. Overnight polling showed the American people approved and supported the Modern Crusade by overwhelming numbers. Polling said not since 9-11, or even Pearl

Harbor, had the sentiment been so strong.

Of course, there were many questions about how this offensive would run. Speculation ran high for a short list of international military leaders with the right stuff to command the mammoth operations.

Washington, D.C.

The President and his staff saw Pope John Luke the First create a global Crusade from a single speech. "Plenty of firepower in that speech," said Tom Bostwick. "In a lot of ways I could hear Cody speaking."

The President said, "It looks like he has a strong influence on the pope. I'm planning to make my speech to the nation in two days. Be sure we have a copy of the pope's speech for our writers. I want to rally the nation to this cause in the same fashion as the pope."

"Meaning you want to concentrate on the first and second commandments of God, and not muddy the waters with a lot of Christian hyperbole," said Bostwick.

"Exactly, assembling a coalition is one thing, getting them all to work, as a team, is another matter completely."

"If Cody is going to run the forces of the coalition, he'll have to do that as the Black Angel," said Bostwick, "nobody else would have the credibility or popular support."

"The question is how. He'll have to explain how he pulled off the Iranian operation without compromising either us or the Catholic Church," said Palmer.

"I'll bet he's spending full-time thinking about that."

The President asked, "Do you think the pope really plans to lead his Swiss Guard into battle?"

"This pope is not like any pope in hundreds of years," said Bostwick. "In the first place, Cody knows him so well because he was actually active in their covert operations. John Luke knows the true capabilities of their center, better than we do. Next, he's a young man, in Papal terms. He probably is in very good physical shape. Elected from the chaos that resulted from the attack at St. Peter Square, where many of the Cardinals who expected to be candidates for the Papacy died along with the previous pope, the College of Cardinals knew they were facing a crisis when they convened to pick a new pope. I think they chose the best man to lead them into the near future, when the entire Catholic movement understood their jeopardy. He's no shrinking violet. He's militant, and ready to fight. So, the answer to your question is yes. I think John Luke will be on the front lines, fighting with his men."

The President got a big boost the following morning when Al Jazeera, the principal Muslim broadcast network came out in solid support for the pope and his speech. They concentrated on the fact that no Christian leader in history had quoted so liberally from the Qur'an, or expressed such deep understanding of the fundamental beliefs of Muhammad and his vision of what was truly important to the Muslim faith. They applauded his achievement of a coalition that combined Muslims with Christians and Jews. Most importantly, they condemned ISIS in the strongest way, agreeing with the pope that these were not Muslims at all, but minions of Satan, who deserved death. They emphasized their point with videos of the beheading of 1,000 Christians, and the destruction of St. Peters. The public had seen the videos of St. Peters, but never the gruesome and brutal beheading of 1,000 men, women and children, just because they did not fit into the mantra of Islam as viewed by ISIS.

American television did not show the videos, as they had not shown other videos of executions, however, Al Jazeera was readily available on the internet and millions of Americans saw the horrific carnage for the first time. By the time President Palmer made his speech to the nation, the public was primed and ready for any action the Administration chose to take.

President Palmer was reviewing drafts for his address almost until he faced the cameras. Throughout the previous 48 hours, the speech evolved from an endorsement of support for the pope, to a virtual declaration of war against the Islamic Caliphate, which had declared for years they were a country that deserved recognition from the rest of the world to legitimatize their existence. Now, Palmer was ready to treat them as if they were a hostile country, endangering the peace and stability of the world.

In actuality, the President faced a difficult decision. Popular and riding high in the polls, he knew there was still a large portion of the country that had an entitlement mentality, and expected a bigger, more benevolent government to provide it. The fact the labor participation rate had risen dramatically from its lowest level in 50 years, and a flood of entrepreneurial enterprises were bringing back the middle class with new jobs, did not keep opponents of Palmer from railing that the poor and disadvantaged citizens of the country were not participating in this recovery.

Palmer was not certain Congress would approve a formal declaration of war. He was certain that, as Commander in Chief of the military, he could order troops into battle as part of the pope's announced coalition, and the country would support it in general, even though it meant another war in the Middle East, which previously had disastrous consequences.

What the President really needed was to stake out a position on high moral ground, which made it impossible for a largely secular nation to ignore the very real threat of ISIS. He needed to stand shoulder to shoulder with the pope and his remarkable coalition of Muslims, Christians, and Jews based on it being a Holy war, and a justifiable Crusade.

The question was how to do that. Palmer felt conflicted, and knew from advance polling, he was going to command a gigantic audience that night. His advisors were saying an unprecedented 70% plus of all the people in the country would be watching. Therefore, he reasoned something had to be in his address that was so potent it would galvanize public opinion dramatically. Consequently, he would have a much wider range of operational choices.

He tried out his idea on his staff, advisors, the Chiefs of Staff of the military, members of his cabinet and the leaders in Congress from both parties. The results ranged from accusing him of showing the horrifying display of atrocities that would sicken the nation, to a past time for the American people to see graphically what ISIS actually did. He got vocal opinions from people on both sides. There was certainly not a consensus. Everyone did agree the President had to do something that would shock Americans out of their chairs and demand an immediate mobilization of U.S. military power, but his manner of doing it was not at all something anyone wanted, but many said was the only way to accomplish his purpose.

Left to search his own heart, the President's conscience had to make the decision. He respected Harry Truman's famous phrase, "The buck stops here."

As he was nearing a choice, it occurred to him he had not asked the man who not only wrote the plan, but would also be the one to command those who would carry it out. He called Cody in Rome.

Cody was sleeping. He was instantly alert when the phone rang, and he answered it.

Palmer said, "I'm sorry to disturb you at this hour, Cody, I'm going to make a speech to the American people in a few hours and I'm trying to decide on something in my presentation. I would like your input and opinion of the choice I'm trying to make."

"OK, Carson, let me have it."

Palmer bluntly told Cody what he was considering.

Cody was quiet for quite a while. Palmer waited patiently knowing he was turning his considerable insights in human nature, public opinion, and decades of seeing how people reacted to violence.

Finally Cody said, "What you are considering is unprecedented, and the impact will be enormous. I'm certain you'll get the reaction you want, however, you can make this even more dramatic, and preserve the sensitivities of children and people with weak stomachs if you warn people of what you are going to show them, then put a clock on the screen that counts down from 60 seconds. This will allow families to get their kids out of the room, and will be like a countdown to a space launch for all the rest. The impact will increase reality. Your worries about the political opposition to this are probably not as damaging as you think. All your opponents will leave the room just on principal. The blowback from the press tomorrow will mix opinions. Some will be outraged at what you did, no matter the motivation. Others will applaud your decision as being exactly what the country needed to know about the true realities of the enemy we face. I think the coverage would cancel itself out and leave you in a very strong position. This is something I hadn't considered until you asked me, so I had to think it through. I'm sorry it took so long."

"Your opinion turns out to be the one I wanted the most," said the President. "Thank you for helping me decide."

"I suppose that means you're going to do it; you can bet I'll be your number one viewer." said Cody.

After the harried President hung up, Cody was not able to sleep the rest of the night, checking his thoughts and insuring he'd given advice the Lord would honor.

Chapter 11
The Black Angel Unmasked

Washington, D.C.

President Carson Palmer tried to calm himself, as he shifted through his notes on the Oval Office desk. The room was full. A camera was set up directly in front of the President, and the teleprompter was counting down the minutes.

At last, a tech put up his hand and silently counted down the seconds from five. The lights went on and the President looked into the camera.

"My fellow Americans, thank you inviting me into your homes tonight. This will be a difficult time for all of us, including myself. Tonight we need to have a frank and serious discussion regarding Pope John Luke's appeal in Geneva a few days ago for a Modern Crusade with a global coalition of nations to end the terror that is ISIS. The pope laid out a compelling argument that included passages from both the Bible and the Qur'an, demonstrating his belief we are all children of God, no matter what creed we follow.

In America today, nobody gives it a second thought if one is a Baptist and another is a Methodist, but in the world of Islam, there are real differences between the majority Sunnis and the Shias. They have battled each other since the death Muhammad. This is why Iran, whose majority is Shia, has joined the pope in this Crusade.

The Kurds are the largest minority population in the world with no country to call their own. Today they battle ISIS continuously. The pope has said the Kurds should have a country of their own. This is why the Kurds have joined the coalition in this Crusade.

In Israel, the Jews have fought for their existence since 1948. They know, firsthand, what terrorism looks like. They seek recognition for their country from their neighbors, and security for their families. This is why the Israelis have joined the pope in this Crusade.

All I have just said is true, but the overriding truth of this is that a Roman Catholic pope has reached out to the people of Islam, and shown something we all often forget. This is the first Commandment of God, Allah, and Jehovah. 'You will love the Lord with all your heart and all you soul and put no other god before Him.' The second Commandment is like the first. 'Love your neighbor as yourself.' This is what Moses said, what Jesus said, and it is what Muhammad said.

The pope was able to bridge the gap of differences between the religions and show that God, Allah, and Jehovah are all the same master, and creator of the universe. He is a God who loves each of us with all his heart from the moment we are born until the day we return to Him.

I realize there are those of you watching me now who do not believe in God. That is your privilege and a right granted to you by the Founding Fathers of our great nation in the Constitution.

However, millions of people in the Middle East tonight do not have this choice. They are required to be compliant and agreeable to a perverse rule demanding that if they do not follow the religious beliefs of their masters, they will suffer the consequences, which is often death.

Pope John Luke identified ISIS for what they are. They are not Muslims in the way other Muslims understand it. They are nothing but an evil gang of thugs, thrill-seekers, thieves, murderers, rapists, and power-hungry fanatics who hide behind the façade of religion to continue their acts of terror on a global basis, to bring fear and capitulation to all nations. The pope called them minions of Satan. They very well might be.

This country and a coalition of other Christian nations will join this Crusade and put an end to the tyranny that is ISIS.

Frankly, I do not believe most of America knows how truly brutal, ruthless, and merciless ISIS has become. You may have read the stories in the press of their atrocities and been outraged. Actually, most of you do not know what is behind those stories to prevent you from seeing what we witness here at the White House on a daily basis.

We will join this crusade, and now I am going to show you why. We have prepared a three-minute video presentation that shows in actual detail the brutality ISIS employs on a daily basis to Muslims, Christians, Jews, men, women and children.

I must warn you that what you are about to see, is the worst that men can be. I urge you to take your children or anyone else out of the room completely, who may not be able to tolerate, emotionally, this video. For the rest of you who stay, I believe you will be as infuriated as I am, and will support our mission in the Crusade.

We will now start a clock on your screen, counting backwards from 60 seconds. In that time, you must shield the innocent from this terrible truth. Please do not take my warning lightly."

The television screens of America went blank and a timer appeared. It showed 60 seconds, and then began to run…59, 58.

In households throughout America and in many foreign homes as well, families were having sharp exchanges and mothers were taking children from the rooms where the TV's were on, shutting off others, closing laptops and computers. Many people had the presence of mind to punch the pause control on their TV's so they had more time to discuss, argue and decide what to do.

The second counter reached zero. The first image America saw were two black hooded men pulling a ten-year-old boy down to the ground with his head on a tree stump. One of the men grabbed the boy's hair and pulled it viciously, while the other man took a large sword and cut off his head. What followed were pictures of people beheaded in groups of 20, a deep pit lay below them, and thousands of headless bodies tumbled in. There was mass slaughter on a wholesale level. Other groups of men, women, and children died in pieces from automatic rifles in a city square.

It was the longest three minutes in American history.

When the video was over, President Palmer came back on the screen.

"I apologize and ask your forgiveness for doing what I have just done. It was the most difficult decision of my life. However, I believe you had a right to know what kind of enemy is stalking us on a global basis even at this hour. Remember, St. Peter's Basilica. Certainly, Pope John Luke remembers it. At this moment, he is leading his Swiss Guard into battle to recapture an ISIS town. We are joining him, as we speak. America is on the march. We stand for freedom, liberty, and justice. ISIS will be destroyed … so help me God!"

In polling the following day, nearly all men over the age of 14 and over half of the women stayed to watch. The outcry for action was as immediate and as dramatic as Cody had predicted. He was not entirely right about the mainstream media. The vast majority of the networks had long specials on the address, and said that the President was right in telling the American people the truth. Objectors, pacifists, atheists, and a few brave political opponents of the President, got a lot of coverage, none of it very favorable.

To President Palmer's surprise, the combined house and senate convened the next day and declared that a state of war existed between the United States and the Islamic Caliphate. All over the country, spontaneous demonstrations took place. A number of people who had not seen the President's address, or had not watched the ISIS video, did so now. President Palmer had what he wanted, a truly unified country on one cause, and about 100 million men who were ready to catch the next plane to the Middle East and start tearing ISIS to pieces, limb by limb.

The President went back on the air the next night thanking everyone for their support and cautioning the public the enemy was ISIS, NOT Islam. He said he would not tolerate any demonstrations or violence against the 2 million peaceful American Muslims. He said simply that if any violence occurred, the orders to the police were to shoot to kill.

Erbil

"Aren't you glad you waited for that assault on Bahji?" Charlie said to Rico. "Now we have the whole world on our side."

"It does change the dynamics of this. My Kurdish friends are anxious to get into action. They can now smell the possibility of having their own country."

"I'm just as anxious as you are," said Charlie, "but an offensive of this size won't just appear out of nowhere. We have some work ahead of us before we can launch. Dad is working fulltime on the details. I had a long talk with him last night. He told me everything he is currently planning, and gave me my marching orders. I need to brief President Barzani on what he can expect."

"Kamal says he's anxious to talk with you too," said Rico. "Let's see if he's available."

Barzani was available and Charlie was ushered into his office, along with Rico and Kamal within minutes.

The President looked up from his computer screen, smiled, and waved the three young warriors to seats.

Without much preamble, Charlie began the briefing, "The first major battles of the Crusade will begin here. The Kurds are the most battle tested, and have a decent command and control system. We're going to improve that a lot. As I told Rico, this offensive can't just magically appear. We have a lot to do to get ready. ISIS has had a long time to dig in. They also have about three divisions worth of weapons captured from the Iraqis. This includes some Abrams tanks, Bradley Fighting Vehicles, many Humvee's and all the ammunition. They also have some anti-aircraft missiles. We are faced with the fact we have to battle against our own equipment."

"How do you see the offensive developing?," said Barzani.

"Two brigades of the Swiss guard are coming here. These are the pope's elite Special Forces. The American military is now pouring equipment, ammunition and trainers into Erbil. This includes Abrams tanks, Bradley's, Humvees, and artillery – the works.

"We need to get 15 Kurdish brigades up to readiness to be able to participate in a combined offensive. After that's done, we'll open the offensive against Daesh here in the north, where we are the strongest. The Swiss Special Forces will augment your Peshmerga in our assault to retake Bahji. Dad hopes an early bloody victory will show what we're capable of doing. This is not going to be a slash and run operation, but one that will permanently remove Bahji from Daesh control. It will take some of the pressure off Kirkuk, currently surrounded on two sides by ISIS. We need to smooth out that bulge in your lines.

"I guess you saw the President of the United States speech the other night. I've no idea how it affected you, but it sure seems to have fired up the whole American population."

"I did see it," said Barzani, "his showing of the nightmare that ISIS really is was a very brave thing to do, but it was also very effective in letting the people see what all of Kurdistan has seen for years. Will your father take command of the coalition here?"

"He will, but he's got a trip to Iran to do first. He wanted to do it a month ago, to make amends to the Iranian people for his part in the nuclear explosions, but all of us told him it was a stupid idea, and the pope ordered him not to go. Now that he's had some time with

President Faroush, he believes the risk of death is small enough to go. He needs to come to an accommodation with the Iranians, by revealing who he actually is, and gaining public support. This is now necessary to lay the groundwork for him taking command of the entire offensive as the Black Angel. The very mention of that name brings fear to everyone and will give him all the authority he needs to command the coalition."

"No doubt," said Barzani, "I felt the same way when I met him in Washington. He's a formidable man who inspires confidence in everyone around him."

"It will be his first offensive as commander of the Crusaders. My job is to get the troops ready to fight as one army and then take part in the tactical operation as the head of the Swiss Guard.

"It sounds like he's giving you your first taste of command," said Barzani.

"True enough," said Charlie, "Dad never works on one level, but enters every situation with a firm idea of all his objectives."

"This is all happening so fast," said Barzani, "it makes my head spin."

"Dad is hoping the same thing is happening within the ISIS ranks. The attack on Bahji can begin in about a month, maybe a little longer."

Barzani asked, "You do realize that Bahji is not just a sleepy town, but a big city and it's almost a hundred miles from Erbil?"

"I know that," said Charlie, "If we can take and hold it, ISIS will suffer a major setback."

Tehran

President Manek Faroush heard a secure call from Rome was waiting for him. He punched the button on his phone. It was Cody. Faroush smiled. He liked Cody and had tremendous confidence in his abilities to manage all that lay before them.

"Salam," said Faroush. "I'm glad to hear from you, and get caught up on everything. I found the world seems to accelerate when you're around."

Cody chuckled, and spent just a moment catching up on all the personal news from both families, as they spoke Farsi during the entire conversation.

"I must say," said Faroush, your son, Charlie, seems to have made quite an impression on my daughter, Mitra. She talks about him all the time, and doesn't seem to mind he's a Christian."

Cody said, "I think the feeling is mutual, I suppose we'll just have to see what develops, before we have to face anything more serious."

"You're right," said Faroush, "right now we all have more on our plates than we can handle."

"Manek," said Cody getting to the business of his call, "the grim fact is that I am going to have to take command of the Crusader forces as the Black Angel. I guess I'm happy now for all the publicity in the last few years. My stature with our forces as the Black Angel will be both a surprise and support as the natural leader. The problem with doing this is I must come to Iran and make a speech on your television network. Basically, I'm going to ask forgiveness from the Iranian people for causing them so much pain and suffering."

"At the same time, I need to prevent the world from knowing I was acting for the Church and in such close cooperation with the Americans. The cover story I would like for us to use is true. I have been a freelance operative for many years, and my work was always for the common good, not glory or bravado. We will say I have worked with many governments, which is true, but always on the condition my identity could never compromised. We will also say I discovered the Iranian plot to smuggle nuclear weapons into the United States independently of any knowledge by them that such an operation was underway, also true. We used some U.S special forces to help me carry out my mission, but none of them ever knew the exact nature of the threat and believed they were only providing support.

"The Iranian portion of the operation should be explained as being entirely the work of my own special team who had worked with me for many years. This is also true.

"I will shoulder all the blame for the detonation of nuclear weapons in Iran, and you must explain this action was taken only as the last resort to thwart the global threats presented by your radical Muslim Ayatollahs.

"Having said all that will you help me, and do you think I can convince your people what we did was in the best interests of world peace?"

Faroush said, "Of course I will help you, Cody, in fact, I already have. Ever since our meetings in Washington, I have worked to massage public opinion in your favor. You already know the government of Iran has made it clear that secular, not religious, control of our government is our best option for recovery. Since the American government and other partner nations repaired almost all the damage, it was easy to convince our people the United States had no part in the return of our own nuclear weapons to Iran and their subsequent detonations. Americans walk the streets freely in Tehran and the other cities now. The centuries of abuse by the Sunni majority makes it possible to demonstrate Christian nations want the same treatment we want, which is treatment with respect. The pope's speech in Geneva seen by all of Iran, confirmed Allah's commandment we treat our neighbors as we would ourselves.

"Moreover, we have instituted curriculums in our schools teaching Allah gives justice to people who seek to commit sins against innocent people. We are even saying the Black Angel was Allah's messenger to protect us from ourselves. We poll the population regularly on their view of our tragedy, and the number of people who blame the Black Angel for it has steadily declined over the years. I would say our people are at least neutral to you, and are certainly curious about the strange man who was able to do so much. An actual appearance by you on television will be watched by everyone and if you take the posture of grief and regret as you suggest, I believe the Iranian people will hail you as an angel of Allah, although most of them think you're dead."

"All that is good news, Manek," said Cody. "We will be launching the first major battle with ISIS in another month or so. I have to be there for that, along with the pope. I need to appear as the Black Angel, the General in charge of the Crusade. But I need to come to Iran first, and get that issue out of the way."

"When can we expect you?" asked Manek.

"How long will it take to coordinate with your staff and prepare the Iranian people for a major speech?"

"Give me a week," said Faroush. "However, there's no reason why you can't come now. You could bring your whole family, including Charlie."

"Not a bad idea, at least as far as Charlie is concerned," said Cody, "He's been working around the clock to get his command of Peshmerga and Swiss Special Forces ready to fight as a combined army. I think he could use a rest. He probably will give me a thousand reasons why he can't come now, and it may take him a few days to tie up some lose ends. But there's no reason why Ashana, Rosy and I can't come now."

"That's perfect," said Manek, "call me back with your arrival details."

When Cody finished the call, he went looking for Ashana and Rosy. He found them working in Ops. Cody smiled. "How about a little lunch?"

"I could sure enjoy a decent lunch," said Rosy.

"And I could sure use a little quality time with my husband," said Ashana.

The three walked across the plaza and into the Vatican to their apartment. Ashana poked around in the refrigerator and came out with all the makings for sandwiches and other goodies.

"You've been working so hard, I hardly ever get to see you," said Ashana. "I miss you and I miss the quiet years in Positano."

"Ditto and Ditto," said Cody.

"I've missed you too, Dad," said Rosy. "Is this luncheon a social occasion?"

"Well, not entirely," said Cody, "but I do have some news I think you're going to like."

"Nothing like good news to raise your morale," said Ashana.

"We're taking a little trip to Tehran tomorrow," said Cody. "We'll be staying with Manek and Kevi Faroush."

"I'll bet this is not just for fun," said Ashana.

"Charlie is going to join us in a few days, as soon as he gets all his projects under control."

"That'll be nice," said Rosy. "I'll bet Charlie won't mind seeing Mitra again."

"But you have a reason for going there, and you think our being with you will help, Honey?"

"Never been able to pull one past your Mom," said Cody. "All right, there's something I have to do there before I take command of the Crusade."

"You've got to get the Iranian people to forgive you, and gain their support," said Ashana.

"In a word, yes," said Cody, "However, in order to make my leadership of the Crusade an accepted fact by the entire coalition, I have to appear as the Black Angel."

"Which puts a huge target on all our backs," said Ashana with a sad frown.

"That will be one of the unintended consequences of doing this," said Cody. "I'm very sorry. You'll just have to put up with a lot more security from now on … no more anonymity for any of us.

❖

The sleek white jet, with no markings, set down at a military base just outside Tehran. Cody, Ashana, and Rosy climbed out. Manek and Kevi Faroush were there to meet them; otherwise, there were no other people in sight.

"Welcome," said Manek, "We thought a little discretion at this point made sense."

"No arguments there," said Cody shaking hands with the President. "How are you, Kevi? You look more beautiful than ever."

"Thank you, Cody, however, I think it is Ashana and Rosy who are the beauties."

"Very nice of you to say that, Kevi," said Ashana, "I'm surprised we don't look a fright, as much as Cody has kept our noses to the grindstone. It is good to see you again. Where's Mitra?"

"Are you kidding?" said Manek, "No Charlie, no Mitra, although I was impressed with her excuse. She will welcome you properly when we arrive. If you'll just step in the limousine, we'll be off."

Cody found out Manek's home was the entire top floor of the sprawling government administration building, and that the whole roof was a stunning garden.

"It may seem a little unorthodox" said Manek, "but we have a very nice home here, and I don't have to leave the building to go to work. Plus, we have built-in security."

"It's a very beautiful home," said Ashana. "It has Kevi written all over it, and it's certainly big enough."

"This is actually a great idea," said Cody. "If I end up having to run a protracted war, this is exactly what I'm going to have. It's not the villa in Positano, but it sure does fill the bill for private living, making everyone come to me for work, and having multiple layers of security."

"Those were my sentiments exactly," said Manek.

Just then, Mitra glided into the room. She was wearing a tank top and tight western jeans. She was even more beautiful than Ashana remembered, and dressed in completely Western clothing, she would mix easily anywhere in Europe or America, except her good looks would attract a lot of attention from every man. She went straight to Rosy and hugged her with strength, then she hugged Ashana more tenderly. She ended up standing in front of Cody. She put out her hand for him to shake and said, "So, Black Angel, you've come to prostrate yourself to the entire Iranian people?"

"That's about it," said Cody, "think I'll get away with it?"

"Yeah, you will," Mitra said. "I've seen you speak, and I'll bet you have a real stem-winder planned for your television address. Our people appreciate straightforward, honest speech, and since you're also going to offer a way to kick ISIS's butt, my guess is that you'll end up being more popular in Iran than my Dad, and I like him a lot."

"Count on you to summarize the situation with the bare minimum number of words, Mitra," said Cody, sincerely. "You did the same thing in Washington. I was impressed then, and I'm impressed now. Since we're exchanging honest talk, let me ask you a question."

"OK," said Mitra.

"Were you as smitten by my son as he was with you?"

"Yes," said Mitra.

"If that's the case, I wish both you and Charlie happiness forever, and I will also add that, even though Charlie is my son, I'm not sure he deserves you."

Mitra laughed aloud, "It's going to be a jolly good time, hanging out with you. Just tell me when he's going to get here?"

"The last I heard, he was whipping his subordinates mercilessly to clear the decks long enough for him to come to Tehran. Give him a couple more days."

"I should call him and set a fire under him."

"Do that," said Cody with a sly grin, "Here use my phone, he always answers that. Put it on speaker so I can hear him squirm."

Mitra took Cody's phone and he told her which quick call button to push. He did it and the line rang.

"Hi Dad, did you get to Tehran alright," said Charlie.

"Your Dad got to Tehran just fine," said Mitra, "what I want to know is how come you missed the plane?"

"Mitra?" Charlie said, very much subdued.

"In the flesh, Hero boy, just answer the question.

"I'm in Erbil, trying to get things sorted out," said Charlie.

"Well, unsort them and get your butt to Tehran!"

"Yeah," said Charlie, completely flustered, "Okay. Sorry. I'll be there as soon as I can."

"I'll send the jet for you, day after tomorrow," said Cody.

"Great! Okay! Thanks, Dad." Charlie hung up without another word.

"You do realize, he won't sleep until he gets on the plane, said Cody with a grin at Mitra, "I hope you'll cut him some slack for that."

"No slack, no quarter!" said Mitra. "His dumb excuse of having to plan a war doesn't cut it with me." Then she laughed again, and this time everyone laughed with her.

Cody and Manek spent the next two days looking at the President's data on what the reaction to Cody's "Coming Out" speech would be with the Iranian public. By all indications, Mitra had hit it on the button. The Iranians certainly remembered the catastrophe that fell on their country, but they also resented the cause of it. The Black Angel was not the cause. He was the solution, and nobody in the country wanted a return to the days when Iran threatened the world and caused countless innocent deaths.

Right on schedule, Charlie arrived in Tehran. The whole family was there to greet him, along with Manek and Kevi Faroush. This time, Mitra was also in the welcoming party.

Charlie stepped off the plane. Ashana could see he was tired, but he also had a wide grin on his face. Mobbed by his family, he stood in the center of a circle that hugged and squeezed him. Manek and Kevi came up and Charlie bowed to both of them, touching his heart in reverence.

"Thank you inviting me to come. Dad was right. I really needed a rest and a break from our constant tactical planning."

Mitra had stood aside from the greetings, but now walked up and got right in Charlie's face, "Speaking of tactical planning, mate, your Father pinned me down bloody well the other night. I found my thinking seemed to come into focus, concerning you."

"Is that right?" said Charlie, a little defiantly, "Well, I didn't have to give it much thought at all. It is you, or no other, and I knew it in Washington. I'm glad we have a meeting of the minds."

"That's not all we're gonna have," said Mitra. She put her arms around Charlie's neck and kissed him in the unabashed manner of true lovers.

Cody and Manek both just rolled their eyes and shook their heads. Both Ashana and Kevi put their hands to their mouths to cover the smiles. Rosy went right to the heart of the matter. "Brother, I'm real happy for you. I'm happy for you both. You need to know Dad said, after the call the other night, he wasn't sure you deserved Mitra. I'm not either, but I'm hoping you turn out to be as good a man for Mitra as Dad is for Mom."

"That will be my goal," said Charlie.

"I do expect you to stay alive during this war," said Mitra. "Try not to get your ass shot off."

"I'll be real careful," said Charlie, "especially since I know what I'll find at home."

"That's a decent answer," smiled Mitra, "I think I'll keep you."

"I'm just glad all this happened at a private airfield where nobody could see you acting in such a manner," said Manek. "Now, before this gets worse, could we just get in the car and go home?"

The following couple of days, the two families didn't see much of Charlie and Mitra, except when they came home for dinner, after a day of exploring Tehran and delighting in their being together.

At one dinner, Cody ventured a question to the two, "Have either of you considered the rather great divide there is between your religions?"

"What divide?" said Charlie. "Mitra and I agree we love the Lord with all our hearts and souls and will dedicate our lives to His service. There is only one god, the true God. To that truth, we dedicate our lives. Everything else is kind of window dressing."

"I guess you were paying attention to the pope's speech. His message was intended to bridge more than the coalition of the Crusade, but also to touch individual lives."

"We agree to obey the first commandment of Allah, to worship him and have no other gods," said Mitra."

"We also agree to obey God's second commandment, to love our neighbors as ourselves," said Charlie. "Is there something we've left out?"

Manek spoke up, "This is not without precedent. A good number of American soldiers stationed in Iran have found love with Iranian girls. I had to issue an Executive Order declaring these unions to be Holy, as long as the couple kept their personal faiths. The pope's speech gave life to my decision and made me look like some kind of genius."

"Speaking of you being a genius," said Cody, "I'd like for you to look at my speech and see if you think I've rung the right bells."

"Let's go off to my office and work on that," said Manek.

❖

When the President announced there would be a special broadcast on television that would answer the many questions the people of Iran had on how the country had come to its current state, the news spread like a wildfire. Hardly a person in Iran was not watching when President Manek Faroush appeared on the screen.

"My fellow countrymen, Allah Akbar. Tonight, after so many years of wonder about the tragedy, which befell us 12 years ago, I am here to give you the answers you have sought. I swear in the name of Allah what you are about to see is the truth.

One of the participants in the detonation of six of our own nuclear bombs is with me tonight and will make a statement to you."

The camera panned to a man in a uniform of battle fatigues, with a purple beret on his head. He was standing erect and his eyes swept across the camera as if he could see everyone watching him. He bowed and put the traditional hand to his heart. He smiled, just a little, as if he was nervous and then said,

"Noble people of the great country of Iran may Allah bless each of you tonight. This is the first time in my life my image has ever appeared on television or anywhere else. The reason is simple. I wanted to stay unknown. What I obeyed for God was true justice for the world and peace and happiness for all."

"Over a period of 20 years, my small team and I went around the world and stamped out injustice and suffering wherever we could. We had contacts with many people and many governments, and our only rule was that when our work was done, we could quietly slip away, unknown, but leaving the people we had served feeling better."

"I had come to end of my career as a field operative and was happily ready to retire. But then the intelligence services in many countries began to call for help in stopping a real disaster from occurring."

"The supreme religious leaders of your country conceived a plot by which they would smuggle six nuclear weapons into the United States and detonate them in their biggest cities. With great reluctance, I assembled my team for one last mission. We were able to locate the ships on which the weapons were to be transported to Mexico where drug cartels agreed to smuggle the bombs across the border, in return for 2,000 kilos of pure heroin."

"We were able to infiltrate the cartels and blow up the drugs before the bombs could be transported to the United States. It took Iran two months to replace the drugs."

"With the drugs in hand, members of the drug cartel and units of Iranian special services successfully took the bombs into the United States. I and my team were waiting for them, and with the assistance of American military personnel, who had no idea what the mission actually was, were able to overpower the Iranian soldiers and technicians, and capture the bombs."

"I then had to make the most difficult decision of my life. If we had simply let the United States keep the bombs and say nothing to their people, it was only a matter of time before more nuclear weapons would be on their way to the United States or other countries."

"My decision was to smuggle the bombs back into Iran, place them at the nuclear enrichment sites where they were built and detonate them. The single large city with a nuclear facility was Qom. As you all know, the city was leveled, and nearly all the radical Ayatollahs were killed."

"I must tell you know how deeply I regret having made this decision. But it was the only way to solve the problem. Nevertheless, I am here tonight to beg the forgiveness of the Iranian people, and to tell you how sorry I am for causing you so much sorrow. I apologize, but if the same conditions existed again, I still would have made the same choice."

"Our team raced to the border of Afghanistan to escape. We were not successful. My entire team died attempting to cross the border. I alone, survived, even though I was heavily wounded."

"Following this mission, I did retire, and have remained so until now. Today a new threat, more vicious, more brutal, has risen with ISIS and, as Pope John Luke told the ecumenical council in Geneva last month, they do not qualify as God loving Muslims at all, but are actually agents of Satan, determined to challenge Allah and bring misery to the entire world. This is ISIS. A so-called Islamic Caliphate, which now occupies Iraq and Syria, is the home of many fellow Shias. ISIS is killing everyone who does not bend to their will. The Shias, I'm sorry to say, have suffered even more than the Christians of the Middle East.

"Tonight, brave Iranians and Americans are guarding your border to keep these animals from ravaging you and your families. The pope has called for a Modern Crusade. Not one in which Islam is facing Christianity, but one in which Muslims, Christians, Jews and Kurds are aligned against ISIS, and will destroy them utterly."

"When the war is won, the Middle East shall have the right to divide itself along the cultural, ethnic and religious states that seem most reasonable to them. This is the pledge of the Crusaders, the pledge of the pope and the commander in chief of all Crusade forces. This person is me. I will lead us to a better life of freedom, peace, and the right to worship Allah, or God, or Jehovah, in what manner is right. I am the Black Angel! I am here again to serve mankind."

"Allah Akbar!"

The light went down, and Cody looked across the room to Ashana, Charlie and Rosy. They were smiling at him.

"For a coming out party, you made quite a splash," said Ashana. Mitra who was standing next to her mother came across the room and put her arms around Cody, "I knew you could do it, and boy did you ever!"

Manek followed his daughter and hugged Cody, "All of Iran will honor you, and more importantly, the world will follow you as you lead us to victory against ISIS. I salute you!"

Rosy said, "You spoke very good Farsi."

Fox News Breaking Story

"The answer to one of the most mysterious stories of modern times seems to have been answered. Yesterday, on Iranian television, the Black Angel finally came out of the shadows and told the full story of how nuclear weapons blew up in Iran. The true identity of this man is still not known, but witnesses have come forward in the last several hours to confirm that the man

they saw on television was, in fact, The Black Angel they'd met."

"Over the last dozen years more than 300 books have been written about the Black Angel and thousands of blogs on the internet. We now know that most of these books were complete works of fiction, while a few of them contained at least one of the points the Black Angel made in his speech yesterday."

"His speech was delivered in Farsi, the language of Iran, but several hours later, identical speeches were delivered by the Black Angel in fluent English, German, Italian, Spanish, and Arabic and broadcast to countries all over the world."

"Pope John Luke has requested The Black Angel visit him at the Vatican in Rome. Catholic Church officials confirm the pope has selected The Black Angel to be the commander in chief of all the Crusader forces now in coalition against ISIS."

Other networks across the world carried Cody's speech. Public opinion of the broadcast was overwhelmingly favorable, and there were many endorsements The Black Angel was, in fact, the right man to lead the coalition. Since he had spoken in so many languages, the countries who spoke those languages claimed Cody as one of their own. The only copy of his file, outside the Vatican, containing his identity and all the other details of his life, which disappeared in obscurity over 30 years before, remained safely locked in Tom Bostwick's safe. Bostwick did cherry pick a number of Black Angel operations over the years, and let them leak to press agencies around the world, which only added more credibility to Cody's story of seeking to quietly do good works. Tom also appeared on a number of network talk shows revealing he had met the Black Angel in person when American personnel helped in Zapata, Texas to capture the bombs. He confirmed the man who had spoken in so many languages, was the same man he had met. Ponderously unhelpful, he gave no one a clue to Cody's true background or identity, saying that the Black Angel was as much a mystery to him as everyone else.

Cody made one public appearance in the main plaza of Tehran to a cheering crowd of over a million people. Only Manek Faroush and Charlie, whom Cody introduced as part of his new team, and the tactical commander for operations against ISIS with the Kurds, accompanied him.

Then it was time for the family to leave Tehran and comply with the pope's summons to come to the Vatican. Cody, Ashana and Rosy were sorry to leave, since they had grown close to the Faroush family. For Charlie and Mitra it was incredibly difficult. Neither of them knew when they would see each other again. The fact that Charlie was stepping off into serious danger made it worse. They clung to one another until the last moment.

❖

The jet touched down at the Vatican airfield outside Rome.

"It's so good to be home again," said Ashana.

"You and Rosy can really go home to the villa if you want to, at least for a few days. Adolfo and Carlotta will be happy to see you," said Cody.

"That's sounds like Heaven to me," said Ashana. "We'll leave tomorrow. Both Rosy and I have work in progress in Ops and we ought to check on it."

"Charlie and I have an appointment with the pope this afternoon," said Cody, "after that we'll all go out for a nice dinner at your favorite place."

"Is that safe?" asked Ashana, "you're not exactly unknown anymore."

"I spent a lot of years moving around and blending in with people. I think our dinner can be private."

"Don't count on it," said Rosy. "The internet is afire with every scrap of information about you, and your picture is everywhere."

Bishop Paglioni was alone to greet them as they stepped off the plane. The family mobbed him with kisses and hugs.

"I'm glad to see you too," said Paglioni when the group hugs ended. "Let's get you into the Vatican as quickly as possible. You managed to make your face the most popular in the world. Very bad for a covert operative."

"I've no intention of being covert from now on, Vincent," said Cody. "From now on, the more publicity the better. I hope it scares the Hell out of ISIS."

"It already has," said Paglioni, "the Caliphate is putting out one press release after another saying they have no fear of you at all, and that you are public infidel number one, whom any good Muslim should shoot on sight."

"My goodness," said Cody, "they really are spooked."

"By the way," said Paglioni, "nice speech in Tehran. You seem to have won over the Iranians. Perhaps more importantly, you have also become the hero of all 200 million Shias is the world. They know you aren't exactly anti-Sunni, but you are anti-ISIS and they *are* Sunnis, so they aren't making much of a distinction in that."

The limousine made its way smoothly to the Vatican. Cody was surprised with all the added security and was very happy to see the front of the cathedral in St. Peter's Square looking more like the original structure. An army of workers was furiously working to rebuild the dome. Paglioni said they were using Michelangelo's exact design, but were reinforcing the dome with more modern materials unknown in Michelangelo's time. He said the dome would be as glorious as ever, and a good deal safer and sturdier.

As they drove into the plaza next to the Vatican admin building, Ashana and Rosy went with Paglioni to Ops, while Cody and Charlie went into the main cathedral for their meeting with the pope.

Chapter 12
Glocks Ablaze

Rome

Entry into the office of the pope was immediate; Cody and Charlie found John Luke sitting at his table, talking on the phone. He waved them to seats.

"I'm grateful for your support and good news, Mr. President," said John Luke. "The Black Angel and Ardishur have just arrived. I will tell them about our conversation. Thank you, Mr. President, Goodbye."

The pope looked at Cody and Charlie with satisfaction. "You seem to have made my job of appointing you Command in Chief of the Crusade rather easy. Your appearance in Iran and the speech you made was a stroke of genius."

"Thank you, your Holiness," said Cody. "Were you just speaking to President Palmer?"

"Yes," said John Luke, "he sends you his best wishes. The reason he called was to tell me that the 11th, 12th, 13th, and 15th Marine Corps battalions are now on the ground in Iran. Also, both the 82nd and 101st Army divisions have arrived in Israel, along with all their equipment and are training for an assault on Damascus. In addition, brigades from England, France, Germany, Italy and Australia have also arrived in Israel and are training as a combined force. The Generals in charge of all these units have received your plans for strategic objectives and tactical ways to accomplish them. Until now, they haven't known where the plans came from, but all seem to agree they are very comprehensive and quite sound operational plans. All of them now know the complete Crusade battle plans came from you and are eager to have the honor of serving under the command of the Black Angel."

"What about the Kurds?" Charlie asked.

"I sent both brigades of my Swiss guard to Erbil. The U.S. has been shipping in heavy weapons and both the Peshmerga and Swiss are working with American trainers to become familiar and competent to use everything they have now."

"That sounds great," said Charlie. "It means we can jump off in a short time to attack our first objective of Bahji. By the way your Holiness, why did you call me Ardishur?"

"It's pretty simple," said the pope. "It wouldn't do to have it commonly known you are Cody's son. We need to do everything we can to conceal your family from ISIS, so we lose the name Charlie and replace it with Ardishur, with that beard you look like a Kurd, anyway. That is the way I'm going to introduce you as my commander, Cody, and you Charlie, as Ardishur, commander of the Kurds. You both look like Kurds. Are you having a beard growing contest?"

Cody asked, "When do you plan to make the announcement?"

"Tomorrow, I've had the Vatican press office rolling out the announcement. We will make the presentation from my balcony. That part is public. There will be a huge crowd in St. Peter's Square. The Italian police are occupying every home and window within a mile to insure we don't get shot by some sniper who's as good as you are."

"You seem to have thought of everything," said Cody. "I'm going to take the family out to a nice dinner tonight at the Borgia Antico. Can you make us reservations?"

The pope asked, "Are you sure you want to do that? It seems like an unnecessary risk to me."

"People might know me, but they don't know the rest of the family. I think I can make myself more or less invisible."

"I'm going to station a squad of Swiss guards at the restaurant anyway," said the pope. "In addition to the formidable brigades I sent to Erbil, I also brought in two full companies of Swiss Special Forces to augment our security. You can be sure they aren't wearing their ceremonial uniforms."

"Well, I guess that's better than you ordering me to stay home and have dinner in our apartment," said Cody.

The three talked for another hour with Cody and Charlie laying out the strategy for the opening offense against Bahji, and using that as a signal to begin the general assault from Iran and Israel. Cody said he would get around to all the commands for personal briefings with the officers in charge of the troops to check their readiness. He set the kick-off of the attack, symbolically, on September 11, two months away.

When Cody and Charlie got back to the apartment, they found

Ashana and Rosy had finished up at the Ops center, and were ready to go out for dinner.

"Our reservations at Borgia Antico are set for 8 p.m." Cody said. "We can leave a little early and stroll over there in a nice leisurely way.

❖

At 7:30, Cody and Charlie had both showered and dressed for dinner. Cody put on a black suit with a neutral tie. He also got out a fashionable hat to wear, and topped it off with dark sunglasses. Ashana agreed he was about as invisible as he could make himself, despite his beard, and that he looked very nice. Charlie got by with just a black suit.

The family went out the back of the Vatican and walked around the plaza. Cody quickly spotted the men following them. The pope was taking no chances, since he knew there would be other security men at the restaurant. He noticed Charlie had spotted them too, but Ashana and Rosy were strolling along arm in arm. He decided not to mention the security.

When they got to the Borgia Antico, they went up the elevator to the veranda with the beautiful view of Rome. Every table on the veranda was full except theirs, and one other on the far corner away from the better seats along the railing.

They ordered their dinner, and chatted about inconsequential things while they drank their wine and ate their salads. During the salad course, Cody noticed a group of seven men come onto the veranda and take the one empty table over in the corner. They were dressed in suits, were clean-shaven and seemed innocent enough.

Then, Cody, who sitting on the side of the table next to Charlie, saw one of the men look up and stare at him. He had seen that look before. It was one where the observer was watching in a way in which he did not want to appear to be watching. Their clothes were wrong. Their behavior was wrong. He leaned over to Charlie.

"Those men in the corner are here for us. Very carefully slip your Glock under the table to Rosy."

Ashana heard the exchange, "Something happening?"

"I'm passing my gun under the table to you. Charlie is doing the same for Rosy. When you have the guns, both of you get up and head for the restroom. Watch that group of seven behind you. The minute they move, and they will all move at the same time, both of you shoot them. Then get under cover."

Neither Ashana nor Rosy turned around to look at the table where they sat. It was a credit to both of them. They reached under the table, careful not to draw attention and grabbed the guns.

"What's the play?" asked Charlie.

"Not suicide vests, they would have spotted them coming. They don't have heavy weapons for the same reason. I think it's most likely they'll use grenades, or very small caliber weapons strapped to their legs. When they move, and Mom and Rosy start gunning them down, we have about five seconds to get to the table and take out whoever is left. I'll go right you go left. Get ready!"

Ashana and Rosy rose from the table very casually and seemed to stroll toward the restrooms without a care. Rosy saw the men at the table begin moving as a unit. One of them pulled the pin on a grenade and tossed it at the table where the family was sitting. When the grenade exploded, the table was empty.

Rosy ignored the grenade blast, raised her gun, and fired. Ashana was right behind her. A hail of bullets flew across the veranda, and four of the men went down.

Cody and Charlie had sprung into action as the girls turned to fire. They raced across the veranda and were onto the three remaining men, while the grenade was going off behind them. One of them pulled out a knife. Cody kicked it out of his hand, and chopped the man in the throat. He went down.

Charlie engaged the other two men. With lightning strikes, he battered both men, sending one of them to the floor. Before either Cody or Charlie could reach him, he pulled a grenade from his sock and pulled the pin. "Allah Akbar!" he cried.

Charlie threw the man he was holding on top of the man with the grenade and then jumped over a table, pulling it onto its edge as he did so. Cody dived behind a huge planter filled with foliage.

The grenade exploded with a thunderous blast, blowing up the man who had it, and the man Charlie had thrown on top of him. That saved them. The falling man took most of the blast, but shrapnel splattered across the veranda, hitting several people, as had the first grenade explosion. The heavy table he had upended protected Charlie. It was full of splinters and cracks. Cody was able to look up from behind the planter. There were people on the floor with blood on their clothes. Most of the rest froze in place. The entire incident had started and ended within less than thirty seconds.

Ashana and Rosy looked around the corner of the wall leading to the restrooms. Shrapnel fragments peppered the wall, but neither of them sustained any injuries.

The Swiss guard detail burst into the room, guns drawn. Cody stood up and walked over to the attackers. Four of them were dead, shot by Ashana and Rosy. The two involved in the grenade blast were unrecognizable corpses. One man injured with a bullet wound in his shoulder, was still alive. Cody waved to the Swiss security force. They moved in, handcuffed him, and hauled him to his feet. The rest of the team surrounded Cody and his family and hustled them off the veranda. Shrill sounds of many police cars filled the air.

On the following afternoon, Cody and his family were sitting quietly on couches in the pope's office. John Luke was seething with rage. Infuriated, he stormed back and forth across the room.

"I can't believe it! I just can't believe it! We came *this* close to losing you all! And now we learn that a person in this building tipped off ISIS you would be at the Borgia Antico."

"Credit Rosy for finding the guy," said Rosy. "Most people who work at the Vatican don't know all calls coming in or going out are recorded. Rosy was able to find the call coming out of a Vatican office. All it said was 'Black Angel at Borgia Antico, 8 p.m.' She isolated the phone and did voice recognition on everyone who worked in that office. Our perp is an alienated Monsignor who believes you have abandoned Christ to Islam, and felt strongly enough about it to make the call."

"How did he know *who* to call," shouted the pope, "and how much other sensitive information has been leaked to ISIS."

Rosy continued, "The interrogation of the man we captured at the restaurant, and the Monsignor, was conducted by the Swiss Special Forces. Their methods are most severe. The first to break was the injured ISIS soldier, who was already in great pain from the girls' guns. He turned out to be the leader of that cell, and admitted to having contact with our monsignor. The priest did not have access to any sensitive information, he just wanted all this Crusade stuff to stop, so he made a few calls and ISIS recruited him. The only thing they really got was the intelligence about us being at the restaurant."

"Which was almost enough!" said the pope.

"With all respect, Holiness," said Charlie, "My Dad had that bunch figured out before they got their menus. He knew exactly what to do and our training allowed us to stop the threat. You should know better than anyone that these kinds of situations are common among all your agents. It's all in a day's work."

"Did you tell him to say that?" asked John Luke.

"No, I didn't," Said Cody, "but I trained them all to react exactly as they did."

"I've never killed a man before," said Ashana, "I always thought I couldn't do it, but last night my family was about to die. I pulled the trigger without a second's hesitation. I don't believe the Lord will hold me responsible for what I did."

"You are a remarkable family," said the pope more mildly. "I think we should start referring to all of you as the Black Angels."

"Unfortunately, that holds more truth than you might think. The surveillance footage from the Borgia Antico tells quite a story. It made quite a splash on television this morning, worldwide. ISIS got vital information after all. Now they know my family and see what they look like. From now on, we're all hunted people."

"I am very sorry about that," said the pope, "but now I'm sure you should stay in the safety of the Vatican."

"Fair point, John Luke," said Cody, "by the way I'm sorry to have messed up your big announcement today."

"I've rescheduled it for tomorrow. After last night the audience should be twice as big."

❖

No humble looking old man came to the balcony of the Papal apartment the next day. Pope John Luke the First came to the window and felt young, vital, and brimming with energy. He spoke in a commanding voice. People jammed St. Peter's Square in multiple crowds overflowing for several blocks away.

The pope began. "Children of God. In the thousands of years the Catholic Church has stood the test of time and troubles, there has never been a moment such as this. Today, we begin the pathway of our Modern Crusade. It is like no other Crusade in history. We shall defeat

ISIS, and send them all to Hell, where Satan rules. I have come today to introduce you to the man who will lead this Crusade. I believe I can say, without a doubt, we could not have made a better choice. He is a man with no country. He has no other allegiance but to go forth now and become the champion of God and Allah and Jehovah. As you already know, he is a fierce and deadly warrior, but he is also a man who has spent a lifetime protecting the innocent. I give you the commander in chief of our Crusade, The Black Angel!

The roar from the hundreds of thousands in the plaza of St. Peter roared their approval as Cody stepped on to balcony wearing a fresh set of battle fatigues. He wore a semi-automatic weapon strapped to his thigh. Charlie came out with him.

"People of the world," cried Cody, "we have suffered long enough with the curse that is ISIS. Today, armies from all over the world and of all faiths gather together to say, NO MORE!"

The crowd roared again.

Charlie came out onto the balcony, also dressed in the traditional Peshmerga fatigues. "This is Ardishur, commander of all the Kurdish military forces and my second in command. I pledge that, with your help, the days of ISIS are now numbered. FREEDOM!

The crowd shouted itself hoarse in their cheers.

Cody, Charlie and the pope came back in the apartment. The pope poured 100-year-old cognac into three glasses, with his own hand, giving Cody and Charlie a glass of their own.

"Let us drink to our victory and pledge ourselves into the hands of God."

They all drank their glasses empty.

❖

Cody asked, "What do you mean, you're going with us?"

"Because I must," said John Luke. The people need to see me, dressed for war, and ready to engage in battle."

"You would be a lot more helpful staying here," said Cody.

"Perhaps," said the pope, "but not more inspirational. Here we are, about to begin our great offensive. What could be more symbolic, and more fitting than to have the Christian Pope first take arms with the Muslims?"

"It will be symbolic alright," said Cody, "but we are heading off to the front lines, not the safest place for you to be."

"Give it up, Cody," said the pope, "this is a closed subject."

❖

Erbil

Two weeks later, a silver jet landed at Erbil Airport. President Barzani and Rico were there to greet them, along with an honor guard of Rico's Peshmerga, and Charlie stood at the front, at attention. Another tight, disciplined company of a hundred men from the Swiss Special Forces also lined up facing the Peshmerga. They had the look of trained warriors with grim looks on their faces.

The last to leave the plane was Cody and the pope. Both of them were dressed in battle fatigues with majestic purple berets and semi-automatic Glocks strapped to their thighs. Barzani was not surprised to see Cody dressed that way, but seeing the pope of the Catholic Church wearing such clothing was striking. The two of them cut an air of authority as they approached the welcome party.

"Howdy Masoud," said Cody shaking the President's hand and putting his hand to his heart in traditional Muslim greeting fashion.

"I would like to introduce you to the pope of the Catholic Church, John Luke the First. Your Holiness, this is President Masoud Barzani, President of Kurdistan."

The two men shook hands and exchanged formal embraces.

"Welcome, your Holiness," said Barzani. "Your arrival is the greatest symbol I can imagine to give life to the Crusade."

"I thank you," said John Luke, "Thank you for the heroic battles you have fought against ISIS. I'm sorry to have not come sooner. However, I am here now and may Allah bless us in the coming struggle."

"Most kind," said Barzani. "Would you consent to speaking a few words to my countrymen who have come to welcome you?"

"I would," said John Luke.

The pope stepped up onto a podium. In addition to a worldwide press corps, were thousands of Kurds who had come without any urging from Barzani to greet their new ally. They cheered and waved enthusiastically. John Luke stepped to the microphone and began speaking in very good Arabic.

"In the name of Allah and God, our mutual creator and master of all life, I am honored to be in your country. I am here to begin the destruction of Satan's slaves. Too long have they tortured us with their

- 159 -

evil ways. I am just the first of many, many soldiers from all over the world who have come to fight as one in our Holy cause. We are Christians, Muslims, Jews, Kurds, but we are all one people, with one mission, which I pledge we will see to its end. Hail to the people of Kurdistan!"

A reaction from everyone present was an outpouring of cheering, expressing respect for the man who had made this Crusade possible. John Luke bowed in respect, and put his hand to his heart in the Muslim acknowledgment of Allah. There was no question, that John Luke had properly begun the quest that laid before them.

The motorcade proceeded to the Presidential palace with large crowds lining the way and shouting their support. When they reached the Palace, both Cody and the John Luke were surprised to find the entire compound surrounded shoulder to shoulder with citizen Kurds, with knives, and crude weapons.

"What's all this?" asked Cody.

"The Kurdish people not only pledge their support for you, but have spontaneously augmented our security to insure your protection," said Barzani. "Such a demonstration for the leader of the Christian Church is somewhat unprecedented, but your speech at the airport in Arabic was also a very impressive gesture."

"All of this is going out worldwide to a very hungry public, who wants to see everything," said Cody. "I think we've made the most of our entry into the Crusade."

"Now we have to prove there is more to us than just uniforms and inspiring speeches," he continued, "This afternoon we'll meet the commander of the Swiss guard and your Peshmerga commander to go through the tactical battle plan for taking down Bahji."

"Rico and I have planned our assault," said Charlie, who had jumped in the car with Cody and the pope. "It's been a busy two weeks. We are conducting a briefing for you this afternoon on how we expect the battle to be conducted."

Later that day, the Swiss and Peshmerga commanders arrived at the Palace. They went immediately into the war room; its walls held photographs, maps and troop disbursal displays. Charlie went to the front of the room and began the briefing for Cody and Pope John Luke. Colonel Joseph Mueller of the Swiss Guard and his Peshmerga counterpart, Colonel Oman Koshiri, were also in the meeting.

"This will be the biggest offensive yet mounted by the Kurdish forces, and the opening battle of the Crusade. The Kurds, reinforced by two brigades of Swiss guards, have trained with the Peshmerga and our American trainers for our heavy weapons, the Abrams tanks, and the Bradley Fighting Vehicles. Our training is intense and focused. We would like more time to prepare, but we believe what we have will be enough. Before they arrived, the Swiss Guard had three weeks of intensive training that began after the attack on St. Peters.

"Our objective is strategic. It is the city of Bahji. We want it; they know it. We are going to take it. ISIS will do everything it can to keep us from doing it.

"Bahji is a city of about 200,000 inhabitants. It is located 100 miles south of Erbil, on the main road to Mosul. It is a major industrial center best known for its oil refinery, the biggest in Iraq, and has a large power plant. Bahji is a junction of the national railway network. We need to capture the refinery intact, along with the power plant and the rail station. Resistance at these points will be the greatest. When ISIS sees they are about to be overrun, they will likely try to destroy these facilities. We must do everything we can to prevent that. By taking this city, we will severely disrupt traffic from Mosul to Bagdad. It will take pressure off Kirkuk, and, best of all, give us oil refinery facilities, which the Kurdish government can use to bargain with the Turks and other countries that need refined Middle Eastern oil. This will make the Kurdish position much stronger in the entire region.

"Make no mistake," said Charlie, "the Daesh are tough, veteran fighters, at least two brigades. They will resist our invasion with everything they have, which is considerable. They have a fleet of Bradley's, at least a dozen Abram tanks, heavy caliber machine guns, mounted on trucks, plus the ISIS ground forces, which have a big supply of RPGs, and their own personal automatic weapons. Additionally, they have probably covered the town with bobby traps, IEDs and concealed explosives, which they will use to cover their retreat as we advance.

"Our most effective strategy is surprise. We need to move so quickly they won't have time to mount effective defenses. We also will be coming at them from more than one direction.

"Beginning tomorrow night two companies of Swiss guards will parachute into the oil refinery, some five miles north of Bahji. These companies will overcome the resistance there and hold the refinery until the main force arrives.

"ISIS will expect us to use highway 1 as our main means of bringing in our heavy equipment and we will. The main force will leave Erbil tomorrow at dusk. We think they can speed along highway 1, for at least 60 miles before encountering ISIS forces.

"However, before reaching Bahji we're going to turn off the highway and hit the town from the west and east. We believe our Bradleys and Abrams can maneuver over this ground and avoid most of the mines and explosives ISIS will have planted along the highway.

"As the operation begins, we will begin an artillery barrage from our towed 155 mm Howitzers, which have an effective range of about 20 miles, and two batteries of 105 mm Howitzers with an effective range of about six miles. We will also have close air support from Blackhawk gunships, and F-22's from Incirlik in Turkey. From our reconnaissance, we have located the main centers where ISIS troops, their artillery, tanks, and Bradleys are stationed. We hope to wipe out those centers and reduce their fighting force. As the artillery is falling we will send in our Peshmerga and the balance of the Swiss guards."

Charlie pointed to the map, "We need to relieve and reinforce our Swiss paratroopers at the oil refinery. Your Peshmerga will enter the city from the west and east. This is the most dangerous of all offensives. We can expect to have to fight, literally from building to building. We want to drive the ISIS fighters toward the city center. There's not as much cover for them there. If we move quickly enough we should be able to drive them to this spot, and wipe them out."

"We will have overhead cover from Rico and his shooters, who will move from location to location to provide long range fire at defenders. Rico, you can set up initially on this hill over the town. You will likely be spotted and draw mortar fire, so you will have to be prepared to move, into the city, and coordinate with the ground troops to the places you are needed the most.

"As I said we will have air support from Blackhawk gunships and F-22's from Incirlik. In addition to hitting their heavy equipment, they will destroy any ISIS forces trying to escape the town.

"We will attack with three brigades of Peshmerga and the two brigades of the Swiss guard. This gives us about 15,000 men. Our latest intelligence says that ISIS has from 5000 to 7000 fighters in the town. We outman them, outgun them, and I'm sure will outfight them.

"Now," said Charlie. "Our tactics in this operation is to take no prisoners. We want the ISIS fighters to die. We do hope to capture a few high value targets for interrogation, to drain all their knowledge of everything they know. After they have given up their information, they will face a war crimes tribunal. ISIS must know from the outset that we intend to give them no quarter or allow them to surrender. If we do this in Bahji, word will spread through the ISIS command, lower their morale and make them fight with fear. Are there any questions?"

"I think you have a sound battle plan, Charlie," said Cody, "You're certainly right speed and surprise, are our best weapons. How are you going to move the troops?"

"With troop transport trucks. Our big ones will hold 50 men, not very comfortably, but we hope to make the move from Erbil to Bahji in about two hours. The Troop transports will be mixed in with our Abrams, Bradleys, and Humvees, to provide cover as we get closer to Bahji."

Cody did some quick math. That means you'll need about 300 troop transporters. Do we have that many?"

"We do," said Charlie. "We are also going to use both lanes of the highway. We figure whatever traffic we meet will be quick to get out of the way. Or we will blast them as we move and shove the wreckage aside."

"Our command and control will be in the rear. We've tested and retested our communication systems. I expect to have continuous connection with our advanced elements. As we secure portions of the city, we'll move closer to the action. We also have two dozen Huey helicopters that will carry about ten men each. They will move just ahead of the main force and provide cover for our troop transports as they enter the city."

"What's my job?" asked Cody.

"You stay back here in Erbil and coordinate all the other offensives from Kuwait, Iran and Israel."

"I've already done that," said Cody. "I suppose you think I've been hanging out at the pool for the last two weeks, but I've actually been making personal inspections of the other commands. The pope accompanied me. We've listened to several battle briefings, all like yours, with the objectives outlined. When you jump off tomorrow, it will be the signal for all the other forces to begin moving as well. The Iranians and their Marines will attack from the east with Bagdad the final objective. The airborne divisions will move north from Israel, into Syria, targeting Damascus. The Israelis will launch their air force into Syria, and move their army past the Golan Heights and into the Becca Valley."

"All that sounds great," said Charlie, "all the more reason to stay in Erbil to keep track of your other operations."

"You should know better than anyone that I'm not wired to sit on the sidelines and watch what's happening. Your main weakness in this plan is the exposed Swiss paratroopers at the oil refinery. I intend to take one of your helicopters and provide overhead for them."

"Your job, Dad," Charlie said firmly, "is to avoid exposing yourself to any risky situations. You are the one man who's not expendable in this mission."

"I'm going with Cody," said the pope.

"That's incredibly stupid," said Charlie, "you aren't expendable either, and don't have Dad's experience in these conditions."

"Nevertheless," the pope said firmly, "I'm going with Cody."

Charlie sighed and then said, "Major Mueller, detach a squad of your best men to go with these dumb men."

"I will," said Mueller.

That night, Cody called Ashana in Rome and brought her and Rosy up to date on the operation. Both of the women expressed their fear for husband and father.

"This is what I do," said Cody, "besides, Charlie is running this attack, and has me and the pope in the rear, taking potshots at whoever puts his head up."

"I'm just as worried about Charlie," said Ashana, "even more so, now I know he's going in with the troops."

"Charlie will be alright," said Cody, "but the pope is insisting on coming with me. I wasn't able to talk him out of it."

"Good Lord," said Ashana, "make sure you keep an eye on him."

❖

At dusk of the following day, the massive convoy pulled out of the Peshmerga army camp. It roared with precision and hit the road at top speed.

As planned, the Swiss paratroopers took off an hour later to secure the oil refinery. Cody, the pope and a squad of Swiss Special Forces got into a helicopter and moved south.

Charlie's Peshmerga and Swiss force moved quietly down the main road to Bahji, doing better than they planned. They got to a dozen miles from Bahji before encountering any ISIS fighters. In unison, the force split into two forces several miles from the city, and moved into position to the east and west of the city. The western force was the first to meet heavier resistance along the Tigris River, where the city of Bahji crept right to the water's edge. Soon the battle was joined and the ISIS soldiers, who were caught sleeping, quickly recovered and began fighting back with heavy fire.

Blackhawk gunships and F-22 fighters roared over the city and hit the main centers of the ISIS forces. They were able to destroy all the tanks, most of the other vehicles, and gun down hundreds of scurrying ISIS soldiers.

The Swiss paratroopers came down close to the oil refinery. When they landed, enemy soldiers immediately engaged them. Some of the paratroopers died before they even reached the ground. It was obvious to Cody, watching from the Huey, the refinery had heavy defenses, more than expected.

He had the helicopter land on a bluff overlooking the refinery. The entire compliment was out of the ship in seconds, and the helicopter flew off. Cody plopped down in heavy grass. His Ghillie suit made him and the rest of the Swiss special forces, also wearing Ghillie suits, effectively invisible. The pope had on a Ghillie suit as well.

"Range," said Cody to one of the Swiss spotters.

"To the outer fence, 550 meters. Our two companies are pinned down along a line at the fence."

Cody pulled out his Timberwolf. The pope had a Glock 17 with a 100 round magazine. He also had a pair of high-powered binoculars to see the action and to serve as a lookout for Cody. He sighted through the scope and saw ISIS fighters setting up mortars to shoot at the Swiss. He quickly fired at two of the mortar positions and took down all their personnel. Then he scanned the rest of the field and found many ISIS fighters moving to attack the Swiss, who had just broken through the fence and were now inside the compound and dropping Satan's soldiers on their own.

The Timberwolf continued to fire. Cody reloaded his magazine often. His targets were the ISIS soldiers attempting to flank the Swiss and get them into a crossfire. The Pope watched through the high-powered binoculars, fitted with a night scope, as was Cody's Timberwolf. In the dark, the Pope watched with amazement as one enemy soldier after another went down, mostly with headshots that blew their brains in all directions, from Cody's deadly sniper rifle. The Swiss Special Forces on the bluff, were also now firing, and men were falling all over the field in front of the refinery.

When the Swiss Special Forces gained the advantage, they moved quickly toward the heart of the refinery. Clearly, ISIS fighters would blow up the refinery rather than allow it to fall into Crusader hands.

Cody shifted his sights to the refinery itself and spotted men trying to get explosives attached to vital parts of the refinery. The Timberwolf began barking again, and the saboteurs went down. With the way cleared, the Swiss companies rapidly moved into the refinery and took out the remainder of the ISIS force guarding the refinery.

Suddenly, the sound of gunfire stopped. The efficient Swiss had overrun and captured the refinery intact.

"Is that it?" asked the pope.

Don't think so," said Cody. "ISIS will send reinforcements to try and take back the refinery or at least destroy it." He scanned the main road leading to the refinery with his riflescope. It was empty for now. He was certain Charlie's assault was well underway and in contact with ISIS fighters. However, Cody knew the command center of ISIS would know about his attack and detach a force for the refinery eventually.

They had lain in their position for about an hour and the pope was beginning to fidget. The Ghillie suit was hot and uncomfortable, and he was unused to lying on bare ground. Cody reached over, and put his hand of the pope's shoulder and mumbled to him in German. "Stay as quiet as you can, Robert. This is the real deal and we're sure to see a counterattack."

"Sorry," said the pope, also in German, "I know you went all through this before we left, but this is hard, and I have to admit I'm scared."

"Me too," said Cody.

"That's seems hard to believe."

"Trust me. I'm scared to death every time. Maybe that's why I lived so long."

"I have to pee," said the pope.

"Just go," said Cody, "it'll wash out."

The assault on Bahji was brutal. In the dark, the night scopes of the Crusaders allowed them to spot many targets and to break up massed attacks ISIS was trying to form. The pincers attack from the east and west caught ISIS by surprise. Charlie's decision to avoid the main road was correct, and avoided heavy mines and bobby traps. By flanking the city from the sides, which were the least defended, the Peshmerga and Swiss penetrated almost to the city's central plaza. Here the resistance became the greatest and the Crusaders often found themselves in individual fights with ISIS soldiers, who were no match for them.

As day dawned, the Crusaders found many of the ISIS had managed to hide. As the coalition went by, they came out with RPGs, grenades and heavy assault weapons. It became a street-by-street fight, and then a house-to-house clash. Rico's Timberwolf and those of his team of shooters blasted away at targets from long range, and provided overhead cover for the advancing troops.

Blackhawk gunships, armed with rapid-fire guns, poured thousands of rounds into parts of the city before Swiss and Peshmerga moved in to clear each sector.

The largest skirmishes came at and around the big power plant and the main train station. ISIS mounted a stiff defense at both those locations. The Crusaders had them surrounded, however, and the numbers of the enemy were dropping fast.

Back at the refinery, Cody used his binoculars to scan the road. Apparently, at least some of the ISIS command and control was still functioning, because by mid-morning he spotted at least five trucks, full of soldiers and two pickups with 50 caliber machine guns mounted in the back, racing toward the front gate.

Cody radioed the Swiss commander to alert him to the new threat approaching. The Swiss commander quickly disbursed his troops to defensive positions inside the refinery compound. Cody also radioed the air cover and two of the Blackhawks detached from the main city and came toward the refinery.

At maximum range, Cody took a bead on the pickups with the deadly machine guns. His first shot missed, but his second shot hit the gunner in the back of the pickup right in his face. Cody switched to the second pickup coming behind. He took a breath and waited more patiently for this truck to come into range. His shot hit the gunner in the throat and decapitated him.

The Blackhawks were now on station and pouring fire into the troop transports. Three of them exploded. However, two more reached the perimeter fence and smashed through it, turning to each side where black-shirted ISIS fighters came pouring out. The Swiss companies now began shooting at these groups. Most of them went down, but Cody shot one man with a large satchel of explosives headed into the refinery to set off his charge. He spotted another sapper trying to do the same. He was using all the cover he could, moving in spurts from one defensive position to another. Cody was finally able to catch him in the open for just a few seconds and his shot set off the satchel of explosives the man was carrying. He hoped the explosion was not close to anything vital.

The battle for Bahji was still going on the next day. Charlie had not slept all night, constantly coordinating his combined forces against ISIS strongpoints. Casualty reports coming in said the Crusaders had 500 dead and about the same number wounded. The estimates of ISIS dead were 7,000.

Charlie knew the battle was over when a convoy of trucks, SUVs, and other vehicles started racing south, out of Bahji. He called the air cover commander who confirmed the information.

"Is there one or two vehicles better than the rest?" he asked.

"Roger, two of the cars in the center of the convoy are black Range Rovers," said the air commander.

"Have your Blackhawks take out all the vehicles in the convoy except those two. I think the ISIS leaders are in them. We need to capture them, if possible."

The Blackhawks and at least two F-22's went to work on the convoy. They destroyed all the vehicles trying to escape, except for the two command vehicles. Charlie dispatched two Bradley's to the fleeing convoy. They came up on the command cars and neatly shot out all their tires. The Range Rovers rolled to a stop. The men inside knew there was now no escape, so they exited the vehicles with hands up. The soldiers on the Bradley quickly took custody of the men, checked for weapons or explosives, handcuffed them, and threw them into the Bradleys. Altogether, they snatched almost a dozen of the senior ISIS commanders of Bahji.

Charlie came into the city center and got out of his Humvee. In one corner of the square were about a hundred captured ISIS fighters. Charlie nodded at his Peshmerga commander, and a group of his soldiers moved up to the trembling men. Then they opened fire and killed every one of them, just as Charlie had ordered. No prisoners, no quarter, all ISIS fighters faced a death sentence.

For the next several days, the Peshmerga and Swiss swept the city, finding ISIS fighters, hiding in houses and backstreets.

The people of Bahji crept out of their homes and hiding places, jubilant at their rescue. Life was very hard in Bahji when ISIS moved in, and many, many innocent people had died. The population pointed out ISIS soldiers who had shed their uniforms for common clothing and were attempting to hide in the crowds. The people of Bahji cheered as these final few were marched to a nearby wall and executed.

Cody and the pope flew on a Huey picked to the city center. Thousands of residents had assembled in the square to get a look at the Black Angel.

Cody climbed up to the top of some stairs on one of the buildings and spoke loudly, "I am the Black Angel. The Crusade has begun. All of you are now free from ISIS. Soon all the lands of Middle East will be free from ISIS. You can tell your children and grandchildren this was the first victory of the Crusade. Praise Allah! You are free!"

Chapter 13
The Crusade Begins

Erbil

"Ardishur! Ardishur! Ardishur!" The crowd kept chanting as Charlie stood on the back of a flatbed truck that moved slowly through Erbil. In front of him was a marching band. Behind was a long line of troop formations, Peshmerga and Swiss, marching proudly in unison. The entire city turned out to welcome home the heroes of Bahji.

The procession stopped in the grand plaza of the city and Charlie jumped down from the truck and up onto the reviewing stand to watch his soldiers marching by. On the stand with him were President Barzani and his wife Enwa, Cody, and Ashana, and Pope John Luke I.

President Barzani stepped forward to the microphone as thousands of flashes went off from the Press and joyful Kurdish people shouted.

"People of Kurdistan! My brothers and sisters, we are here today to celebrate our great victory in Bahji. Today, the people of Bahji are free from the oppression of ISIS and rejoice to Allah the first victory of the Holy Crusade."

"We are here to honor the leader of our forces, Hail to Ardishur!"

The hundreds of thousands of people in the plaza cheered and waved Kurdistani flags.

"We also are here today to celebrate our soldiers, the Peshmerga and the Holy Father's soldiers, the Swiss Special Forces and guards. Their bravery gave us this victory!

"The Crusade has begun, and already the evil forces of ISIS are feeling the sting of defeat and retribution for their sins against Allah!"

There was another thunderous roar from the huge crowd.

"Before we hear from Ardishur, I want you to listen to the words of Pope John Luke, whose steadfast leadership has brought us all together."

Pope John Luke stepped forward, still wearing battle fatigues and a purple beret. He spoke in Arabic to the crowd. "Dearly beloved brothers and sisters, Allah Akbar!"

When the crowd had yelled itself out again, the pope went on, "I speak the name of Allah with honor and respect. He is god, the true God. In my world, we speak his name in another way, but he is the same for all of us. The first commandment of our Creator is that we worship Him and no others. This is what is guiding us to victory over the evil minions of Satan in this Holy Crusade. It is the reason we are able to stand together today as one and serve our God with all our hearts, and all our strength.

"This Crusade is being led by the greatest General God ever given us. He is the man who commands the forces who will rewrite history and the boundaries of the Middle East, and give to the Kurdish people what you have been denied for so long ...a country of your own! Join me in triumph as I present The Black Angel."

Cody walked to the microphone and waved at the crowd. "People of Kurdistan. Today we add a new piece of territory to your country, the city of Bahji. They will join you as part of the new nation of Kurdistan. As we speak, the Peshmerga and Swiss soldiers and many, many of our relief workers are in Bahji, to protect them and to begin to heal the wounds caused by mindless barbarians who only took and never gave. Today we are giving aid and comfort, where before there was only butchery."

"I can tell you other parts of the Crusade are in motion. The Iranians and U.S. Marines have crossed the border of Iraq and are driving toward Bagdad, even as the American army is pouring out of Israel headed for Damascus.

"In the west, the Israeli army passed through the Golan Heights and occupied the Becca Valley in Lebanon. Their air force is striking at the heart of ISIS in Syria. All of our Crusaders fight in the name of Allah, God, Jehovah, different words, but the same God, who will stand with us and lead us to victory!

"Now let me introduce the man who gave us this great victory, the conqueror of Bahji, the man whose plans made it possible for us to take such a great stronghold of ISIS in only three days. He is my son, but he is your Ardishur!"

As Charlie walked past his Father to the microphone, Cody said, "You did good, kid. Try not to trip over your tongue when you open your mouth."

Charlie patted his father on the shoulder and shook his hand as he hugged him on the way to the microphone. He gave thanks to God. He praised his troops. He pledged more victories. He spoke and did not step on his tongue. The adoring masses seemed ready to follow this Christian wherever he led.

When the public celebration was over, the Crusade leaders returned to the Palace for more serious discussions. Cody led the talks in a large conference room, which included the pope, President Barzani, Charlie, and the two Colonels commanding the Swiss and Peshmerga forces.

"While we were busy taking Bahji," said Cody, "the rest of the coalition jumped off and began their operations. Ten Iranian brigades, supported by two brigades of U.S. Forces and three battalions of Marines moved across the border and worked south into the largely Shia regions south of Bagdad. As they moved, a large number of Shia militias joined them. They sense southern Iraq, including the biggest city of Basra, will be a haven for Shiite's when ISIS is defeated.

"The two American divisions moved north from Israel and are moving toward Damascus. We don't need to worry much about the sparsely settled desert of western Iraq. However, they are almost completely Sunni and there is evidence some of the Sunni tribal leaders are being pressured to throw in with ISIS. I think that unlikely. The pope's message was very clear. This is not a war with Islam. He got assurances from both Sunni and Shia clerics in Geneva that this was the message to all Muslims. He emphasized nothing would damage the coalition more, than a continuing conflict between Sunnis and Shias while we were busy taking out ISIS. From everything, I've learned in feedback the pope is getting, this is still the case.

"We're not seeing Sunni/Shia clashes occurring in other parts of the Muslim world. Saudi Arabia is quiet, as is Indonesia and India. My sense of this is that everyone is waiting to see what they have to gain and lose in land and resources when the war is won.

"If I can just return to Bahji for a moment," said Charlie. "We dealt ISIS a major defeat. They poured in reinforcements to hold the city and we wiped them out. We estimate they lost about 7,000 men. For us, we had 500 killed, and 1,000 wounded, but many of those casualties will recover and return to their units.

"More significantly," said Charlie, "we captured the biggest oil refinery in Iraq intact, the big power plant, and we now control the major rail hub between Mosul and Bagdad. This gives the Kurds an immense advantage. They will be able to use their oil reserves, refine them, and build pipelines into Turkey. The Turks and the Kurds may be longtime enemies, but if the Kurds don't provoke Turkey in the west, where they are the majority population, the Turks will come to realize that wealth from oil is a powerful incentive to find ways to get along with the Kurds."

"If I may add something to that," said Colonel Oman Koshiri, Commander of the Kurdish forces in Bahji. Our victory at Bahji was significant, that is true, but we weakened our defenses in Syria to get it. ISIS still has a very potent offense in many places, and Syria is one of those places."

Cody said, "Right now, two divisions of American soldiers driving toward Damascus. Since we have fewer forces in northern Syria, I think you should withdraw them to west of the Euphrates River, and take as many civilian Kurds with you as you go."

Koshiri said, "But we face the danger of Turkey invading Syria on its own. Turkey has a powerful military. Easily, they could have defeated ISIS in the early years. What kept them from doing so was the presence of Kurds in northern Syria. They didn't like ISIS, but they hated us more, and were willing to let ISIS wipe us out."

"In my opinion, Turkey will invade Syria," said Cody. "But when they do, I don't think they will target the Kurds."

Charlie said, "The conflict between the Kurds and Turkey is one of the most vicious battles in modern history, however things have changed lately. After a century of trying to eliminate, assimilate, and pacify the Kurds, and getting nowhere, Turkey has taken a more expedient method of dealing with their problem. The Kurds were included in the national vote for Parliament in the last election and now hold a 10% representation. The Public opinion in Turkey just wants the Kurdish problem to go away. There have even been rumblings inside their government to give the Kurds the independence they want. Most of the Kurdish population is located in southeast Turkey in about seven provinces."

"That's exactly right Charlie," said Cody. Was that part of your international studies at William and Mary?"

"Since the Kurds are largest minority population in the world without a country, it got a lot of attention."

Cody asked, "What do the Kurds have that Turkey wants?"

"Oil and natural gas," said Charlie. "In fact, that's already happening. When the Kurds took Kirkuk, they negotiated a pipeline to

Turkey. Now with Bahji in our hands, it would be possible to increase that dramatically."

Cody asked, "John Luke, were any Muslim clerics from Turkey at the Geneva conference?

"Several, I think," said the pope.

"Naturally, they joined in the fight with ISIS, along with the rest, but their support didn't include the Kurds."

"It never came up," said John Luke.

"Of course not," said Cody. "Well, I have the feeling Turkey will be part of the endgame before the end. I know you are worried about them now, but trust me on this and just get all the Kurds east of the river."

Koshiri said, "As you command, Sir. I've no idea what you plan, but we trust you."

"That's all I ask," said Cody. "John Luke, you and I need to go back to Iran."

"Can I hitch a ride with you?" asked Charlie.

"Sure," said Cody, "you're the hero of the day right now, but your command needs a little rest. A few days away won't matter much."

Cody called Manek Faroush in Tehran and asked if he could come visit him. He said the principal reason for him was to get to the front lines in Iraq to see how the Iranians were doing. He also mentioned the pope would come with him and open a new conversation.

"Charlie also begged a ride with me," said Cody, "I can't imagine what that's all about."

Manek laughed and said he would be glad to see them. Cody said they would be there tomorrow afternoon.

When the jet set down at a Tehran military base, Cody found it abuzz with activity. Troops were moving, military planes were taking off and landing. It was evidence of a full-scale operation underway. President Faroush, Kevi, and of course, Mitra were there to meet the plane.

Cody came down the steps and warmly greeted Manek and Kevi. "Mr. President, it's my honor to present the Pope of the Roman Catholic Church, John Luke the First." The two shook hands, and Manek welcomed the Pope to Iran, saying it was an historic occasion.

Charlie and Mitra had their own personal welcome. They fell into each other's arms and held on tightly before giving each other a huge kiss.

When they got back to the President's compound/home, they went directly to the residence and enjoyed some hot tea and biscuits.

"Our offensive into southern Iraq has proceeded very quickly," said Manek. "Having a Shia population made overpowering the thin ISIS forces an easy job. We've captured Basra and are using the airport there to bring more men and equipment in. I think ISIS figured out they were not going to be able to hold southern Iraq, so they pulled out, back to Bagdad. We basically, have the city surrounded."

"I need to get to your forward headquarters as soon as possible," said Cody. "The troops need to see the Black Angel on the scene."

"I thought as much," said Manek. "We'll fly you in there tomorrow morning."

"What about me," asked the pope?

"You need to come along also," said Cody. "There are lots of Americans who need to see you, and for you to tend to their religious needs."

"I guess that just leaves you and me," said Mitra.

"Yes, indeed, it does," said Kevi, "Manek and I need to talk to you both about your future."

"Looks like we have to face the music on the consequences of falling in love," said Charlie.

"You're a fine young man, Charlie," said Manek, "we could not have picked a better choice for Mitra, but there are complications to this union, even if I wasn't President of the country."

"I can appreciate that," said Charlie, but I don't get the feeling you're trying to stop it."

"Of course not," said Manek. "We only ask that your children know their heritage and the culture of Persia, and be given the choice to choose which life seems more important to them."

"I agree, sir," said Charlie, because this is what both Mitra and I believe as well. Our children will be aware of both worlds. We will raise them to honor and worship in both religions. We've no idea what a strange dichotomy that will present, but they will always have the choice."

"Then you have our blessing," said Manek, "and we will count you as a son."

❖

The following morning Cody and the pope, along with a security guard of Navy Seals, took off for Basra. When they arrived, there was a contingent of senior Iranian and American officers to greet them, and a very big crowd of soldiers from both countries. They cheered when Cody stepped off the plane and chanted "Black Angel, Black Angel!" Cody smiled and waved.

The Commanding General of all Crusader forces, an Iranian, stepped up and smartly saluted. Cody returned the salute sharply, and then the two smiled and shook hands.

"We are very happy you're here," said the General, "as you can see, it's very good for morale. We are also eager to go over some operational plans with you."

"That's why I'm here, General," said Cody. "How about I go over and meet some of our men?"

The General and his staff followed Cody to the barricade lines. When the troops saw him coming, they pressed for better positions against the barricades in hopes of shaking the hand, or just touching The Black Angel. There was a lot of jostling between Iranian and American troops, but nobody was mad at anyone for wanting his chance.

Cody worked the ropes for over an hour, shaking hands, chatting with Iranians in Farsi, and Americans in English. He got laughs, cheers, and people were actually on their hands and knees, trying to reach under the crowd to touch The Black Angel.

The pope also got into the act. Many didn't recognize him in battle fatigues and wearing a Glock on his hip, but soon the word spread who was among them. Soldiers, Christians and Muslims crowded about him. He was the man who was giving them the opportunity to right wrongs, to heal and unify all creeds, all religions. Where Cody was the swashbuckling Commander in Chief, the pope was the heart of the Crusade.

"I must say," said the General when they arrived at the Ops Center, "you two do know how to inspire men. We are very fortunate to have you."

"Why General," said Cody, "you're the one doing the fighting, making the split-second decisions that mean lives saved, battles won. It is us who salute you, sir."

"Most gracious," said the General, "However, sir, may I point out we are following, almost exactly, the tactical battle plans you wrote months ago. I, all of us, just marvel as we approach an objective and apply your tactics. They work."

"Well General, all of that is about to come to end soon, and then we're all going to have to bear down and figure it out," Cody said firmly.

The General asked, "Can you explain more fully?"

"Your occupation of southern Iraq was facilitated by the willing support of a largely Shia population. To your credit, you and your officers here around the table have followed the most important part of my plan to the letter. There is still a considerable Sunni population here in the south. We made sure there was a smooth transition of government operations into your after-action policies. We instructed you to allow no blood feuds to break out between Sunni and Shia, and the Sunni minority be allowed to continue their lives with the least amount of prejudice, or discrimination.

"Admittedly, some ugly incidents have happened, such as the bombing of several Shiite Mosques. But there was no wholesale retaliation. Your police and military police conducted proper investigations and made some arrests. The most important principle of this war is to understand we are fighting in the name of Allah, and God, against evil. This is not a war of Shia against Sunni, or Muslim against Christianity, or of either against the Jews. You could not have accomplished this without explaining to the people what the Crusade is doing. It looks as if you've done a good job."

The General replied, "In actuality, it turned out to be the Sunnis who stopped most of the violence. When Shias did not respond to Sunni attacks, and we explained that even though we were the majority in this part of Iraq, it didn't mean Sunnis would bear discrimination. After all, Shias are the ones who were the victims of Sunni oppression for centuries. We said we understood what a horrible thing that was, and were not going to repeat the same mistake. It was a concept that was difficult for the Sunnis to understand, but in the face of our moderation, it proved to be successful."

"Exactly what we want," said Cody. "Now we have to do the same thing in Bagdad, the capital of the ISIS Caliphate. What we don't want is a slaughter of a lot on innocent Sunnis or Shias in Bagdad. What we do want is to remove ISIS from control of the city. They have a number of strongpoints, which we intend to attack and destroy. However, Bagdad is a large, cosmopolitan city, and the majority of its residents have not supported the medieval kind of Islamic society ISIS has imposed on them. The incredibly strict forms of Sharia Law they are using with no music, no entertainment, no public gatherings, and the brutal manner in which they have enforced their will is not popular at all. The Shia population has suffered the most, but all other religious practices not fitting the ISIS mold are producing atrocities on all other religions. In short, we believe Bagdad is ready for a popular uprising.

"Currently we have the entire city surrounded with Crusader troops. ISIS remains trapped in its own capital. All that is getting in is food, water, medical supplies and electricity. Most likely, ISIS will move to the largest Shia part of the city, take it hostage and threaten to kill them all, if we don't stop our blockade.

"Sadr City is the biggest Shia community. Move your army to that part of Bagdad on the east side of the Tigris River, and attack. My hope is it will prevent the blanket killing of Shias. Once we control that part of Bagdad, we'll drop millions of leaflets telling the Sunnis to throw off ISIS control, or at least evacuate to Sadr City, where they will receive the same fair and equal treatment Sunnis in southern Iraq have received."

"There will still be a lot of Shia deaths as we enter Sadr City," said the General.

"I have an additional plan to disorganize and confuse ISIS," said Cody. "We've already bombed the airport and made it unusable for ISIS. We're going to conduct a much bigger airstrike, using cruise missiles and other high-tech smart bombs, to hit the principal command and control centers of ISIS in Bagdad. I think ISIS will be so busy trying to save their own skins their orders to the rank and file troops will be disrupted or not delivered at all."

"Will these airstrikes occur before our assault?" asked the General.

"Just before," said Cody, "and right after we drop more leaflets telling the people of Bagdad to get under cover, and stay away from the ISIS centers."

The General asked, "You actually believe your leaflet campaign will work?"

"Not completely," said Cody, "We are also running an extensive campaign of radio and television announcements to reach the maximum number of people.

"Also, we've been slipping a lot of Crusaders into Bagdad for the past month. Most of them are Muslim clerics. Some of them were actually in Geneva when the Crusade began. They are conducting a whisper campaign to tell the people and former leaders in Bagdad, what's about to happen. Their job is to mobilize popular uprisings all over Bagdad to inspire the population to act. Most people don't know what to do in a crisis until someone tells them. Our corps of conspirators is already reporting a good deal of success."

"You seem to have thought of everything," said the General, "What's the timeline on this operation?"

"I have two more places to go before we launch everything we've got. Give me a couple of weeks. In the meantime, continue your program of establishing an all Arab, Shia government in southern Iraq."

The Iranian General said, "We will await your orders to carry out our part of the mission."

The next stop for Cody was the forward base of the American Command, comprised of the six brigades of the 82nd and 101st airborne, brigades from England, France, Italy, Germany, and Australia, plus three battalions of Marines. This force was the biggest and had seen some of the heaviest fighting. They were at maximum alert. They were currently occupying Damascus International Airport as their main base.

Cody's operational plan for this Crusader army raised many eyebrows when he proposed it. With Israel as a part of the coalition, Cody decided to use the geography of the region to get a strait shot at Syria. Israel had held the original Syrian territory, the Golan Heights, for many years. The distance from the Golan Heights to Damascus was only a few hours' drive.

His reasoning was to have the American and other Western nations, stage in Israel itself, and then move north to Damascus, the other major strongpoint of ISIS, besides Bagdad.

When the army was assembled, and conducted unified training operations to make them a single command, Cody had them storm through the Golan Heights and directly to Damascus. ISIS was entrenched in the city, and had been, for some years, following their overthrow of the Assad Regime. A substantial part of their force was in Damascus and ruled over most of Syria from this base. The only part of the country they had not been able to capture was the Kurdish held lands in the northwest portion of the country.

The Israeli army followed the coalition forces and took control of the big Becca Valley in Lebanon. Their air force pounded ISIS targets in and around Damascus for weeks.

Exactly like Bagdad, the forward ISIS units in Damascus were surrounded and cut off. The Crusader army slowly tightened the circle, taking suburbs of the city and engaging in furious fighting on a street-by-street and house-by-house operation. Small units of ISIS fighters were constantly on the move with heavy weapons, in hopes of isolating Crusader forces also in smaller groups. The tactic worked part of the time, and Crusader casualties were mounting. However, ISIS was losing a lot more men. It was a never-ending series of attacks and counter attacks. Slowly, the assault turned in the favor of the Crusaders and the hard core of ISIS was now concentrated near the center of the city.

It was into this maelstrom that Cody and the pope flew, landing at the Damascus Airport headquarters.

Major General Francis Gordon was in command. General Gordon and his entire staff where there to welcome the Crusade commander. Across the tarmac, behind barricades were hundreds of soldiers who had gathered, as in Basra to get a personal look at the legendary Black Angel and the Pope.

Cody returned General Gordon's snappy salute and saluted the rest of the staff. Gordon walked up and said quietly, "Great to see you again, Cody. I'm sure you remember me from Texas when we took out the Iranians and snatched their bombs. I was in command of the Special Forces troops that night. I was only a Captain in those days, but that mission put me on a fast track that ended me up in this awful place."

"I do remember," said Cody, "as I recall they call you 'Flash' Gordon. I'll bet that annoys you as much as my handle."

"You're right about that," said Gordon, "that's why I used your real name. I'm one of the few who know it, and I won't use it again."

"I'll try to never call you 'Flash'," laughed Cody. "May I introduce Pope John Luke?"

"It's a great honor to meet you Your Holiness. I'm a Catholic boy myself and I sure have been proud of how you managed to put this coalition together."

"Many thanks," said John Luke, "it's always good to meet a fellow of the faith."

As before, the pope and Cody made their way to the barricade lines set up to restrain the soldiers. They took their time moving up and down the lines, talking to soldiers, hearing about their hometowns, and something of their background. As usual, all the troops were astounded that Cody was able to call up from his prodigious memory, interesting tidbits, about the hometowns of the Americans. The pope blessed many soldiers.

Cody and the pope were both gratified the troops on the ground seemed to have a very clear idea of their mission and the reasons they were fighting. Their restraint when engaging Sunni militants soon brought a cease-fire for Christian and Muslim forces, and both had now turned on ISIS.

There were other engagements going on around the world. Navy Seal Teams, Rangers, British SAS, and groups from other countries were dropping into all the countries where ISIS had a presence. Often with the cooperation of the national governments, ISIS strongholds and influence was eroding. A combined force from Nigeria and Chad moved into the ISIS controlled parts of their countries and engaged in fierce battles.

Without weapons resupply, money, and no popular support from local peoples because of the barrage of press releases pouring out of a front operation of the Catholic Church, the entire infrastructure of ISIS began to crumble. Only in their stronghold, cities of Damascus and Bagdad were they still able to fight.

The final and most critical phase of the Crusade was about to get underway.

Chapter 14
Taken By the Enemy

Ankara, Turkey

President Carson Palmer was welcomed to Turkey with the usual fanfare and pomp. He was there to meet with the current leader, Prime Minister Farid Sensek. Officially, he was there to discuss a new trade alliance and to discuss Turkey's relationship with NATO. Unofficially, his agenda was far more extensive.

Sensek was a western educated, cosmopolitan leader, known for his quick mind and his ability to get things done in a country that had a thousand special interests. He was in the group that greeted Palmer as he came down the stairs of Air Force 1. The two had met before in Washington to discuss common issues and problems between the two nominal allies. He liked Palmer for his brilliant mind, and willingness to take decisive action.

"Welcome, Mr. President," said Sensek in perfect English, "I hope your visit to Turkey will be an enjoyable and useful event."

"Thank you, Prime Minister," said Palmer, "It's always good for two nations with many common interests to meet."

There was probably more press in the welcoming group than spectators. Palmer didn't mind a bit. He waved at the crowd and got into a limousine with Sensek that drove off to the official residence of the Prime Minister.

After an aide showed him to in his room, the President, pulled out a thick pile of papers from his briefcase, and reviewed them. There was an email from Cody, which said, "I'll be there tomorrow afternoon. Keep talking to him about how poor their oil reserves are and the continuing strife with the Kurds."

Soon the aide was back to escort the President to the formal photo session with the press and then to sit down for talks. Palmer came into a big room with a lot of press. He went through the ritual of shaking hands with the Prime Minister, and speaking in vague generalities about the purpose of the President's visit. When the photo session was over, Sensek led the President into his private office where they sat on soft couches facing each other.

Sensek got right to the point, "Since the Crusade began we've found our relations with the Kurds have been the quietest in decades. They're so busy fighting and grabbing territory in Iraq, they aren't thinking about us at all. One of the issues that concern me is that the United States has so heavily armed the Kurds, we are afraid, when ISIS is defeated we will face a very dangerous situation."

"Part of my reason for being here is to assure you when the Crusade if over, your relationship with the Kurds will be completely different. If I may say so, Prime Minister, your country is paranoid on how threatening the Kurds are. You can't imagine any other scenarios. The truth is your country could end up being one of the biggest winners in this struggle with ISIS."

"I'm afraid I don't understand you, Mr. President," said Sensek.

"How do you feel about the Kurds now controlling a full 10% of the votes in your parliament"?

"Honestly, it makes our parliament somewhat dysfunctional. We are constantly forced to deal with Kurdish issues."

"That's what I thought," said Palmer. "If I might move to another major issue for Turkey, I know the big oil companies have pulled out of their search for oil in the Black Sea. They've been in there for three years and have come up with nothing."

"We had hopes of finding oil reserves in the Black Sea to provide us more independence on importing foreign oil. It was disappointing."

"To make matters worse, your efforts to find oil in the Aegean Sea have proved more promising, but have put you in direct conflict with Greece over who has the rights to drill for the reserves."

"You are unusually well informed on our affairs, Mr. President," said Sensek, "but what does any of this have to do with the Crusade you mentioned earlier?"

"Because a solution to your two main problems could be resolved tomorrow when the Black Angel arrives in Ankara."

"The Black Angel is coming here?" said Sensek. His voice almost seemed to quiver as he said it. "At the present time he is the single biggest fact in the Middle East. His military maneuvers are occurring with incredible speed, and they're working. ISIS seems doomed. If he wants to talk to me, he wants something. It's a frightening prospect."

"Don't let the image of this man intimidate you," said Palmer, "I just said he thinks he can solve your two biggest problems. I've worked with him a great deal in the last few months, and I can tell you I sincerely trust his judgement when it comes to strategic maneuvers."

"When he's finished with us, our country will never be the same," moaned Sensek.

"When he's finished, the entire Middle East will never be the same," said Palmer, "maybe the whole world."

"Is this one man that important?" asked Sensek.

"His planning, strategies, and clear results with an impossible coalition have made him that important," said Palmer.

"And you've come all the way to Ankara to let this modern day Alexander the Great loose on me!"

Palmer laughed at Sensek's obvious overstatement of Cody's role in the war with ISIS, "You're making entirely too much of his image. The Black Angel is not a fire-breathing dragon, but rather a pragmatic and well-grounded man with deeply held religious beliefs. He told me just the other day that the Turkish military could have beaten ISIS easily without any help by him at all."

"Even if that is true, I would never have been able to take the political risks. The Black Angel has no such limitations."

"He's very nervous over this meeting with you. He says you're the key to making everything work."

"Do you have anything you can tell me about what he's going to say?" asked Sensek.

"Only in the most general terms," said Palmer. "I will share with you the email he sent me." The President pulled the email out of his portfolio and handed it to Sensek, who read it and shook his head.

"You've done exactly as he asked."

"I guess we'll both just sit back and watch the show tomorrow."

❖

The following day, a jet set down in Ankara. Both President Palmer and Prime Minister Sensek stood a little uneasily as the plane came to a stop on the tarmac. Inside the plane, an equally uneasy Cody, puffed his cheeks and headed for the stairs. As he exited the plane, he saw Carson Palmer grinning at him. Next to Palmer was Prime Minister Sensek, with a grim look on his face.

Nevertheless, Sensek walked forward and smiled thinly.

"Welcome to Turkey. Your arrival here is a surprise for me."

"You were expecting the big, bad Black Angel, but the truth is, Farid, I'm not really that person. My name is Cody Frost, and I've come with some ideas I think will solve a bunch of your problems as a country. I ask you, in all sincerity, to let me try to convince you my motives are truly noble."

Sensek did not know what to say. When Cody had come off the plane, he looked like he had just stepped off the battlefield. His fatigues seemed well used, and he had a Glock strapped to his leg. He was tall, and glowed with charisma. He was exactly what Sensek expected, a very terrifying warrior. Now he was standing in front of the man, who had dissolved into a perfectly normal person, calling him by his first name and introducing himself with his real name. He was speaking to him in an almost pleading manner. Sensek felt his shoulders relax, and put out his hand. "Nothing like I expected," he said shaking Cody's hand with real warmth.

"I speak several languages," said Cody, "but Turkish is not one of them, would you feel more comfortable with Arabic, Farsi, Italian, French, Spanish, or German?"

"Plain English is perfect for me. I had a Western education," said Sensek.

"Of course," said Cody, "you did your undergraduate studies at Yale, and then took your Masters at Oxford in England. You're an expert in political studies, international relations, and agriculture. If that includes gardening, you and I are kindred spirits."

Sensek laughed in spite of himself, "It does. It's nice to meet a fellow who suffers from dirt fever."

Cody laughed too, "I tell you, when I'm not out squishing the bad guys, there's nothing I like better than a day in my garden. Allah, forgive me, I'm sinfully proud of my garden at home."

Sensek laughed again, "I hope I have a chance to show you my garden."

Cody slapped him on the shoulder, and said, "I'll look forward to that."

President Palmer was a fascinated observer to this exchange. Cody was always full of surprises. In less than a minute he'd managed to disarm Sensek, calm his nerves, make himself a brother in something totally unassociated with serious business, and even throw in a Muslim prayer.

The three of them walked together to a waiting limousine, as if they had just greeted old friends.

An hour after arriving at the official residence of the Prime Minister, and posing for a huge crowd of press, Sensek, Palmer and Cody retreated to the quiet of Sensek's office.

"President Palmer and I were here yesterday, and when I heard the Black Angel was coming to see me, I had to catch my breath. I didn't sleep well last night worrying about it. I must say, I don't feel at all apprehensive, now I've met you in person."

"Carson probably felt the same way the first time we met," said Cody. "Now we're good friends and loyal partners. He calls me Cody, and you should too, Farid. It's really silly to preface everything by reminding each other who we are."

Sensek asked, "But aren't you here to talk about very serious matters?"

"Even more so," said Cody, "When people sit in the presence of God to discuss life-changing decisions, He never honors posturing from His children."

"Well spoken," said Sensek, "alright, Cody, why don't you tell me why you're here?"

"Actually, Carson has already set the table for us. Turkey is a strong country with many good things going for you. You are among the world's leading producers of agricultural products; textiles; motor vehicles, ships, and other transportation equipment; construction materials; consumer electronics and home appliances. Your economy is one of the strongest is the world."

"Carson told me to expect you to bring a remarkable insight and intelligence to our meeting," said Farid. "You are better informed than he is."

"I could go on for ten minutes about your strengths," said Cody, "but I'm here to talk about the problems Carson mentioned. You are spending a good deal of money buying oil and you have a nagging problem with the Kurds."

"Are you telling me you intend to do something to improve our position in these areas?" asked Farid.

"Well, of course," said Cody, "I'm not here to go over old ground. In case you haven't noticed there's a war going on just south of you."

"One of the most unlikely coalitions in history," said Sensek. "The pope of the Catholic Church made the most inspirational speech I've ever seen. Somehow he was able to find common ground between Christians and Islam, and turn it into a modern Crusade to destroy the abomination that is ISIS."

President Palmer said, "For your information, Cody was directly involved in the writing of that speech, and the pope tasked Cody with finding a strategy that would defeat ISIS, and that's what he did. Then the pope had the brains to pick him as commander for the Crusader forces. He's not allied with any country, and smart enough to put together the strategic and tactical plans to make it work. Our Black Angel used his formidable reputation to put terror into ISIS and now will bring them to the brink of defeat."

"I've heard stories of ISIS soldiers turning and running just at the rumor the Black Angel was among the attacking forces," said Sensek.

"A lot more of that is truer than you would believe," said Palmer. "Our greatest fear is that Cody may find himself in mortal danger and risk getting killed or injured."

"Enough of this," said Cody. "Farid, I would like Turkey to join this Crusade."

"What possible reason would we have for doing that?"

"Just what I said before, it will solve your Kurd and oil problems."

"You're going to have to explain that to me," said Sensek.

Cody looked into Sensek's eyes and said, "I can guarantee the Kurds will withdraw from all political activities in Turkey."

"How would you do that?"

"Simple," said Cody, "the Kurds will no longer be a part of the country. All you have to do is to cede your seven eastern provinces to the Kurds."

"That's preposterous!" said Sensek, "Turkey is not going to give away any of our country's territory."

"Even if you acquired more valuable land?" said Cody.

Sensek said, "I'm completely lost."

"I think that's understandable," said Cody. "Follow my reasoning. The political picture in the Middle East was the result of the actions of England and France at the end of World War I. They carved up the entire region with no consideration for the cultural, geographical, ethnic, or religious affiliations of anyone who lived in the Middle East.

It could never have worked. The rise of a radical form of Islam was inevitable. It happened in Iran, who attempted to upset the balance by developing nuclear weapons. I stopped that. However, the vacuum created by a weakened Iran, and an equally disrupted Iraq, produced the environment for ISIS to develop. A dozen years later, ISIS had conquered both Iraq and Syria."

Sensek replied, "I don't know of a single country in the world who thinks ISIS and their Islamic Caliphate is a legitimate political entity."

"There's no doubt in my mind ISIS is nearly defeated," said Cody, "the real issue requires no screw up of the endgame. We have to insure the Middle East is divided up this time along the correct lines."

Cody pulled out his phone and transferred the graphics on it to a big screen TV in Sensek's office. "This is how I see the way the Middle East should look after ISIS."

The graphics showed the Middle East in its current configuration.

"Since we are talking about Turkey," said Cody, let's begin there."

The graphic flowed and showed Turkey expanding to the south into Syria.

"The new borders of Turkey would look like this," said Cody. "You would annex northern Syria from the present border, along the Euphrates River and south to Lebanon, all the way to the city of Homs. What you get from this is approximately half the oil reserves of present Syria. You also get the off-shore territory where there is natural gas."

Sensek looked at the map with fierce concentration.

"This will be the new country of Kurdistan," said Cody.

The graphic showed Kurdistan running along the entire northern region of Iraq, as far south as Kirkuk, and Bahji, and west into Syria up to the Euphrates River. To the north, it enveloped the seven eastern provinces of Turkey.

"In this scenario, you are acquiring substantial oil reserves of your own and jettisoning the hill country of the Kurds in the east. This land is not particularly valuable in terms of agriculture, and especially oil. The Kurds then build more oil pipelines to Turkey and will deliver 20 million barrels of crude oil to you, every day for the next 25 years at 10% over the actual production and transport costs. Currently, worldwide oil prices are running about $75 dollars a barrel. This oil, you'll get for less than half of that."

"The Kurds would never agree to that," said Sensek.

"They already have," said Cody. "The Kurds are the largest ethnic group in the world with no country of their own. This agreement, signed as part of the larger Pan Middle East treaty for all countries, will receive the approval of the General Assembly of the United Nations."

"The Kurds also agree to withdraw from all political activities in Turkey, since they will no longer have a reason to do so."

"I must admit your plan is very seductive," said Sensek. "The only problem I see is actually occupying the northern half of Syria."

"Which is currently held by ISIS," said Cody. "We need you to join the Crusader coalition and destroy ISIS. Of course, while you are doing this, your armed forces will be under Crusader command, meaning me. After ISIS is gone, we expect you to respect the rights of other Muslims, Kurds, Christians, and all the other religious groups in the area. You must guarantee that all people currently living in the new Turkey have the religious freedom to follow as they choose. It's not much different from what you are already doing in your country, except for the Kurds."

Sensek said, "As commander in chief of the military, I could order an assault into Syria, tomorrow. However, all the other components of your plan would have to be approved by Parliament."

"I know that," said Cody, "you should order your troops into action immediately. I doubt many of your generals will disagree. In fact, I know a lot of them have urged you to take this action for a long time."

"That's true," said Sensek.

"In the meantime, call a special session of Parliament and give them this deal. The Kurds in Parliament will ratify what I've told you about what Kurdistan is prepared to offer. I actually think this is an offer you can't refuse."

President Palmer was silent through Cody's presentation, now he spoke up, "The United States is prepared to offer you any assistance you may need in this transitional period."

"Did you know what he was going to say?" asked Sensek.

"As I told you only in a general way, I've stopped trying to keep up with Cody's mind. He thinks on so many levels, most of us just try to keep up. You just got an example of that."

"Are you a gambling man, Cody?" asked Farid.

"Not really. I try to compute outcomes based on probabilities."

"That sounds like the same thing to me," said Sensek. "Based on your probabilities, what are the odds of me being able to pull this off?"

"The probability of you launching your army is almost a sure thing. The probability of your Parliament approving my plan is about 80%. The downside is the hatred many of your legislators have for the Kurds, and even though the deal is a slam-dunk, they could reject your proposal because they don't want the Kurds to have a victory. They would go on hating and killing them out of pure spite."

"How do I shorten the odds?"

"Take the attitude of 'good riddance', then bear down on all the money you're going to make. If that doesn't bring out a chance for grabbing some of the goodies for themselves, then I've misjudged this entire proposal."

"Small chance of that," said Sensek. He looked again at the map of the new Turkey, and thought of the oil fields, and the gusher of cheap oil that would pour into the country.

"You really are as important as Carson says you are. I was a skeptic an hour ago, and now I regard you as a friend and ally."

"You have three brigades on the border with Syria, just waiting for an excuse to attack ISIS. All it will take is one phone call from you to get them moving."

"I've no idea how you know that," said Sensek, "but you're right, and I'll make the call."

Cody hung around for a few days to make sure his scheme was accepted. He also had several conversations with the commander of the Turkish forces and provided him with a battle plan to facilitate the invasion and save innocent lives. The Turkish Generals were as impressed with Cody as Sensek. They launched their operation and found themselves in immediate contact with ISIS forces. It was bloody business, but the Turks were advancing toward Aleppo and Raqqa. Sensek did a masterful job with the Turkish Parliament and found strong support among all political parties. The Kurdish representatives assured Parliament the offer Cody made was legitimate.

With this final piece of the puzzle in place, Cody contacted all the Crusader force commanders and set them to moving forward with the major operation. The Kurds attacked from the north. The Iranians and

Americans began their assault on Bagdad. The American divisions moved forward to duplicate the same strategy delivered in Bagdad with dropped leaflets, internet messages, and public broadcasts on all major media outlets, in Damascus.

"The Black Angel is once more on the move," said Sensek. "I've enjoyed your time here and a chance to know you better. I appreciate you letting me listen in to your calls. It gave me a much better understanding of the size and scope of the Crusade."

"No problem, Farid, you used the information to knock heads together in Parliament. I'm sure you won't have any more problems in that regard from now on."

"I don't understand why you didn't make a personal appearance yourself," said Farid.

"In the first place," said Cody, "you didn't need my help. In the second place, remember your feelings when I arrived here. Did the larger than life figure who stepped off the plane turn out to be true?"

"Not at all," said Farid, "It's just your reputation proceeded you and made me feel a little afraid."

"Then you've answered your own question," said Cody. "If I had swaggered into your Parliament, they would have felt the same way, and it wouldn't have helped. Just the opposite I think. It was better for me to hang around your place, lay low, and let you steal the show."

"No doubt my personal stock has risen somewhat," said Farid, "I got to show a way to solve our Kurd problem, while the same people were cheering me on, and I delivered a windfall of new revenue to the country."

"Allah has a plan for all our lives."

"You always use that term, Cody, when I know you're Christian."

"Would you rather I say 'God'? That's how we were able to put this Crusade together. God is God, no matter what name you use. The only people who don't believe that are the men of ISIS, and they are dying by the thousands."

"Praise the Lord," said Farid.

"That's the spirit, my friend."

"Have you got everything?" asked Farid.

Cody picked up his bag, "I travel light."

"The motorcade is waiting to take you to the airport. If it were me, I would have taken a helicopter to the airport, or at least traveled with three or four cars and a police escort."

"As far as I know, nobody knows I'm here, except you," said Cody. "Besides, I think we're taking the right precautions leaving in the middle of the night, with other identical SUVs going out at the same time, but in several different directions. It's a ploy I've used often."

"The staff certainly knows you're here," said Farid. "Let's hope there are no covert agents hidden among them."

"If that were the case, they would have shot both of us the first night," smiled Cody.

He held out his hand to say goodbye to Sensek. "I'm afraid that's not going to quite do it." Farid hugged Cody. They both smiled and Cody went out the side door to the waiting SUVs.

The five SUVs drove out the front gate and went in five different directions. An armed soldier drove Cody's SUV. There were three other men in the car, heavily armed. Cody tried to relax as he thought of the several stops on his itinerary to all the forward bases of the coalition. He had heard that night from all of them, Operation Desert Fire, was underway.

As they turned onto the main road to the airport, Cody expected there to be little or no traffic. However, there were two cars tailing behind. He had not noticed when they had started following.

"Anybody here speak English?" Cody asked.

Two of the men spoke back to him in English.

"I think we're being followed. We could be driving into an ambush. Everybody get out your weapons and be ready."

All the men in the car pulled out their automatic weapons and chambered a round.

Directly ahead was a side road that merged onto the airport road. As they approached it, two big SUVs pulled out and screeched in front of Cody's car. The two cars from behind sped up and blocked the way.

"This is the real deal, men!" shouted Cody. "Get on your radio to your headquarters and tell them what's happening. Crash into that car on the left as soon as we hit it, blast the car and kill whoever is in it, then we all will hit the ground and use both cars as shields to shoot at the other cars!"

The driver accelerated and smashed into the black SUV on the left side of the road. Cody was out of the car before anyone else, and started shooting into the SUV. There were four men in it, and Cody shot them all.

The Turkish soldiers were right behind Cody, and dashed around to the other side of the smashed SUV and opened fire on the three carloads of men who were jumping out of their own vehicles. There were at least 15 men in the remaining three cars and they began firing the second they got out. One of the Turkish soldiers took a shot in the head and fell dead at Cody's feet. Cody grabbed the automatic weapon and rushed to the cover of the SUV.

Furious gunfire erupted from both sides. The Turkish soldiers were special ops men, so they were effective in taking down targets. Cody was steadily firing and men were falling. The ambushers moved closer and closer to the cover of the SUV and two more Turks went down, including the driver. Cody was now alone with at least six men still moving in on him. He shot two more, and then they were on him.

Cody fought, hand to hand, as he had never fought before, but suddenly he felt the shock of a Taser hit him in the chest and fell to his knees. The remaining four men moved quickly to tie and gag Cody and drag him to the undamaged SUV. They threw him violently into the rear. One of the men brought out a hypodermic needle while the other three men held him. Cody felt the needle jammed into his neck, then felt consciousness falling away from him.

The last thing he heard before passing out was one of the men saying in Arabic. "We have him. Call it in."

The SUV roared off into the night and was soon out of sight.

The Black Angel was alive, but taken by the enemy.

Chapter 15
Debate and Resistance

Farid Sensek was just getting ready to go to bed when his phone rang. It was the military headquarters calling.

"Prime Minister, the Black Angel's car was ambushed on the way to the airport. We got a call on the radio about the attack. We had troops at the scene in minutes. We found all our special forces detail dead, and 14 other unidentified men. None of the dead is the Black Angel. We can only assume he's been captured."

"Order the borders sealed immediately!" said Sensek. "I want a perimeter set up 20 miles from the ambush! Get every helicopter we have in the air five minutes ago! Find that vehicle!"

The news about the Black Angel's kidnapping sent shock waves around the world.

In the Vatican, the phone in Ashana and Rosy's apartment rang just before dawn. It was the pope on the phone. He broke the news to Ashana, and said every resource in Turkey was part of the search, the borders were sealed, checkpoints set up on every road, and dozens of helicopters were in the air. He said regretfully, "The location of the ambush was on the main road to the airport, where there's no surveillance video.

"Cody's strategic plan to defeat and decimate ISIS is working," said the pope. "In fact, there's news that ISIS fighters are running away, deserting their posts. Only a few strongholds remain in Bagdad and Damascus, and even those are squeezed tighter and tighter every day. It would be a tragedy, on the eve of victory, that the man responsible for it all should be lost."

"It would be a tragedy if I lost my husband and Charlie and Rosy lost their father," snapped Ashana.

"I'm sorry, Ashana," said John Luke, "I should have thought of the personal part of this first. I can assure you a worldwide effort is being made to find Cody."

"Have we heard anything from ISIS?" asked Ashana.

"Nothing," said the pope. "I don't know if that's good or bad."

"I need to call Charlie," said Ashana. "Rosy is still asleep. I'm not looking forward to waking her up, but I can tell you she will be very angry. Look for her down in Ops within the hour scouring over everything that will give her a clue about finding her dad."

"I'll keep you informed," said the pope. "Try to be calm Ashana, the Lord is with Cody, and he's been in situations like this before."

Ashana was right about Rosy. After having a good cry and a prayer for Cody's safe return, she raged through rooms, and in less than an hour was in the Ops Center sifting through anything that might provide the slightest clue to find her father.

Her first step was to check all satellite imagery. Ankara, Turkey was not a hotbed of surveillance, but the nearby military base attracted more attention. Rosy scanned the images in detail, for 24 hours prior to ambush. The pictures were not great, being at the edge of the imagery scan, but with video enhancement, Rosy was able to locate a group of men standing beside two SUVs at the road intersection where the attack took place, on the day of the trap. The resolution was not good enough to identify any individuals, but the type and make of vehicles was possible. More importantly, the rear bumper of one SUV had damage. For the next 20 hours, Rosy searched for this vehicle in every satellite image of Ankara she could find.

She finally found another image of the SUV on the traffic surveillance videos in Ankara. From this, she was able to switch from one surveillance camera to another and follow the SUV around during the day.

As night was falling on the day of the ambush, Rosy saw the SUV parked at a cheap hotel in the outskirts of Ankara. Within an hour, three other vehicles pulled into the hotel parking lot. Two of them were local cars, the other a match for the black SUV with the damaged bumper. Several men went into the hotel.

When she first found the SUV, Rosy contacted the number she had for the Turkish intelligence agency. They told her to keep them informed on her progress. Now she called back and gave the intelligence contact the new information and the name of the hotel. Then she went back to follow all four target cars around the city. Her team of analysts in the Vatican Ops helped her with this and used city surveillance to try to keep up with where the cars were going.

A call came in for her, on a secure line. Turkish intelligence and police had raided the hotel and arrested one man. They were interrogating him as they spoke, and said they would call back if they were able to learn anything.

A breakthrough came several hours later when one of the Vatican analysts was able to spot one of the local cars stopping at another house to pick up four men. It drove to the residence of the Prime Minister and waited until the group of SUVs came out driving in different direction. The local car seemed to know which SUV Cody was in, and began to follow it. Soon, the other local car, also filled with men, joined it. Rosy lost them both when they drove out of town toward the airport, and out of city surveillance.

Rosy was exhausted. Her eyes hurt from looking at computer images. She sat back in her chair and closed her eyes, using the relaxation techniques her father had taught her. She actually dozed for about half an hour, when her phone rang and she was instantly awake. It was the Turkish intelligence officer.

"Rosy," said the man in good English, our interrogation of the man at the hotel reveals information we didn't know. Apparently, the man was the contact between ISIS and an informant inside the Prime Minister's residence. We got his identity and brought him in for interrogation. He says he knew the man at the hotel, and received a great deal of money for information about the departure of the Black Angel. He insists he did not know his acquaintance worked for ISIS and has no knowledge of the ambush. It looks like the employee at the Residence was just greedy for all that money. In any case, we don't think he knows more.

"The other man gave us more information. He admits he worked for ISIS, and arranged for the cars used in the trap. We were able to get one name from him, Anwar Ghazi. We have nothing on him, but you might with your better resources."

"Thanks," said Rosy, "we'll see what we have on him."

Rosy went over to her mother, who was reading the complete file of all known ISIS leaders and operatives. She had worked almost as long as Rosy.

"Mom," said Rosy, "do we have anything on a man named Anwar Ghazi?"

Ashana open a different file on her computer and put in the name. "Here he is," she said, "It says here he's a mid to upper level operative for ISIS. He's an Iraqi. His specialty is kidnappings and abductions. His last known location was in Raqqa, but that's several months old."

"I doubt he's there now," said Bishop Paglioni, who was working with the rest of the people in the Ops center for most of the time Ashana and Rosy were there.

He came over to them now. "The Turkish army took Aleppo, two days ago, and is now in Raqqa clearing the city."

"If his headquarters was in Raqqa," said Rosy, "That means ISIS is moving, or has moved, dad to Damascus. They must have dumped the SUV shortly after they grabbed him and switched to another vehicle. It would have to be one that is innocent looking and may have gotten through the checkpoints at the Turkish border. Once they were in Syria, they could probably move freely, around the fighting, and somehow got through the checkpoints all around Damascus."

"I don't see how they could do that," said Paglioni, "Damascus in locked down tighter than a hangman's noose. It would have to be something completely different."

"We're wasting time," said Rosy irritably, "we're no closer to finding dad, then we were 24 hours ago."

"Both of you are worn out with work and worry," said the Bishop. "All of us are scanning every satellite image we can find, and monitoring all the chatter on ISIS phones and radios. The best thing you can do right now is to get something to eat and have some sleep. I'll wake you the moment we hear anything."

Reluctantly, Ashana agreed and took Rosy by the arm and back to their apartment. They ate a breakfast Paglioni ordered for them. When they were finished, Ashana said, "I need to talk to your brother. He's probably tearing his hair by this time."

She called Charlie on the secure phone. He answered immediately, "What's up! Do we know anything?"

"Not much," said Ashana, "we now know how the information about your father's departure from the Prime Minister's residence was leaked, and to whom. Our best guess right now is that he may be in Damascus, but we are only guessing about that, and the trail runs cold around Damascus. What are you doing?"

"I've taken operational control of all the Crusader forces.

Operation Desert Fire was already underway when they snatched dad, so there's not much I can do but monitor the fighting. I will say one thing. Just at the time when we have ISIS on the ropes, they pull this stunt. I couldn't imagine anything that would infuriate the Crusader coalition more. Bagdad is mostly secure and the Iranians and Americans are tearing up the city looking for dad, even though it's very unlikely he's here."

"We expected a long campaign in taking Mosul, but it looks like most of the ISIS fighters are trying to hide among the population. A large convoy of troops and heavy equipment pulled out of the city last night. The Iranian, American, and Israeli air forces shot them to pieces."

"Your father will be proud of you, son," said Ashana.

"I just pray I have a chance to hear that from him."

After saying goodbye to Charlie, Ashana and Rosy went into the big bedroom and collapsed together on the bed, holding each other tightly, until they fell asleep.

Just four hours later, the phone rang. Ashana was awake instantly and snatched the phone. It was Bishop Paglioni. "We've had a break. Come to Ops as soon as you can."

Both Rosy and Ashana were back in Ops in minutes.

Paglioni was at the door, and said, "One of the analysts was scanning satellite imagery of the area outside the 20 mile perimeter, Prime Minister Sensek ordered. They spotted the SUV running at high speed on a back road and across some open land to another road. There was an ambulance waiting there. We could see men taking an unconscious man out of the SUV and into the ambulance. Then the ambulance made a run for the border, with lights and sirens blazing.

"From what we've been able to learn the ambulance was permitted to cross the border on the pretext it was needed to transport wounded Turkish soldiers back to Turkey.

"This is where we were able to pick up the ambulance on a number of satellites monitoring Syria. It drove straight south, stopping for gas once, and then driving directly to Damascus."

Ashana and Rosy watched the images as Paglioni spoke.

"Here's where it gets interesting. The ambulance drove to a medium sized hospital outside the Crusader perimeter. It has continued to operate because of all the injured people. American forces swept it twice and declared it a neutral site. Now, watch this. Our subject ambulance pulls up to the emergency entrance and a gurney, with a man on it, rolls into the hospital. Look at the enhanced image of the man. It's Cody."

Rosy said, "They used the most obvious vehicle to cover their tracks and nobody figured it out."

"All of this is misdirection," said Paglioni. "We must have bombed two dozen buildings inside Damascus trying to hit the Command and Control center for ISIS. It never even slowed them down. Now we find there is an almost certain probability ISIS and its leaders are hidden behind all the patients in that hospital."

"We can't just bomb the building," said Rosy, "there are lots of innocent people in there, and now we know dad is there too. We need a special force to take it out."

"An entire Seal team is on the way there now," said Paglioni. "I spoke to President Palmer a little while ago and brought him up to date."

Rosy asked, "How long before a Seal team breaches the hospital?"

"We can't get everyone is position and ready for about 24 hours," said Paglioni.

"Cody could be dead by then!" Ashana cried.

"They didn't kill him at the ambush site and went to a lot of trouble to sneak him back to Syria and Damascus," said Paglioni. "My guess is they may interrogate him for a while, and then pull some spectacular act, like beheading him with great ceremony. I think we have the time. Remember, they are talking to the best field agent in the world. Cody will know we are doing everything we can to find, and rescue him alive. He may be able to use his wits to buy himself some time."

"If that's the case, I'm going with the Seals," said Rosy, "and I'm going to call Charlie and get him there as well."

"A noble thought," said Paglioni, "and under the circumstances I would feel the same way. However, you aren't better than the Seals, and there's no reason to put your own lives at risk."

"In the first place, Charlie and I are better than any Seal," said Rosy with grim resolve, "and in the second place, we are going because that's our dad in there, and I intend to get him out alive. I'm not going to argue with you about this, Vincent, or you either, mother.

I'm going to call Charlie right now and get him to Damascus. He'll feel exactly the same way I do."

"Then may the Lord be with you. All of you will be lucky to live through it."

Rosy called Charlie and he completely agreed. He said he'd be on the first plane out. "I'll bring along Rico to provide us with some overhead."

❖

Slowly consciousness was beginning to return. Cody recognized he was coming back from a long period of sedation. His thought process was impaired and the effects of whatever drugs they used still held him in the grip of a dream world.

The first reaction from other people would fight to rise to full awareness, and struggle to get control. Cody was not other people. He had been drugged before. His captors would be watching him for the first signs of life, and then begin a barrage of questions before he was fully conscious in hopes of gaining information, or whatever they wanted him to disclose. He quietly relaxed, but did not move or jerk, the common reaction. He needed time to orient himself to whatever circumstances he faced.

For long minutes, he remained motionless and continued to give the appearance of still being asleep. During that time, he concentrated on the last things he remembered. He recalled his alarm at realizing his car was driving into a trap set for him. There was the gunfight where his outnumbered guards were overwhelmed by superior forces of at least a dozen. Cody recalled bringing down several of them himself.

Then there was the close-in struggle when he'd handled all but a few of the men. Then he remembered the Taser, which incapacitated him, followed by a needle being plunged into his neck. This meant the ambush was for the purposes of capturing him alive for whatever his captors hoped to accomplish by doing that.

His mind was clearing as he went through the facts. He was obviously the target of ISIS. Perhaps they expected to ransom him to gain some kind of control over what remained of their shattered caliphate. Without his leadership, the Crusader coalition would be in disarray, and his image as a great liberator might be large enough for ISIS to demand such terms in return for some kind of independence.

He considered this possibility. He knew Charlie would smoothly assume a central leadership, and keep the coalition on-task to complete their mission. He wondered if ISIS knew that. Probably not, he concluded, so the ransom ploy was still an option.

The second most likely probability ISIS would use, knowing they were defeated, was to make a final statement of hatred and vengeance. If they could publicly execute the immortal Black Angel, it might produce a shock to the world that would derail his plans for the reconfiguring the Middle East.

Using this worst-case scenario, Cody knew his only chance of survival was to buy enough time for the considerable intelligence resources of the world to locate him and effect a rescue attempt. He was not optimistic about living through such an effort, but some hope was better than no hope. Now through his fully alert mind, he began running possible options that would buy him time.

He could tell he was securely bound to a chair in a room that rang with empty hollowness, and there was a sack over his head. Physically, he appeared not to be injured. All his normal aches and pains were right where he left them. He was still thinking when he heard a grunting voice, speaking in Arabic.

"He should be awake by this time. The doctor said the dosages we used would last until now."

"Perhaps he is awake, but stalling to gain time to reorient himself," said a calm and authoritative voice. "Remember who he is, and how long it took for him to lower his guard and make a mistake in judgement. Even a great mind, such as his clearly is, can still take unnecessary risks."

Cody thought about that. Whoever was speaking was right. He remembered laughing off Farid's advice to let him take a helicopter to the airport. He realized he had behaved foolishly. He heard the sound of a chair pulled across a concrete floor and the same voice spoke in broken English, "You, Black Angel, you awake, I know, time to talk."

The hood was jerked off his head and Cody was looking into the black, but obviously intelligent eyes of a man dressed in black with a mask across the bottom of his face.

Cody spoke first, in fluent Arabic, "Your English is terrible. If you intend to have a long talk, why not use a language you're more comfortable in. By the way, somebody forgot to pull off your hood. That's a very rude thing to do. Muslim custom and the words of the

Qur'an say that when you are speaking to an enemy leader, in victory or defeat, you must face them with no deceit."

The man's eyes squinted a little in either anger or understanding. However, he reached up and pulled off his mask and turban. What Cody saw was a man with a closely cropped beard. He was a handsome man whose eyes glowed with intelligence and a fierce magnetism that filled the room. The other two men in the room might be part of his inner circle or just guards, but they obviously deferred to his authority.

"Ah," said Cody, "Hassan Al Aswiri himself, the actual leader of ISIS. You were born in Mosul on July 10, 1980, to a middle-class family. You were educated in a Muslim school and had a goal of becoming an imam or caliph or perhaps even a grand Mufti. This was not to be, as the view of your interpretation of the Qur'an seemed too narrow and ultra-traditional. You did not meet the measure of more progressive Muslim leaders. This has always been a huge insult to you.

"Over the years, your particular brand of Islam, which is positively medieval, along with your natural charm and personal charisma brought many others to your belief. When the unrest of the Middle East and two invasions by American troops and others brought chaos to Iraq, you grabbed the vacuum left by the departure of American soldiers to seize control of an obscure branch of Al Qaeda and turn it into ISIS. You were fabulously successful. Soon, you were powerful enough to begin an offensive of your own.

"Since nobody stopped you, either by underestimating you, or for purely political reasons, you have managed to overrun two countries, and install the kind of Sharia Law your early interpretation of the Holy Qur'an said was correct, calling it the truest form of Islam. Of course, this interpretation made it impossible for you to tolerate any other form of religious beliefs. So you have made it your business to execute every Shia, Christian, Druze, Jew, or any other people not in line with your beliefs.

"Did you honestly believe the rest of Islam and the world would forever tolerate this? Now your caliphate is in tatters, your followers are deserting you, and ISIS is about to be obliterated in the name of Allah, by Shia and Sunni Muslims, Jews, and Christians alike, all acting under the first Commandment of God, that you will have no other gods before Him."

Aswiri sat back in his chair and smiled then said, "Finally, a man worth killing."

"Just like that?" asked Cody. "Are we not to have an intelligent discourse, a noble debate over the very points which we now are fighting. I would have expected more from a man of your stature and obvious intelligence. Look at your minions. They are positively quivering in fear that someone, anyone, has had the fiber to meet you on your own terms, and speak to you in such a manner. Are you not greater than that, and able to respond to my challenges to your interpretation of what the Holy Prophet Muhammad taught?"

Aswiri glanced over his shoulder and could see the terror in the eyes of his trusted lieutenants, who had followed him from the beginning. The Black Angel was right, and had to be defeated on purely religious terms. He knew the Black Angel was a Christian. He could not imagine him being able to withstand a debate of Islamic principles.

"Very well, Black Angel, you shall have your debate, but know this, you will lose … and the penalty for that is death."

"I accept your terms," said Cody, "a battle to the death!"

Before Aswiri could speak again, Cody said, "Since you are actually willing to have a conversation with me, which is very much to your credit and demonstrates you are a man of honor, and deeply held beliefs, I have some requests of you in the tradition of Islamic courtesy."

"What are your requests?" asked Aswiri.

"First, I request that I be allowed to use the toilet and to cleanse myself as you do before prayer."

"That is reasonable," said Aswiri.

"Next, I request that we both pray together, in the Sunni tradition of the first four Caliphs, so that our words can be heard by Allah, who will judge us both."

"Very strange for a Christian," said Aswiri.

"'There is no god, but God, said Muhammad.' We should pray in that manner."

"I will agree," said Aswiri, "but only because we do so in the true Muslim manner and in the name of Allah."

"Finally, I have fasted without food or drink for two days," said Cody, "I humbly request we share both in the name of Allah as noble adversaries, and surely, since we will likely speak at some length, we both would be more comfortable than sitting on these metal chairs."

Aswiri actually laughed at that, and Cody sensed an opening.

"You could also just let me go," he said with a big grin.

Aswiri grinned. "Unlock him and take him to the bathroom."

A guard stepped forward and released the handcuffs behind his back, and the ropes wrapped around him. Cody stood up and stretched to unfold his cramped muscles. He squatted to the floor to loosen his legs and a nervous guard lowered his rifle at Cody.

"You guys are pretty jumpy around a starving middle-aged man."

"Stop!" said Aswiri sharply.

Two guards escorted Cody to a restroom. They went up three floors on an elevator. When the doors opened, Cody was surprised to find he had come from the basement of a hospital. There were nurses and doctors scurrying around and there were wounded people everywhere. They filled the hallways with gurneys.

Cody went into a restroom with the guards. It was reasonably clean. He used the toilet. The guards would not let him shut the door. When he was finished, he got up and went to the sink. He looked at himself in the mirror. He felt as tired as the image coming back at him. He turned on the faucet and splashed water in his face and used soap to wash his hands and face. He ran his hands through his hair and straightened his fatigues. All this made him feel better. "Allah Akbar," he said to the guards. "If you fellows have finished enjoying watching a man take a dump, I'm ready to go back downstairs."

Beside themselves, the two guards snickered. Cody's personality was infectious. He smiled at the men and said, "Any of you need to go to bathroom. I promise not to watch."

The guards were much more polite to him as they went back to the elevator and down the three floors. Despite, his jokes and good humor, Cody was keenly watching everything. There were no visible guards on the hospital floor, but there were several when the elevator opened. The hallway ran in both directions from the elevator and Cody could see light at the end opposite from where the guards were leading him. Along the hallway were a number of other steel doors with heavy bars across them. Cody could hear sounds coming from inside the rooms as he passed by. Possibly other prisoners were in this dudgeon. He filed it away.

When they came back in the room, the metal chairs were gone and replaced by two comfortable chairs with a table between them. The table had plates of food, a carafe of water, and a pot of tea. Aswiri was smoking a cigarette.

Cody sat down in the chair. Aswiri made no motion for him to be handcuffed again. Apparently, Aswiri believed the two, armed guards with machine guns behind him were protection enough. Cody snickered to himself. Aswiri was a fool. He could easily have killed all three men in the room in about 15 seconds. However, there were many other guards just outside the room and he did not like his chances of making it to the hospital upstairs. His only real option was to stall long enough for his people to find him. Even with that, there was no good chance he would survive such an assault.

"I very much appreciate you allowing me to clean myself. Our God honors those who come to him with clean hands and face."

He looked at the food, and especially the water on the table. He knew Aswiri was waiting for him to lunge at the food and drink. As badly as he was dehydrated, he ignored the food and water.

Cody looked around the room, "I'm sorry, I don't have a prayer rug for our devotions. Can you help?"

Aswiri told one of the guards to fetch a prayer rug for Cody. He dashed out the door and was back in just a few minutes with a prayer rug in his hands.

"You'll have to guide me on the direction of Mecca," said Cody. "I was not able to orient myself when I arrived, obviously."

"Mecca is in that direction," Aswiri, pointing toward one of the far walls.

Cody glanced at the two guards, "Should we all not have the opportunity to worship Allah as men of God."

This seemed to cause Aswiri pause for thought. The guards were there for his protection. If he allowed them to join in prayer, they would have to shed their weapons. Cody saw the indecision in his eyes and said, "No man would violate the call to prayer and its ritual. In this we are all children of God."

Aswiri shook his head and then said to the guards, "Get your rugs, you will join us."

The guards seemed to regard all this is as very strange, but one of them left the room. He returned in a few more minutes with two more rugs.

"Shall we pray?" Cody rose from his chair and went to a corner of the room Aswiri had indicated. The guards shed their weapons and all four men went to the prayer rugs spread on the floor. Cody fell to his knees. Aswiri followed him and the guards did the same. Together, the four performed the entire ritual of the Muslim prayer. Cody could feel Aswiri's eyes glancing at him as he prayed.

When they had finished Cody stood up. He ignored the guards quickly retrieving their weapons.

Now that we have honored Allah with our prayers, I think it would be a good idea if we were formally introduced."

He put out his hand and said, "My first name is Cody, Hassan. I'm glad to meet you."

Aswiri seemed even more confused. His great enemy had just told him his real name. It was a mystery to him. But he took Cody's hand and shook it.

"I'm very grateful for the food and drink," said Cody. "You have been true to my requests, as have I. May we now eat and drink?"

Aswiri pointed to the chair and Cody sat back down, waiting for his host to serve the food in the traditional manner. Aswiri prepared a plate of meats, unleavened bread, a bean dip, and a selection of fruits and vegetables. Finally, he poured a glass of water for Cody.

"You are most kind," he said.

The two men ate and drank in silence. Cody ate with measured movements, not hurrying or gobbling the food. He finally took his glass of water and drank most of it. Aswiri knew, full well, what Cody had been through since the ambush, and could not help but be impressed with the restraint and dignity Cody displayed in eating.

The guards were hungry and thirsty too, but Aswiri made no indication they should participate. Cody pointed at them, "It must be difficult to watch others eat and drink when you're hungry yourself."

Aswiri hesitated a second, then waved for one of the guards to remove the food tray from the table. "You may have what's left."

The guards took the tray to another part of the room and held it between them as they stuffed food in their mouths.

Cody took the opportunity to fill his water glass, and drink some more. Then he looked straight at Aswiri.

"Tell me, Hassan, before we ate, what did we do?"

"We prayed to Allah."

"We were praying to God."

"Allah is God."

"Yes God is Allah and Allah is God. Did we not pray together to the same God?"

"Not your God," said Aswiri.

Cody looked at Aswiri and said "God says in the Holy Qur'an: *'Say, O Muslims. We believe in God and that which is revealed unto us and that which was revealed unto Abraham, and Ishmael, and Isaac, and Jacob, and the tribes, and that which Moses and Jesus received, and that which the prophets received from their Lord. We make no distinction between any of them, and unto Him, we have surrendered. And if they believe in the like of that which ye believe, then are they rightly guided. But if they turn away, then are they in schism and God will suffice thee against them. He is the Hearer, the Knower'*."

"The Holy Qur'an says that those who are not of the faith shall be called infidels, and Allah's servants shall strike them down," said Aswiri heatedly.

Cody responded, "The Prophet Muhammad did not say that, Hassan. We know the Qur'an orders believers to fight in combat against those who are the oppressors, aggressors, and terrorists, and those who are assaulting and killing the innocent men, women, and children. But it also gives our clear order – NOT TO Fight, against those who are not fighting against you, also in the Qur'an."

Cody continued, "There is not such a meaning in the Qur'an, ordering or even permitting Muslims to attack innocent people whether they are Christians, Jews, Kurds, Shia, or any other faith for that matter."

"The American's are not innocent people," said Aswiri, "they invaded our homeland, twice, and many innocent Muslims were killed. The Prophet declared we should declare jihad on such actions and that whatever was required to defeat them would be as Allah has decreed."

Cody answered, "Scholars of Qur'an tell us the verses dealing with this topic are specific and not intended to imply a general meaning for just anyone to decide to go around combatting non-Muslims.

"It should also be stated the usage of the word 'Fitnah' denotes a horrible condition, not unlike what we find today where there is terrorism and tyranny against the moral and just society at large. It would be easy to understand properly the meaning as *'engage them in combat, even killing them, until the state of Fitnah, or terrorism, no longer exists in the society and people are free to worship Allah by their choice."*

"Those are exactly the conditions that existed in Iraq and Syria before the Islamic Caliphate began to regain control of our tortured lands from the infidels who were occupying it," said Aswiri, pointing his finger at Cody's nose.

"We are not the ones to declare Shia Muslims to be heretics, and murder them," said Cody evenly, "We are not the ones who behead Christians. We are not the ones to set fire to another Sunni Muslim who was captured while flying his jet for the Jordanians. We are not the ones who have attacked and killed innocent people in Paris. We are not the ones who attacked Christianity's most Holy Church and killed their Holy leader."

"In Jihad there are many deaths," said Aswiri, "The justification for legal executions under Sharia Law is clear, no matter what the religion of the guilty party."

Cody quickly replied, "In the Holy Qur'an, God Most High tells Muslims to issue the following call to Christians, and Jews—the *People of the Scripture. Say, O People of the Scripture! Come to a common word between you, that we shall worship none but God, and that we shall ascribe no partner unto Him and that none of us shall take others for lords beside God and us. And if they turn away, then say, Bear witness that we are they who have surrendered unto Him*

"Clearly, the blessed words: *we shall ascribe no partner unto Him* relate to the Unity of God. Clearly also, worshipping *none but God*, relates to being totally devoted to God and hence to the *First and Greatest Commandment*.

"In other words, Hassan, Muslims, Christians and Jews should be free to each follow what God commanded them, and not have 'to prostrate before kings and the like', for God says elsewhere in the Holy Qur'an: *Let there be no compulsion in religion*. This clearly relates to the Second Commandment … to love one's neighbor of which justice and freedom of religion are a crucial part.

"God says in the Holy Qur'an, *God forbiddeth you not those who warred not against you on account of religion and drove you not out of your homes, that ye should show them kindness and deal justly with them. Lo! God loveth the just dealers."*

On and on it went. Aswiri seemed to enjoy the exchange, especially since his opponent, a Christian, seemed to be able to quote at will from the Qur'an. The two exchanged opposing viewpoints from the Qur'an in detail. Both Aswiri and Cody eventually used the toilets in the hospital above.

Once again, Cody took in the entire scene. He glanced at the clock. Ten hours had passed since he was last there. This time he spotted several black-shirted Jihadists roaming the halls with weapons ready. His instincts told him the sharp analysts in the Vatican, led by Rosy, had figured out where he was. He also knew an attack on the hospital carried a big risk of hurting many innocent people. The Special Forces team would have to be very careful.

After praying again, with the guards, the two had another meal. After it was over, Aswiri, finally, seemed to be tiring. Cody tried another delaying tactic.

"Hassan, we've done a better job of analyzing the Qur'an today, than most Ayatollah's. I have enjoyed the exchange and have actually learned a lot, particularly your understanding of why ISIS was the answer for Middle Eastern politics. Perhaps, there are ways in which some accommodation to your Caliphate can be made."

"I don't know what you mean by an 'accommodation,'" said Aswiri, "You're unholy alliance between Muslims, Christians, and Jews in you're, so-called, modern Crusade, have brought nothing but death and destruction to the warriors of the Islamic Caliphate. I don't believe you intend anything less than our complete annihilation.

"Ultimately, the world will witness the public execution of its mighty leader crucified, as the criminal Jesus died. At dawn tomorrow, you will die." With that, Aswiri left the room. The two guards followed him out and Cody heard the door bolt shut.

Chapter 16
Liberation

Damascus, Syria

Charlie and Rico rushed off the plane at Damascus Airport. Rosy and Ashana were there to pick them up and take them to a waiting Humvee.

"What's the latest?" asked Charlie.

"We know your father went into that hospital just outside the Damascus perimeter. He was on a gurney, probably drugged," said Ashana.

"We've got that place locked down tight," said Rosy, "Nothing is going or coming except the regular hospital personnel. We're certain dad has not left the building."

Rico asked, "Any idea where they're keeping him?"

Rosy said, "It looks like the bottom two floors, including the basement is the Command and Control center for what's left of the ISIS forces. He's probably in the basement under heavy guard."

Charlie insisted, "Let's get to our Command center and take a look at their assault plans."

They drove across the airport to a building formerly used as the administrative offices for the airlines and airport officials, now used as the quarters for the brigades of the 82nd and 101st airborne divisions for the duration of the war.

The three went in past the guards at the doors and into a first floor conference room serving as the battle center. There were a number of senior officers standing around the table, looking at maps, photos, schematics of the hospital. They stopped as the Frost family came into the room.

"Attention!" called the general in the center. All came to their feet and stood quietly. The two-star general walked smartly to Charlie and saluted him. Charlie returned the salute and said, "As you were, gentlemen." The officers went back to work on the plans they were discussing.

"Ardishur, I'm General Francis Gordon. I command our two divisions. It's a great pleasure to meet you. Back in the dark ages, when I was just a Captain, I led the team that captured the Iranian bombs in Zapata, Texas. I know your father pretty well, well enough to know his real name and how truly effective he is.

"Our job now is to affect a rescue of the Black Angel from the hospital where he's being held, and also serves as the secret Command and Control center for ISIS. Most of their senior leaders are there, including the ISIS Commander, Hassan Al Aswiri."

"It's good to know you are a friend of my father, general," said Charlie, "meet the rest of the family. This is my mother Ashana, my sister Rosy, and my lifelong friend and brother Enrico."

General Gordon shook hands will all of them, "Welcome to Damascus. I wish the circumstances were different."

"So do we," said Rosy.

"If you'll come over here, I'll show you what we are facing," said Gordon.

He first showed them a map of Damascus, "We've been working our way very slowly into the center of the city. We're facing heavy opposition and have to fight literally from house to house. Right now, we have the hardcore of the remaining ISIS army, bottled up near the center of the city, all around the old palace and headquarters of the Assad regime. As you can imagine, though it was heavily fortified by Assad, we think ISIS made it even stronger.

"Our intelligence told us the Command and Control of ISIS was located in the center of this array of fortifications, but that turned out to be wrong. ISIS leadership managed to slip through our lines and into the hospital, just outside our perimeter. Our troops swept the building twice and found only a hospital. The blueprints don't show two full floors under the hospital, and the entrance is very well hidden, so we missed it."

"What's the plan for breaking in?" asked Charlie.

"We were just discussing that," said Gordon. "Obviously, ISIS is hiding behind a lot of innocent patients at the hospital. So going in the front door is not an option."

The commander of the Seal team, pointed to the building. "They are dug in for a last stand. We've spotted two mortar emplacements on the roof. ISIS has set up their defenses in concentric circles around the hospital. Their troops occupy each of the circles. We must break through each troop's circle with crossfire machine gun emplacements. As you get closer to the hospital, there are more defenses, and more fighters. They know where the IED's and mines are, and we don't."

"What entrance is used to bring people in an out?" asked Charlie.

"It's a loading dock and garage at the rear of the hospital. It's right in the middle of the building. Undoubtedly, they drive cars into the garage to move their high value personnel safely. We've used infrared scanners on the garage and loading dock. There are two entries to the underground center, one on each side. If we could get our men to those entry points, we think we can go down and take out their defense from two directions. The problem, of course, is getting through the encircling troops without setting off alarms."

"How big is that perimeter around the hospital," asked Charlie.

"At least a thousand yards."

"If we could clear the roof of those mortar squads, we would have a third way into the hospital. We could drop men from helicopters onto the roof to move them down into the hospital. Then, take out whatever ISIS barricades are there." said Charlie.

"There are two squads of three men on the roof manning the mortars at all times," said the Seal team leader. "We have to make our assault at night. I just don't think we can get them all fast enough to keep them from pushing the alarm button."

"Rico and I can take out those mortars in about 15 seconds."

"At night, from a thousand yards away, using silenced sniper rifles?" said the Seal leader grimly. "That's a real big if."

Rico and I have done it before," said Charlie, "Do you have any men who might be able to do the same?"

"We have good shooters," said the Seal, "but I'm not sure I'd risk a roof landing based on their skill sets."

"Alright," said Charlie, "let's go through the rest of your plan."

"That's just what we were working on when you came in," said General Gordon. "The problem is to penetrate that perimeter without getting your dad killed while were doing it. As soon as ISIS knows an attack is in progress, they'll kill him and any other hostages they might be holding. We assume he's still alive."

"He is," said Ashana, "Cody is the most resourceful man I know, and I just know he's managed to find a way to buy enough time for us to rescue him."

Charlie was staring at the maps and photos of the hospital, "I don't think we have to break up this whole perimeter, just a piece of it."

"Show me," said Gordon.

"If we come straight in to the loading dock and garage with a big Seal team, I think we can overpower the ISIS guards in that section. If we do it quietly enough, it won't alert the rest of the men guarding the rest of the perimeter. As we move the Seals through the gap, you can bring up a flanking force to watch for ISIS who will rush to the garage when the shooting starts inside the hospital. They don't need to attack. They can wait for the soldiers to come running and cut them down as they come into range."

"Meanwhile, the Seals split into two groups as they get into the garage, heading for the two entrances you mentioned. If those doors are locked and reinforced, we'll have to blow them open. That will wake up everyone and ISIS will know we're there. After that, speed is what we need. We have to put enough men in the building to kill the defenders and drive to the lower level before they can shoot dad."

"When the doors blow, we drop our team onto the roof, and let them occupy all the ISIS actually in the hospital. This will give us four attack points."

"You lost me," said Gordon.

"If you think the Black Angel is going to just sit around waiting for the cavalry to arrive, you don't know him as well as you thought," said Charlie, "At the first sign a rescue is underway he'll start an offensive of his own."

"I think we might have come up with this plan on our own," said Gordon, "but since you've done all the thinking for us, is there anyone here who has something to add?"

The room was silent.

"We have to go tonight," said Charlie, "I think dad has probably bought all the time he has."

"Which way to the equipment room," said Rosy, "I need some armor, a night scope, and a better weapon?"

"There's no way we're going to let a women go in with the Seals," said Gordon.

Rosy shrugged her soldiers and turned on the two closest Seals. With lightning speed and a flurry of blows and leg kicks, she had both of them gasping on the floor in a matter of seconds.

"You got any better men?" said Rosy straightening her fatigues. "Charlie and Rico are better than I am."

"I guess the Black Angel raised a pretty deadly team," said Gordon with a smile.

Rosy helped the Seals to their feet. "I'm sorry fellows. I hope I didn't hurt you, I tried to go easy, but you know how it is when you get to close in fighting."

Gordon looked at Ashana, "I suppose you want to go too?"

"Cody would be very annoyed if I got hurt," said Ashana. "I can shoot almost as well as Charlie and Rico. When they leave to join the Seal teams, I'll stay behind and continue to provide overhead."

"I'm going to put my best snipers with you," said Gordon.

They spent the remainder of the day polishing the plan, determining the exact route they would use to get to the garage and loading dock, bringing in the 50 Seals who would do the actual assault, and thoroughly briefing them. The Seal briefing was in an empty hanger at the airport. Charlie, Rico, Ashana, and Rosy joined them, fully armed, wearing protective vests, and helmets with night scopes.

One of the senior sergeants in the team said, "You don't really plan to go with us, do you, little lady?"

"I'm getting real tired of this," said Rosy. She spun around and pulled out her Glock with a smooth and rapid motion. Then she emptied the clip on an empty barrel 50 yards from where the group was standing. Her shot pattern was less than three inches wide.

There was a murmur of amazement among the tough Seals. Finally, one of the men spoke up and said, "Could I go with you, Rosy?"

Night fell, and the Seals moved in a convoy of Humvees, around the outer road surrounding Damascus. By midnight, they were in position at the far edge of the ISIS perimeter surrounding the hospital. General Gordon moved two full companies of Airborne Rangers into position to follow the Seals into the gap they expected to open, and provide flanking cover.

Ashana, Rico, and Charlie, along with two Seal snipers left the group and went to the top of a building overlooking the hospital. In his reconnaissance, Charlie had found the right building to give them a full field of fire on the two mortar crews on the roof of the hospital. They went quickly and quietly with their faces blackened and their Timberwolves wrapped in strips of cloth.

All of them lay quietly on the rooftop and waited.

"H" hour was set for 3am.

Charlie scanned the roof of the hospital with his binoculars. He could see both mortar installations, and the six men assigned to operate them. It would be a clear shot.

While he watched, the door to the rooftop opened and two more men came out onto the roof. Charlie saw the door was just a bar across the door. That meant it wasn't locked, easy access for the team coming down from the helicopters.

The two men went to the mortar crews, spoke for a moment, and then walked to the edge of the roof. A two-foot tall wall surrounded the roof. Each of the men went to opposite sides of the roof and sat down. They took out binoculars and began searching the ground for any activity.

Charlie mumbled to one of the Seal snipers. "Call it in, the rooftop door is unlocked, and we have two more targets on the roof."

He turned to Rico, lying next to him and said, "They'll have radios to alert people inside about any ground movement. They're our first targets, otherwise the Seal assault force might be seen approaching."

"Right," said Rico, "we'll have to take them together and then target the mortar crews."

"Eight men," said one of the Seals, "from this distance with silenced rifles and night scopes. I wouldn't want to take that shot."

"Just hold your fire until Rico and I finish," said Charlie, "we can't risk a miss to let those guys sound the alarm or start plunking out mortars. There'll be plenty of targets when the Seals drive a wedge in that perimeter."

Charlie looked around Rico to Ashana. "When the show starts with our taking out the rooftop guys, Rico and I are going to hightail it down to the Seal team making their assault. We're leaving you here with the Seals. You need to keep an eye on the roof in case more men come up to use the mortars. Think you can handle that, mom?"

"Just get in there and find your dad, bub, and try not to get your butt shot off. Keep an eye on your sister too. I might not be the eagle eye of you and Rico, but I can sure hit a target from here."

"I'm sure you can," said Charlie. "You guys take care of my mom or I'll kill you."

"I believe it," said one of the Seals.

Charlie looked at his watch. "Ten minutes."

Down on the ground, 50 soldiers of the Seal Team moved quietly from building to building. All the structures in this part of Damascus had seen heavy fighting when the Assad forces were making their final stand against ISIS. Now all the buildings were deserted.

"One klick to go," said a quiet, calm voice in Rosy's radio built into her helmet. The only difference from her and the other black-suited Seals was she was a little shorter. She moved as they did, only quieter. She was a shadow moving from place to place. She paused for a moment to use her night vision binoculars on the buildings ahead. She didn't spot anything moving or out of place.

The Seal who'd asked if he could go with her had done just that. His problem was keeping up with her and finding her in the darkness. He almost bumped into her as he moved up.

"Careful, dummy," she mumbled. "This operation is supposed to be covert."

"Where did you learn all these skills?" asked the Seal.

"My father taught me."

"The actual Black Angel?"

"Don't let him hear you call him that," said Rosy. "He hates it. His real name is Cody, and he's my dad."

"I heard the scuttlebutt around the barracks about a special team coming in to give us a hand on this mission. I had no idea, you, and Ardishur, and the other guy were the team, and I sure didn't know the Black Angel had a family."

"Well, he does, and I'm gonna bust him out of that hospital."

Rosy turned to the young man, and found him handsome even under all the blackout cream, "What's your name?

"I'm Matt."

"You married, Matt?"

"Nah, don't even have a regular girlfriend. Being a Seal is a full-time job."

"Well, let's get back to Sealing," said Rosy, "the hospital is just around that next building. We should expect to see ISIS guys pretty quick."

The radio cracked again, "Moving into final position, the hospital is just around the next building."

"You got a map in your head or something?" said Matt to Rosy.

"I pay attention at the briefings, and I've had more of them than you … plus I was the one who found this hospital in the first place."

"No kidding," said Matt.

Another radio message, "Units 1, 2, and 3 to the left. Units 4, 5, and 6 to the right. Five meter intervals. Advance two by two. We move when the helicopters come in over the hospital."

"How come we're waiting for the helicopters?" asked Matt.

"Because the ISIS guys will see them too, and come out from where they're hiding to shoot at them," said Rosy, like she was talking to Fourth grader. Matt felt like one too.

Rosy looked at her watch. It was just five minutes until three.

"Charlie and Rico will take out their overhead, the mortars, and anything else they have on the rooftop at exactly 3 am. The choppers will be coming in as he's firing. When the ISIS come out to start shooting, you concentrate on the short-range targets. I'll take the ones further away."

"Yes ma'am," said Matt.

Both Charlie and Rico checked their firing conditions one last time then each took magazines and loaded them into their Timberwolf. They flipped down their night scopes and chambered a round. Both of them began sighting in on their targets.

"I'll take the guy on the far side of the roof," said Rico.

"Let's see if we can get all our rounds downrange, before anyone hears the firing," said Charlie.

"Thirty seconds," said one of the Seals. Charlie could hear the faint sound of helicopters in the distance.

The seconds ticked by torturously.

"Fire," said the Seal.

The two Seals were watching the rooftop through their binoculars as Rico and Charlie began shooting. They were astonished at how fast they were. Through the night scopes on their binoculars, they watched as first the two spotter's heads exploded. They turned to the mortar crews who had just managed to begin moving before all six of them were dead, mostly with gory headshots.

"Man!" said one of the Seals, "that's good shootin'!"

Charlie and Rico did not even hear the man. They were already on their feet and running down the stairs with Glock 17 machine pistols, strapped to their thighs. They left their sniper rifles behind.

Almost immediately, Ashana saw two helicopters lower over the hospital roof and a string of Seals slide down the ropes. There were a dozen of them. They ran straight to the roof door and disappeared inside. Shortly after, they could see the glare of a flash-bang grenade and knew the Seals were engaging.

Rosy, Matt, and the rest of the Seals saw the helicopters too. Almost on cue, ISIS fighters came out of their cover and began shooting at the helicopters. That was the signal for the Seal to begin firing. A dozen ISIS went down right away.

One man jumped out from behind a wall and tried to slice Rosy with a long knife. She parried the thrust and flipped the man onto his back. Then she hit him hard with the edge of her hand in his throat. He did not move.

While Rosy was dispatching one fighter, Matt shot two more, closing in on them. They were near the point of the formation so they reached the loading dock and garage first. There was a machine gun emplacement on the loading dock and Seals were going down. Rosy dodged behind a tree, as splinters of wood flew everywhere. She pulled the pin on a grenade and stepped out from the tree to lob it onto the loading dock and eliminate the gun emplacement.

The ISIS fighters still seemed to be surprised and dazed at the speed of the Seal's assault. Rosy took the chance to pull open the door to the loading dock, gun down two of the enemy, and push the buttons to open the garage doors. The Seals flanked on both sides of the garage and threw several flash-bang and high explosive grenades into the garage.

At that moment, Charlie and Rico rushed up. They had covered the distance from their sniper point to the gap opened by the Seals in less than five minutes. Charlie could see the 82nd Airborne Rangers moving in to set up flanking protection for the Seal attack. They ran past them and were soon inside the garage.

Ahead of them, the Seals split into two groups and went through the big doors on either side of the garage, giving them access to the hospital itself. A barrage of automatic fire poured out of the doors as they pulled them open. There were ISIS fighters inside, but they had constrictions from the width of the hallway. Seals on both sides of the doors lobed grenades into the hallway and then rushed in, gunning down soldiers as they rushed down the hallways.

Down in his locked room, Cody heard the sound of the muffled guns firing, and knew the assault on the hospital had begun. In all likelihood, Aswiri would send men to the lower level to kill him before a rescue team found him. He jumped out of his chair and stood behind the door. In short order, the door opened and he could see the barrel of a rifle poke into the room. He grabbed the rifle barrel and pulled the man into the room, a quick chop and man went down. Cody grabbed the rifle and put it around the edge of the door, shooting as he did. No immediate shots came from the hallway, so he grabbed several magazines from the dead man on the floor and stuffed them into his fatigue pockets. Then he made a quick look down the hall and saw other ISIS fighters throwing open the doors that lined the hallway and were shooting into the rooms.

There was no one else in the hall behind him. He'd been in one of the end rooms. Facing him were ISIS soldiers intent on killing people inside the rooms. Cody opened up with his rifle and shot down a half dozen of the men. Then he ran down the hall, pulling open the bars of the rooms the enemy soldiers had not yet reached. As he pulled open one door, he was overwhelmed with the stench coming from the room. It was a combination of feces, urine, and the smell of death. There must have been fifty people crammed into the cell, smaller than the one in that confined him.

He yelled in Arabic, "The Crusaders are here! You're free! Help each other to leave, but stay out of the hallway until it's clear of Daesh fighters. He repeated the instructions in English.

With an eye on the end of the hallway for more ISIS soldiers, Cody moved down the hallway opening more cells, where he found much the same conditions. In the one near the end, the cell was full of girls and young women. Cody shuddered to think of what they'd been suffering. He realized that this lower level was nothing but a prison for people captured and held by ISIS.

Cody peaked around the corner. This was the end of the hallway where he'd seen light the day before, so it must be a stairway to the next floor. As he looked up the stairs, he saw two Seals moving to come down.

"Don't shoot me!" yelled Cody in English. I'm who you came to rescue. The two Seals came down the stairs quickly.

"Are you the Black Angel?" one of them asked.

"In the flesh," said Cody, "this entire lower level is nothing but a prison. There must be a couple hundred people in those cells along the hallway. When we've secured the hospital we can come back and tend to them."

"What's going on upstairs?"

"We have ISIS trapped between two Seal teams working their way down the hall and all the offices in between. It's a bloody fight."

"Radio your command and tell them I'm OK," said Cody, "then tell them I believe the ISIS leadership has retreated to their command center. We need to capture as many of them as we can alive, and we need to move quickly to prevent them from destroying all their computers, and servers. We're going to need all that information to take out the many ISIS cells currently operating internationally."

The Seal reported all Cody had said to the Command center.

Ashana lay on the building's floor with her two Seal protectors. She watched the helicopters swoop in and drop their Seals to the hospital rooftop. She could see the Seal Teams opening the gap toward the loading dock and garage.

With all the Seals now inside the hospital, the Rangers of the 82nd Airborne lined the gap. They were in a furious fight with all the ISIS soldiers who had converged on them from around the building.

She looked back at the rooftop. Suddenly, a group of the enemy broke through the door, and ran for the mortars. Ashana had no idea how they had escaped the Seals in the upper floors of the hospital, but it was understandable since only a dozen men had come from the helicopters.

Ashana picked up her Timberwolf and sighted in on the men trying to get the mortars into action. She squeezed off several rounds and three of the men went down. The other two Seals now saw what she was doing, and leveled their sniper rifles on the rooftop fighters. Between the three of them, they soon cleared the rooftop again.

"Very good shooting, Ma'am," said one of the Seals, "I think you only missed once."

They were relieved to find more helicopters lining up to land on the roof and soldiers climbing off the choppers. Soon, there were 50 soldiers on the rooftop. They would secure it with a few men and the rest could join the fight inside the hospital.

Rosy and Matt were still at the forefront of the assault. They moved from room to room in the ISIS headquarters. Surprised by three ISIS fighters as they entered one room, the men attacked with knives. Apparently, they were not close to their other weapons when the surprise attack had begun.

Rosy waded into the three men, jumping from one to another with cat-like speed. She took a deep, nasty cut in her shoulder, but ignored it and was throwing men down to the floor, leg licking in two directions with blazing speed, and had overwhelmed all three men in only a few seconds. Matt did not have time to get into the fight. Rosy was just too fast and efficient.

Matt had time to say, "Boy, Rosy, remind me to take you with me everywhere I go."

Almost knocked down by Charlie and Rico running down the hallway, Rosy and Matt felt relief.

"You got here, pretty quick," said Rosy.

"We wouldn't want to miss all the fun and let you hog the spotlight, sis," said Charlie. "That's a nasty cut on your arm, why don't you go back to the garage and let one of the medics fix you up."

"It's just a scratch," said Rosy, "I don't want you to hog all the cheering either."

"Could we have a little more family courtesy," said a familiar voice behind them. All three of them ran to Cody hugging and kissing him.

"No family reunions just yet," said Cody, "we need to get to the Command center and secure the ISIS leaders and all their intelligence.

Several other Seals now joined them and paced the deadly quartet as they moved with incredible speed from corridor to corridor, in the much larger upper floor of the ISIS nerve center. They shot down a number of ISIS fighters along the way.

Finally, they arrived at the elevator. "This is in the center of the hospital. I think the Command center is just at the end of that corridor."

They found a locked, steel door at the end. One of the Seals put explosive charges on each corner, and they all ducked into an office. The explosion was deafening. Cody and his family rushed to the broken door and into a large room, filled with computers, maps on a conference table and at least 20 ISIS men inside the room.

One of the soldiers at the corner of the room began firing his automatic weapon. "Look out," said Rico, shoving Charlie out of the hail of bullets. Several of them hit him in his armor, but two rounds caught him in the neck and his leg. Charlie whipped around on the shooter and blasted him with a burst from his Glock. Then he kneeled on the floor to check Rico. It looked like the neck shot had nicked his carotid artery. He was bleeding heavily. Charlie grabbed a cloth from the table and shoved it into his artery to stop the blood flow.

He turned to two of the Seals who had just entered the room and shouted, "Get this man to the medics STAT. If they don't stop that bleeding in about a minute, he'll bleed out."

The Seals gathered up Rico and carried him from the room.

Meanwhile Cody leveled his Glock on the remaining men in the room and said, "Anybody else want to die right now? One of the men went for his gun in a shoulder holster and Cody shot him right between the eyes. He fell in a bloody heap on the floor.

Cody spotted Aswiri, standing behind his men. "Order them to drop their weapons right now, Hassan, or you'll be the first to die!"

Aswiri threw his gun on the table, and the rest of the men in the room did the same.

More Seals burst into the room. "Secure these prisoners, said Cody. Quickly all the men had restraints. Cody could still hear the sound of sporadic gunfire, but more of it was the thump of the silenced Seal weapons than the sharp sounds of ISIS rifles. Cody sensed the Seals were mopping up.

He knew the battle was over for sure when the elevator opened and ten Seals came running out.

"Is the hospital secure?" asked Cody.

"Mostly," said a senior sergeant, "We're sweeping all the floors now. We have quite a few prisoners."

Cody pushed through the crowd of glaring ISIS officers and up to Aswiri. "As I said, Hassan, this would be a battle to the death. It turns out it won't be my death, nor yours either just now. That's for an International Court to decide."

"All that debating we did was just to buy time for this assault. You tricked me," spat Aswiri.

"I admit that was part of my intentions," said Cody, "but I also wanted to know the root of your radical, and poorly reasoned Muslim principles. I thought, perhaps, I might be able to convince you of your errors in judgement. As it turns out, you stuck to your beliefs. There are thousands of people around the world and in the Middle East whose deaths are on your hands."

"I need to go check on Rico," said Charlie, "Come on along Rosy you're injured more than you think."

"Give me a hand, brother I'm getting kind of dizzy."

Charlie scooped his sister up in his arms and carried her out the door, headed for the medics waiting in the garage. Blood was now running heavily down her arm.

When he got to the garage, Charlie found the medics working furiously on Rico.

"How's he doing?"

"That cloth you jammed in his carotid artery bought him enough time for him to have a chance," said the doctor, "We've clamped off the artery for now and are giving him transfusions of whole blood. However, he's still in critical condition. We still have the complication of his leg wound. It looks like the bullet hit the bone. The Dust Off helicopters are coming in now. He'll be the first one out."

Charlie looked around at the busy triage center. "Tell me the worst."

The doctor looked up, "We have twenty dead, both Seals and Rangers, and about fifty more wounded some of them critical, like your friend here."

"What about the ISIS?"

"Don't know about that," said the Doc. "You'll have to ask one of the officers working the whole perimeter."

"Can you get someone to look at my sister?" said Charlie. "She's got a bad cut in her arm."

The doctor waved at another doctor, who came over to where Charlie had laid Rosy. The doctor looked at her arm. "Lots of blood. Probably cut an artery. However, I think we can stitch this up for now, give her some blood, and send her off with the choppers."

Charlie looked at Rosy, "Hear that, sis? The doc says you're going to make it."

"I'm getting dopey from the painkiller they gave me," said Rosy.

"What's a woman doing in this operation?" asked the doc.

"We belong here," said Charlie, "Our dad is the one we came to save."

"Are you family of the Black Angel?" asked the doctor with astonishment.

"Do not let him hear you call him that," said Charlie and Rosy together.

The doctor chuckled, "And this man," pointing at Rico?

"He's also my brother," said Charlie.

"I've heard some pretty unbelievable stories about your deadly family," said the doctor. "Now I think they must all be true."

Just then, Rico opened his eyes, "Did we get 'em?"

"We did," said Charlie, "From now on, I suppose I'm going to hear you tell everyone how you saved my life."

"In that case, I guess I'll just have to pull through, so I can torture you forever," said Rico with a little smile.

Charlie leaned over and kissed Rico on the forehead, "We sure did a job here this night."

He got up and walked out of the garage. The sun was just coming up and it looked like it would be a glorious day.

Chapter 17
Saving the Family

Fox News

"In an overnight raid on a hospital outside of Damascus, American Seal Team Six and elements of the 82nd Airborne Division, rescued the Black Angel and 490 other people held hostage, and captured the entire senior leadership of ISIS. For more on the story we bring in our Middle Eastern correspondent Brent Williams."

"Robert, this story reads like an action movie script. Using intelligence gained from international sources, Navy Seal Team Six attacked a hospital on the outskirts of Damascus last night and were able to, not only rescue the Black Angel, who was kidnapped in Ankara, Turkey three days ago, but also discovered 490 other hostages being held in brutal conditions in the lower levels of the hospital. Intelligence had learned that this hospital was serving as the central command and control center for ISIS."

"The Seals conducted an overnight raid on the hospital, killing at least 1,000 ISIS fighters. They were able to slip into the hospital and surprise the entire senior leadership of ISIS, including their leader Hassan Al Aswiri."

"Our sources say the Black Angel, himself, mounted a one man offensive of his own after the raid began and was present when Aswiri was captured. We've also learned the Black Angel's own family, were involved in the raid. His son, known as Ardishur by the Kurds, and his daughter, Rosy, an apparently formidable warrior herself was also involved and was seriously injured, but is said to be recovering. One report, which we can't confirm, was that the Black Angel's wife was also present in the raid, and did more than just watch from the sidelines. Back to you Robert."

"This raid on the ISIS headquarters is the culmination of a six month Crusade, set off by Roman Catholic Pope John Luke the

First. In this coalition, the pope was able to unify Shia Muslims from Iran, Kurds from northern Iraq, Israeli Jews, and American forces of the two most combat ready divisions in the U.S. Army, the 82nd and 101st Airborne, along with six brigades of Marines. The United States was joined by forces from ten other western countries."

"After over a twelve year rampage of atrocities by ISIS on Muslims, Jews, Christians, Kurds and other religious groups, the Middle East is quiet tonight."

"In other associated news, the entire intelligence structure of ISIS was also captured. Defense Department correspondent, Tony Willis has the story.

"Robert, the capture of the ISIS headquarters in Damascus yielded the largest cache of intelligence ever found regarding terrorist activities around the world by ISIS, Al Qaeda, and a number of other jihadist organizations. The Defense and State Department are reporting arrests are now being made on hundreds of terrorist operatives around the world in the largest manhunt in history, Robert.'

"So what does all this mean? ISIS is defeated and destroyed, but what about the future for the Middle East. For that we turn to our Fox News Senior White House correspondent, Amber Whitley, Amber?"

"Robert, the White House has made no official announcement yet, but our sources tell us all the leaders of the Crusader coalition are on their way to Washington for high level talks on the future of the Middle East. A West Wing official would only say that a major change in the political and geographic picture of the Middle East is the likely outcome of these talks. Back to you Robert."

"Across the world today, there are huge crowds of spontaneous celebrations in many capitals both Christian and Muslim. There's a sense of relief as the most unlikely of all coalitions made up of Muslims, Christians, and Jews have managed to totally destroy the biggest terrorist organization in world history."

❖

President Carson Palmer switched off the TV, and picked up the analysis and recommendations for what should be done following the defeat of ISIS. Cody worked on it, off and on, throughout the Crusade. With changing circumstances, he would amend his analysis and demonstrate how these solutions represented the most stable and profitable outcome for all parties, either fighting the war or victims of it. Throughout all the various iterations of his plan, he always made the point of the outcome of American involvement in the reconstruction of Germany and Japan after World War II, as well as the Colter Plan for Iran, and the lack of finishing the job in previous involvements in Afghanistan, Iraq, and the rest of the region. He pounded away on the need for the proper endgame that wiped out the unilateral choices of the Western, Christian nations of France and Britain following World War I.

Convinced by Cody's logic, President Palmer determined to get global approval for the detailed plan Cody suggested, as radical as it was.

He had not spoken to Cody since the hospital raid, but the reports coming to him from the Joint Chief of Staff of the military painted an astonishing picture of what really happened at the Damascus hospital. Palmer was not surprised at the gushing reports on the exploits of the Frost family. Nothing this group of remarkable individuals did was surprising. All he knew was that both Cody and Pope John Luke had survived this war. Without them, the task could have been impossible.

❖

At that moment, Cody couldn't care less about Middle Eastern politics. He, Charlie and Ashana were languishing in a waiting room at a large hospital in Tel Aviv. After airlifting to Israel, Rico and Rosy were receiving superior service and care for their injuries. Rico was just holding on from his injuries. He had undergone two operations to repair the damage to his carotid artery, and his leg would require a different operation to repair his shattered bone. Even though this was very important to do, the doctors could not risk another operation while Rico was still in mortal danger from the other wound.

For Rosy, it was now a question of trying to control the septic shock from her knife wound. She'd ignored it and kept fighting, which only made it worse. Now the doctors were afraid she might lose her arm. Cody and Ashana clung to each other. Charlie sat intensely across the room in another chair. Tears filled his eyes.

It seemed like days passed, although it was only a few hours. At last, a surgeon came into the waiting room. There was a smile on his face.

"The second operation was able to repair the temporary job they did in Damascus. Don't get me wrong, those guys did a truly heroic job, and saved Rico's life. It was just a patch, and we had to go in and rebuild his carotid artery as well as all the tissue damage surrounding it. We have him in ICU now and are monitoring him carefully, but I think I can say this crisis has passed."

"What about his leg?" asked Ashana.

"We need to get to work on that as soon as he's strong enough to undergo another operation. We think we can repair the broken bones, but the longer we wait the better the chance of infection setting in and him losing his leg. Why don't you all go get some sleep? It's not like you've been on vacation the last few days.

"May I just say, sir, the people of Israel regard you as one of our own? I know you often have said you are a man without a country. You will always have a home with us."

"Thank you, Doctor," said Cody, "about the good news for Rico and your kind invitation to live in Israel. We would consider that a privilege. But you're right about us needing some rest. I'm out on my feet."

There was a limousine waiting for them as they left the hospital. It took them to a luxury hotel in Tel-Aviv, where they had to push their way through a mob of employees and citizens who wanted to celebrate the famous family.

By the time they got to their spacious suite, they plopped down in soft chairs.

"Tell you the truth, you didn't look like you were out on your feet at the hospital," said Charlie.

"A lifetime of adrenaline rushes, I guess," said Cody. "People think the war is over. Well, it's not. The fighting may be over, but the biggest battles of them all are waiting for us."

"How so?" asked Ashana.

"Destroying ISIS will only create another vacuum. We have to make sure the changes we make this time are ones that people will support, and then we have to help them learn how to do it."

"I guess we haven't talked about this very much," said Charlie. "Exactly what do you think needs to happen?"

"Pretty simple," said Cody. "The Kurds need a country of their own. The Shias of Iraq need a country of their own. The Palestinians need a country of their own. The Sunnis of Iraq need a country of their own. Israel needs to receive recognition as a country by other Muslim nations and everyone has to share the oil and other resources."

"That's a lot more easily said than done," mused Charlie.

"We aren't going to solve the problem tonight," said Cody, "and I just realized I'm truly exhausted, adrenaline or not."

"Let's go to bed," said Ashana. "I'll give you a nice bath and then rub you down."

"That sounds like the best news of the day."

"I'm going to bed," said Charlie. "See you in the morning."

Ashana was tired too, but was desperately worried about her husband. The strain of the last several months, plus the intensity of what he had endured in the last week made his bravado seem very hollow to her. She soaked him in the big tub, and then had him lay on the bed while she worked on his knotted muscles. It was no surprise to her when Cody started snoring softly in just a few minutes.

All three of them slept long and well. Cody woke and found he was the last one up. Charlie and Ashana were sipping coffee and a big breakfast was waiting for Cody. Ashana had ordered it when she got up.

"How are you feeling?" asked Ashana.

"Good," said Cody, "best night's sleep I've had in a long time. Was it the same for you too?"

"Yeah," said Charlie, "we feel great."

"We got a call from the hospital," said Ashana, "Rico is out of ICU, and they expect to work on his leg tomorrow. He's awake and asking for us."

"What about Rosy?"

"She's awake also. They filled her with antibiotics overnight, and now think she's well enough to be released tomorrow. Rosy thinks it should be today. I talked to her and she's getting anxious to move on."

"You've also had other calls," said Ashana, "President Palmer called to see how you're doing. He sends his best. Also the pope called wanting to know when you can come to Rome."

"All of this cause I slept in a little?" said Cody.

"The front desk of the hotel called and said they are overwhelmed with the Press, wanting to know when you're going to make a statement," said Charlie. "I would be interested to know, myself, what you're going to say."

"I'm not going to say anything until I've talked with President Palmer, and John Luke," said Cody. "Tell you what, why don't you two get dressed and head over to the hospital. Have the hotel slip you out the back way. If the press catches you, just say I'm OK, and will have a statement for them later today. Be happy and gracious and thank them all for their interest, but don't get caught in anything that has to do with what we do next."

"Got it," said Charlie.

"Say hello to Rico and Rosy. Tell them I love them and will come as soon as I can."

Ashana and Charlie got ready to leave in just a few minutes, and left Cody writing on his laptop.

There was no chance Ashana or Charlie were going to be able to avoid the press. They had camped out at every exit. So, Ashana decided to take them head on. She and Charlie arrived at the lobby and conducted an impromptu press conference.

"Ladies and Gentlemen," she said, "I thank you all for coming, and for your kind concern for my husband. The Black Angel had a good night's sleep, the best he's had in months. We are going to the hospital now to check on our daughter, Rosy, and Rico, who is really a part of the family. Both of them are doing well, and we believe they will recover from their injuries, even though it was touch and go for Rico for a while. He is the real hero of the day. He shoved Ardishur out of the way, and took the shots intended for him, himself."

"The Black Angel is trying to get caught up on everything, and is talking with world leaders as we speak. He wants me to remind you he was just the field commander of the Crusade, and many other people played important roles in the war with ISIS.

"All of you must know that winning the war was just the beginning of the huge job of bringing peace and stability back to the Middle East. That will be the Black Angel's mission from now on. In fact, he's starting the process right now, and says he can't really say anything until he's spoken to other world leaders."

"I know you have thousands of questions. Trust me, my husband is in the same boat. He says he will try to come down later and answer as many questions as he can. Until then, please be patient, and let him work with a clear head."

"Please let us go now. I have a couple of hurt kids who need us, and I really can't tell you more than you already know."

Ashana and Charlie stepped away from the microphones and ignored the many questions thrown at them as they passed through the lobby of the hotel to the waiting limousine outside.

In his room, Cody was trying to gather his thoughts. He made a number of entries on his laptop. Then he called Rome and was put through to Pope John Luke immediately.

"Well, Cody, you managed to put an enormous exclamation point on the end of the war with ISIS," said John Luke. "Are you alright?"

"I'd say I was back up to speed, and ready for all that comes next," said Cody. "What are your plans?"

"I was thinking of reconvening the conference of all the people who came to the first one in Geneva."

"We need something more from them than just confirmation they were right, and our thanks for giving you the chance to right the wrongs of the Islamic Caliphate. We need their pledge to work with us in the same spirit as we go about reorganizing the Middle East. You've got a lot of clout right now and we need to use it to push for the reforms we've discussed."

"President Palmer is saying much the same," said John Luke.

"You've spoken to him?"

"Twice, he's anxious to talk with you."

"He called me this morning while I was sleeping. As soon as you and I finish up, I'll call him."

"It's the middle of the night in Washington," said the pope, "but I'm pretty sure the President is working late. Let me know what he says."

"I will," said Cody. He broke the connection with the pope and called the White House.

"I've been napping," said the President when he came on the line.

"Sorry for the time difference, Carson, I just think we need to get an immediate handle on all this before everyone else comes up with their own ideas."

"Fortunately, most of the ideas I've heard fall into line with your strategy. It's also helping a lot the press, is concentrating at this moment on surveying the damage in the ISIS controlled areas, they haven't gotten into in years, and reporting the long list of really awful things they're finding. In addition, the Crusader forces are still mopping up in a few places where there are still active ISIS cells. All the information you recovered from their command center has given us the intelligence we need to run smaller operations. Best of all, we now have a very clear picture of all the activities of ISIS around the world. A couple dozen countries are acting on this intelligence and are arresting thousands of people. In quite a few cases, ISIS has tried to make final stands, so the death toll is mounting. In some cases, popular uprisings of people have taken the action out of our hands. ISIS supporters are dying."

"There's no question we have them beat," said Cody. "Now we need get our plan out to the public before the next news cycle occurs."

"What's the next move you propose?" asked the President.

"You need to send invitations for a major conference with the leaders of the countries that have the most skin in this game. If you can get them to Washington in the next week, I plan to present them with my proposals. Am I right, I'm still the biggest single influence?"

"You are," said the President. "Who do we invite to the conference?"

"We need Masoud Barzani, President of the Kurds, Prime Minister Farid Sensek from Turkey, President Manek Faroush from Iran, Pope John Luke, and Ari ben Cannan from Israel."

"Shouldn't we invite some of the other members of the coalition?"

"If this plan is going to work at all, those are the people we should talk to first. If I can get the Turks and the Kurds to agree on the new borders, we'll set an example for the rest of the Middle East to follow."

"Solve the problems one at a time?" said the President.

"Exactly," said Cody. Let me know when you've set up the conference."

"You realize this is going to be a hard nut to crack?"

"All of those men trust me," said Cody. "They'll come just to hear what I have to say, and to see if I'm willing to keep all the promises I've made."

"I'll call you when I've got everything arranged."

"Do it as fast as you can, Carson, I can't have these countries having second thoughts. In fact, I'm going to have a press conference this afternoon and say the United State is sponsoring a major meeting with the combatants of the Crusade, and we expect to be able to make some major announcements."

"No pressure," said the President.

"A lot of pressure, Carson, but you're the man to pull it off."

"The Russians and the Chinese are raising holy hell about being left out of all we've done."

"They're going to be my prime victims when we get this completed plan to the United Nations," said Cody.

Despite the hordes of press around the hotel, Cody was able to make a get-away disguised as a deliveryman. He put on a coverall, a baseball cap and dark glasses. Then he just walked out through the kitchen, got in the company truck and drove himself to the hospital. He got into the hospital the same way. He stripped off the coverall, and took the elevator to the floor where Rico and Rosy were resting.

Actually, resting was not quite what he found with Rosy. She was out of her bed and sitting in a chair, still hooked up to an IV bag.

"Really, dad, this is a bit much. I want to leave."

"Just cool it, kid," said Cody. "You got a big infection from that knife wound because you kept fighting and tore it up some more. That IV is full of antibiotics, which you need today. They can give you pills after that. Don't worry, you aren't gonna miss nuthin'. In fact, you're another family hero, and the press wants to talk to you almost as much as I am asked. I've heard stories from the Seal Team, and a nice fellow named Matt, who says the Seals want to adopt you."

"Where'd you hear that?"

"From General Gordon he's been handling the press, on the hospital assault. You're famous among a group of men who aren't easily impressed."

"I liked Matt," said Rosy. "He's my kind of man. I'd like to see him again."

"The Seals have a big welcome planned for you tomorrow. If you'll just cool your jets for another day, you can go. Otherwise, I'll send you home to Positano."

"You wouldn't dare!" said Rosy noisily.

Cody laughed, "Just kidding, honey. I wouldn't keep you from your big welcome, but you still have to hang around here till the docs say you're OK to leave."

"OK, you win, but you don't win fair," said Rosy.

She sat in the chair for a while, and then turned on the TV to get the latest news. She was interested in how much the press actually missed, and how superficial it was. As she was watching, a voice spoke from the door, "Hi there. Can I come in?"

Rosy turned and stared at the man in the door for a minute. Then she recognized him without all the camouflage, "Why it's my man Matt himself," she grinned.

"We're having a big welcome for you when you get out here," said Matt, "but I wanted to come by on my own and talk to you privately."

"Have a seat," said Rosy. "Tell me the news I wasn't getting much of it from the TV."

Matt pulled up a chair and sat down close to Rosy.

"I've been with the Seals for three years," he said, "we've jumped in and out of some pretty hairy situations. None of them was like what we went through at the hospital. I just came to say I've never seen anyone do the things you did. Even with your arm sliced almost in half, you went on as if nothing had happened. You saved my life twice. A fellow gets real close to people in a hurry under circumstances like that."

Rosy blushed a little, "That's nice of you to say. I was pretty impressed with you as well."

"I was just wondering," said Matt very quietly, "if you might like to spend some time together, when we're not shooting bad guys?"

"Are you actually asking me for a date?" Rosy asked.

"I am. Look, Rosy, I sort of looked through the battle cream and got a good look at you while they were fixing your arm. I want to know the woman behind that fierce warrior spirit. You're awful pretty, you know. Guess I sort of felt a connection between us, and I really like you."

"I like you too," said Rosy. "Trust me, that's saying a lot. I've never really had a real date. I've been way too busy to bother with any personal relationships. I'm thinking I might make an exception for you."

"That's great!" said Matt. "I was scared to come here and see you, because I was afraid you might not feel anything for me, like I do for you."

"I was hoping to see you again," said Rosy, "maybe for the same reason."

"Maybe we could do something after my teammates get through slobbering all over you tomorrow, and declaring you to an official, unofficial Seal."

"I'd like that," said Rosy. "I think I know now how my brother feels."

"What's that," asked Matt.

"Kind of a long story," said Rosy. "I'll tell you all about it tomorrow."

Cody's next stop was to see Rico. Charlie was in the room with him. "Ahh, the warrior brother's reunited."

"Hi Cody, How's it going?" said Rico.

"You boys have made quite a name for yourselves."

"Just doing the stuff you taught us," Rico said smiling.

He had a big bandage on his neck, and his leg was elevated from the bed.

"I heard from the docs they're taking you down to have your leg fixed this afternoon. That's good news. It means they think you're strong enough from that mess…,"he pointed at the neck bandage, "to stand another operation.

"The doc said he was sure they could repair the bone in my leg. It didn't take a direct hit, just shattered off a jillion little pieces."

"It's the small bone fragments that made them worry about infection. Now it looks like your bone will grow back good as new. I want you to get on your feet as fast as you can, because you're going to Washington with the rest of the family. You even get to stay at the White House."

"That sounds great," said Rico.

"You did a great job in the hospital raid," said Cody.

"Sure did save my life," added Charlie, "Thanks, bro."

"All in a day's work," said Rico, "You would have done the same for me."

"I'll leave you guys to tell war stories," said Cody, "remember Rico, I'm going to need you in Washington next week."

"I'll be ready."

Cody went back to Rosy's room and found Ashana there. "I missed you when I was here earlier."

"I went down to make sure Rosy would be able to leave safely tomorrow."

"Everything, OK?"

"The infection is under control and her wound is healing nicely. You'll have a scar to explain," said Ashana.

"Badge of honor," said Rosy.

Rosy has an admirer," said Ashana. "His name is Matt. He fought with Rosy at the hospital, and came to ask her out on a date. She said yes."

"Really," said Cody, "I have to meet this guy. Anybody who can break through you're armor, must be pretty special."

The family visited for a few more minutes before Cody led Ashana and Charlie out of the hospital and into a limousine. When they got back to the hotel, it was funny to see all the press crushed around General Gordon, who had pinch-hit as the Crusader spokesperson for the last day. Gordon was good with the press, but without anything new to add to the overall situation found himself answering the same questions repeatedly.

Cody, Ashana, and Charlie managed to slip into the press crowd without attracting any attention. Finally, Cody laughed and yelled out over the crowd, "Hey Flash, why don't you tell 'em what you really think?"

Gordon scowled at the use of his nickname and then spotted Cody standing unnoticed among all the intense journalists trying to wring every drop out of Gordon. A big smile filled his face. He held his hands up to get everyone's attention. "The question was why I don't tell you what I really think. What I really think is that you people are like ISIS you've never learned the gentle art of sneaking up from behind. The Black Angel did that all the time. It was a wonder to watch his brilliant tactics. But who am I to talk about the Black Angel, he's managed to sneak up on all of you." Gordon started laughing as the press looked around. Not only was he laughing but also so were Ashana, Charlie and Cody.

Cody made his way to the podium, Ashana and Charlie joined him. The press was roaring, many of them were laughing, but most were trying to get Cody's attention. The press learned the hard way that Cody despised the term Black Angel. Since nobody but a select, few in the world knew his real name the press started just using the term "Sir." It was just one of the many mysteries surrounding Cody. He was a man with no country. A few details had come out about his life, and everyone knew he was the man that conceived and executed the operation that foiled the Iranian plot. Now, he had led the Crusaders to victory over the previously invincible Islamic Caliphate who had absorbed two countries, Iraq and Syria. The final battle at the hospital that rescued the Black Angel and crushed ISIS, made Cody the most popular man in the world.

When Cody held his finger to his lips, everyone went silent.

"The first thing I want to say is that our long time family member Enrico Moretti is now in stable condition. He will have to undergo another operation this afternoon to repair the bullet wound he received in the thigh. I should add that Rico was actually shot five times, but his armor protected him from three of them."

"My daughter Rosy received a very serious knife wound in her arm near the beginning of the assault on the hospital by Seal Team 6. Yet, she continued to fight to the end and killed several ISIS defenders. She is recovering from this wound and will leave the hospital tomorrow. I understand the Seals have a special party planned for her. She's been adopted as an official Seal."

"Now that I've gotten the important personal announcements made, let's move to more official business. It's critical you know ISIS, Al Qaeda, and a number of other fringe terrorist groups are finished. Arrests and manhunts are underway all over the world. The intelligence we recovered from the ISIS command center gave us vital information of whom and where these people are located."

"Ladies and Gentlemen, the fighting is over. I offer congratulations and thanks to the noble men and women who were part of our Crusader coalition. When the moment came, the Lord God Almighty, by whatever name He is known entered the hearts of people who worship Him and came together as never before, to defeat an enemy whose motives were so evil and profane their existence could not be tolerated in our world."

"Now even though the fighting is over, we must come together as a family of nations to insure peace, harmony, and freedom reach the embattled people of the Middle East. In just a few days, we will offer a comprehensive plan showing how these goals can be achieved. I can tell you this plan will give us a very different Middle East, but one that takes into consideration the cultural, ethnic, geographic, and religious factors of this troubled part of the world. All of you have given strong support for our Crusade, and for me. I'm very grateful, and so is my family. Now I ask you to stand strong as we attempt to thread the needle to a lasting peace. It will require good will and a spirit of compromise to accomplish what will come next. Don't ask me, I'm not free to act on my own, as I did when I commanded the Crusaders. Many others have a part to play. Just stay sharp and make sure you report the complete stories, the world is depending on you."

Chapter 18
Pan Middle-Eastern Treaty
Washington, D.C.

A week later, the whole Frost family, plus Rico wearing a leg brace and using crutches were at the White House. The dynamics of the negotiations were very tense.

The Kurds did not trust the Turks; the Iranians were worried about their own borders with the Sunnis in Iraq; the Israelis wanted recognition of their existence from their neighbors. It was the same situation as had existed before ISIS. Cody was determined to change the paradigm. He spent two days with John Luke in Rome. The pope was busy trying to reassemble the same conferees who attended the meetings in Geneva that set off the modern Crusade. So far, he received confirmations from almost all the delegates.

Their idea was to wait until some consensus appeared in Washington on the political solutions, and then mobilize a global effort to implement it. The plan called for an army of volunteers, willing to go into the region, to nurture infant nations to maturity. They would be unarmed civilians with no interests other than the political and social health of each nation, as well as diplomatic relationships with other nations. The Catholic Church was prepared to open public, secular universities to train new leaders from a young age to take their place within the governments, as they grew older and more mature.

The main sticking point of this and all the rest of the negotiations was an equal status for all women as well as the right to vote.

President Palmer stood between the pope and Cody just outside the large lounge were all the invited leaders drinking coffee, tea, and nibbling on an assortment of pastries.

"I don't hear anybody yelling," said Cody, "we ought to count that as a good sign."

"Think you can remember the plan?" said Palmer to both Cody

and the pope.

Both of them laughed a little.

"It won't get any easier, if we just stand out here," said Palmer. "Let's go in and test the waters." He opened the double door and all the leaders stopped as the architects of this day walked into the room.

It was Prime Minister Farid Sensek, who got to Cody first, "I offer my most sincere apologies for allowing you to be kidnapped in Turkey. It was a national disgrace."

"As I recall," said Cody, "it was you who wanted me to go to the airport in a helicopter. The disgrace is mine. I had come to believe I was invulnerable. Of course, I was wrong. If it's any help to you, I'll come to Turkey and make a public speech apologizing for my stupidity."

"That is most gracious of you, Cody," said Sensek.

The exchange broke the ice in the room. Cody, the Pope John Luke, and President Palmer made the rounds with everyone, complimenting all for their efforts, and sacrifice of blood and treasure in decimating ISIS.

The President spoke above the conversations, "If you gentlemen will just go into the conference room, I think we can get started."

There were nametags at each place around the large oval table. Cody had meticulously seated all the leaders strategically. Since the table did not really have any edges, there was no distinction between the placing of one leader next to another. For himself, he had picked a seat near the center. The pope sat across from him, and President Palmer sat next to him.

"Before we begin the job of creating a new Middle East," said Cody, "I have an announcement I would like to make. Entirely too much of the spotlight for our struggle against ISIS was focused on me. I permitted this, along with the term 'Black Angel', since it was valuable for morale. All of you men in this room know my real first name, please use it today, and use your own first names as well. I hate pomp and posturing. When we have completed our work, I fully intend to go back into retirement with my family. I have no interest whatsoever, in continuing in any official role. I came from nowhere, and I'm looking forward to getting back there at the first possible moment."

There was more than modesty in Cody's remarks. He knew what

kind of unique position he held in the world. Saying he was eager to give it all up, and slip into obscurity, was a sign to everyone in the room he did not intend to use his power to manipulate any of them. Unconsciously, everyone in the room sighed, a breath of relief.

"Having told everyone I'm tendering my resignation, let's get started."

"All of us have met together before, except for the Prime Minister of Turkey Farid Sensek. I welcome you, Farid and thank you for all your country has done to allow us to set the keystone of our new Middle Eastern geography in place."

The Prime Minister stood, placed his hand on his heart, and said, "When Cody first came to me with his proposal, it seemed like a preposterous pipe-dream. However, the more he talked, the more I began to have hope, it was possible. I ended up ordering our military into northern Syria. We were able to defeat ISIS in some of their biggest strongholds. As Cody and I agreed, we advanced south to the border of Lebanon, stopping at the city of Homs, and going no further east than the Euphrates River.

"Because of that, we gained important reserves of oil, and the cleared the way for off-shore development of large reserves of natural gas.

"Cody assured me we would be able to keep this land and its resources. With this accomplished, I was able to put forward the framework for an accommodation with the Kurds in our Parliament."

After Farid returned to his seat, Masoud Barzani, President of the Kurds said, "Prime Minister Farid Sensek made direct contact with me and we were able to come to an agreement of the Kurdish lands of eastern and southern Turkey. In return for ceding this land to the Kurds, we agreed to supply Turkey with more oil pipelines and deliver 20 million barrels of crude oil, every day for the next 25 years at 10% over the actual production and transport costs. We also agreed to withdraw our elected representatives in the Turkish parliament, since there would be no Kurds living in Turkey."

Cody said, "Kurdistan will now become as one with the leaders in the Middle East, each will have about 30% of all the oil in Syria and Iraq. The country will run across the entire northern border of Iraq, Syria, and to the Euphrates River. Masoud has traveled throughout Kurdistan and received support from all the splinter groups, which had their own agendas. The two countries have now signed the Pan Middle-Eastern plan I have envisioned. Interestingly, the one issue, which caused the most difference of opinion in both counties, was the status of women in their society. Fortunately, both countries are much further advanced in this regard than other Middle Eastern countries, and will set the standard for the rest."

Masoud and Farid were sitting next to each other. Now both of them stood and shook hands to seal the deal.

"As I said, solving the problem of Turkish Kurds and the shortage of oil in Turkey is the keystone to our larger agreement," said Cody. "When other areas of the Middle East see that such an impossible problem is solved, it will allow us to negotiate with others in the same spirit of accommodation and compromise.

"By the way," said Cody, "I've made a separate agreement with the Kurds to relocate and rebuild the Aswan dam, now in their country. It was a foolish placement of the dam in the first place, but we intend to put it in a better location, so that vital water supplies can be delivered south without continuous fear of the dam collapsing and leaving an entire population to the south without water or power. It's part of the display of goodwill and vital aid for what will remain of the old Iraq."

"Additionally," said Manek Faroush, speaking up for the first time. Iran has experienced its own problem with the Kurds. They have experienced discrimination and repression for many years. In the Pan Middle-Eastern Treaty, we have agreed to cede the small portion of our country, known as western Azerbaijan to the Kurds. Almost all of the population is Shia Muslims, but Masoud assures me they will be regarded as Kurds first, and will be free to practice Shiite practices in the new Kurdistan."

Cody spoke up again, "I believe now is the time to show you all our vision for the restructured Middle East. He punched a button on a remote and a picture of the entire Middle East, as it would become, flashed on the screen. Cody paused for a moment to let the new reality sink in.

There were sounds of surprise and wonder about the table.

Several men got up and stood close to the graphic, tracing the borders with their fingers.

"Is this truly what you envision?" asked Ari ben Cannan, Prime

Minister of Israel.

"It is," said Cody, "this is the way the Middle East should have been partitioned at the end of World War I. This map, not only divides resources more equally, but it also divides along ethnic lines. People can live with this configuration.

Cody continued, "We are creating three new countries and altering the borders of four more. Parts of Iraq, Turkey, and a small part of Iran as you can see now, will become Kurdistan.

"Down here, in the southern part of Iraq, south of Bagdad, the population is almost totally Shia. I've arbitrarily given it the name of Sumeria, a title derived from the history of the area. The people can select whatever name they like. Its capital city will be Basra. The current population of Sumeria is about 30 million people.

"To the north is Bagdad, the new capital of the consolidated country, which I have returned to its original name, Mesopotamia. Again, the people can choose whatever name they want. From Bagdad, north the country ends just outside of Tikrit. This land is almost totally Sunni. In this scenario, Mesopotamia retains about 60% of current oil reserves, which will put it on a par with Kurdistan.

"Syria will become about half the size it is now, but retaining a third of their oil fields. If you are wondering who will populate this land, since about three million fled Syria during the civil war and subsequent occupation by ISIS, we have at least a million refugees eking out an existence in Europe. There were far too many ISIS terrorists imbedded in that mass of people. We are busy identifying them now. For the rest of them, they will be happy to come home, and a lot of them are from this part of Syria. They also are mostly Shiites.

"I propose we give the Palestinians a country of their own, here in Jordan. Over half the population is already Palestinian and the King will have no choice but to govern according to the wishes of the Palestinian majority.

"For Israel, I propose the Gaza Strip be abandoned as Jewish lands and given back to the Egyptians. However, Israel will remain in the West Bank and move its borders to both sides of the Dead Sea. Also, they will annex the Becca Valley, which they have already occupied.

"Finally, as a buffer for the Iranians bordering Mesopotamia, I believe they should occupy the Zagros mountain chain, and hold the high ground."

Farid Sensek said, "Do you realize you're doing all this planning without consulting either the Iraqi or Syrian people? We are the ones who will have to absorb the culture shock and deal with the refugees."

Cody replied, "I know that, Farid. Keep thinking about the oil you will own, and how the decades of strife with the Kurds will not be part of your political structure. Gentleman, the floor is open. We welcome your comments, suggestions, and criticism."

"How do you see all this working politically? asked Manek Faroush. "It seems to me we have done everything necessary to defuse possible points of dissension among the new countries. Many of the age-old pressure points are gone.

Farid said. "There are still other countries in the Middle-East who may not appear to be directly impacted, but who might oppose this new order. Have you given any thoughts to them?"

"Saudi Arabia is the biggest of the countries. They are also one of the most oppressive in their treatment of women. However, there's not much, they can do about it and we might see some relaxation of their cultural inflexibility. One thing is for sure, we got nothing but support from most of the countries around the Arabian Peninsula. Bahrain, The Emirate's, Kuwait, Oman, even Yemen, watched with wonder as we assembled a coalition made up of Muslims, Christians, and Jews, based on our dedication to the one true God, and effectively used it to destroy the Caliphate. They were the enemy of everyone."

"That's what is the most astonishing to me," said Manek.

"You can credit the wise men of Islam for that," said Cody. "They have corresponded, over the years with the Catholic Church and other Evangelical groups. Their premise was simply for all of us to remember we worship God, who is the same God for us all. When you begin from that conviction, a lot of the ritual of worship ceases to be all that important."

"Since such a large number of Muslim leaders from all over the world signed the letter," said the pope, "it motivated us to agree with them. We were all facing a common enemy; the coalition was not all that hard to form."

"Is there any member of the coalition, present today, who cannot support the way we have restructured the Middle East?" asked Cody.

The room was quiet for a moment, then Ari ben Cannan spoke up. "We agree the reorganization makes sense to us all. However, Israel still faces the same problem we had in 1948, when the country was formed. Not one of the Muslim countries has recognized our right to exist. If we proceed with your plan, Cody, Israel can't easily support it without a change to this attitude."

"We saw Israelis fighting and dying, side by side, with Muslims in our destruction of ISIS," said the Iranian, Manek Faroush. It seems archaic to me not to recognize the new reality."

"The Kurds have always enjoyed a good relationship with Israel," said Masoud Barzani. "Of course, we didn't have a country of our own until now. I will tell you, Ari, Kurdistan is ready to establish a formal diplomatic relationship with your country."

"We were constrained by the politics of the region also, and as a Muslim nation we stood with the rest of the Muslim world in rejecting Israel's right to exist," said Turkish Prime Minister Sensek. "We are no longer going to follow that mantra. We are now stronger and more independent than anyone. Turkey will join Kurdistan and Iran in recognizing the sovereignty of Israel."

"My guess is that most of the other nations in the Middle East will adopt the same attitude," said Cody. "Look around you. You now have three partners you didn't have five minutes ago."

"I am most grateful for your support," said Ari ben Cannan. "With this beginning, and the solution to the Palestinian problem in hand, I believe we can move forward with the rest of the Middle East for a bright new tomorrow."

"I'm pretty sure Syria, Mesopotamia and Sumeria will adopt the same policy," said Cody.

President Palmer spoke up for the first time, "This is all excellent, Cody, but how do we go about getting international support for this profound facelift for the Middle East?"

"The most important component in accomplishing this is to present a unified position to the world. What I have in mind is a Pan Middle East Accord. Every one of you present have constituents of your own to satisfy, and independent self-determination to protect.

"However, there are some issues upon which we can agree. The first, and perhaps the most important, is freedom of religion. Christians need to feel safe to worship in the midst of overwhelming Muslim populations. Also, the Shias should feel equally safe. We have seen how awful the daily lives of people become when the policy of a single sector of Islam motivates the behaviors of their religion. They do not follow the principles of the first commandment of God: that we will worship him and have no other gods before Him. The second commandment is like the first: we must love our neighbors as ourselves, and understand how their ways are not like our ways. We accept that. If we don't follow these commandments of our common God, then the war we've just fought was to no purpose."

"We can also agree that control of the government must in the hands of secular political leaders and not the unilateral decrees of Ayatollahs or other religious leaders. Government must be separate from religion. The most recent example of why this does not work is the heartache, pain and misery Iran experienced.

"I actually don't object to Sharia Law, when it is confined to the home and families, but not the government. Sharia Law has to do with personal behaviors and is far too limited to apply as general law for a whole country. Therefore, the women of the new Middle East should enjoy the same rights and privileges as men. They all should have the right to vote, and to be able to seek justice as individuals from secular courts who establish laws that recognize all men, and women, are created equally."

"If we put these key components in our treaty, constitution, articles of confederation, or whatever you want to call it, we will present a unified and common face to the rest of the world."

"How exactly are we going to accomplish this?" asked Manek Faroush. There were other comments around the table that echoed this roadblock.

Cody turned to Ari ben Cannan, "How did the country of Israel come to be?"

"It was a general vote by the General Assembly of the United Nations."

"Why did it come to that?" asked Cody.

"The Security Council could not agree," said Ari. "They ended up hopelessly deadlocked."

"That is exactly right," said Cody. "I will tell you the Security Council is going to end up the same way in this issue. Both Russia and China will oppose it, while the United States, France and Great Britain support it."

"The charter of the United Nations says that in the case of

deadlock in the Security Council, or if the Council does not act, when International peace and global security is involved, the General Assembly can take up the matter independently of the Security Council, and vote to produce a resolution of their own. In order for an issue of this magnitude to pass, we would need a two-thirds majority. There are currently 193 members of the United Nations, which means we need 128 votes."

"How do-able is that?" asked Farid.

"Every country has their own self interests," said Cody. Those nations who rely on a steady and predictable flow of oil from the Middle East will vote in favor. Nations who now have a better feeling of security from the destruction of the Caliphate will favor it. Many nations who have no particular interest in either will be glad ISIS is no longer terrorizing the world, and will be in favor. In short, I think we have a very good chance of ramming this through."

"So what's the next step?" asked Barzani.

"I've taken the liberty of writing a draft resolution of our Pan Middle East articles," said Cody. "I want each of you to take a copy, study it, call whoever you need to test the waters of support. Then bring it back to me, with your corrections, changes, or objections. This group, the heart of the coalition, has a lot of clout in the world right now. If we can agree on our document, submit it to your people and get a vote, up or down … call it 'The referendum of peace'.

"Assuming, your voters approve it, we will have millions of voices to stick in the face of the United Nations. If we can get other Muslim countries to sign on to our agreement, it will certainly help. The influence of the United States would be the key to have peace."

"We will do everything we can," said President Palmer. "Do you think the people of the United States should vote on this as well?"

"If it passes," said Cody. "Otherwise, if your polling shows it's a loser, then I would recommend deciding this with the people of the region, and not conduct a vote."

"That's probably good advice," said Palmer.

"We need a consensus among ourselves before we move any further," said Cody. "Would a week, be enough time for everyone to study my draft, and then reconvene for a final debate?"

There was general agreement at the round table.

"Great." said Cody, "Here's the proposal." He opened his attaché case and distributed the draft to everyone.

The group sat in dumb silence. Finally Masoud spoke up, "This is only three pages long."

"Sorry," said Cody, "I wanted it to be as short as the American Constitution, but I was a little long-winded."

"I doubt it will take me a whole week to absorb this," said Farid.

"On the contrary, my friend, every word in this document carries a deep meaning. You will have a difficult time," said Cody.

As the meeting broke up, President Palmer, who had already read the document with Pope John Luke, lingered behind.

"You're right, Cody," said the President, "Those men will struggle to comprehend the depth and scope of your proposal."

"What do you two think?" asked Cody.

"Quite up to form, Cody," said the pope. "It has everything a Republic should have to be successful."

"I've already done some polling on this," said the President. "The numbers say we would get American approval for this easily. I'm sure a large number of people will volunteer to go to the Middle East to teach them how a good government is supposed to work. In fact, I think there are at least two elements you've included, which ought to be amendments to our constitution, like term limits for elected officials, and a requirement for a balanced budget."

"I suppose that's a battle for a different day," said Cody, "but I think you're right and ought to try and get those ideas through Congress."

"Once we have an approved document, "said John Luke, "I can convene my assembly of religious leaders. I plan to remind them what God can do if people of goodwill set their minds to a goal. We have accomplished our first goal, which is the commandment of God that he is God, and nothing else but total dedication to him really matters.

"Then I'm going to address the second commandment, 'Love your neighbor as yourself.' I believe this will make it easier to set up volunteer groups. Universities of learning established to concentrate on civics, political compromise, and public dedication would prepare an understanding to the greater good."

"That sounds exactly right," said Cody.

"One last thing, Cody," said the President. "When we have a completed document in our hands, approved by the people of each country involved, it has to be presented to the United Nations. There is just one person in the world, everyone will listen to…you. Call it your swansong before you slip out of the public eye, but this speech to the world has to be yours."

"He's right, Cody," said John Luke. "The Black Angel has one more job to do."

Cody said, "It's a speech yet to be written. We have a long way to go before we can say we've finished the Lord's task."

Chapter 19
God Is One

Washington, D.C.

The members of the coalition took their week, and talked to each other as well as Cody about the fireworks buried in the three short pages of the proposal.

Farid and Masoud talked to each other the most, regarding the separation of the Kurds from the Turks. While both men were pleased with the overall document, because it gave both of them almost everything they wanted, there were still some questions. A lifetime of animosity between the Kurds and Turks made it a tricky situation. The routes of the pipelines coming out of Kurdistan could be a joint project, or the work would take place by each country within their own borders. Both men actually favored a joint project since it was the simplest and most cost effective. But the idea of having Kurds working inside Turkey, across lands owned by individuals or companies might create conflicts. In the end, they found a solution.

Farid suggested before the end of the week, "Let's consider putting the new pipelines next to each other." The disruption of lives, where the pipelines would go were minimal, and the jobs it brought to Turkish workers made it easier to seal the deal. The separate contract on the previously agreed amount of oil, the terms of its price, and the length of the contract satisfied both men.

It was the easiest part of Cody's document to conclude. The language of the document had all the elements of the Bill of Rights in the American Constitution including the right of freedom of religion, and the separation of church and state. Additionally, the right to keep and hold arms, the right of free speech, a free press, and the right to petition the government for redress of grievances would satisfy the needs of a new nation. Since the language of the document gave these rights to all people, women were included without having to say so. It was a significant departure from what wives had known for a very long time.

In the end, the allies agreed only the best of the past should remain and a new beginning begun for all. In this, it was the Israelis, who led the way. They already were operating their government in the manner specified by the massive agreement, and all the allies found themselves seeking out the counsel of Ari ben Cannan. This made the recognition of Israel as a legitimate government much easier. It was exactly what the Israeli's wanted, a chance for an honest exchange of views. Israel had long held if previous non-negotiable matters became negotiable, then accommodations of all kinds were possible.

Meanwhile, all the leaders spent a good deal of time talking to various opposition groups in their own countries and, as expected, found the extreme groups on both ends of the political spectrum the most vocal. What were not vocal were the rants of Islamic clerics, imams, and Mufti's. Cody gave all the credit for that to the Pope, who was spending 14 hours a day on the telephone speaking to Muslim religious leaders, many of which were in Geneva. Without lighting the fuse of religious intolerance, the opposition found its efforts crippled. In general, the people in the allied countries felt justice was done, and they were the winners.

When the big meeting ended, the simple adoption of the Pan Middle-East Accord turned out to be almost predictable. Cody had already made a number of changes to the resolution, mostly to clarify some expressions that seemed overly dramatic or would not translate well into other languages. But the simplicity and the clarity of the document played well, not only to the Allied leaders, but also to the common man or woman on the street.

President Palmer and Cody cooked up a planned leak of the resolution to the press, and Cody was surprised with the results. Palmer summed it all up, "What you did, Cody, was to deliver three pages of sound bites. I'm not surprised it's playing so well with the mainstream media. The fact you remain off-limits to the press for an interview, only makes them hungrier to spit out anything you say."

"The media doesn't know I wrote the draft," Cody said, "we've always said it was the result of a collaboration of Crusader Allies."

"Which you led," said Palmer. "They might not know you wrote it, but they suspect you did and are acting accordingly."

The reaction of the American people was overwhelmingly favorable. It was written in words the people could understand, and could read in about five minutes.

Simultaneously, the map of the new Middle East worked its way into the press, along with explanations of how the lands would change. Russia and China vocally objected to the whole plan, saying, "It was a plot by the United States to rig the system for its own advantage." President Palmer calmly replied, "If it was oil and gas they were talking about, then those countries should bear in mind the United States was oil independent and between them and Canada were the largest producers in the world."

Pope John Luke stayed long enough in Washington to ensure the political process was going to be stable. He set his reconvention of religious leaders in Geneva for two weeks later. His last conversation with Cody concentrated on exactly what the delegates to the religious summit should do.

"Remember, John Luke, "It was this group who made the Crusade possible and they should feel God was working within them to have everything turn out the way it did. They have every right to feel a deep sense of satisfaction. You need to play on that. The first issue addressed in the letter to the Church from the Islamic religious leaders was to agree that god is God, and we all worship Him. You were able to brand the Caliphate as the evil minions of Satan, and the Crusade launched to destroy it.

"That part is complete. The second commandment of God is to love your neighbor as yourself. This is where we produce tolerance for different forms of our worship. All true dedication to God flows directly to Him no matter how it is spoken or practiced."

"I know all that, Cody," said John Luke. "How about I ask you to mind your own business and let me handle this. You've gotten so used to people doing everything you tell them to do you forget who you're addressing."

Cody bowed deeply and went to his knees in front of the Pope. "Your Holiness, I ask your forgiveness for my behavior. I doubt the Lord would honor it. Of course, you know better than I how to accomplish your task. It was wrong to suggest otherwise."

"Oh get up, Cody," said John Luke. "There's nothing to forgive. You were only following your heart and offering sincere advice to a good friend. For your information, a lot of the delegates have already started working in all the new states. They are finding their jobs a lot easier without having to deal directly with Sunni and Shia differences. In case you haven't read, a lot of Shias are moving into Sumeria, and a lot of Sunnis are busy consolidating Mesopotamia into a cohesive state."

"I've read that," said Cody. "I just hope we're not creating countries that will use their influence and wealth to bully and threaten others."

"Not much chance of that," said John Luke. "You division of wealth and resources was so equal, I think the new countries will spend a lot of their money on making their country beautiful. The Lord knows how much damage and destruction ISIS left behind."

"Well, may the Lord be with you in your labors ahead," said Cody, "let me know if there's anything you need."

"I will," said John Luke.

The Geneva conference had coverage from swarms of press. It proceeded over two weeks, with meetings that often included all the children of God, whether they were Christian, Muslim, or Jew.

In his opening address, John Luke summarized the goals of the conference.

"My brothers and sisters, we have two principal tasks to accomplish at this conference. First, we need to consider the practical and day-to-day nurturing of our flocks, which are expressed in the Pan Middle East Accords. The ratification of this body of law, for all affected regions, gives us all a framework, from which we can establish relationships with all Middle Eastern countries. If other nations not taking part in the Crusade, wish to adopt our Accords then so much the better."

"Our second goal is to rebuild the former countries of Syria and Iraq, which were so inhumanly abused by the Islamic Caliphate. This will require a global effort by many nations. The armies of the Crusaders will disband and return to their own lands. In their place, we need to bring in a new army of unarmed, well-meaning civilians with the skills and equipment needed to transform the region into beautiful places, where jobs are plentiful; cities are properly run, and national governments function with transparency and honesty."

"There are numerous injunctions in Islam about the necessity and paramount importance of love for and mercy towards our neighbors. Love of the neighbor is an essential and integral part of faith in God and love of God, because without love of the neighbor there is neither true faith in God nor righteousness in Islam. The Prophet Muhammad said, *"None of you has faith until you love for your brother what you love for yourself.* And, *"None of you has faith until you love for your neighbor what you love for yourself.* Without giving the neighbor what we ourselves love, we do not truly love God or the neighbor."

"The message is the same for Christians and Jews. We cite the words of the Messiah, Jesus Christ, about the paramount importance, second only to the love of God, love of your neighbor. *'You shall love your neighbor as yourself.'*

"It remains only to be noted that this commandment is also to be found in the Old Testament, as revered by the Jewish. In Leviticus we see, *'You shall not hate your brother in your heart. You shall surely rebuke your neighbor, and not bear sin because of him. You shall not take vengeance, nor bear any grudge against the children of your people, but you shall love your neighbor as yourself: I am the LORD.'* Thus the Second Commandment, like the First Commandment, expects generosity and self-sacrifice, and *'On these two commandments hang all the Law and the Prophets.'*"

With this, the conference began. The delegates labored to find ways to make the Pan Middle East Accord, the law of the land for all three of the new countries as well as those who were part of the coalition. There were many intense arguments as traditional Christians, Jews and Muslims fought to maintain the status quo. Nevertheless, the Middle East was going to change because the Crusade made it easier for the more progressive clerics to drive home their points. No one wanted to return to the chaos of the past with dictatorships and intolerance, so the progressive groups argued acceptance of the Accord as law, and the dedication from the resources of many represented countries ought to commence as soon as possible.

Finally, these terms almost unanimously adopted, received consent in less than two weeks.

❖

President Palmer and Cody took the news with real satisfaction. "It looks like John Luke has gotten what he wanted," said Palmer.

"Now we need to conduct a referendum on the Accords here in the United States as well as all the countries directly involved in the Crusade."

"If we get the kind of approval I'm expecting," said Cody, "we can go directly to the United Nations General Assembly and see if two-thirds of the countries of the world agree with us."

"The fact the Security Council is so deadlocked and unable to resolve the matter, gives you the platform you need to go directly to the General Assembly," said Palmer. "I hope you give a nice speech."

"Yeah, no pressure," said Cody.

A month later, the referendums conducted in 15 countries, and all the Crusader coalition allies, and the three new countries created under the Pan Middle East Accords, made it clear the referendum was going to pass with overwhelming support. The General Assembly of the United Nations voted, with few objections, that it had the authority under the United Nations charter to take up the matter and rule on it.

It was determined The Black Angel would speak for the acceptance of the revised borders of the Middle East, and for the adoption of the Accords in the Pan Middle East Treaty. Several other countries demanded the right to speak in opposition. All of them had their demand granted, but the final speaker would be the Black Angel.

The day and the moment finally arrived. Cody was standing away from the huge podium with all his family, and Rico. Ashana, rubbed Cody's beard and smoothed it, "I know how you feel, sweetie," she said. "Just know you have many, many friends in that packed hall out there. What you have accomplished is so much more than anyone ever expected. I love you, and there's no doubt in my mind you will win this final battle."

Cody kissed Ashana and the rest of the family, "I'm glad you're all here."

"Break a leg, dad," said Rosy. Charlie just smiled and nodded his head.

The Secretary-General gaveled the General Session to order:

"My fellow delegates of the United Nations, it is a distinct honor to introduce the leader of the Crusade, which destroyed the ISIS Caliphate. He has also proposed the General Assembly make its ruling on the borders of the new Middle East and the manner in which it shall govern by a referendum of agreement from all parties who were involved in the Crusade. Please welcome, The Black Angel."

Cody walked out to the podium to thunderous applause. He was wearing a new set of battle fatigues and his purple beret. He took it off when he reached the podium.

Making a significant show, the Russian, Chinese, Venezuelan, and Indonesian delegations all walked out. This was not a surprise for Cody. He expected it. As they left, Cody shouted goodbye to them and said to the audience, "What a disappointment. I worked on this speech for a month." That got some intermittent applause and a good laugh from the remaining delegations.

"Ladies and Gentlemen of the General Assembly of the United Nations, I appreciate very much this opportunity to speak to you. Isn't it strange that a man with no name, no country and no self-interest, nevertheless, is given the chance to address you?

"I do have a name, a family, and a home, but none of those matters anymore. In the last two days, you've heard fiery speeches, from some of the same delegations who just walked out, condemning our plans, hopes, dreams, and prayers for the stricken people of the Middle East. I wish they had stayed and afforded me the same courtesy you did, to listen to their reasons why the Pan Middle East Accord had no value.

"In truthfulness, some of those delegations are the very reason we are here today: greed, self-interest, colonialism, and a shocking lack of compassion for what the people of the Middle East have endured for the past twelve years. Let me show you how bad it really was.

On a giant screen above him, Cody pointed to the images. What the delegates saw were pictures of men, women and children lying headless in a trench. They saw men and women chained to Christian monuments and blown to pieces. They saw families falling, victims of machine-guns outside their homes. They saw looting, pillaging and wonton destruction on a scale not seen since the Second World War, and ending with the explosions that rocked St. Peter's dome in Rome and caused it to collapse into itself.

When the video was over, Cody said, "This was the face of the Islamic Caliphate as it decimated two entire countries, and terrorized countless other places in the world, screaming they were doing all these things in the name of Allah, God and Jehovah."

"Last year, a group of clergy from all faiths who call God the

Supreme Creator of the Universe, gathered in Geneva to declare ISIS did not represent God, at all, but was hiding shamelessly behind his name, so they could commit the atrocities you have just witnessed."

"From this conference, the Modern Crusade was born. Formed from a coalition of Muslims, Christians, Jews who believe it was their duty to bind themselves together in the name of God, no matter by what name He is called, and despite the differences in how He is worshipped, they determined to wipe this scourge of evil from the face of the earth. So, men of strong will took up arms against the Caliphate and emancipated the people of the old Syria and Iraq.

"Now we come to the rebuilding of these shattered cities and destroyed lives. There was a time when the world faced very much the same conditions.

"At the end of World War I, the victors unilaterally chose how the Middle East would be divided. Their motives were based on the same motivations of the delegations you just saw walking out of this chamber…greed, self-interest and colonialism. These choices did not take into consideration any of the truly different ethnic, cultural, religious, or geographical conditions that existed in the Middle East.

"How could we have possibly gotten a different history than the one we have endured for over a hundred years, based on these motivations?

"There have been 20 wars in the Middle East since the end of World War I. The people of the Middle East have hardly known anything else but war with grieving. The rise of ISIS was an entirely predictable outcome of these conditions, and the people of the Middle East, and many other countries suffered as a result.

"Now the Islamic Caliphate is no more, and the world, once again, has to make a choice. Will we mindlessly try to put everything back the way it was, minus ISIS? Or, will we finally meet the true and real needs of the people of this region?"

A new graphic appeared on the giant screen. It showed the map of the Middle East very different from the familiar one.

"This is the way the Middle East should look. The Kurds, the largest ethnic people in the world with no country will have one. The Shia Muslims, who are the vast majority in old southern Iraq, will have their own country. The Sunni Muslims, who are the overwhelming majority in northern Iraq, will have their own country. The

Palestinians, who have fought for decades for a homeland of their own, will have one. The Israelis, whose nation was created by a vote of this very body, will finally have peace and the recognition of their state as being their legitimate home.

"You have before you the document spelling out the rights and responsibilities of all countries, new, and who were part of the Crusader coalition. It gives rights they have never had among their people. It restrains authoritative governments from denying these rights to all, men and women equally, and it divides the resources of the region in a proportional manner so that everyone can benefit.

"A few weeks ago, a referendum was held among the people of all nations who had a stake or will have a future in a modern Middle East. There were over a billion votes cast. The results were an overwhelming approval of the Accords by every nation.

"The Security Council of this United Nations has not acted and is hopelessly deadlocked. The Charter of the United Nations gives the General Assembly the right to vote in absence of agreement from the Security Council when world peace and stability is at stake. There has never been a time when peace and stability was more at stake than right now.

"I ask you to ratify these new borders of the Middle East, as the people have, and allow the millions of men and women, who are eager to restore what was lost. Muslims, Christians, Jews, all will work together, not as an armed force, but as innocent and otherwise defenseless civilians to fulfill the Commandment of God to love your neighbors.

"This is the final public address I will ever make. I resign as Commander of the Crusaders. I seek nothing further from any of you. After today, I intend to fall into obscurity and live out my life in peace, joy, and a daily communion with God. That was all I ever wanted in the first place.

"I have done the work the Lord gave me to do. Now it is time for you to do the same."

Cody left his purple beret on the podium and walked off the platform.

The stunned General Assembly sat in shocked silence for a moment. Then in growing numbers, they rose to their feet and gave Cody the ovation of a lifetime.

Epilogue

"I sure like you better with short hair and no beard," said Ashana.

"Yeah, dad," said Rosy, with those sunglasses and the bland shorts and T-shirt, not a single person in this huge crowd has recognized you."

"I didn't recognize you," said Matt, standing with his arm around Rosy.

"I was always good at blending in," said Cody.

Shouldn't you be up there on the podium with your mom and dad?" Charlie said to Mitra.

"I would say my proper place is with my husband," said Mitra. "Besides, pregnant women look stupid in public."

"I've thought you never looked more beautiful," said Charlie.

"I love you so much," said Mitra.

"It a good thing we have such a big villa," said Ashana. "With new families stuffed into it, we've needed the room."

The Moretti family stood together with Cody and all the rest of the expanded family.

"We're not inconvenienced at all," said Adolfo. "We're all very comfortable in our own home, where we've always lived. It's wonderful to have Rico and Alia back safe and sound."

"Well, you're going to have the place to yourself again," said Charlie, "what with all of us scattering again to join the different groups working in our new Middle East."

"I'm still trying to learn how this family views human behavior," said Matt. "We fight a war, and then jump right back into the same region to serve a humanitarian mission. Rosy and I are off to Sumeria, Charlie and Mitra are going back to Kurdistan, and you, Cody, are returning to the very same hospital in Damascus where you almost got killed."

"It's not The Black Angel going back to Damascus," said Cody, "It's just Cody and Ashana Frost, pitching in to do what we can."

"What has surprised me the most," said Charlie, "is the outpouring of so many people from so many countries going off to live in pretty primitive conditions, just because they feel the same way we do."

"Having so many very serious Peace Keepers from the United Nations is sure making security a lot easier," said Ashana.

"It's a little strange," said Cody, "the United Nations is not the same organization it was a few months ago. The idea they should assume additional responsibility for world peace and stability has made the General Assembly much more active in world affairs. Their solidarity in approving the Pan Middle East Accord, and ratifying the people's will in so many countries, to establish their own borders, served as a wake-up call to stop deferring to the Security Council for all important decisions."

"I think it's kind of funny the new countries chose to keep the names you gave them," said Rosy.

"Those were the names of those countries for thousands of years," said Charlie. "It's not surprising at all.

"Quiet," said Cody, "the ceremony is about to start."

As the family stood among the hundreds of thousands of people in St. Peter's Square, Pope John Luke the First walked briskly up a ramp built for him to speak to the crowd before him. Joining him were Manek Faroush of Iran, Ari be Cannan from Israel, Farid Sensek of Turkey, Masoud Barzani from Kurdistan, King Assad from Palestine, and a number of Muslim religious leaders from the Geneva Conclaves.

"Dearly beloved," said John Luke, "We are gathered here tonight to rededicate the Church of God. It is entirely fitting I am joined by the men who understood that god is God. He is the same God for us all. May this unveiling of our dome represent a new understanding and tolerance that, although we call God by different names, and worship in different ways, He is still our God and we shall have no other God before Him. Let this ceremony represent the new peace and security of our world. We fought together, died together, and from that learned a great lesson from our Creator even though we all cherish our own singularity. In the name of God, here is our St. Peter's church restored."

The big lights focused on the church, as the gigantic shroud pulled away from the dome. Then all the lights went out, and the shining lights of St. Peters and its beautiful dome gleamed into the night.

"Nice show," said Cody, "Let's go home."

Meet Phil Walker

A lifelong career for him began when he was only 13 years old, as a radio broadcaster in his hometown, Fort Collins, Colorado. He says this was the year his voice changed. Over the next 58 years, he continued a much-celebrated career at radio stations in Colorado and Nebraska. He received recognition by state broadcaster's associations, for forty straight years, culminating in him chosen as Colorado Broadcaster of the Year in 1997.

Writing began early. He estimates he has written 10,000 radio commercials and several million words of news copy. His first book, a non-fiction work on American Western history was the best-selling book in Fort Collins for nine years and reprinted seven times. To this, he added eight, hour-long CDs with music, sound effects, multiple voices - sweeping sagas of history. Over a hundred thousand CDs have sold to date.

Serious writing of fiction novels began in 2002. Six more books comprising the *Starlight* Series joined his first book, *The Galilee Foundation.* Phil admits writing in the genre of Religion and Science Fiction was something of a tough way to crack the market.

Then came the critically acclaimed *The Black Angel, Crusade of the Black Angel, The Rangers are Coming,* and the latest book, soon to be released, *The Magic and the Misery.*

Phil Walker lives with his wife, Verna, a nationally known artist, in The Villages, Florida. When he's not writing, he loves the days in his garden.

If you have finished reading this book, I would like to hear from you. I don't want to know what you liked about the book, although that would be nice, but rather what you didn't like about it. Please feel free to send your comments to my email address: walkhouse@yahoo.com

Enjoy these books by Phil Walker

The Black Angel
Crusade of The Black Angel
The Rangers are Coming
Lions and Tigers, and Bears, OH GOD!
Out of the Emerald Cathedral

The Starlight Series

The Holy Mission
The Galilee Foundation
The Galilee Garden
Island of the Angels
Terra Rising
Heaven's Angels
The Galactic Quest

Coming Nov, 2016
The Magic and the Misery

Non-Fiction History

Visions Along the Poudre Valley
Modern Visions Along the Poudre Valley